Graveduggery

Lula Lucent

Ghost Festival Press

GRAVEDUGGERY

Part of the Graveduggery™ series, Book the First

Published by Ghost Festival Press

Cover art by Les Solot

ISBN: 978-0-9906078-0-9

First edition: August 15, 2014
Duggery Day

Printed on Earth

For Leila, wherever in the ground you lie.

It is always glorious when we go gravedigging. Most of the time it rains great pouring streaks that pockmark the dirty backwoods roads we take. This lends a natural bleakness to the proceedings. And I credit Sik; she specifically waits for nights like these when the mud squeals for us to stop trampling it. The worse the better, as she takes them.

"Hurry up, Red, we're there nearly."

I'm never sure if she's showing off when she says that. Every tree looks the same and if there was a path underfoot the storm saw to destroying it last night. For me the whole world is black and unchanging except for when she lets a little light out of her shuttered lantern and looks about. In those moments, I pretend we're seated in the backroom of Darvin's, the door has been brushed open by a passing body and a sliver of firelight illuminates her pointy nose, and maybe she's smiling.

#

"There are chiefly four things in life that make a person happy. Enough food down your gullet, a bit of warmth, and somewhere comforting to lie your head." Sik tips her hat back and leans against the shovel. "But it's a wicked, blissful few who can profit all three by seeing someone else miserable or, in this case, dead."

1

The rain and I clap.

"It's a lovely graveyard," I say.

Sik digs back into the grave. "Isn't it?"

We've avoided this place pretty much the duration of our partnership. Well-guarded, well-known, well-stocked with all sorts of named individuals I personally have never heard of, but maybe you have. For those reasons, it's ironic that these cemeteries are often the most lacking in forgotten offerings. I suppose the more one's name matters in life, the less it does in death.

I've never seen a cemetery quite so detailed. The stairway that led from the lower level was flanked by statues of faceless robed figures with their heads bowed humbly. As if to whet the yet unknowing appetite, they appear at equal intervals with equal proportions, equally pious. They are all the same. But then, at the summit, the wide plateau spreads into the distance with an exploding mass of angels.

They are perched on walls, kneeling on tombs, standing next to columns. Always in groups, always together. Clad in simple togas that wrap their bodies like gusts of spring wind. In the more mournful corners that Sik and I had trodden after our ascent, there were sorrowful angels consoling each other. Sagging wings. Holding hands. I began to feel that we had stumbled into a city that was the world, and the world had passed away.

Sik clears her throat and spits on the ground. "Hey, dreamer, you gonna join me?"

I start to dig.

A place like this is hit-or-miss. Probably pointless. What Sik has taken to calling our, ahh, "Starvation Fund Despairitory."

Underneath us, hiding, is a man who up until two weeks ago was sucking air. Apparently everyone loved him, but I never knew about it. Sik hadn't either, until he died. They say he wore a brown linen robe from dawn to dusk, living plainly, acting as the kindly benefactor to the common man and woman. Even in death he was simple, asking nothing other than to be buried with his fellows with no pomp and no grave-marking -- exactly like the burial of the poorest poor.

"A touching story," sighs Sik when I mention it.

"And it is said that his wealthier brothers and sisters felt *so distraught* that they couldn't give him the send-off they always give each other..."

Sik curls around the shovel, shuddering with passion. "His friends!" she gasps. "What beautiful friendships! I envy him."

"But he's dead."

"I don't envy the sod that, obviously."

"And my friendship?"

"You're okay," she says, but shudders again, knees near collapse. "Such lovely, stalwart, magnificent friends! But... I mourn. I mourn for them!"

"I mourn for them too."

"But I mourn for them more!" she cries at the thunder-wracked sky. "They have riches. The man doesn't desire a rich interment. What to do! What to do! Pray, my dearest Red, what to do?"

"Why," I flourish, "since he had forsaken riches in life, they would grant it to his body in death."

"Such... beauty!"

"But alas. Corpses have no need for money."

"What an oversight."

Sik laughs devilishly and does a profane dance.

It's said that we gravediggers are just fools happily digging our own graves. I'm sure there's some truth in that. Every dig is a gamble, this one more than most. Still, we try to keep our fingers on the pulse of the dead and dying and, as with most other darkling professions, sometimes a little craziness pays off.

#

We wedge the shovel under the corpse and throw our weight down.

"Come on, you bastard, wake up! Rise and bloody shine! Damn, Red, he's heavy. Hrrnnnph! Resurrect, damn you. Reh-zur-ect! Unngh!" Finally getting the corpse unstuck from the muddy slush, she cheers. "That's it, that's it! Get the lantern!"

We both immediately regret the light.

"Oh gross... gross..." she says weakly. "A rotter. The bloody thing's a rotter."

"Rather... impressive buoyancy."

"If I— if I touch him, he'll explode. Oh gross. Gross gross gross."

"I'll do the check," I say.

"It's fine..." Rubs her nose. "Only... keep the light away from his face."

"Sure. As soon as I find it."

Sik runs gloved hands over the burial shroud. Prodding various parts with a finger. Looking for coins, rings, trinkets. Looking for our livelihood amongst the dead. Plucking a thing too dark to see, tossing it out of the pit. Springing to another part of the body. Flitting shadow, darkness daughter. Searching. Plucking. Tossing. Searching. Plucking. Tossing.

She raises the corpse's hand to me. "Give me a hand," she says without amusement. "Ha. Ha. Ha."

The finger is bloated twice too large for the ring. I hold the wrist and finger. Pull, wiggle the joint, bending, bending, bending... Resists. Pull harder, damn thing's stubborn... Jerk back, snap the bone. The finger breaks away, goo impotently ejaculating from the wound. I pluck off the ring and toss the finger away.

Sik stalks away, up and out of the grave. I hold the ring into the lantern's light, but it's a useless gesture. My partner's arched shoulders are appraisal enough.

Worthless.

#

"What the hell is this shit," Sik says, the miniscule pile of coins flat across her outstretched palms.

I toss another heap of dirt down into the dark that swallows it immediately. Wonder if there's a point to this. The rain worsens and it'll fill the grave for us, given time.

"Fuck it. This is Sik's Sorrowful Drink Fund."

I finish the job. Jam the shovel into the ground to act sentry to our blessed benefactor.

She shakes the coins at me. "Now taking donations!"

I put my arm around her. "Guess it wasn't an honest Devil's Night, huh?"

"But it was," she mumbles. "Perfect night. Perfect weather. Perfect everything! Well… 'cept what I figured."

The rain beats a livelier tattoo atop her hat, then splatters my cheek. I wipe it off. More rain splatters. "What do you think?" I ask.

"I'm trying not to," she says.

"Since we're here…"

"There won't be anything," she sighs. "That's why these places are always rot. The money is spent on the elaborate tombs and stuff. It's kinda obvious, but, well, ya know, you figure there's so much money flying around there's gotta be a way for us to catch a bit." She shoves the coins in a pocket. "A bit…"

"Have a vendetta," I suggest.

"Eh?"

"Go take the pickax and break stuff."

That gets her laughing.

"Geez, I'm not *that* petty." Glances up at me from under the hat. Tries to hold back a smile. "Ahh. Red, Red, Red. It really is tempting to open these crypts. It's all words to say it's useless back at home, but now that we're here? Surrounded by 'em? I start… I start to feel *that*. Ya know? It just feels like there has to be something inside."

"You know what," I say, "there probably is. But we don't have the equipment to get in and if we did, or if we do, no way to keep the Watch from hearing. We've only been able to do that in unguarded spots."

"And even the thieves have already picked through those clean enough."

"So, as you know…"

"… back where we started."

I give her a sandwich.

"Ah, thanks. Was starting to get a headache."

We sit down on a gravestone overlooking the lower levels and eat. Sik kicks her feet back and forth, acting like she hasn't a single care in all the world, drinks coffee and passes the container back to me.

Between those weathered graves and ancient trees, the lanterns of the guards swing to and fro. From this distance I can pretend they are lost souls, slowly floating through the cemetery, searching for a way out, but ultimately resigned to stay within the confines of the flagstone pathways.

"We're going about this all wrong," I say between swallows.

"Mphmmphh?" Sik asks.

I gesture at the lights. "Get a job like them, we can go digging on the sly."

"Mphhsss mmrrphhmphhm," Sik says. Swallows, clears her throat. "Not as romantic."

After dinner, or whatever this is, we huddle together and watch the storm deepen. To go home empty-handed? Depressing. Best to brood a while longer. But each blast of lightning reminds me with increased frequency that Sik will tire soon, and there are many hours of weary footfalls on the long slog home before I can tuck her in bed and stoke the fireplace.

"Shit!" Sik jerks me upright. "Is that an inspection patrol or raid or something?"

A mass of lanterns, momentarily blossoming at the fog-drowned entrance, is now trudging down the path that leads to the stairs below us. If I figure one lantern per wielder…

"… so that's why they don't patrol up here after nightfall," I say. "They do it en masse later."

Sik's frown is nearly audible.

"Would take forever to get in a crypt and if you *could* without making a noise, you'd still be deep inside when they came. Those clever fucking lazy execrations."

A thin cry pushes past the heavy blanket of mist. Sobbing shakes the rain. Somewhere, thunder has murmured in commiseration. The lightning brightens a faraway patch of cloud-cover and then is still.

"That's a funeral procession."

"No freaking way." Sik scampers along the edge for a closer look, but she's as familiar with that painfully slow pace as I am. Someone has died. Someone now mourns.

"I'm not gonna question it," she says when she returns. "They want to do this in a downpour, that's their weird business."

"You're amazingly calm for that gleeful flash in your eyes. What's wrong," I tease, "little Sik is having a good feeling about some luck?"

"N-nothing in anything like that," she says emphatically. "It'll be m-more rot again, I bet. Y-you'll see."

"Oh good, your voice caught up." I poke her side and she jumps away. "I was worried you were half-asleep."

"N-no sleep 'till death!" she exclaims.

No sleep 'till death.

Isn't that so?

#

The service of the dead doesn't last long. Though unmentioned, the nature of her death was not doubtful. Those burials are always done at night. I'm not sure why, but even Sik admits there's a dreadful poetry to it.

Fortunately she was not fated to be interred beyond our grasp. As Sik and I stalked the procession further and further into this plain of towering tombs and monuments, the thunder reflected my mood. But in a lonesome hollow they halted and began to dig. Between the willowy trees, a solitary angel covered her face and wept silently. Sik and I hunkered beneath her wings.

The body has been lowered into the pit. Someone stands with a shovel, in a pose uncannily similar to Sik's earlier, off to the side. Executioner? As much as I squint, I can't make out the telling blade or scarf.

The conclusion comes.

"And so let us send her away, borne aloft on all our dreams," the orator says.

"Requiem," the crowd intones.

"All our hopes."

"Requiem."

"All our love."

"Requiem."

"Requiem," Sik whispers.

With lanterns in hand, the funeral march flows back along its wake and back towards a land that promises, at least one day, to be warm again. After the hole is filled, the final straggler reclaims its lantern and dutifully trails behind. Rain bleeds down on the freshly-turned gravedirt. We wait a time, until it feels safe enough.

I pat Sik's shoulder. She nods, hands me the shovel.

"They could have saved us the effort," I complain.

"That's half the fun, though!"

"And they always bury these ones deeper."

"Pah-lenty of time," she says.

Like Sik, I become covered in more dirt and mud than clothing the deeper we dig. But right now my face aches more than my body. Maybe shock. Fatigue. Or, as Sik says, insanity. None of the words sound right. And then I land on joy. It sticks in my mind, such simplicity. It's here, where the muck drags me down, that I find home.

Once we reach the dead girl, Sik starts scraping dirt off the body. I lift it up, feel underneath for any scattered offerings. Rain washes the face clean.

Skin almost like that of the marble angels, surrounded in flowing hair now the color of the grave. She lies in repose in a lilac dress, the only sign of spring we'll see for many months to come.

"She's no older than you," I say.

"Damn," Sik mutters. "Damn it. She's prettier than me."

Cradled in the girl's hands is a goblet.

I raise it into the light.

"Silver, at least," I say, and rub the dirt away.

"Oh ho!" Sik jumps.

Circling the side of the rim are generously-sized crimson stones. Sik snatches the cup, hugging it to her chest. She dances around the corpse, singing her favorite digger shantey, though wordlessly and interspersed with bouts of laughter. I pick around for scattered coins. Sik fills the cup with rainwater, flings it high, laughing wild as the wind when it splashes on her hat. Above us, the sky shudders. The ground drips down on us. We are crows.

I climb out of the grave, reach back for Sik. Grinning, she offers a hand, but when I'm about to take it her expression fades. She turns back. Looks down at the body. Says something. Waits a moment. Glances back at me, then at the body. Sharp intake of breath, then kicks the dead girl's stomach as hard as she can, and says it again.

"Stupid bitch." The words venom-thick.

But when Sik finally takes my hand, and I pull her out, she slips on the mud and slams into me. I stagger, knocking into the lantern, and the fire flares as oil is spilled. Shadows of ourselves writhe and claw at our backs and then our faces as it swings back and forth.

Her breaths come in quick, short pulses from her nose, frosting in the air. For the first time tonight, I become aware of the bitter cold. Sik must too, because she shudders and gives a kind of sigh. Her heartbeat pounds against my own.

Midnight has gone. Dawn will come. The heavens peal a warning. But Sik and I are still standing, still staring back into the grave where we watch our shadows hold each other and flicker.

"And me too," we say. A triptych of words.

#

The pipes are humming. Sik is humming. I collapse in my half-broken armchair, its comfort directly proportional to its wear. The room is as cluttered as it is warm.

Home, in all its dilapidated splendor.

The firelight flashes malformed images behind my eyelids. Stories of spooks and nightmare creatures and all manner of strange things that frighten Sik. Poor girl. Terrors of myth and imagination are more real to her than the respective nooses awaiting us in the legal reaches of time. I smile. Now these stories catch in my mind, as they often do, as I stare into the fireplace and think about nothing at all.

"You're gonna fall asleep there."

"Will not," I grumble.

Sik is draped in a light robe and sprawling atop the carpet. Her shortened hair sticks up in complete disorder, as it always does wet or dry unless she takes uncharacteristic efforts. She watches me silently, eyes slowly blinking.

"You look tired," I say.

Scrunches up her face in the very picture of a walnut. "You aren't supposed to say that to a girl."

"Even if it's true."

"Say 'you *sound* tired.' That way, it seems kinda cute."

"You *sound* exhausted."

She stretches, makes overly-dramatic groans, and jumps to her feet. I settle deeper into the chair.

"Geez, can't even see the docks. I wonder if they floated away," she says.

"Maybe we're the ones floating away," I yawn.

"Ohh, that sounds so nice. Floating... floating..." Her forehead lightly falls against the window, slides down, down, down. "Cold," she complains.

"Siiik."

"What."

"Siiiik."

"Whaat."

"Can't you hear them?"

"Who."

"Your pillow and blanket. They're calling you. They're promising floating dreams."

"Pillows lie," she mumbles, "and blankets are in cahoots."

"Get some sleep," I tell her. "We'll go to Darvin's once you wake up."

"Okay," she says, but doesn't move. Her forehead slides farther down the window. "What if I don't wake up?"

"I'll hoist you over my shoulder and take you anyways."

She makes an amused sound -- something between a snort and a fart -- and, finally relenting, stumbles along the wall towards bed. At the threshold, she pauses. "If you fall asleep there, you'll get a crook in your neck."

Scant years ago we would not have been able to find such respite as we enjoy right now. The night can continue to be blind and to howl like a desperate, dying animal. It can claw at the roof and the door and the windows, but in vain. Sik is dry and warm and safe.

I open one eye and peer out the window. It's obscured, but somewhere out in that impenetrable gloom a young woman yearns for spring underground, not very far from a man whose broken finger points at nothing.

#

The sun is dipping when we depart. A shivering breeze stirs the cloud-raked sky and the signposts of the shops we pass by. Sik wobbles beside me, sometimes stomping on an errant puddle, but usually pulling her wide-brimmed hat low and shoving hands under armpits.

Darvin's is only superficially open at this time. He will let you take a spell, maybe fix you up something if he likes you. But at the end of things, he is a businessman and setting up for the night. It's those few of us that stay out of his way that can come and go as we will. Being avid regulars, for you will find me and Sik here most workless nights, we have the special privilege of permanent seathood.

"Anything," Sik says to Darvin the moment she is through the door.

He waves us to our favorite table in the corner and calls back into the kitchen. His toothy grin stretches a chestnut beard which has never seemed to grow as long as I've known him. In a world of interchangeable troubles and pains, he is always that understood and subtle constant.

We shake hands over the bar.

"Darvin."

"Red."

"How's business?"

His deep laughter shakes the floorboards. "I should ask you," he says as Sik staggers across the room.

"She'll be alright," I say.

"Good news? Bad news?"

"Good, I think. We're going to figure out what to do with it this evening."

Drums his fingers atop the counter. "Hmm," he says after a moment. "*It.*"

"One is better than none."

"And sometimes an insult, but," he says, seeing me grinning now, "looks like it was a good piece."

"We'll see," I laugh.

"Not that you're not," he says, leaning towards me, "but be discreet. Some upstarts were fooling around Crypt Dun while you were gone. It was on the low for a while, but the Watch is keeping a sharper eye for you, ah, diggers."

"Well that's always that. The idiots looking for a fast turn stir up the hornets and we all have to keep our heads down for a while." I chew the inside of my cheek. "Shit. If they were stupid enough to try for the Dun, it *will* be crazier around here. We really did get lucky last night."

"Brightwater?"

"Darrow."

"Ah, good ground that. Had a friend up there once."

"Tradesman?"

"Dead. Though not esteemed enough for that particular plot." Darvin pours a tall glass of stout and another of milk. Hands them to me. "And don't trust Bors."

"Who the hell does?"

He shrugs meaningfully.

I turn back to see that Sik has managed to reach a chair. Her head is half book-ended by the tabletop. I set the milk in front of her. She pushes it away.

"Urrrreuunngggghhh," she whines.

"Sik…"

"Urrrruunnngggggggg!" she whines louder, pushing it away farther.

"It's not alcohol."

"Too early," she moans.

"Wake up, it's not alcohol."

She peers over the rim. "It *looks* like alcohol."

"It does not. It bloody well looks like milk and you know it."

But she's already glugging it down, pausing only to make delighted *ahhhs* and take a breath.

Darvin reenters from the back with a hastily-prepared platter and crosses the room in a few strides.

"And what is the matter, my girl?" he asks.

Blackened eyes stare up at him over an empty glass. "Metabolism headache," she says.

He presents leftover slices of meat pie, berry pie, and a generous pile of fried sweet potatoes.

"Eat and be full!" Darvin tells her with a hearty laugh.

"Food!" she cheers.

"The only thing," I note, "that shuts you up."

Her smile is surrounded by full cheeks and hidden by pie crust.

#

"It's the waiting time," Sik is saying, leaning back in her seat and taking a long draw from her pipe, "before the conversations, sound of glass, fireside. Darvin's isn't yet awake until the white noise."

"But we," I say, "will have to light out before then."

"Yes. Yes! What are we to do with *that*." Points a heel at the cloth-wrapped goblet.

"Not Bors."

"No shit. Not after last time."

"Not ever again after his latest stunt too," I say. "Apparently he tried to have some one-year-out dredgers hit the Dun."

"Shut up!"

"And so, my dearest Sik, this little piece is worth more for us now." I roll it between my hands. "It has to hold us over until we can go out again."

"Yeah yeah, *if* we can go out again. I'm not even dumb enough to do that. Did they get anything?"

"Death-sentences I assume."

I wait for her customary string of curses, but instead there is smoke and the faint *puh* of parting lips. *Puh. Puh.*

"The Executioners will be stroking their blades over this for as long as they can." I sigh. "He really has to fuck with everyone, doesn't he? That's not how you keep customers."

"He's a fence," Sik says. "Whaddaya expect? I'm surprised he was as 'honest' with us so long as he was. Patient man, I guess."

"If that's so, he's more patient than you."

Puh. Puh. "You just compared me to Bors," she groans, then fidgets as if her chair needed coaxing back to sleep. "Naw. I'm not patient. I just have... resignation."

"We may need that before this is through. Hey," I point at the door, "it's half of Picker and Stealer."

Sik vaults to her feet. "Where? Where?"

A woman who looks either very shifty or very observant, which depends how well you know her, is busy unwrapping herself of an absurdly long scarf and knee-length coat. Her personality is exactly as patchwork.

"Oi!" she waves, still half-wrapped.

"Jackal!" Sik dives into the confused mess and embraces her.

"Hey, girl! How's my fave crazy?"

"Good! Good!" Sik drags Jackal, practically tripping on the scarf, across the room. The planks squeak in anticipation.

"Hey, man. Ya keepin' my Sik happy and safe?"

"Despite her best efforts," I say.

"Jackal! Jackal!"

"Yeah, I hear ya! Calm down a sec. There. That's better. Oi, Darvs! Got any drink heated up? Colder than a bitch's heart out there! Yeah, yeah, I acknowledge your presence, little one, now... come into my arms!"

"Jackal!" And again Sik dives deep.

"Didn't expect you guys back, not until next week. Errr..." Tugs at a crimson twintail. "I got my dates wrong again, huh?"

"About a week wrong," I say.

"Can't be helped." She kicks up a chair, spins it around. "So tell me, tell me. Tell Big Sis Jackal whatcha got her."

"This!" Sik presents the night's offering.

"Let's see, let's see... Ohh, ohh." Hers are the hands of a professional. Even though the pub is empty aside from us, out of habit she keeps part of the goblet wrapped at all times and angles it so it catches the light but no one's interest. "Oh that is fantastic."

"Eeh hee hee hee," is about all Sik is capable of saying in her unbridled greed.

"I really, *really* want to steal this from ya," Jackal confesses, "but I think ya guys are in it a liiiittle deeply."

I roll my eyes. "So what *is* this Dun business? What the hell's going on?"

Jackal hands the piece back. "Nothin' yet, that's the problem. We're all of us waitin' to see how it goes down. Until word leaks out on what the Executioners are doing and what the Sovereignty lets have happen, all the fences dance the good-little-citizen-dance." Slaps her hand on the table in emphasis. "Every damn one!"

"Is no one buying?"

"The legit ones are... is what I want to say." Shakes her head. "Don't need to say it, but ya know ya can't offload *that* with *them*. Not right now."

Sik's face turns ashen. "W-we can't sell it?"

"Sorry." Jackal shrugs. "It's tough for us too, ya know. Oh, here it is, heeere it iiiis." She takes the steaming mug from Darvin and raises it respectfully. "Aaahhhhh! That's it! I love this new crop of apples!" And drains it before Darvin can return to his work. "Aaahhh, sooo gooood," she purrs.

Sik is frowning.

"It's alright, Sik," I say.

"It's all rot," she says.

"Listen." Jackal's tone now takes on a quality as dull and frigid as a millstone: Picker and Stealer's business voice. "Know a fellow. Killjoy. He's a bit of a divvie," she says. "We got in good with him only last month. If ya think Darvs's shrewd with who he deals with, you've seen nothin'."

"And he's buying?" I ask.

"Expressly, no. He runs the city's auction house. Perfect front, actually. Always hide your valuables on the mantelpiece." Smirks at Sik. "Bit of advice for ya from our side of the night." Reaches over and ruffles Sik's hair; she flinches, but perks up after a moment and touches Jackal's hand. "Anyway, I think he'd consider it, comin' from me. We've become fast fiends. Like I say, he's not buyin', but he could auction it and then take a cut. Hey... am I an asshole if I ask for a finder's fee?"

"There goes all the profit," I say.

Sik puts her pipe away. "How much."

"*Extremely modest*," says Jackal, batting the question away with the back of her hand. "Like... five percent. Food money. Got no interest in screwin' over what few friends I have. Yeah?"

"Yeah," I tell her, "yeah, five percent's not bloodthirsty."

"Jackal!" cries Sik, once more pouncing. "You're the best." And now assaults the hapless Jackal's breasts. "And I want your boobs! We're throwing them into the deal too!" Jackal's face flushes and she barely stifles a pleasured moan under Sik's attention. "Why can't I have boobs like yours? It's because Quinn feeds you so well, isn't it? Red doesn't feed me very good. And look at him, he's all strong and stuff. I know he's hiding food from me. I've looked!"

"You eat as well as I do," I say.

"Ahh ahh, Sik, you need to st-st... ahhhh." But whether Jackal actually wants Sik to stop, I'm never entirely sure. "We, we can go see him right nn... nnngh!"

I push my chair back. "Lead the way."

And so Jackal does. Somehow, with Sik in tow. Darvin waves us out in the manner in which he waved us in. This place has become a strange hub for those of us who work in the shadows -- doubtlessly stranger for that mostly-honest man who is always a half-step away from laughter. Still, it's not rare to leave his haunt in high-spirits, whether you were drinking or not.

#

Old City is a city that sprawls, lazily. At peak business hours, the wide streets can never truly be said to be crowded. Only during festival seasons will you find your gait impeded, but even then there are so many sidestreets to take. It may be underestimation to say 'city' since it stretches all the way south to Old Kingdom -- and where the one ends and the other begins is an academic question I leave to cartographers with too much time on their hands.

If nothing else, Old City is a place of long, long roads.

"What's Quinn up to?" I ask.

"Dockside." Jackal says and smirks, meaning to say no more in public.

Killjoy's auction house is set deep within the artisan quarter. It is a uniquely constructed building compared to the rest of the city, a grand cylinder covered in creeper vines and mossy eaves.

Sik tips her hat back, turns in wide circles, taking in everything. "Why do I recognize this place?"

"Old theatre. Renovated when Killjoy bought it up."

"Wow," Sik says. "We haven't been here in ages. Looks so different during the day."

"Yeah." Jackal nods feverishly. "Used to light it good, they did! He plays things a bit more subtle. And believe me, we prefer it that way." She ushers us into an alcove and knocks on the rear door.

A lilting voice answers. "Speaking?"

"Jackal and two friends."

The door squeaks open. Viridian eyes peek out at us. "Hey, miss Jackal."

"Oi. Hiya."

"He's finishing some business," the diminutive girl informs us. "Wait in the hall?"

"Right, right," Jackal says, clicking her tongue. Perhaps in deference to the auction house's origin, she dramatically bows to us, arm extended towards the doorway.

The organized chaos is staggering. Sik whistles, the sound of it muffled almost instantly. Crates litter the room. Some are covered in dyed cloth, so many dark and rich colors, but most are stacked high and left dusty. Various antiques are perched atop the colored cloth, unique numbers dangling from them like insects trapped in spiderweb.

"Are they still renovating?" I ask.

"Naw, naw, it's the look of it. Kinda charmin', ya know?"

"We're done setting up for next week's auction," the girl says blankly. She pulls a small ledger from her dress. Then a pen from the back of her hair. Then, with more concentration than seems necessary, she flips through the pages. Stops. Stares me in the eye. Waits. For what, I can't imagine. Finally, she says out of nowhere: "Name?"

"Red."

Holds ledger close to her face. Scribbles a word. Peers over the ledger at me, as if that would confirm my identity. Turns to Sik.

Sik is oblivious of course. She's busy cocking her head side to side, wondering -- like me -- if anything we've ever found has passed second, third, or fourth-hand through these doors.

"Hey," I call to her.

"What." Glances over a shoulder.

I point at the expectant girl.

They stare at each other. They blink. They wait. They keep waiting. I wonder how long this can go on. Finally, the girl says at her own pace: "Name?"

"I'm Sik."

The girl lowers the ledger. "Hmmm," she says noncommittally, then scampers out of the room.

"Okay then," Sik says, and goes back to milling about. "I remember this room being bigger, but I guess it really has changed."

"Auction house, workshop, home. Mine is a tiny world and I'd have it no other way." A man clad in a leather jacket cracked with age, nearly as much as his face, strides out from what used to be a stage. His face splits into a smile. "Killjoy. It's a pleasure."

"They're my friends," Jackal says. "Sole people other than Quinn I'd vouch for."

"Splendid," he says. "Only now completed the day's last order of business. I was looking for my assistant, but... she seems to have wandered off again. No matter. Please, step this way."

"I'm told you're something of a divvie," I say.

"That's right," Killjoy remarks. "I take in the proceeds and divvie up the profits."

The guts of the old theatre grow progressively darker. Footsteps resound down one of the corridors we pass, but which is impossible to say. Somewhere a door creaks open, then shuts. Or maybe it's a trapdoor. But eventually we reach a room, if possible, messier than the main hall, filled with various works of art in a varying degrees of completion.

Killjoy's workroom smells smoky, pleasantly, as of years of endlessly burning candles.

"Pardon the visual noise," he says. "It helps me think. Ahh, there she is. Have you the provenance?"

His taciturn assistant hands over a yellowed sheet of paper, then walks to Sik and offers a cup of hot tea. The girl rubs her throat. "It's good for here," she says. Blinks a few times and then, apparently finished talking, disappears among the statuary and easels.

Killjoy regards the paper in his hands, nods once, twice, and promptly folds it up and tosses it into the nearest brazier.

It disappears into blue smoke instantly.

"Authenticity be damned?" laughs Jackal. "Ya really do burn them all!"

"Unfortunate truth, my dear. If it's of questionable origin, I can't in principle run it through here. Best to leave a wisp of a hint of the genuine with the buyer -- or else my reputation will be put to the torch. Now then!" He claps his hands. "May I see the item?"

I hand him the wrapped goblet.

"Well let's take a look. Oh yes. Yes. Very good," he says. "This is a surprise." Glances up. "And a cursed blessing that you bring."

"You recognize it?"

"Recognize it? Of course. A piece like this doesn't travel very far in the trade without raising an eyebrow or two."

"Are you interested, then?"

Killjoy grimaces. "It's not that I'm not," he admits. "You'd do well enough at auction -- honestly, I'm favoring canceling next week outright, too much uncertainty -- and I don't know if your esteemed colleague told you, but I am not, for the same reason, presently in the position to buy such a piece -- though it breaks my heart. Ah, look at that craftsmanship..." he breathes. "Gets you right here." Taps his chest. "Like beautiful music or a beautiful woman."

"Or an Executioner's blade," Jackal retorts.

"How apt of you," Killjoy says gravely. "This is... well, it's part of a set, in fact. The rest have been... ambling about the city for the past three years or so."

"Any *amble* through your hands?" Sik asks.

"Not *through*," he discloses. "Not yet. As with most of everything that came out of that province, at the time, it would have consisted of five goblets. Least ways, that's the educated assumption: she was, time to time, somewhat... schizophrenic in her output. At present, I have procured three -- four, if you'll permit me. Therefore, we miss only the final piece."

"That was a quick jump from 'I' to 'we'."

"Naturally. If we're in this, we're in this together, my boy."

"So, basically, what you're telling us is…"

"My position is this," he says, "I cannot go to auction with an incomplete set. I've come down too many… paths to risk the loss now. I am not comfortable buying it for the same reason no one is buying right now -- which is why, if I could point you to another party, self-interest forbid I ever be so masochistic, you would have no better luck elsewhere."

"Stating the obvious I expect, but if we insisted on running it through your hall, you'd refuse. Correct?"

Tilts his head back, longingly, yet deeply, deeply annoyed -- with me, with circumstances, with himself, but likely all at once.

"Again, the self-interest part."

"And the only other auction house…?"

"Is this one. Again, the self-interest part."

"Hell," Sik says. "All this work and it's only worth the drink we can piss into it. *Unless we find another one.* Geez."

"That," Killjoy states, "is the salient point. I *know* where the last resides. And the answer to your next question is the last thing any of us wants to hear."

This really is the way of it, isn't it? A desperate job turns up nothing. A bit of random luck has the sheen of good fortune. So this is where a burial at midnight was leading us, all along. No wonder the cup was buried with the dead. That's probably where it will remain. But one of us has to put a foot forward to keep going, even if it's up the scaffold.

"Where?" I ask, already suspecting.

He hands the cup back in unspoken apology.

#

Beyond the shrine, the land dips down and there lays that contemptible grassy hill. Here in the mornings, the embankment all around is filled with fog and the very top juts out like an island in the clouds. As the sun rises, it transforms each wisp and tendril into a gentle pink that glows brighter, and brighter, and brighter, until the mist becomes a river of gold. When it evaporates, the island is illusory, a half-remembered dream, or possibly a memory.

But to the eyes of a gravedigger, it is sadly a hateful thing. For while countless dead are interred inside, the Executioners protect that lonesome mound of earth above all else.

Crypt Dun.

The Hill of the Dead.

… fucking hell.

Sik kicks an errant rock over the edge. "Why did we come up here again."

"To brood."

"Is it working?"

"Frown."

She frowns at me.

Sigh. "Not deep enough…"

"Ya… people… have way… fu— uughh… way… too much… endur… fu— oi, listen to… when I'm… ughhh." Jackal finally mounts the last step.

"You didn't have to come," Sik says.

"There's an… easy jo— in there… too ti— to bother… unghh," she sputters and slumps against the wall.

"Did you hear how they tried to get in?" I ask.

"Lotta… sedatives."

"N-not half bad," Sik snickers.

"I have to admit, that is pretty inspired."

Half-opened, bleary eyes gaze over at the hill now painted in the waning rays of sun. "Pretty… lonely… in the even… nuh… haahh, I'm si… sittin'," Jackal says, sliding to the lacquered floorboards.

"So, brooding's productive and all, but what now, Red?"

"Well, we aren't going to starve, but we're as piss poor as always. I'd like to say 'screw it' and go out again tonight, hit a few far out areas before... damn, see, that's it, isn't it? We can do what we normally do because nothing's changed yet and we can't do what we normally do because we don't know what and when they're going to change."

"Maybe they won't?"

"It's the *Dun*, Sik."

"Yeah, I know." She nods.

"They aren't going to sleep over this one."

"Yeah, I know! Shit, I'm not stupid, you asshole."

"I... yeah I know, I... ah, screw it, let's wait."

"Wait?" Her face plummets.

"We wait."

"Ugh, I hate waiting," she whispers.

"There were places farther than Darrow I thought about, if we were going to muck around longer, but we don't have time for that." I glance back at our weary thief. "We don't have time you think, Jackal? Will this come down soon?"

Jackal raises her arm and drops it like an axe.

Well, that was certainly easier than the monosyllabic. She can debate Quinn soon.

I rub my eyes. "Sorry, Sik."

She shrugs. "Sure."

"I wanted... to see that damn hill again. See the bell that was rung before the echo rebounds at us. No matter what the Executioners say, no good ever came outta the Dun. Which, given our luck, will be seen."

"S'fine. Keep telling ya you don't have to explain yourself. I'm happy tagging along."

"And maybe I thought it would give me a plan."

"Burn plans. Let's relax. Lately's been real stressful."

"Good plan." I say.

"Yep." She grins.

"Your plans are always better."

She shrugs again. "'Cause they aren't plans."

Her needle-thin shadow stretches towards Crypt Dun as she walks away to the hundred-some steps that lead back down to the city. I follow and surely my shadow is much the same behind me, yet unlike hers I feel like mine does not recede, instead stretches thinner and thinner to the point of snapping, hastened only by the horizon-bound sun.

"O... oi! Didn't we ju— get up he— oi, don't... leave," a voice calls after me.

#

We talked over the next days. Jackal stopped by once, cradling a bottle of wine she claimed Quinn had lifted for us. I asked her if it were possible we could work together, circumstance permitting.

"Oh, yeah, we've talked 'bout that," she grinned. "Lotsa fun! Only..." She tugged at a twintail for a while before finding the right words. "There aren't... burials on people's property much. Actually, never seen it... Part of Executioner puh... puh-rai-vih-ti... shun? Um. Mmm," she nods. "Life is for the livin', yeah? Why put stuff like that in your home? Naw, we'll let ya know if we find underground stuff or diggin' stuff for ya to help with. Promise."

Soon after, word came down.

My anxious reluctancy to even go and listen...

The message-runner climbed atop an empty crate the greens merchant in the adjacent stall gave her. She kept brushing back her flaxen hair, clearly distressed in a crowd. A black scarf, shot through with a single crimson line, had been hurriedly tied around her upper arm. At first I mistook her for an Executioner, until I saw another more benign pastel scarf swaying from her side. Honestly, the satchel should have given her away, but seeing those threatening colors always makes me too nervous to think.

I noticed Sik pinching my sleeve.

She wasn't much better off...

"A runner..." she murmured. "Bet the whole city's full of them this morning."

I didn't say anything.

"Ever seen 'em wear *their* colors?"

"Never."

"Me neither," she whispered. Two city rabbits hopped up to the crate and began to nibble at fallen leaves. The runner cleared her throat. The rabbits ignored her. "She'll be off to the towns outside before noon. Probably weeks... months, before she tells everyone and can come home."

And then it started.

The real beginning of our story...

"Regarding the recent incident at Crypt Dun and its aftermath," the girl announces in a crystalline voice, its power reminiscent of a cavern's depths and surprising considering her earlier demeanor, "I will speak.

"Fifteen days ago, two gravediggers sought unlawful entrance to the burial space known as Crypt Dun. In so doing, they disrupted the peaceful interment of potential cursed, risked provoking confirmed cursed, and threatened the security of Old City. The Executioners discovered the intruders before damage had been done to any vault; Crypt Dun remains secure.

"However, the Executioners have contested that the status quo cannot persist where there exist individuals that actively disturb the dead in pursuit of financial gain or otherwise. After deliberation, the Sovereignty agrees; the Executioners are to be granted expanded authority as follows.

"All graveyards fall within Executioner domain. The Executioners may coordinate with, or replace, the Officers of the Watch as is deemed appropriate.

"All corpses fall within Executioner property. The Executioners may exhume, transfer and inter any and all as is deemed appropriate.

"All vault construction falls within Executioner oversight. The Executioners may create burial chambers, built to Executioner code, regardless of location.

"Finally, Pauper's Pit is to be transferred to Executioner control effective immediately. Its conversion will be subject to no objection or obstruction."

I can't believe what I hear, even as the words of the runner echo down the street and into the silence of unseen distances. Everything? Two idiots try to steal from the Dun and this is how the Sovereignty responds? It gives the Executioners everything they have ever wanted, when years of debate only granted them an inspection of the recently dead, a presence at burials, and a stupid sodding hill to burrow around?

The girl brushes her hair back again and steps down from the crate. One rabbit dashes off into the crowd, the other ignores them both. "Please circulate this," she requests before everyone disperses, "we want the City informed before nightfall. Thanks." And with that, she runs off to another quarter to carry on her message.

I pull Sik away roughly.

"Whoa, hey, what the hell!"

"Take the rest of our money," I tell her. "Buy food."

"E— ehh?" She stops tripping over her own heels and finally matches my hurried pace.

"One, no, no, two. Two months."

"Two wha—?"

"No, see Darv. Call in a favor. Three months."

"Thre— Darv? Uh, but we only got one favor with him."

"Doesn't matter. Use it."

"Whaddaya mean 'three'?" I stop. She slams into my back. "Uff!"

"What are you talking about?" I let go of her hand and flash three fingers. "Three. Three months."

"E— ehh? I... we can't carry that much food."

I weigh emptiness in both hands. "Ask Darv, that's why. The favor. And we eat it. Eat the food, more space. More space, less food. Less food, more loot. We eat. Come home. All loot."

"Wai-wai-wait, I know I'm the crazy one, but you're insane!" she protests.

"Please. You heard her. We're living in an age of panic. A little insanity is salvation."

Sik thinks for one second, then flashes her beautiful devil-grin. "Like it when yer like this."

"Ha, that's ahh… yeah, me too."

The message-runners were running. Sik was running. Undoubtedly, the Executioners were running, probably had been, slavering gleeful piss-drunk ecstatic, moving their plans out into the yawning daylight. I stood there, squinting as it lanced through the dark, dappled cloud-cover. One beam of light hung like the hand of a frozen clock, illusionary stillness captured in an imaginary needle.

They'd be at our backs, the Executioners. Winter would be too, howling behind us and whipping up banners of black and crimson. But if we gravediggers chased the sunrise hard enough, we would stay ahead of them all.

And the dead?

Well.

They'd wait for us.

And the frozen clock hand lurched.

#

I mulled over the cup while Sik was gone. There was a good chance Killjoy might be interested now. The message-runner had said nothing of inspections that might impede our proper business dealings, but there was no assurance there wouldn't be. It's true that Executioners, almost to a fault, strike at the source. Until now, shady goods were mostly the Watch's concern, thievery falling wholly within their jurisdiction.

To risk the loss now, he had said.

There would be some who would risk the loss. Wouldn't even consider it loss. A waxy, gray visage appears in my mind, its musty unkempt beard frowning. I snort reflexively. *That's* not happening.

"We'll leave it with Picker and Stealer," I tell Sik later, tossing the cup between my hands.

She throws two full packs on the bed. "We can't."

"Sure, it's perfect. They'll keep it safe, get itchy to take it for themselves, slip word out to Killjoy or whoever else to let off some tension, the dealers'll get famished for it, as they are for anything good, and when we're here again it'll have a fine, desperate price on it."

"Uh uh, Red."

"Insurance. Finally we aren't entirely broke," I gesture at the packs, "your transaction notwithstanding."

"Naw, I mean we can't. Jackal, she and Quinn are out on a gig."

"What, now?"

She nods. "Went to go say bye, but there was a note on the table. I doubled back to Darv to let him know to tell them."

"He'd tell them," I say.

"Well, yeah, but I also wanted to apologize."

"Ehh?"

"We got in an argument."

Dubious phrasing. She reads my look instantly.

"Fine, fine, *I* got into an argument with him, *I* did. Geez."

"Why?"

"Tried… stiffing him outta two favors."

"Why? All we needed was the one."

"I… I didn't want to use it, okay? So I tried tricking him he owed us for something else. He's—" Waves a finger at me erratically. "He's got a really good memory!"

"Course he does. Why do you think no one does business in there?"

Silence.

She rubs her hair. It sticks up in disarray. "Sorry."

"So…?" I lead.

"So?"

"Everything patched up?" I ask.

"Huh? Oh, yeah, he and me are cool."

And she forgets her anxiety that fast…

Wish I could do that.

"Right, details bedamned," I announce. "Let's shog."

"Oh!" Sik cheers, eagerly bouncing at the door.

#

Our shortest stay after a dig and we were off again. Sik, rueful of the fact, affectionately cuddled a city-rabbit… who honestly didn't mind where it was going.

It wasn't the way I wanted to leave things, but I buried the cup in the basement inside the mushroom bed. The mantelpiece idea did seem idiotic enough to work, but, well, habits you know?

Once we exit the city proper, Sik raises the rabbit on high. "Liberation!" she cries.

It's rare to see anyone out here, rarer still to cross paths, instead we appear as distant shadows to one another, silhouetted by ambivalent horizons. It isn't that the Sovereignty discourages travel, it's… there isn't any real reason to. True, trade exists, except localized and irregular enough to be forgotten in the day-to-day. Old Kingdom, and Old City by extension, is unique in affluence. Towns are mostly simple, cultivating enough and only enough for existence. The border cities, the shantytowns… who knows. I haven't been there. I don't think anyone has.

That's kinda the point.

"Do you think they'll enforce a curfew while we're gone?" I ask.

"Ehhh, I doubt the Execrations'll care. Didn't need one before and now they have a huge playground. When there's something horrible happens, like… a buuunch of cursed get loose, then they'll call for emergency practice."

"I still don't believe it," I try to say inaudibly enough to let the subject die without—

She groans. "Yes, my dear, I know. Execrations only inter bodies 'cause it's fun! Whoo! They're like us… only… reverse!"

"Has anyone seen one? At all?"

"I fucking hope I don't. Shit." The rabbit squeaks. "Ah, bun. You okay?" She scratches its ears. "Anyways. Red. No one's *seen* the plague either, but it's down there, beyond the Gap, if there *is* anything down there anymore. Or anywhere."

"That's what's said, though I'm not sure I believe that either."

"Be a nicer place to live, if you're right." Halts, looks back at me, dark circles under her eyes more prominent than usual. "'It's all a conspiracy. The Sovereignty's consolidating its resources for some big thing. The Execrations are reaving the dead to get at their offerings to fund whatever the hell it is they do and exert further influence over everyone. And the Blaggards are skulking, somewhere, until midnight to murder us all.' Sing we now the names of the dead." She blinks. "The world already ended. We don't have the luxury of subtext. Plaguers. Cursed. Simple. Sorry."

"That isn't what I think."

"No? Sure seems like you think there's more to things than there is."

"We're ignorant of reality," I say. "We're on the fringe. We can only know what we know."

Waves of grass roil the fields.

Each blade sighs a lazy susurrus.

She strokes the rabbit's ears. "That's true too. I'm not all that smart, so what I know is minimal. I know there's more to things simply because I don't know much. Still. It's not me alone, though, ya know? The Execrations can't say why a corpse becomes a cursed, or if it's cursed beforehand, or why one is cursed and not another."

"That's why I don't trust them," I mutter. "Or part of it, leastways."

"Yeah, that whole wanting to kill us for messing with their pretty little graves makes it real difficult to be friends."

"Makes it easy enough to be poor, though."

She shrugs. "We get by." Sideways glance. "We get by, right?"

I bump into her.

She bumps back.

"Ready?"

"Almost." Strokes the rabbit's ears a while longer. "It's not the same, ya know?" Gives a sad smile.

The vibrant city waits for us to return from where we have to go. Sik places the rabbit on the ground. It hops away once, eats some grass, and starts bounding on its way to wherever. She doesn't stand.

"What a happy thing," she says.

#

In an obscure ditch within an unremarkable patch of trees surrounded by absolutely nothing noteworthy, we pick up our hidden tools of trade.

Time was this wasn't necessary, but as the voice of the message-runner sang this morning, time will always change. When the stigma of gravedigging became too dangerous, we felt uneasy keeping shovels at home and moving about at night solely to hide our identities. That became the worst tactic. When only two types of people work outside the confines of the city at night and one happens to be an Executioner, and you're not an Executioner...

If curses do exist, their exposure to the dead apparently doesn't infect them. Neither does ours us. We have that much in common at least and it's enough for me and Sik to shirk paranoia. Still, doesn't mean the general populace wouldn't panic at us for fear of transmission, if that is a correct analogy.

"I love these things."

Sik is scarfing down, catching crumbs in her palm and licking them up.

"It's the honey," I explain.

"It's the everything. But, yes! The honey… ughh, I… mgpphn… mmm! I miss sugar, damn it all!"

"Seriously, Sik, I'm not letting you binge. They're compact for a reason. We needed them like that, remember? And…"

"I know."

"Aaand you eat a lot, *you'll* be compact and miss shitting more than sugar."

She barks a laugh. "Honestly, I love these because they're so filling. I eat this and I know I won't get hungry for ever. Ughh, bliss isn't that?"

"I wouldn't really know."

"Yeah, well…" Mutters some unintelligible, crass words. "It's annoying. And so I will devour everything… unto death! And then beyond death, in the great chasm of my stomach, the churning void of acid and shifting lands where to leave is to enter other darker, forbidden places."

I can't help smirking. "Are you finished yet?"

"I'm pretty pumped, though, right? I've been aching to get at Avershym long time now, long time!"

"More than Darrow?" I ask.

"Fuck yes more than Darrow. Darrow was a piss, never had real hopes for it, fun though it was to try at last. But Avershym? Ohh ho ho, ahaha, no one knows what's in those vaults."

"While yet before we're there. Plenty of stops along the way. First—"

#

"Stalwart Ensbryng," Sik snickers.

"Time to get to work," I grin.

Crumbled walls and ivy laying claim to every visible surface is how this cemetery greets you. Not nearly so old as it masquerades. The winds from the east, the flash-floods from the north, and ultimately poor planning have forced everything to totter into twilight years far too early. Oddly moving in its desolation, laudable in the way it stands, raising its head not in abject defiance but to see daybreak one more day, one more day.

That is Ensbryng.

"I can't remember the last time we've done this in good weather," I say.

Sik scrunches up her face. "Weird, huh?"

The guards are plenty apparent, chattering and joking the night away -- loud enough to offset their lack of visibility. High-mounted torches transform their shadows into dumpy, fearful children hiding underneath the protection of their legs.

Broken walls make good peepholes.

We split up and take the perimeter.

"Never a stir, Red," Sik says when we meet back up.

"You say that," I reply, "as though you had something to do with it."

She offers a grin and a piece of parchment. I unfold it and read a short list of recent dead and their new homes.

"It was... unattended," she explains.

"Uh huh."

"It was!" Her insistent shadow of a face juts out of the darkness.

I give up.

"I didn't see anyone over on the other side. And a couple of these are in that section." I shake the list. "Them first."

"Got it." Sik salutes.

Digging is so much easier without the slush-mud the dirt becomes in a storm. Conversely, the Watch doesn't skive patrol duty either, so…

We take turns, alternating between shovel and lantern. When a guard comes close, we throw a tarp over the hole and wait. Sometimes, Sik scouts around and leaves me to it, then flashes the shutter in my eyes when I need to hide. The guard leaves; Sik follows. I dig in darkness. Then she dashes back to help at a frantic pace.

Before long, we've unearthed the dead and found an assortment of coins. About as much as last time, but Sik won't complain. This is the beginning of the journey. Set expectations low. Hope for the best, plan for the worst.

"They never date the dead."

"Figure it's taboo?" Sik asks.

"Not sure. I always thought it was that the *who* mattered more than the *when*."

"Guess so. The Execrations probably keep records now. You're wanting a twelve-year, eh?" she teases.

"Don't we all," I say under a breath.

"Ungh, seriously. Enough of those and we'd never dig another day in our life."

"Yeah right." I smile. "As if that would ever happen."

"Ha," she laughs, "you're right."

"Last one's over— ah."

"Over whe— ah."

I point. "I was not informed of this."

Sik blinks rapidly at the entrance of a burial vault. "That's… not Execration. Uhh. Is that? Is it?" I almost chide her for opening the lantern full-bright, but the paralyzed lump in my throat balks a comment and my flurried thoughts smother it into oblivion. "Doesn't look Execration. I mean, it does and it doesn't. This is…"

"When the hell was a vault in Ensbryng?"

"… really, really unexpected."

The construction certainly resembles that of the Executioners. And yet… too ad hoc, not practical enough. If nothing else, that beige stone is far too brittle for their purposes especially given the environment. There is, however, one glaring point that is decidedly un-Executioner.

"It's open," I say in awe.

"Let's go before they pop the lid on!"

"Don't rush in, you d—"

But she doesn't listen. She never listens.

#

It's dank. The ceiling glistens in the lantern-light. I don't know how long the guards have left the entrance gaping, but the air shouldn't be like this. Not until far down. Either the vault has been exposed for months or the construction really was amateur. We pass recesses in the walls that appear half-finished or never-started. None of them are filled. No bodies, bones or dust. The whole place exudes abandonment.

Hallways split off to dead-ends.

Ditches, wide enough to be graves themselves, lay about at random.

Holes like giant eye sockets watch us from the ceiling.

I hoist Sik atop my shoulders and she sticks her head in one of them and peers about, but says she doesn't see much.

"I feel like this place is going to cave in on us."

"Two diggers never to be dug for," Sik says ominously. "How fitting."

"Shh, lights out!"

Sik closes the shutter in less than a thought.

The chill that only a grave can have wraps around us, licks our eyes in the pitch-black world. I hear nothing beyond my heartbeat and the soft exhale of Sik's breath. Seconds tiptoe around us. Nothing. I reach out for her hand, then stop when I see it. A dull glow. Green? Surely an afterimage from the lantern. Wait. No, that would be blue.

I squint and nudge Sik.

"I think it's safe," she whispers.

I nod, unseen.

We creep towards the source. As my eyes adjust, the light reflects off the moisture on the walls, then the ceiling. Still and quiet but for us. I stop at the corner. Sik holds a pale green finger at her pale green face. I nod. Look around the corner. No torch, no guard. Instead, some growth on the floor, resembling cave popcorn, emits the light.

"Hey, look at that." Sik bends down. "Weird crystal." She pokes it. "Gruuengh!"

"Did you cut yourself?"

She makes a face, unreadable in the dimness except for the tongue jutting out. "It... squished."

"Huh." I peer at it. "Think it's a mushroom."

"Not eating it."

Definitely poor lighting, though impressive for a... whatever this thing is.

The lantern blinds me with its sudden appearance.

"We go," she says flatly.

As we work farther into the vault, we discover a stairway leading lower. Along its walls: more incomplete delving at intervals where you might expect a doorway to open upon a new level. None do. And so the stairs go down, down, down.

At the bottom, the air is clammy. The path divides into five separate directions.

"This isn't Executioner at all," I say.

"I wonder," Sik says. "Then, who made it?"

"The guards if it's as newish as the cemetery."

"And if it's olderish than?" she asks.

I struggle to answer. "Some bored, obsessive miner."

"Makes sense."

"Which one you want?" I gesture broadly at the paths.

"Ehh? We only got the one lantern."

"There's enough of these glowing—"

"Stop," she says. "I get it. This way. You go opposite and come back here if you run out of... *yeah*."

My pace is slow, but the green glow is surprisingly efficient. At these depths, reflective moisture pools and drips onto the floor, and the mushrooms -- the word I've chosen for ease of calling them something identifiable -- seem substantial enough. I thought to take some with me, but the glow dies out when their... body... is disturbed. For now, there's enough by which to see and very little worth seeing else. The walls here lack recesses whatsoever and it's all I can do to keep my bearings as the path splits again and again.

"I don't think there's much point to covering more ground at the same time," I tell the Sik-not-there.

"Feels more productive to say so, though," she tells me.

"If you say so," I tell her.

"They went down here."

At first I'm not sure what she means, quick to realize it wasn't her who said it.

"I didn't see nothing." A gruffer voice.

"I'm sure of it." The other voice is on a warpath.

"Sure as shit I'm not. I hate this place."

"Claustrophobe."

"*What* did you call me!?"

"Relax." A third voice, bored and tired.

"You heard him!" Gruff protests.

"It means you don't like closed-in places," Bored says.

"I— I know what it means!"

Freeze.

Don't make a sound. Don't even breathe.

Three guards are blocking my way. Two mill around, searching carefully, but Gruff whips her torch about erratically. Upset, unpredictable: she's the dangerous one. If she comes this way fast, I can't get away without running. Don't breathe, damn it! She darts out of sight. My shoulders relax. Not by much.

Sik, I'm not sure where she is. Possibly far enough away, but these aren't necessarily the only guards patrolling. And they know we're here.

"Let's hurry up," Gruff calls.

"Go back if you want," Warpath snorts.

"And let you get everything for yourself? Right."

Need to meet up with Sik. I start to creep away.

"I like her, you know," Warpath sighs.

"I know," says Bored.

"But she gets really, really annoying."

"You get used to it. Eventually."

"Really?" Warpath asks.

"… no. She's getting worse lately. I just wanted to say that. Come on, let's check the buried section next."

Buried section.

I start to creep after their shadows.

That sounds profitable.

#

The guard won't leave. Stands sentry at the entrance, dust blooming from his stamping foot. The other guard said he'd be back in a few minutes after he checked a riskier area himself. Wouldn't let this new guy follow. And so there he stamps and waits, too lost to leave alone, with me stuck in the darkness of this cave stamping and waiting on him.

At least he's not an Executioner.

The buried section turned out to be literal. Cave-in, additional evidence of dismal construction quality. I tried to pick around as they looked through the area, but soon it was clear that nothing of interest was here for either of us. Unfortunately, as they had the sole light, they made to exit quicker.

And so, here we are.

One good whack of the shovel…

… I could take his torch too.

Sik would like that one.

Still, they don't know I'm *here* here. And… but I could frame a rock for it, plenty of them here. That's a good— That's stupid, I'm lost too. Even if it would feel good to knock sense into him… I bet it's like a melon it would make a satisfying thump I wish that idiot would hurry and—

"Come on."

"Took you long enough," I growl.

"Took you long enough," the guard says.

"Don't rush into hazards." Bored responds to Warpath's complaint with a clap to an unprotected ear.

I let a little sadism tug my lips upwards.

"This is balls. We're leaving," Bored says.

"We have to find her first." Warpath keeps his distance, rubs the side of his head.

"We'll seal her in too," Bored grumbles. "Teach her to run off on another fit…"

Hoping that they always left this vault open did seem too easy. Unused as it is, why do they even bother?

I need to find Sik. Now.

But they make straight for the staircase, calling out to their missing companion. Maybe Sik will take that as a cue and at least come see what's going on. It's these three alone. We could take them. Knock one out at the start and Sik impales a leg with the pickax. Leave the newbie last, he panics, we lay into him. Three bodies on the floor, sadly the only ones in this vault, all alive and one, maybe two, conscious. At these depths, no one would hear a cry for help. Gives us time to dig up that final corpse, wherever it was, obviously not here.

"Hey," Warpath whispers to the other. "Is that one of them on the landing?"

Shit. Sik, if that's you, I'm going to kick your ass later.

As torchlight floods the stairway, shivering shadows flee for fear of drowning in it, leaving someone else in view.

"What are you *doing* here?" Bored asks her.

That frantic guardswoman is sitting on the first step, hugging her legs. She jolts at the noise. Her voice is deadened. "Let's go."

"Where's your torch? What's wrong?"

"We're going!" she shouts, finally looking at them, face wet and eyes pink.

"What happened? Hey! Get back here!" Bored shouts.

"Leave her alone, alright?" Warpath hurries to her side.

"Le… 'leave her alone' he says. That's what I've been bloody telling him…"

The guards file up the stairs. I look down the hallways for a sign of Sik. Surprisingly, she's right next to me.

"Yo."

"'Yo' yourself, they're about to seal us in," I tell her.

"Hmm? But I refuse."

"I'm sure they don't care," I say.

"I didn't find anything."

"Me neither."

"I found her though." I can hear her malevolent smile.

"Huh?"

Sik makes one of her amused sounds. "I was screwing with her."

"That really helps our situation, seeing as they're ahead of us and she's wigging out."

"I got some money off her," Sik says, rummaging through her pockets as if that alone can allay my concerns.

"Good. The diggers will have some offerings to strip from us when they come for our bones in a few years. Shut up and hurry up already."

"Yes yes," she says.

We follow the guards, none of them checking their backs for us and none of them slowing down. The moisture pooling on the ground splashes underfoot. That's a problem. If we speed up now, they'll hear us without fail. Despite its demented architecture I do understand the layout of the upper level, so we can book it then and assault them -- at least, we have to. Quiet subterfuge will only get us as far as a sealed exit.

"You're sure?" Sik asks of the plan.

"Unless you think you know the grounds better."

"No, I'm bad with directions."

I take the lantern from her. She takes out the pickax.

"Ready?" I ask.

"Go, Red."

I let the light spill out and race down the uneven ground. The maze of dead-ends engulfs us, but the pattern is familiar, repetitious, it unfolds in my mind as a paper figure might: complicated when viewed yet simplistic once you know the trick. I feel like I dug these halls. It's linear. A single line, twisting, breaking itself, breaking upon itself, but continuing without falter. The dead-ends? The recesses? Aspects added later. Visual trappings. Ignore them.

Even so, I make two wrong turns.

Then a third.

Sharp staccato stabs my heart.

I adjust the map in my head. We'll be fine. Sik gives my shoulder an encouraging slap. And we run.

Before long, we hear our prey again. Slow down. Edge around the corner. We'll sprint here. Sik hands me the shovel. The final corner. Time to fight. I tense my leg and Sik and I—

"Shut up!"

— come to a halt immediately.

The guardswoman slams her fist into someone's face and whoever it was goes down with a pathetic yelp. Torchlight casts her shadow along the tunnel a frenzied dance. She shakes her fists at the entire group surrounding the vault's entrance, begging another newcomer to give her extra shit she doesn't need.

"You didn't even find one," someone protests.

"I said shut up!" A finger spears her companions. "Neither did they."

"You said you'd find them this time," another accuses.

"I...!" Finally, shoulders droop. Reverts to being the girl at the base of an unlit, miserable staircase. "I... fucked up. Alright? I fucked up."

The group shifts around. Uncomfortable with the situation or caught off-guard by the admission.

After a long silence, someone else asks: "So what do we do now?"

"We... close it."

No one likes the answer, but no one objects.

"I'm... sorry."

She helps them slide the massive block into place. For just a moment, she looks back at us standing in full view. There's no reason why she shouldn't see us, yet she doesn't. She stares at something past us, something veiled from her in the shadows, while we stare past her at the light being compressed into a single, thin line until -- the finality of immovable stone settling into place -- whatever we sought is lost to both of us.

#

"I won't panic," Sik says to herself.

It's implacable stone that seals the way out. Thick, heavy. Exactly what you want for someplace you don't plan on ever opening again. Against my palm, it isn't coldness that I feel emanating from it but a terrible permanence.

"I won't panic," Sik maintains. "Can we break through if we have to? With the pickax? Red?"

"If we have to," I lie.

"Oh, good. Honest, I was a little freaked."

"I hadn't planned to be on this side yet," I mutter.

"Yeah, I know, right?"

She doesn't laugh.

Distract her.

"The question," I start, fumbling for a topic, "is how often they open this place up."

"Why."

"Maybe there's a schedule to it," I offer.

"No, I mean: 'why would they open it to begin with?'"

"There's nothing here," I say.

"Right?"

"That we found."

"Yeah."

"Bad timing? Coincidence?" I ask.

"Maybe. But maybe they do inspections of what's here."

"Of the nothing that's here," I say.

"Y-yeah… look, I don't get it either, but there's some reason they came inside."

"If it were proper Executioner they'd be interring, but I didn't see any sign of that," I say. "So, they always leave the vault wide, saw us, and tried to find us?"

"M-maybe," she stutters. "Something I still don't get, though. That guard, he said something like not finding us this time, but… this is our first time here."

I didn't notice that.

"Other diggers…?" But my voice trails away as I think over everything I heard, and didn't hear, from the guards.

Sik asks the question. "Red, did they even know we were here?"

"They acted like it. I think."

Sik perks up. "Something's in here!"

I want to snark at her, but I wordlessly follow her stomping heels instead. This might be her way of coping. Looking for a thing that's not there is better than calculating time of survival based on food supply. I slow her down enough so I can scratch out an approximate sketch of this place by the lantern's impatiently jumping light.

By the time we reach the staircase, I've studied enough of the complete design to understand that the layout isn't meant to be as desultory as its execution. From appearance, the architects were trying to force a structure that the rock they bore through wouldn't allow. The clumsy turns, the dead-ends, simply a result of the natural landscape of Ensbryng.

"Amazing. That is pretty *boring*, huh?" Sik quips.

Regrettably, our search is as fruitless as the last. It's an empty vault, top to bottom. The only thing I can think of is to try to crack the entrance and, ultimately failing that, hope a passing guard discovers the disturbance. This is assuming they really don't know we're here and sealing us in truly wasn't their decision. If not...

"I *knew* it!" Sik cries out.

"Ah?"

"Up there!" She focuses lantern-light into one of those many ceiling-holes we've been passing by.

"What about it? You said nothing is up there."

"Well, yeah, it's empty. 'Cept there's doorways and hallways, I guess, or somethin'."

I cuff the backside of her head.

Lantern oil spills and hisses at me.

"Hey!"

"Moron!" I say. "Tell me when you spot shit like that!"

"Yeah, well, it wasn't interesting at the time. It wasn't crypt-like at all. No bodies! No money!" She shuts the lantern tight. In the darkness, the air moves upwards and her invisible hand smacks my forehead. Lights back on and we're glaring at each other. Really want to lay into her, punch her in that special way that knocks her air out...

But I relent. "Hop on."

She nods, starts to climb up my back.

"Hey," she says.

"Eh."

"Don't call me a moron."

"Even if it's true," I say.

"J-just… don't do it. Alright?" she presses.

Once she crawls up a level, I pass her the lantern and our supplies. Her skinny arm juts down and she helps yank me up. I blink a few times. It really isn't crypt-like.

"It seems to parallel… basically… everything below us," I say to myself.

"Bet there's not a parallel entrance."

"No, but there's probably another way in. In fact, it's certain," I say. "We were thorough. No other ways up here but to climb."

"Hmm. Weird tunnels. You think this is a new interment place? Hallways first, then recesses?"

"Likely enough," I remark. "New addition…"

"Every home needs an attic, the dead are no different!" She pauses. "We don't have an attic."

Not long until the monotonous rooms lead to the first good scrap of luck: a door.

"Bolt hole," I announce.

"Oh!"

Metallic, rusty, no visible way to open it.

"Oh, come on. It opens on the other side?"

"Huh? Oh hey, a door!" Sik announces.

"Yes, a do— what were you looking at?"

"The bolt hole." Points at a hole burrowed through the wall, about a foot from the door itself. "I thought you were being literal."

"I meant it metaphoric," I say.

"Well, so what, we have a way out."

I peek into the actual bolt hole. "You do. I can't fit."

She says it with a sober face, a serious voice:

"Then, this is goodbye."

… and cracks straightaway.

"Funny," I say.

She struggles to stifle the giggles.

"Sorry, sorry. Look, I'll go and find the way to open it."

She lights a torch, drops to her knees and wriggles through the hole. When did she get a torch?

Her muffled voice cries, "I'm stuck! I'm gonna starve to death! Aaahh!"

"Through yet?"

"Yeah," her voice calls back. "No way to the door here, though."

"Course not. That would be convenient."

"I'll poke around. Be back."

I try scouring the level for anything we missed, but I only turn up a fresh sense of boredom. Lacking a better plan, I stare at the door, willing it to unlock.

It decides to remain uncooperative.

I drop to the floor. Staring. Nothing happens.

I eat a snack. More staring. More nothing happens.

I swallow.

Silence, silence upon silence.

No wonder the Executioners prefer interment to burial. The quiet is lulling. The cursed can sleep on and on, never to wake for sun or sound, a breathless sleep that is deeper than ours, the pounding of ones heart a dull reminder submerged far below the defenestrating waves overheard of an ocean of memories if the dead can truly be said to remember, but why would they when the living cannot?

#

Still she dances in red-brown-red trans-crimson mourning as the sun sinks and rises in the chill, chill waters. I watch the seaweed dress her skin. Whither goes the dirt of dawn, washed to holdfasts where to remains of a corpse, even now lingering in the half-light of sunken beams? I reached out for them, forgetting she was there, despite her eternal importance. She leaves. I look back. She is gone, and grief, but the current shifts and I recede.

Flowing into a crack. A rock. A stone. A grave. Marking of where we've been. Marking of where I go. Down, down,

down, no breath, no heartbeat. The bodies do not sleep, but they are not awake.

Still she wears soot on her face. Her hands are dust. Her arms are clay. I call to her. She jumps. Eyes sinking into deep, deep, deep, the light is gone and she despairs.

Your despair is beautiful. I tell her that. You're despair it's beautiful.

She cries. The catacomb's entrance is sealed, the tears cannot escape. They fill, fill, fill and we drown alone together. I open my mouth for my final breath. I taste happiness.

I am filled to bursting.

"What is your name?"

#

"LOOK!" the drowned voice bursts through the door shatteringly start awake to terror held and sight beating.

The massive rabbit stares down at me and I swing the shovel.

"Oh oh, watch it!" Sik snaps. "Don't hurt him."

"Blighting ears and!" I say.

"Huh?"

I rub my face. "Unngh. Nothing." I look again.

Sik's arms are awkwardly wrapped around an impossible rabbit, half her size and very nearly too heavy to hold.

I'm unsure how to respond to this, so I gather our things.

"He's the Rabbit King!" she says cheerfully. "He knows the Pumpkin Cat King." And she repeats it to the poor animal. "You know the Pumpkin Cat King. You do."

"The exit?" I ask.

Lost in excitement, Sik is bewildered. "Exit?"

"Not surprised…" I say to myself.

"LOOK!"

"Come on."

"Come on," she repeats to Rabbit King.

They follow me through the door and out into similar hallways. The rooms here are derelict too, filled with broken rotting barrels with moldy indiscernible contents. Somewhere a breeze, however thin, beckons. Inviting though the scent, our unwilling companion struggles to hop in the opposite direction.

"Quit wrigglin'!" But her protests fall flat on huge, twitching ears.

When we find the fresh air's origin, the gap in the earth is predictably Rabbit-King-sized. A few blows with the pickax, a few shovelfuls of mud, and the vaulted-ceiling of the sky surrounds the living once again.

"Yaah, quit it!" Sik exclaims.

The moment we exit, Rabbit King's squirming becomes unrelenting. Somehow he manages to twist around and kick Sik onto her ass, hopping away to a clump of grass in the same movement. As he munches on it, I imagine his bold whiskers trembling in annoyed disdain. Then, unceremoniously, he sniffs scorn at the night and flops back into the vault.

"We couldn't have taken him with us," I say.

"Well, yeah, but," Sik protests, "he'd've had an amazing adventure."

"He already is. Doesn't need us."

"How come?" she asks me.

"Think where he's living."

"Ahh!" Sik puts a fist to her chin and nods in approval. "I understand."

I tug on her hand, to reassure myself of its presence rather than to pull her from reverie. But she holds on anyways, hums a shantey.

I smile.

"Should we double-back for that last corpse?"

"Naw," Sik says as we turn away from Rabbit King and his hidden throne, "we'll leave it."

She doesn't let go.

Eyes shut, she beams at me.

"He's a digger too, ya know!"

#

After our involuntary interment, the following digs were far less stressful and had particularly lessened amounts of fearing for the length of our meagre lives. True enough, there was the occasional Executioner -- as is expected these days. Even so, they were stationed and had been. No sign of the Sovereignty's proclamation traveling in these lands on quick legs.

"Not today!" as Sik is fond of cackling.

The weather had turned, however, and quickened itself into the pulse of the darkest season and its worrisome inevitability: frozen deepness. Rain no longer splattered lazily. The droplets lanced, at times cutting our exposed skin despite our bundled preparations. Sik always took care to find the offending sleet and snap it between two fingers before wiping the blood away.

We had to take additional breaks now. On days when the rain was liquid, it was freezing and soaked deep. Risk of chill had to be precariously weighed against opportunity.

For now we wait out the newest storm as wind claws at the door of the shrine in which we hide, wheezing at us.

"Ground's gonna freeze through soon," Sik tells the fire, then yawns. "Not possible to dig that dirt."

"Should be fine," I say. "This is about when I wanted to hit the crypts."

"That'll be good when we can't ma-aa-aake the shrines. Ughh, I'm tired…"

"Don't get used to it. I hate sleeping here."

"Paranoid."

I laugh. "You're immeasurably worse. What are you talking about?"

"Stop… worrying…"

These shrines, made of wood felled and erected long enough ago to earn the description 'ancient', used to be places for travelers to rest. Their dead and buried architects envisioned them little different than how Sik and I use them today -- albeit without gravedigging in mind.

Only the message-runners frequent them now. Locals, where they can, maintain the structures and leave preserved foods to aid them on their way, to say thank you, or perhaps to yearn for a time when more than one set of lonely footprints trampled the earth and dirtied the floorboards. Where they can't, time has weathered disuse into disrepair.

Which kind of shrine is more numerous, you've probably seen firsthand.

Sik interrupts my thoughts. "Relax. Get some sleep."

I mumble something noncommittal.

"No one is gonna stop here. Too remote..." She snorts snot and swallows. "'Sides, the Execrations would go straight to Crossroads... is... only like... half-a-mile away..."

"We'll circle Crossroads. I don't want to touch it."

"Really are... paranoid... heh..." Her lips curl.

I lie down. "Yeah yeah..."

"Hey... Red..."

"Huh."

Soft breathing. The fire crackling... *snap-snirk-snap*... She falls asleep faster on the road. The light... the shadows... the heat... I'm not sure if that makes me feel good or bad. The warmth... She sleeps.

"Red..."

Not yet? "Uh huh..." Nothing. "Sik?"

"I... uhh..." She stirs, settles back. "Forgot..."

"Oh."

"Forgot..." she repeats.

"It's fine."

"F..."

"It's fine," I tell her.

"F... f... f..."

"Shh, sleep now."

The fire flares.

"Fuck, it's cold!" She arches around painfully, furious and wide awake.

The sliding door slams. "Sorry!"

Sik's eyes dart at me. I make a quick glance over my shoulder at the partially-unconcealed shovel. The newcomer shrugs out of a pathetically-thin coat, ostensibly oblivious of the weather outside considering her bare legs, and reveals an Executioner scarf wrapped around her upper arm.

Sik makes a strange, swallowed sound.

I pull the tarp over the shovel and let out a breath.

"Th-the hell's wrong with you?" Sik whispers.

Ignore her agitation. I recognize that hair color.

"Sorry," the message-runner says. "Didn't expect anyone else here. Um, I'll sleep over here. Okay?"

She hunkers down with her satchel in a far corner, completely wound-up fidgets aimlessly in no way relaxed enough to sleep, glancing, glancing, glancing at us and... does she think we don't notice?

Even if she's simply representing the Executioners, we don't need the suspicion nor the scrutiny.

"There's enough room at the fire for you to—" I start.

"Thanks, no!" she pipes up, almost a squeak.

Sik pretends to go back to sleep.

She's biting a nail, scowling at me. Sorry, Sik.

"Um," the runner plays with her fingers. "I'm plenty warm. Thanks."

Tree branches crack and cackle in the gusts of wind outside the shrine.

"In that?" I ask, not faking the incredulity.

"Yes." Instant response. She's a true message-runner. "They give us good clothes. Technocracy stuff." Pauses. "Is what they call it," she explains in case I don't understand. If it wasn't for Quinn, I honestly wouldn't.

"The Executioners?"

"No. Um. The message-runners."

"Ahh. I thought that was Executioner. Nevermind."

She pauses again. Damn, she's a calculating one... Did she see through that?

Sik scowls deeper.

"Oh, this?" The message-runner touches the scarf, sadly. "They have everyone doing this."

"I heard about your announcement." I shake my head. "Bad news."

"I don't know." Gives me that odd look again that says she's thinking more than she should. "Maybe good, maybe bad. Depends for whom." Shrugs. "It's a message."

Sik gives me a pleading look.

"Most of our messages are good," she continues. "Or not bad. That's what I think."

"Are you done running yet?"

"No. Not close, even. Not at all. 'To the last city and back.'" Her eyes blur, staring through the floor.

"Bury it, Red, I'm exhausted."

I whisper behind my hand. "Right, give me a—"

"I know, but seriously... just drop it for now."

"She's the *same* one. She should be far ahead of us, so why here... why now?"

"Unnngh, I don't know, alright?" One tired eye squints up at me. "But she doesn't feel like a vanguard does she? Bury it."

"Alright, alri—"

"Idiots," says the message-runner.

I start at the word. Sik stops breathing, unsure how to respond to the insult.

"Never made us do that before," the girl is commenting to herself, "and they make me—"

"Ah...?" I try to get her attention.

"I never even...!" And instead of talking to some unseen thing below her, she addresses the empty space next to her. "And and and you said, you said..."

"Are you alright?" I ask.

"It's not the same… it's not—"

I clap my hands together. "Hey."

The runner jerks at that and finally turns to me. Her focus is back, but she looks like she's going to cry. "I… I… I have to sleep now, I have to wake up early and start again, so, so… so."

"Fair enough."

She doesn't move.

"Goodnight then," I say. "Such as it is."

"Um!"

I stop lying down. "What?"

"Are, are you a Black Guard!?" She asks in such an overexcitable flurry, I have to wait a few seconds to process what she said.

"No."

"Oh. Oh…" She relaxes.

"You know the Black Guard?"

"No." She shakes her head.

"The hell'd you think that?" Sik mutters so low I can barely hear her.

"Because," the runner explains, glumly, "I was scared."

"What do you know of the Black Guard?" Sik prods.

"Nothing. I don't know what they look like at all, so I didn't know if maybe you were." She brushes her hair back.

Sik, wobbly with fatigue, sits up. "Shit, you bloody people, I swear to fuck."

The runner's face goes blank. "I'm sorry?"

"No one knows what they look like. That's the point. *No one knows*." Sik spreads her arms. "And, this is my favorite bit, we don't even know what they *do*. Me, I think they don't even exist. Or!" She holds a finger up, accusatory to a point. "Or maybe they're a branch of the Execrations."

"Huh?" The message-runner is fully lost. *I've* heard this rant many times before, so I can only wish her luck.

"Think about it. We never heard about Blaggards before the Execrations, right?"

"I... Um."

"Right?" Sik presses.

"Okay."

"Right!" I don't know what Sik looks so happy for. Wasn't she a blink or two away from unconsciousness? It's not like the poor message-runner knows what the hell she's on about.

Unless that addled look happens to be her default face.

"Sik, it's too late for your crazy talk."

"Any time is a perfect time."

"We're moving on," I remind her, "storm or not, so get a few hours at least."

"Where are you going?" the runner asks.

I say the closest city's name.

"Ohh, that's not too far. I might be going that way too."

Crap. This is heading exactly where I don't—

"Want to travel together?"

"Hehhh~? You wanna journey with the nasty, scary Blaggards?" Sik wiggles her fingers. "Huu, huu, huu."

I smack her. "But you'd be going through Crossroads." The ordinary path for anyone.

"Sure," the runner nods. "Of course."

"We'll be cutting through the woods around there. It's faster, but dangerous. Are you armed?"

"Not really."

"We aren't exactly bodyguards."

Sik nods the affirmative. "Nope, we're Blaggards!"

I smack her again and she quiets down.

Instead of a frown, the girl gives us her first real smile. "You do understand I'm a runner?" Laughs delightedly in her hand, hiding that same smile. "Show me where." Pulls out a map from her dusky satchel and unrolls it in front of us. "We like shortcuts."

The intricacy is astounding. Orienting myself with Old City, I have to carefully track the line of our path before finding Crossroads.

"Where are we?" I ask.

"Here." She points out a symbol that looks like a roof.

"All these markings are confusing."

She laughs again. "Really gets that way, even for me. I don't know how they deal with it."

Nervous heat warms me self-consciously. I place my finger and begin to draw the fake trail from a random spot below Crossroads, up and around to our destination. It isn't remotely believable.

"That can't be correct," she notes automatically. "Roads aren't maintained out here, but they would be considerably shorter."

"Sorry." I rub the back of my neck. "I guess our map is inaccurate."

I raise my eyes to hers, expecting that calculating look. Instead, she smiles reassuringly. "That's expected, I suppose. You shouldn't purchase any scrap for anything outside a mile of home unless you find a cartographer out here, that is. We find lost sorts sometimes. I don't know why we don't make our maps available. But... I tend to forget it's usually just us runners outside." The smile collapses on one side. "Makes me sad."

Sik has been unnaturally silent, rebukes notwithstanding. I look. She's definitely wide awake now. Eyes unblinking, fingers trembling at parted lips.

"Do you... mind if... we copy this?" she says, emotionlessly.

"Please." The message-runner pushes the map closer and stands up. "Rrrnnnggrrrr," she stretches. "Haaa, I'm dead," and stumbles towards the door.

"Red!" Sik hisses. "Are you seeing this?"

"What?"

"This! This thing! This isn't a message-runner map. It's Exe-fucking-cration!"

"Bullshit."

But it's true, the more I look at it. Graveyards have their own symbol, as do crypts and tombs, and... There are places here I've never even heard of. Executioner vaults I'm not sure anyone knew about. And here! A private mausoleum. Ten miles away, if that. Untouched? Is it untouched?

Sik is already frantically scratching the new locations on our map.

I turn to the runner. "What's your name?"

"Me?" She withdraws a crimson paper talisman from her satchel. "You can call me Eddy."

"Thanks, Eddy. This helps us a lot."

Beaming. "Of course, we're here to help!" And then she slaps the talisman over the crack between sliding door and wall. A sweet, slightly rotten smell saturates the room.

"Incense?"

"I wish," she says. "It keeps the plague out."

That stops Sik. "*Plague*?"

Eddy waves about agitatedly. "Don't, don't worry! I, ah. 'All is well,'" she recites. "It's more habit than precaution. Plus it will seal the entrance from being blown open. I... hope no one else comes by. Well, they'd knock, I suppose."

"Have any of those that open doors?" I ask.

One embarrassed smile later: "They... don't really work like that."

She takes a rice cake from a small cupboard behind us, sits against the wall and unwraps it. Sik has resumed sketching, no indication of stopping. I sink to the floor and wonder over this new fortune offered by an unwitting messenger for no price at all. The linear path we had planned suddenly blooms before me in half-images that branch one way, then another, then blur into a single form as they grow, as they shiver in the breeze of shifting daydream.

When Eddy sleeps, she isn't next to the fire, but she is a little less distant than she had been previously.

\#

The storm has mostly passed by dawn.

And we need to ditch our new companion.

Eddy trots lightly upon the weed-punctured road. She ignores the bitter cold and I'm starting to believe she truly doesn't feel it. Instead, she happily leads us exactly towards the center of Crossroads and me further from any good, suspicionless excuse to circumvent that.

Sik is no help, the walking corpse. Bumping into me, all unfocused. Zigzags are the only straight lines she can follow.

So, the map was not without cost.

But to walk into, and hopefully out of, Crossroads with a message-runner may be a passable idea.

Would you approve, Jackal?

She'd give a fitting, Quinn-like nod. "Mantelpiece," is all she'd say, grinning spectacularly.

Crossroads, as far as I understand, had an accidental foundation -- and plenty of accidents along the way. Once a major thoroughfare for trade in all directions, a kind of hub for the larger cities on their way to Old City, it was merely one stopping point along a long journey. Some people stopped a little too long, however, and haven't moved on since.

I couldn't count how many stories I've heard.

Crushed by a fallen branch the size of a large man. Engulfed by a campfire while sleeping. Suffocated by a sinkhole -- saved the Executioners some effort. Choked to death on an apple from a nearby tree. Poisoned by a devilspot that sprouted overnight and belched its spores into ignorant lungs.

After hearing enough, I'm starting to think none of the deaths are embellished. Pull any random scenario from your ass and surely some wight found the same inglorious demise here in Crossroads. There's that saying you probably know, though phrased somewhat more poetically.

"'Every fool's ill fortune will cross Crossroads before the final fool is dug for.'"

I'm surprised to hear that come from Eddy when it's Sik who will quote Scriber any chance she finds, usually with a sadistic glee not meant in its original context. The tone of Eddy's words is somber. As expected of a girl who lives a life awash in daylight and wears a pastel scarf at her hip.

She sighs. "That's so morbid."

And so those that died stayed. With a cart packed tight, there is no room for a corpse. With a cart packed tight with foodstuffs, there is no tolerance for one either. A grave here, and here, and here, and soon you have monuments from those who can afford the price and pity, and with an almost depressing alacrity all the roads into Crossroads are flanked by tombstones and angels in never-ending wakes, a path marking the cold road we must suffer with reluctance.

We pass an apple tree, its limbs weighted down by spotty, grayish fruits.

I shouldn't be here.

We openly pass guards changing to a morning shift.

I shouldn't have come here.

There's plenty of tragedy underfoot, as there is everywhere, and certainly more than we can know. It bleeds into the land so gradually yet can dry in an instant. In reality, it may well be that the majority of the buried haven't actually died here, I want to imagine that, but stand at the midpoint of this accidental graveyard and take a road -- any one road -- and tell me you still believe that at the other end.

An old man with a pair of shears waves at Eddy.

"Back already? Can't keep up with your lot," the twisting beard grumbles.

"Sorry?" Eddy holds a hand to her chest. "I haven't been. Did another runner come by?"

"Runner, missy? Phffft." The beard puffs out. "One of those damnable gravediggers." A gnarled finger stabs at the Executioner colors.

"Gravediggers?" Clutches at the scarf. It trembles before she lets go. "I'm not one of them, but I am representing the Executioners."

"Same damnable difference! Digging up my graves. Let the dead sleep, yeh damnable bloodsuckers. Ain't there enough wrong with the world? Phffft. So?"

"Um."

"Why are yeh back?"

"I, I told you, I'm a message-runner, I'm not back, I'm passing through."

"Executioners. Phffft. What are they executing? Orders? The dead? They have to kill the dead now? What times. People living past the end of the world. The hell we still here for? And the dead want to come back to this? What times. Used to be orchards here. Now look at this. I'll be glad to leave it."

"Um."

"And yeh telling me I'm gonna come back? Why? The hell I'd come back here for. Phffft." Taps the shears against a nearby headstone. "So? What are yeh around for, message-runner? Plague? Wouldn't surprise me. Never good news no more."

"All, 'all is well,'" recites the flustered message-runner. "We're, we're heading to..." She swallows. "Let me give my message first. Are many people living in Crossroads? Could you gather—"

"What yeh take this for, a stage, missy? Crossroads is what it is, a crossroads. Ain't no city, ain't no town. Not for the living leastwise. And I ain't gathering up all them dead for yeh to spout nonsense at! Go talk to the guards or your digger friends with their fancy table-knives if yeh like." Eddy is about to respond, but he keeps going. "And don't bother wasting breath on me, I'll have none on it either. I'll learn what it is eventually? Good."

"The Executioners left?" I ask.

Bushy eyebrows rise, then furrow. "That's right, son. They come, they go. Like the living. Like the dead. Why? Hell if I know, certainly don't care. Starts feeling peaceful-like, but then they show up as sure as frost on an angel's ass and out farts snow."

Sik laughs after a delay, once the words worm through sleepiness, but is ignored.

"Maybe they returned," the beard sways back and forth. "Keep finding my graves open and the dead staring at the sky, as if there's something worth seeing up there in this damnable weather, but they ain't moving the bodies. Hell with 'em! I say. And fill the grave to the brim all the same. Shiftless bastards. Job half done? What times." Puffs out a breath. "Keeps happening."

"Graveburrower."

"Eh?"

Shit.

Sik holds up a finger and wobbles. "Graveburrower," she repeats.

"The hell's that."

Sik, shut up!

"S'animal. This big." Stretches arms wide, stumbles and almost falls. "M'arms not long enough. Anyways..." Voice drifts away to whispering.

"Speak up, missy."

Bad idea. I lightly touch Sik. "Hey, Sik, we—"

"Don't interrupt, son."

Fuck's sake... Sik, please shut up...

"I said!" she says. "Eats corpses, but it's a... shitty digger." Smiles at an inside joke that, thankfully, she doesn't share. "Soooo it eats the gravedirt until it gets to the corpse. But! Too full to eat, so it leaves."

"Well ain't that a thing."

"S'why they bury six-feet-deep now! Mostly. 'Cause only five-feet fit in their stomachs."

"Thought yeh weren't Executioners."

"We aren't," I jump in, hoping to deflect from the obvious, "but she's an enthusiast."

"Huh. Strange hobby for a girl. Yours?"

"Sort of," I say.

"Yeah? Well keep her from digging, don't care how enthused she is. No good comes from the dead. Lot of foul odors and dark moods, that's what." The beard swings up and down. "Right, I'm not waiting for them Executioners and I hate talking to them. Come along, son, let's hunt those graveburrowers or whatever-the-hell."

"We aren't really—"

"Experts enough as far as I want. Come along."

Sik follows without complaint. I'm about to as well when I feel a tug on my sleeve.

"Um." It's Eddy, a little more bewildered than when the conversation left her. "I'm going to head on. I can't stay."

"Sure."

"Don't tell anyone you saw me."

I stop at that. It's a suspicious remark that Sik or I would say, or at least want to say, to Eddy.

"Why?" Sik asks, just suddenly *there*.

Both of us jump, Eddy dramatically.

"Can you please, please not tell anyone you saw me?" she pleads, avoiding the question.

"How come?" Sik pesters.

Message-runners are supposed to be frank and this guardedness and evasion is, from eyes-that-won't-look-at-us alone, something Eddy is having trouble coping with.

"Just don't. Please." she says. "The truth is that I'm not supposed to be… anywhere near this place. I strayed off my route. A, a few times. They won't find out, though! Delays are expected in runs, especially when we're going out to the edge of the world it seems. But…" Bites her lip. "Please. If I say it, I'm going to… please, let me go, I, I can't deal with this. Please."

Sik hugs Eddy.

"I understand," she says.

"N-no, please," Eddy tries to push Sik away. "I can't deal with this," she maintains, but Sik doesn't let go. "I, I." But Eddy's resolve weakens. She tears up. "Thank you…" And returns the embrace. Sik whispers some words, then a few extra, and Eddy nods. "Thanks, but really I'm okay."

"Okay." Sik backs up.

"It's just… difficult… out here." Eddy rubs the tears away and I think I see a sharp-edged spark behind them now. When our eyes meet, I'm sure of it. A gust of wind stirs a memory, of the one who started us on this crazy journey, the crystalline voice of a young, flaxen-haired girl who stood above us all for a significant moment and called out our future. The echo hasn't faded and resonates even here in Crossroads.

"Thanks, Eddy," I say.

"What for?"

I shrug and laugh. "For kicking us in the right direction, I guess."

"I don't really get it, but," she smiles, "you're welcome."

"So what do runners say when they part?"

"Nothing special, I think," she says. "Um. 'Don't run into a ditch' is what I've heard my, ah." The smile falters. She stares through me, but then slaps her cheeks forcefully. Flushed, she smiles wider. "Right! I'll have to do my best."

"Huh?" Sik says.

A fierce look meets mine. "Don't run into a grave!" Eddy exclaims.

"Huh?" I echo.

"The… burrowerthing. Good luck with that."

"Of course," I stammer. "Yes, we'll do our best too."

She waves and backs up. Turns without another goodbye, jogs away some distance, then runs off. The *clomp-stomp* of boots the same rhythm as the last autumn rain.

That makes me homesick.

"Even Sik has women's intuition, eh?"

"Huh?" she says.

I jerk my head at the old man. "Guess this one's mine…"

"What did you mean?" Sik asks.

"The, uh, what you said to her."

"What I said to her?"

"Yeah."

Her face scrunches up. "I don't get it."

I'm about to ignore her, assuming this is sarcastic-exhaustion-mode Sik, but I look at her instead. She's truly mystified by the topic.

"You were saying something to her."

She shrugs. "What did I say?"

I'm not sure what my expression is and, not sure what expression I should have, settle for shaking my head.

"This is why I'm always telling you to sleep."

"Huh… you're weird, Red."

The old man fusses with a scraggly bush, more thorns than foliage. It appears as entirely dead as my patience, but still he snips and snaps at it.

"All done there, son?"

"Yeah, one of us is…" I make an ambiguous gesture. "You own this place or something?"

The beard puffs. "More a caretaker, I reckon."

"Kinda anachronistic."

"Family trade. Old habits, innit?"

"Old habits," I agree.

"Last one was yonder. Hurry up."

He totters deeper into the graveyard, occasionally pestering a guardsman out of the way or yelling at a guardswoman to stop leaning, stop yawning, stop trying to sit on the tombstones. Despite words to the contrary, he certainly acts like he owns this whole plot.

And his cantankerous venom keeps anyone from taking a hard look at us gravediggers, so really...

"Right here?" I ask.

"Sure as dying."

I scan the area. Ground's pretty flat. Not much in the way of shrubbery, unlike elsewhere. Innocent mushrooms cluster and hide around trees with roots that arch painfully, as though they struck some terrible thing deep underground and refused to tunnel any deeper. No hilly parts to be seen, discounts normal burrower patterns.

Hmm.

"Strange."

"Well?"

"It's true they don't feed near their burrows, but maybe patrols make them choose a grave based on opportunity of the moment."

"Sounds familiar," Sik states profoundly.

"Well, where will we find it?"

"Anywhere bushy. Still, it'd be better to simply wait. They're nocturnal."

"Sounds familiar!" Sik giggles.

"Honestly, the ground will freeze soon enough and that'll fix your problem. The burrower will move on... or hibernate. Not sure which they do. Maybe both."

"At the same time," Sik jokes.

"Shut up already," I tell her.

The beard bristles, threatens to spark into a blaze. "Won't happen. They seeded it."

"Seeded... what does that mean?"

"Hell if I know, son, present times make themselves too complex for me. All I know is they were shucking bagfuls of crap all over, nigh a week. Said it'd keep the dirt pliable.

Smiled when he said it! Like I'd be pleased to death! I was *something'd* to death, that's certain. Pfff."

Luckily, Sik has stopped commenting on things and is quietly humming, otherwise I'd have to smack her.

"I'll take a crazy guess." Not even trying to keep the annoyance out of my voice. "The ground freezing. It pisses the dead off."

"That's it!" Fingers snap, pointing at me.

The beard wags.

"What a stupid stor— a few years ago it was fire! That burning them pisses them off! What bullshit!"

"That's so!" He slaps me on the shoulder. "Yeh've got it right, yeh've got it right there. They've been spreading the manure thick as flies, now they're sowing it with some seeds? Some crop's coming, alright!"

"A crock's coming, same one they've been squatting over all this time, then freely offering us with a cheerful face."

"Makes me sick," we say.

In a graveyard at a crossroads two men stood and, perhaps having nothing more in common than a momentary understanding, nodded in commiseration.

#

Ultimately, I decided to risk a few hours in Crossroads. Sik was in no condition to protest and whenever I saw her struggling to keep up, eyelids drawn down by gravity's ravenous pull, my stomach tried to twist away from the swallowed guilt.

"F-fucking Execrations are gone!" she yells at me in my imagination, instead sullenly trips on a rock in reality. "That's not the time to be bold, 'cause we have no clue when they come back. Dipshit!"

She's right. I'm always pushing us too hard and she just goes along with it until the screaming voice in her head, that tiny bit of sense floating around and sometimes bumping into things in there, finally makes itself audible, warns of unavoidable danger.

I'm taking advantage.

I want an edge.

I hear the proclamation of the Sovereignty.

I'm doing this for her.

We need money.

My thoughts are jumbled.

This winter will grow worse.

Too much to think about.

Too much to figure out.

Too much to agonize over and over and over and it's:

Only when she smiles, everything feels calm.

I squeeze her shoulder and make my face into the shape of a smile. She doesn't return it. I'm selfish. And an asshole. We need to leave. Listen to Sik when she doesn't talk to you! Why can't I go? Why is it always like this? Am I trying to force this on her? Am I doing it to make her stop me? Is it that hand that grabs my own shoulder, the head that shakes back and forth, the hat that dips down in a frown she doesn't give, or won't, or is scared to, that I wait for night after night because I never know our limit?

How far is too far?

How far is enough?

Why do I make her define that?

Is she waiting for me to answer that?

Why am I so terrified of saying anything at all?

"Can we go?" she asks.

A quiet voice, emotion-bleached from tiredness.

"Soon," I lie.

"Yeah," she says. "Okay."

I turn away, again, until I sense the familiar presence of Sik following and I feel... relief.

And I hate myself for that. But I'm getting used to it.

#

We don't find a single sign of the burrower. Had I looked, I may have. Instead I walked next to the old caretaker, craning my neck, splitting the grounds into arbitrary divisions and landmarks, scrawling a haphazard map in my mind.

I never wanted to come here, but now…

If we could snatch a bag of those seeds, well, we'd screw some Executioners over, always a worthwhile project, but the graves of winter would open themselves to us. No more would we have to endure the icy, suffocating fingers that only loosened their grasp of the ground when spring yawned. Two manic idiots with stupid grins and unblinking, crazed expressions could be the harbingers of a false spring right in the midst of gale-screeching, rain-lancing, frost-frozen misery. And that, that is what the graves would open their eyes to see.

Damn it I love that image.

We shake hands when we part.

"I'll throttle those wasters until they find that thing, sure enough," the cackling beard tells me. "Be back this way, yeh figure?"

I try to suppress the disturbing grin lurking beneath the surface of my skin. "Absolutely."

"Where're yeh bound?"

I say the opposite of the closest city's name.

"Well then," he says, nods pleasantly, turns around and instantly turns into the cross in Crossroads. "Get that fat ass off that stone, yeh damn slob! That were a chair, we'd've sat the corpse on it, wouldn't we?"

"Alright, we're done here, Sik. I'm thinking on our way home we—"

She's not here.

"Sik."

She doesn't answer.

"Shit, shit, she was… shit…"

I hold back my instinct to bolt. The Watch saw you with their cantankerous, would-be taskmaster. No suspicion. Be natural. Natural steps, natural glances, natural— fuck it, Sik, I'm lenient with your stupidity, but not now in this place you fucking idiot, not— shit! And I can imagine it: Sik has been carrying the shovel. She'll be in some secluded area, inside a copse or something, assuming she's not so bleary to forget caution, any caution, a vague caution, just... I'm sure of it. That's where she is. She'll be a foot deep. Singing a fucking shantey while hazy visions of treasure smile back like blinded skulls and stop singing you fucking idiot and try being silent for once damn it all why can't you sense the tension in the air it's not another storm it's you and me getting fucked over by what we do!

But there stands she, underneath an apple tree, staring up at the glassy sheen of sky, so quiet, so quietly reaching.

The branch sways.

She plucks the apple. The skin of the fruit is gray, covered in black splotches. Eyes closing, a fragile smile forms. She raises it to parted lips.

I rush over and slap it out of her hand, but I miss the apple and strike her spindly fingers.

"Stop it, Red!"

"Hell is wrong with you."

"Hungry," she mumbles.

"That's disgusting. Did you even look at it?"

"It's an apple. Looks like a bloody apple..."

"Who do you think its roots are sunk into? Huh?"

"Big deal. I'm not eating the corpse that fed it."

"Hardly a difference. The tree is sick! Didn't you look at it? And if it isn't, I don't even want to know what's wrong with it."

"Heehhh~?" Cocks her head. "I'm a tree now?"

"You know what I mean."

"Tchhh. Sure, 'f you say so."

"What is with you?" I cool my voice down. "You've been out of it before, but it's like you're sleepwalking today with a blindfold on."

She says nothing.

"What's wrong?"

"Ehh."

"What's that mean?"

"I'm fine."

"Alright."

"I'm fine," she repeats.

"Are you?"

She says nothing.

"Are you sick?"

"Whaddaya mean," she mutters. "I'm always Sik. Red's weird. Eh. Ehe eheh heh heh."

"Right, well, in any case," I say, "you could have said something."

"I'm hungry. You weren't here."

"You weren't where I was."

"Whatever."

"Hey."

"Whatever!" she shouts.

"Fine."

"You're being an ass to me."

"Wha— in what fucking way!?"

"Fuck you," she whispers.

I bite my cheek hard. Coppery taste. "Yeah and fuck you too, Sik. And we're leaving, since you were too busy drooling over diseased apples to notice."

At first I figure she won't, but she does. Uneven gait, barely keeping pace with mine, but even so she walks next to me. I hand her one of Darvin's honey bars.

At first I figure she'll take it, but she doesn't. Not even to throw away or stamp on. It stays in my hand.

Uneaten, undiscarded, hanging there between us.

#

Deep wilderness.

Such woodland maintains a strange relationship with winter. Even now a delicate film of snow dusts the treetops, but when the snowstorms truly begin it will pile atop the canopy overhead. The compact roots we pick through will stay untouched, unless a weak spot in the branches gives way and down cascades a deadly snowfall. For now, tripping is our sole concern.

I'm mindful that the mausoleum may be filled with Executioners, or at the very least visited by those that left Crossroads. Other than its location, it's impossible to know anything until we see for ourselves.

Sik, placid despite the arduous landscape, climbs over the roots carefully.

I wait below to help her make the jump down. She stops at the edge, looking disoriented. She's been doing this for an hour now. The moment always passes before I can figure it out, but I keep feeling like I'm missing the obvious. In a few seconds, she will touch fingertips together, frown, and go on without a word.

"Where's Rin?"

I blink. "What do you mean?"

"Where did Rin go?" she presses.

"She didn't go anywhere." *Rin, her stuffed toy...*

"Yes, but, no, she was just with us. She ate a… dumpling. We had dumplings, didn't we?"

"We… no, we didn't do that." *Rin, at home in bed...*

"Uhhh… but we, no… yeah."

"Come on, squat and I'll help you down here."

"But I don't wanna leave her again."

"Sik, I realize you're exhausted," I plead softly. "We'll rest soon, right? I promise. Just a bit further."

"But! She's… she's waiting for us. Is… isn't she?"

"Who?"

"Rin."

"I think you mean Eddy."

She stops. "Ed-dy?"

"The message-runner girl."

"No, see, that's why I understand. Because of Rin."

"Come on, give me your hand."

"I… don't think I should." Takes a step back. "We have to—"

"Sik, please focus. Eddy was the girl that came into the shrine when we were there. We went to Crossroads and split up. You hugged her."

"Who?"

"Eddy."

"I…" Fidgets with a strand of hair. "I don't… understand that. I only hug Rin."

My intestines are starting to knot themselves into balls of scratchy yarn. This conversation is seriously screwed up.

"You hug Jackal too."

"That's different!" she protests, now angry and upset. "And, and… and I need to go home. I'm… I'm going…"

"He— hey, Sik! Be careful, you—!"

But she trips backwards over the root, tumbles unseen to a crashing halt: the crunch of skinny, fallen branches and withered leaves and a terrifying silence.

I try to scale the roots I climbed down, but they are slick with ice. I shout her name again, making another futile scramble up the embankment. Cursing, I run down the burrow to find another way up. When I do, I make a slipshod dash through the uneven, twisting path and nearly collide with a tree.

Sik is curled up, panting heavily.

"Shit. Shit." I check her body. She doesn't look injured. "Did you hit your head?" I check. Seems fine. "Not like it would matter, right?" She doesn't scowl at me or laugh. Panting, panting. "Sik… are you okay…?"

It's instinct, not actual thought, that moves my hand to remove the glove, to place the shaking palm against her burning forehead.

"Fuck," I say. "Fuck fuck fuck fuck fuck."

"Aaa, aaa," she says.

"Idiot. Idiot! Course it's this. Idiot, pushing her... she's not... shit, shit, okay, okay, we have medicine, we have... I... I was carrying it. Okay. Okay."

I rummage through my pack, throwing out everything that isn't what I'm clawing for.

"Aaaa... aaaa...."

"It's alright," I say. "Here, drink."

The liquid in the vial looks like white mold.

I pour some in her mouth.

"Gruaaa... pllllll..." she sputters.

"I know it sucks." I cover her mouth, try to force a swallow as gently as possible before she spits it out. "But it works. Is what she said, at least."

"Eeeuuwaaa..."

"Sorry."

"Euug... aaaa... aaa..."

"Sorry, Sik..."

I unroll the map, but end up simply staring at my feet.

"We're supposed to watch out for each other. Since we're both screw-ups... in our own way. Sik covers for Red, Red covers for Sik, and everything is o-kay. The lame take care of the blind and then we're a whole person between us, huh? Right... we're a team... But that only works when we're both working, otherwise we're two cripples walking into things. So unless one of us is perfect when the other is in trouble, it doesn't work. It doesn't balance. Isn't that so stupid?"

Fitfully sleeping, she doesn't answer.

"What should we do? We're about... here."

I touch the map, feeling no closer to anywhere.

Halfway there.

"One foot in," the Sik-sitting-across-from-me says.

"Crossroads is out. Executioners notwithstanding, it isn't safe. Could we reach the shrine?"

She shakes her head, frowns. "Execrations use those too, ya know."

"You said not to worry."

"I was tired. Duh."

"Right…"

"Keep going, then?" she asks.

"Where? You need shelter."

Points at the map. "Mausoleum."

"I know," I say. "But I can't carry you and everything else at once."

"Guess you'll have to choose." Stifles a laugh.

"Be quiet."

"Isn't it so?"

"I take you, then come back, you might wake up and wander off. I leave you, then come back, same thing."

"Or you could take me, and then…" she leads.

"Oh."

"Piece…"

"… by piece. I get it."

She grins. "I'll think light thoughts."

I carry Sik a short distance, then set her down carefully. While she dreams, I retrieve our equipment and then alternate again and again, always keeping her in sight when she isn't in my arms. She stirs occasionally, often babbling incoherently. When I rest next to her, she'll turn to me and say something that makes sense, but not really because her fevered context is intangible. And then she sleeps, on and on, breathes in rhythm with the wind, while the light draining through the forest's canopy grows thinner -- and feeling so tiny beneath the roots that loom above in whispering judgment, I wonder if I sleep too.

#

I shouldn't be surprised by the distressing accuracy with which the Executioners mark their maps, but once the pitted stone of the mausoleum frowns at me from across the hollow, exactly as predicted, my spine seems to fuse to the ground and I almost drop Sik.

So is this how it feels to behold your rival's obsession and to see that it's the same?

Twisting, interwoven branches obscure the sky to the extent that I cannot determine if the weather is calm or now storming. This enclosure dulls my senses; the light is wan and constant, makes the hour uncertain, as if this little voided portion of the world has been plucked away and is secreted from everywhere else familiar.

Crimson ivy coils up the face of the structure, strangles what pillars languish in unended vigil, all the while shadows hide the main portal which gasps for air.

I prop up Sik's head on a makeshift pillow, fold my arms, and stare at the door.

Far too old to be Executioner… which means nothing to say since most everything predates them. But even if it was, I don't know the trick to opening it. Handles, levers, any type of logical mechanism that would trigger entry are nowhere to be found. Ignore the fact that such a thing defeats the purpose of a mausoleum to begin with…

Nothing around the door itself.

Nor the alcove that houses it.

I'm stupid enough to climb a tree, jump onto the roof and search there. Still nothing.

Sooner than I want to admit defeat, I'm kicking the solid stone that blocks our way.

"Open the fuck up," I demand of it. "Open the fuck up right now."

"Yer sure… swearin' lots…"

"Yeah. Yeah, I do that sometimes," I say. "Picked that up from you."

"Meee~?" Sik asks innocently.

I sit down across from her.

"But I'm... so nice and well-behaved."

"And when you make trouble for me?" I ask.

She sighs. "I'm sorry in the way in which I'm not."

"Ha."

"Heh."

I lean in. "How do you feel?"

"Like shit. Am I ill? I'm all... fuzzy. Can't think. Where is this? Weren't we at the shrine? Ugh. So fuzzy."

"You don't remember?"

"N-no, not... really? I see images, but... I'm confused." Shakes her head. "I dreamt we were in Crossroads?"

"No, we did that."

"Really?" Her voice now confused *and* weirded-out.

"The short of it is you were up all night revising our map, didn't sleep, probably got sick from that on top of the cold, and then I forced you to walk all over Crossroads because I thought you were fine."

"O-oh..."

"I thoroughly screwed up, Sik," I tell her, "but we're going to keep you here until you're on your feet again and your craziness sounds like normal."

"O-okay..."

She tries to smile, but it doesn't fully happen.

"Red..."

"Yeah."

"When I wasn't... um... *here*... I was... talking?"

"You were in and out for a while there. It didn't make much sense."

"What about?"

"Nothing specific." I scratch my nose. "Although you kept getting Rin and Eddy mixed up."

She looks away. "I talked about Rin?"

"I think you were more trying to talk *to* her."

"Umm. Okay. I was talking to Rin, okay. Umm… Red… if I said anything else, I really… really want you to not lie to me, okay, you should tell me. So, did I talk about Rin or not?"

"I don't think so."

"And so… so I didn't talk about… umm… you know."

"Oh."

She keeps looking away. "So…"

"No, you didn't."

Looks back. "Promise?"

"Sik," I say, "even if you ever started to out of delirium, I'd cover my ears."

"Thank you, Red." From the quavering voice, I half expect to see tears in her eyes, but no, they're merely tired as they usually are, only more so.

I groan when I stand, regard the newest impediment in our journey. Always obstacles. It can never be a simple dig anymore, can it? Stretching, I let out a breath. "But it won't do us much good if we can't get out of this fucking cold tonight."

"More swears," she notes.

"I'm in the mood."

She starts fidgeting off the covers I buried her under.

"Don't do that."

"I'm all… sweaty!" she whines.

"I want you that way."

Agape. Then with pursued lips: "Pervert."

"To sweat out the fever."

"Suuuure."

Roundabout strategy. I was never as good as Jackal or Quinn with that concept. I've reached the point that the logic of it grows -- no, that's a poor word, too organic, more like: pieces itself together in the effort, such as the planks of a bridge laid one by one -- a few annoyingly floating away in the process -- until enough cobble together passage. Sketchy. Effective. That's how my thoughts work, apparently.

Even so, I'll never have the second-nature those two have. It's how they breathe and why they'll never be caught.

I'm a little jealous, but when the pickax slams into the stone and coughs splinters at me, I feel somewhat better.

After a few minutes, Sik asks, "This'll work?"

"Dunno," I pant.

The corridors of life are teeming with dead-ends, most crafted lovingly by our singular ignorance, and all the off-shooting paths lead nowhere happy and the deeper we dig, the deeper we dig. Waste. Uselessness. Oblivion. Pathetic.

My arms burn as the night falls.

My mind blisters.

This dead-end, at least, I can break through.

#

Old weathered stone is as resilient as a fevered will, but both crack eventually.

"I don't wanna be naked," she protested.

"It's getting colder," I said.

It runs a good optimistic length, but we can't squeeze through yet.

"Stop touching me," she protested.

"Let me wipe you dry," I said.

I need to start up again before the fog comes.

"I love you," she protested.

I didn't know what to say to that.

"You were always listening to me." Gripping my arm tighter. "Don't leave me again." And, already dreaming of someone else, she sleeps.

I wipe the beading droplets from her forehead.

A sigh, unsure who it came from.

And worming free of her grasp, reluctantly, I rise. It isn't safe yet and I'm the only one of us not destroyed by sleep deprivation. So I light a fire and throw in branches until it feels hot enough. As a precaution, I wad up some cotton and stop up her ears.

I strike. The stone chips and flakes.

And the light sleeper breathes in, then out, oblivious for once in a good way.

"Didn't actually think that would work," I say, risking a smile, and striking again.

But despite my better spirits, it takes over an hour before the break is wide enough for the willowy Sik, to say nothing of me.

#

She begins coughing.

At first I think she's merely stirring, but it immediately turns into a fit. She doubles over, gripping a breast, and flecks of ice shoot out of her mouth with each convulsion. I drop the pickax, and throw the rest of the wood into the fire. Embers flee in panic.

I rub her back until the fit subsides.

"Finished?" I ask.

She nods, sitting up.

I unshutter the lantern.

A thick, opaque fog fills the hollow. Its tendrils drift up the stairs, undeterred by the heat of the fire.

Does the deepness fall so soon out in the wild?

No respite.

"Come on, Sik, up you go. It'll be warmer inside, so we'll shelter here for now, okay? Here, can you squeeze through? You can squeeze through, right? There. Watch your head. Ah! Yeah, that's what I meant. You okay?"

Inside the mausoleum, she looks out at me and nods.

"Stay there."

I hurriedly gather up more branches, trying to carry as many as possible while keeping a hand firmly clasped over my mouth. I hand them to her.

"Can you make a fire?"

She nods, staring at the wood.

I pass a flaming brand through the hole.

"Here, light it."

The branches crackle and snap. Wiry shadows dart about and the jumping colors are yellow and red and pink, and the heat envelops.

"Hungry?"

She doesn't nod.

"Eat anyways."

While she snacks I push whatever will fit through the crack, which isn't much, but enough for the makeshift bed at the very least.

I ignore fatigue and strike harder and faster.

Behind me, the fog is creeping closer.

#

Fissuring veins along the stone multiply, but the hole I'm desperately beating through the entrance remains the lop-sided, toothless grin it has been, paralyzed and mocking. With the fog now twisting around my chest, I can no longer struggle against its rise. I must wait it out, until sunrise.

I kick the largest fractured stone towards the fog.

"Drown this, bloody cloud," I sneer.

It clatters down the stairs and thumps against the dirt.

"Sik, sorry, but wake up."

Her arms are flung wide, limp.

Jaw hanging down, she snores.

"Sik!" I shout.

"Uweah!" Terrified eyes flying around.

"Calm down."

"H-hahh…"

"Hand me the tarp. Gonna stop up the hole." I take it from her. "Go back to sleep."

She nods, disappears when I wedge that thick material into the top of the crack, working it along pinched edges all the way down the sides. Then I aim the lantern at a few trees, luckily finding the closest one the easiest to climb.

Breath held and into the fog.

Frigid ice vapor, snowblind explosion lantern-light reflected sun and daggering at squinted sight. Look to the ground. Feet invisible, ground non-existent, trampling solidified nothingness. Step, step, carefully, quickly, step, step, rock. Trip. Forwards, no handholds, knee sacrifices itself for the greater good. Stinging, pulsing. Instinctually sucking air: no air. Fog, little spears puncturing down the throat. Coughing it out: no air. Direction blasted, blind, blind. But the earth raising, uneven unhindered. Clambering now, oxygen-desperate longing for darkness.

I grip a branch and pull my head up, coughing again and filling my lungs with the sweet, soothing night air. Vaulting from branch to branch, I settle into one that can take my weight. Now safe, I recline against the bark.

"How ya doing over there?" I yawn, focusing the lantern at the mausoleum.

The tarp is fallen.

Diving, heedless plunge, into the fog, overtaking the steps in bounds.

I jut my head inside. Within the atrium, the heat is concentrated, no hint of fog yet. It must have only now come undone. I fix the cover, hammering in stones to act as nails. And wait.

Fog is gathering around my neck.

The stones pop out and bounce off the rubble. *Tak. Tak.*

Then the tarp curls and sags.

I take it before it falls again. "Too heavy, huh…"

Holding it up, pushing the rubble together with my feet. I stand on the pile. It shifts, not much, but it isn't high enough. This won't work.

I look back at the tree. Think. Think. Could I get her up there? No, I'll trip again. Could I keep my face inside and keep the hole covered? Maybe, but that position is too awkward and couldn't be held for hours. Think. Think. Fog, tree, hole, rocks, tomb, stone.

"Got it."

A quick job with the tarp. It'll hold for a minute or so.

Down in the fog, I creep towards one of the felled columns, waving a hand before me. I stop when my leg bumps into it. All the stone fragments are huge, unwieldy, but I feel one out that might work. I lift it, mindful not to grunt or exhale, and slowly hurry back to the lantern.

To stand atop this and block out the fog…

Thuck.

Long night, this is.

Fixing the tarp for the final time, hopefully, I plug the edges and press my shoulder blade against the top flap.

And the sentinel standing upon its pedestal in the form of me crosses its arms and leans against the mausoleum. It spits. Engulfed by the lantern-stained vapors, this is swallowed with an immediacy that makes the gesture lost on all but the statue itself.

#

Dungeon-stuck waiting nothing. Taking a look outside, but the table staggers into placing a mug before them. The drunkard and the drunk. Which was which way did we get here with her on before, on and off, but definitely with feet kicked-up and warm nights in the abyss. There's a pause, blinkard, one eye shining in constellations and clouds, although fog settling and seething as before.

"I give up."

They laugh.

She settles into a pipe, lights up, and the lantern, and the stars, and the sun burst from fingertips and the campfire is ashes and the limbs are stiff as stone, waiting, hazy half-sight of fog, the forest, forgotten stone walls, bleary non-understanding and instantaneous dispersing remembrance.

I rise.

#

Work again already. Sore, tired. Not amused.

"Oi, you awake?" I start shoving the rubble and column fragment out of the way. "Heh. Channeling my inner Jackal apparently..." The bed is emptied and Sik gone. Well, at least I won't wake her up.

Sunlight permeates the cross-work of branches. Shadows play over the remnants of evaporating fog like a gobo effect in the theatre. As they shift and sway, the morning warms in a feeble way and I feel a deep satisfaction for investing in so indestructible a digging tool. There was always the suspicion one of us three would snap, gladder still the stone was the first. And vowing, once Sik is back to health, I'll be needing a good damn break.

When the forsaken entrance is thoroughly penetrated, finally I enter the mausoleum.

The dust of indeterminable years mixes with the stale, dry air. Broken benches line the two rooms that flank the atrium, thread-torn tapestries yet hanging above. Their condition, so dismal, whether originally intricate landscapes or simply pattern-work... hopeless to discern. Perhaps they were intended to be drab pastiches of dying color, another epitaph to the passing of things.

An entirely horrible place that no one sane would ever wish to visit.

I love it immediately.

In its prime, it would have been lovely to anyone. Quartz crystal windows, mostly covered up by the cast-off dregs of the forest, are set into the ceiling. Some let in faint, gray light, having been washed clean by rain -- or my previous stumbling about for an easy way in.

Subdued lighting to console grief. Can you see it? Our artistic bends are not always without nobler intentions.

So, where was Sik in all this?

I expect to find her squatting in a corner, but each room passed by is empty of the living and the dead. If no interment in the building itself, that means...

I find the stairs and start worrying simultaneously.

"Blazes, Sik," I call down the shaft, "if you fell and killed yourself, I'm going to kick your ass all the way back home and bury you in a flowerpot."

Saying that, I feel my heart pounding for another reason. Only extensive burial plots smell like this. I go to retrieve the lantern, pause, then stoop down for the pickax too. It's heavy. Either from build-up of lactic acid or guilt.

"In case," I rationalize.

The middle of the staircase is worn smooth, imperfectly though, to allow a gradual incline. A surprising attribute. Could have sworn that a recent addition by the Executioners. Guess they picked it up along the way and didn't invent carting after all. At the bottom, a crumpled heap of blood, broken limbs and a split-open head doesn't await me.

So she can actually walk and not die.

Grimly impressed.

Unlike Ensbryng, time has been a kindlier companion here. The halls of the mausoleum are finished with stonework that must have been polished to the gleam of marble once and, although dulled, remain durable. The ceiling runs with a disconcerting network of cracks, however, and the more I marvel at the construction the more I remember the collapse inherent in that crypt that almost became our tomb.

And when the hallway begins to split off in multiple directions, I stop and chew on my cheek in indecision.

She didn't used to wander off like this.

First Crossroads, now this.

Sure, she's not well, and it's not really her fault. But the repetition, the repetition. That line, what she said when she tripped, the one about going home… Was that more rambling or something at the heart of her? I stare out the corner of my eye at nothing. This reminds me of my dreams: the way I act in those… Is that the real me or the me that acts when I forget what it means to be myself?

A stupid question maybe, pointless definitely. Similar feeling, though. Similar feeling. The repetition, the repetition.

An echo.

Shit. I wasn't paying attention. Which direction?

"Hey!"

No one responds.

"Hey! Where are you?"

No one answers.

"And what if she wanders by me and out into the forest?" I demand of myself, as I turn to the nearest path. "Take this one, she pops out that one, like that comedy we watched back in…" I hesitate and start for another path. "I…" Dithering at once. "I…" Halting before I move a foot towards another.

I can't choose…

Ah.

So that's it.

That's the reason why I pull Sik along in my wake.

And now that I've admitted it, I can't lie to myself anymore.

I'm always thinking the worst of her. Exhausted Sik who can't pay attention. Stupid Sik who misses the obvious. Greedy Sik who puts us in danger. Idiot Sik who walks into walls. Pissy Sik who argues over meaningless things. Irresponsible Sik who disappears without a word.

"Quit fucking around!" I yell.

"Quit fucking around," the echo retorts.

"Quit fucking around," the echo mutters.

"Quit fucking around," the echo whispers.

And another echo, wordless, from down this same hallway.

Of course, Sik understands being underground. Keep going straight. Never stop going straight, unless you have to, then go right, and keep going right, unless you can't, then go back. Map it all out so you never get—

She could be lost.

She could be waiting.

She values this partnership too, fool.

"Keep making noise!" I shout.

Swinging lantern-light cascades up and down the walls, washing into reflections as I go. She doesn't make any other sounds, but I begin to make out irregular patterns in the dust that can only be her trail. It's the right way. The tunnels can't go on forever and so I'll find her.

I'll find her.

But when the hallway continues and continues, the sweat down my back numbs my former excitement. How many people are interred here? And from where? I haven't seen extended burial in this manner since Old Kingdom's own sepulchre and that was set up from its inception -- before Old Kingdom was Old Kingdom -- having been expanded upon as the decades faded into the ink of the emotionless strokes of a historian's pen.

Was a city here or miles away?

Was a city delved below this level?

Crazy possibilities are always to be entertained in a world of ruin.

In the tumult of death, plague and curses, history has been lost. No one cares what happened yesterday when tomorrow may never arrive. Worth looking up this place, though, if there's anything to dredge up -- or anywhere to dredge.

The hallway forks. I run right.

"Hey!" I call out.

Nothing.

I search Sik's likely path, but too soon I lose her in the dust. Checking the off-shooting paths where she may have gone. None of the vaults have been disturbed. Wish they were... Couldn't start on the first one and see what was inside could you? Would've found you, scolded you, and joined you near the foot of the stairs. But searching is what we do first. Ahh, Sik. My lop-sided grin. Don't start making sense on me now.

"Oi!"

Nothing.

Deeper on, farther ahead. More turns, as logical as possible. I leave permanent markings on the walls, and actually start to miss the orderly Executioner ways.

Shit, this is complicated.

Here the walls are bulging and the ceiling is so cracked it's a breath away from shattering utterly. Whether chips are closer to begin raining down or the ceiling to shrugging support and crushing me, I hate to imagine. In such condition, if Sik is nearby she might be trapped.

Torchlight flickers around the corner.

I rush forward.

But it isn't another corridor. The walls and ceiling have eroded all the way to the adjacent passageway. Stonework, soil and rocks are paralyzed by wormgut spew into a calcified pillar; it has the appearance of bones melted together by some deranged candlemaker.

"Sik!"

Her hat wobbles upwards. Hollow eyes leak and her pale face doesn't twitch.

"Sik."

Her hand limply holds a dangling torch. The other moves, almost unconsciously, reaching through the tangle of hair over her eye, brushes it away so she can see.

"R-Red?"

"You look awful. Why did you run off? Your fever was close to breaking, you dolt." My admonishment too gentle to be anything other than concern. "Did it get worse?"

"Worse," she repeats a little stilted, a laugh caught at the back of her throat. "Y-yeah."

"Promise you'll listen to me until you're well, okay?"

"Okay."

I nod and make ready to break down the pillar.

She doesn't move out of the way.

"Don't!" she exclaims, panicked.

"Let me bust this wormshit down."

From the way her face quirks up, I know she'll start a fight over this. Good to see that spirit again, but now isn't—

The howl erupts from far down the passageway. A nauseating mixture of a reversed scream gasping for breath and a stomach squeezing out internal organs rather than vomit. The pitch rises and lowers, the cadence stutters in disrupted inhalation and screams out again. The floor shudders under the voice and stones begin to crack, splinter, or maybe that's my skull.

"What the fuck...?" My jaw clacks painfully as the intensity jolts in terrible crescendo.

"That's my new friend," she says, face screwing up. "Doesn't like noise." Clutching the torch in both hands now. "Or light. Too bad I can't see in the dark too, huh? Ah ha. Ha ha ha!" Shivering smile.

"I'll get you out."

"No."

"It won't take long."

"It will. Don't do it."

I don't care how many nights I have to dig for this girl. I'm not leaving.

Her hand firmly grips the dangling torch. The other moves, hurriedly, reaching towards me through the twisting mess that separates us.

It opens, the most fragile flower. I hold it tightly.

"I have to go," she says.

"This place isn't Ensbryng," I rush to remind her. "Everything is connected somehow."

"Red." Her calm voice terrifies me.

"Get around that thing and come back the same way."

"It doesn't matter. I can't do it," she says.

"You can."

"I can't. You know I don't have a head for that."

"Sik."

"Sorry, Red. I'll have to break that promise already."

And she lets go of me.

Skips back a distance, lightly, as if spring had come and we were lazing in the balmy weather, caressing winds gliding off the lake. The image holds. I can almost believe it. But finally, tearing eyes away from my face, she rushes down the nearest hole and the torchlight winks out. I shine the trembling lantern, seeing nothing, hearing horrors. Want to follow. Want to flee. The palm that grips the pickax is slick.

IT SCREAMS! IT SCREAMS!

THE BLACK MASS SLAMS INTO THE WALL.

"Stop," I whisper. "St...op." So meek, demanding in the faltering dimness of a worthless flame trapped in metal.

IT WRITHES. IT PEELS OFF THE CRIPPLED WALL.

IT IGNORES THE FEEBLE MAN.

ITS WAIL VOMITS AGAIN AND AGAIN

LIKE AN UNDYING MACHINE THAT WANTS TO DIE.

ITS BLOATED BODY IS A PULSING SHADOW.

And then: simply gone. Its squelching bellow dopplers, the earthquake of its passage lulls, leaves behind bone-jarring numbness. And then that too: simply gone.

I begin to breathe again.

I open my mouth. I try to yell.

Follow me. Follow me.

Instead, only air escapes.

The pickax slams into the pillar. A chunk breaks off, pus squirts out. Another is knocked to the floor, lying there, a lump of half-frozen milk. Rancid stench. I can't remember what I saw or if I saw anything at all. And so I do what I can do, working mindlessly with muscle-memory. Keep going. Keep going. The pickax desperately delving.

How deep we must dig— I say to myself.

How deep we must dig—
Unable to finish the thought, I'm not sure what I meant.

#

Useless.

The pillar is half-broken and each swing causes the remnants of the ceiling to shift. There'll be no way through here for me. There might be enough space for Sik if she presses herself flat to the wall, but… it's useless.

Do I try to retrace her footprints again?

Push on in the relative direction of her flight?

I turn to ask the Sik-standing-next-to-me.

But the Sik-standing-next-to-me isn't there.

And says nothing.

Only emptiness and that unwavering sense of paralysis embrace me.

"Fine," I say. "Enough thinking."

No plans, no maps, no anything organized. I'll ignore it, stop doing what I normally do. Plowing into unknown stretches without any tools except a pickax. What if we need rope? Or another torch? Ignore it, push it back.

No tools? No time. Keep on, on and on.

Damage wrought by infestation increases. Now I find vaults long since breached, but not by any diggers such as the two frantically searching for each other down in these stone-entombed bowels. Eventually the corridors end and the final wall, reduced to pulverized dirt, opens upon a squirming cavern.

Wormguts. Their translucent bodies puff up, pallid organs wobble and twist, then are squeezed back to size while they dream of the many dead that lay behind me, so many countless meals. They are perhaps the worst corpses to unearth, those consumed by wormguts. While a burrower may devour everything, these rancid maggots hunger only to dissolve the bones, leaving the flapping skin and moist innards to putrefy.

A wormgut stirs from sleep.

It shakes itself and stretches towards the mausoleum. Mucus spurts from a hole that is both mouth and anus to lubricate its passing. I creep away from it and begin to cross their lair, unsure if my boots will remain undigested by the oozy mass covering the ground.

I pass spew deposits, gagging at their chalky, sickening odor. For what purpose are these haphazard monuments erected? They litter the places wormguts gather and maybe the Executioners have some theories, but I don't. All I know is that once I see less of them, the sooner I'll know this fetid womb is behind me.

One belches frothy white that dribbles down the wall.

A wall that convulses.

Unghh.

Many deposits frame the passageway that, from the cutting chill beyond, must lead out. Take careful steps. No tripping. I duck under the ledge before I'm spat on and hurry away.

#

Now in a system of caverns that could burrow on forever as the mausoleum before it seemed to. I run my hand along the glittering stone, mostly for reassurance while I parallel the great abyss at my side. The decline is gradual, but with boots slick with unmentionable slop, each slip is frightening. Not the least of which because I dare not make a sound.

"Gllluuuu-p!" echoes the noise from far below in that dark, dark pit.

A moratorium on mausoleums after today.

"Lululu…. luuuu-p!" echoes the noise from far below, asking if I'm still there.

No. No, I'm not.

And yet I descend, not too deep though deep enough.

In my mind, I can't figure the division between cavern system and mausoleum. The latter constructed after the discovery of the first: an easy way to delve multiple levels?

Still, coincidence or not, the likelihood of multiple exits now exists, and that's something of a comfort.

"Rruurl-ruuuu-p!"

Vaguely.

Gray rock, stark shadows, no clue.

Where am I. The hell am I doing.

Another wormgut spire marks my passage, another revolting milestone on a road to nowhere. I give it little heed until I notice my light shining on the wall behind. It blocks my way back out of the caverns. I consider the trail that twists downwards a painful pace along the chasm.

No good. She has to be above me anyways.

I set the lantern down and begin breaking the spire apart, one foul chunk at a time. Without a roof to be propped up, this one is easier to manage. I work at the base of it, the way I've seen lumberers work a tree, until it tilts in top-heavy stupor like some drunk tip-toeing on the edge of oblivious slumber. The thing in the pit makes much of this, but determination bedamned; I can't always be expected to prize stealth above survival. A thing more present is stalking Sik and I don't know how to balance those two needs so when I finish and step away and cover my face and the accumulated tower of spew topples down, I let the crash punctuate the "and fuck you too" of my footfalls that propel me into this next section of mausoleum.

At every corner, I almost expect to find Sik dashing into me and toting some stupid rabbit under her arm. And each time is a disappointment, never lending me encouragement nor offering suggestions on where to go next.

But I understand the direction she ran. She would have kept straight on, labyrinthine as our surroundings she wouldn't risk being run into a dead-end, and found some escape. Sik's good at that, the crazy wight. I can't go distrusting her now. Can't, can't… Just parallel the course, there have to be stairs somewhere, probably lots, this isn't

Executioner construction. That's my hope, pathetic in its simplicity and ignorance -- if not Executioner, then built by whom? Not knowing that is not knowing architectural style and logic. Shit. Wonder if Jackal and Quinn can sneak me into Archives for a week or two to study up.

After a few turns, claustrophobic tunnel-vision opens up on what I've sought. The ceiling extends up multiple levels; the floor drops down once, ending in a stagnant pool covered in an undisturbed film of dust. No stairs. Of course not. That would make too much sense. But it's my way back up.

Back up to—

FLASH OF VOID. SCREAMING.

Cold layer of sweat.

From the memory? The unbroken silence?

Shut up and think.

Sik made it here.

If. If. If.

What would she do?

It's unmistakable. She'd spot a way away from the terror of dead-ends, and climb. But how high? All levels? One level? One level until the thing found another way to get at her and then ascend higher? Assuming it couldn't climb too. What if it could climb... crap, crap, no good.

This silence. No guidance.

Close my eyes. It's been instinct to this point.

Calm down. *Think.*

Nothing comes.

Smell of decay, torpid thought.

Sound of nearly unheard echoes...

        ...teetering on the edge of perception.

Eyelids the color of blood...

        ...diluted by the light of the lantern.

Ah! Her light!

My eyes snap open and fix on the highest point.

That's it!

Trying to make sense of what Sik would do when I never can when she's talking straight at me? Stupid as shit, but it may have worked for once. Torches are as unreliable as her wits in this kind of danger. She wouldn't take any risk of losing hers, and flee as far as possible before it ran out.

Roots hang from the ceiling like withered spider legs, barely low enough to grab from the level above mine. Nothing much around to make a makeshift stool with...

I tap the gray rock with my pickax. Bits crack away and bounce off the floor. *Tak tak*. Breath held, one quick strike. *Kkrcht*!

Listening. Any change?

Wait.

One more second.

Nothing.

I break the rock again and wait.

Maybe *it* will hear me. But maybe Sik will first.

I break off footholds, then handholds. Uniform noise, careful pauses, nothing roused. I toss the pickax to the next level and clamber up. She would have had trouble reaching the roots, but I can't think she wouldn't have tried. One corridor shoots off the way I came, another back the way I think she did. Reckless flight down the next corridor? Or would this open room have made enough visual difference to jar her adrenaline-drenched mind?

I'll trust her to ascend.

Still, can't take both of these. I weigh the lantern and pickax in a shrug of resignation before setting the latter down. Like so much, a bit fucked. With one firm fistful of roots and a precarious partial-grasp of lantern, I hoist myself up -- only to painfully slip down a foot for every two risen. Can't take both? Can't take either.

I hop to the floor before I swing back out over the pool.

Lantern shutter wide, and the cavern wall sparkles.

"Alright, alright..."

Grab a single root and yank. *Snap*. Grab another. *Snick*. Another. *Snak*. Wood, wood... need wood. I see the pickax and grimace.

"Shit, this was expensive."

And well-crafted, hence we bought it. I didn't believe for a second when I was told it was indestructible, but there is no way to split it here. Too heavy and bulky, anyways.

"Something... something..."

Casting about. Nothing, nothing. Empty floor, empty halls, nothing to backtrack to, and why would there be otherwise? A mausoleum, not a supply closet. Not a thing to be stored except dead, forgotten memories and worthless bones.

Ah.

I stifle the laugh. Sik would love this.

The vault is easily opened and its disintegrated occupant without protest. I select a bone, offering quiet yet perverse thanks, twist the roots as tight as possible and thrust it into the lantern. The roots crackle and curl, but the ad hoc torch holds its ad hoc form. Bone wedged between teeth, musty grotty taste, and now I can climb.

Dust is thick everywhere. It coats each floor I pass. And at the top, although thinner, it is a dull carpet -- except for where footprints have torn through it.

I run.

A low moan rumbles.

I run harder.

Leaving behind footsteps of my own. Footsteps that follow alongside hers. Both sets that will, in these lonely depths, remain untouched and exactly where they belong: right next to each other.

I stop at a vault, at a scattering of chipped mortar and a pile of strewn bones. The floor shakes again. The discarded rib cage shifts. Carefully, carefully I remove the cover and bring light into the recess behind.

There, she sleeps.

I call her name.

Then, she stirs.

I reach for her hand. Shakily. I expect it to be rigid and cold, but when I feel the pliable, spindly fingers, the blooming warmth, my eyes sting and her name, needing to be spoken a second time, expands in my throat and is stuck.

"M-mm," she murmurs. "M-hm."

Eyes unfocused, she turns. Stares. Eyes unfocused, she rises. Sobs. Only once, catches herself, one hand clutching eyes unfocused, one hand clutching—

"Let's go," I say.

"M-mmm!" she says, almost sobbing again.

She stands.

The Sik-sitting-next-to-her smiles up at us, up at me.

"That's what I've been trying to tell you," she says. "Dummy," she chides.

Before I can ask what she meant, Sik holds up her snuffed brand.

"Li-light me."

"Here."

Our torches touch.

The fire offers itself freely.

At first, no reaction. But then -- a spark, a transfer, a transformation -- it bursts to life.

And the shadows explode in rebuke, closing in, sundering rock in passing and careening in exultant trumpeting wails. We make escape, adjacent to panic, hounded by horrors. Stricken sprint full aortal seizure eruption legs upsurge and slam into ancient granite heartbeat's paralyzed masonry. The dust a cloud a fog a glow of burning immediacy swallowed by nothingness, silent in its oblivion, silent in its obliviousness. Flashing images -- framing flashing lantern-light on mineral walls, coiling roots -- gone, rejected mind replaced by solidified sound cacophony of imaginary flesh and bones.

Scaling down, now she follows, full in terror and gall by slipping and catching and slipping and catching managing to breathe and watch and follow down down to the familiar level, stopping -- split-second mistake! but following down one more, the prompting: she jumped, hits, crouches, takes the outstretched pickax and becomes the shadow trailing the frantic swingsong burning box.

Beckon! Beckon now the swollen shadows to plummet air shrieking howling begging to feast!

The pool hisses in waterfall jeers and torrent spray of rock beneath exposed and shouting in cracking sufferance. But the ground underneath the corridors yearns to peel back, ablative forces a force of time compacting millennia into seconds splitting and breaking away and earthquaking underfoot, tearing away a false reprieve.

It knows! It knows where they are bound!

The cavern vertigoes and stretches paths to seem too long light to seem too weak and always always the promise of returned horror!

"Rulu-p! Rulu-p!"

No time to looking away around behind, trust her clomp of boot and rapid inhale.

"Gluuululu! Gluuuluu-p!"

And the rising tremor brings it back, prompted by its ally's quailing, scenting upwards a trail of fear like a snail's transparent, reeking shadow left to bubble and fester.

"Don't slip!" I tell her, now edging into slumbering territory, walls and ceiling and floor rousing from the untimely call.

But she does, halfway across, drops her charge and the clang parallel ricochets strident to falling maggots like bleeding rain and they screech and vomit curses of digested refuse. The splash the stomp they are focused and spit at the alarming miss mass outburst and hatred and interloper bones. A hole for licking. A hole for sucking. Fresh ossified candies wrapped in skin-paper with muscle-stuffing. Ignore the nasty blood, children, dig in our presents for sweets!

Mouth anus discharge, thick and pasty, shot too short too far too confused by the new intruder, its swell the foundation of discord. Silence it!

One focuses, puffs up squeeze in and spews. Distracted by the chorus, by Sik's grip on my arm after she falls again, after I fall against her, it splatters my face sting acid cold and immediate irritation eye pulsing blinded and optic nerve agonies.

She pulls me up, through, aiming at the entrance or exit and the nightmare has come unbidden to the lullaby and they set upon it with vile words of phlegm. It blasts the moist, sickly hot air but earless do not recoil the way half-sightless does from the knives of imagination and their impossible angles.

A violence a gnashing squeals of pandemonic battle and two casualties flee and damn either side and every side dashing dashing dashing through the halls. A buckling pillar and findings of the left markings and follow, remembering now, but led more than leading swamped by waves of pain over and over and tidally yanked upright by the rattling whispers in the ear of this way? this way?

Idon'tknowIdon'tknowmakeitstop.

Is this this is this is it this way?

Yes, this way!

Higher higher faded consciousness on faded cries deepness detached left back and air colder air moving, stop moving, slow down, fall. Hand on stairs. A hand on back. Breathing, breathing, he looks up, she smiles eyes focused. He smiles. The air is cold. Bleak. He smiled. Everything subsides. She collapses, slow motion, sitting and letting out a breath held for unknown time, though likely hours.

"Are you okay?"

He says, "No. Hurts like hell."

"Can you hear it?"

He says, "No. Can you?"

"Yeah," she sniffs. "In my head. Pounding. Not gonna stop hearing for a long time I think, too."

"I'm sorry."

"What for?"

"Dunno," he says. "Something," I say.

"Well, um… you can stand?"

Hesitating. "R-right."

"Yeah, yeah, okay, there ya go. Up we go, Red. I'll hold that for ya now, alright?"

"Right."

"Think we… think we dug too deep on this one."

We laugh, genuinely, but forced through a nigh-impenetrable fear, thinning only with each next step up the grand stairway.

"Should we g— ungh, go back for anything?" I ask.

"Yeah. No."

"Let the other diggers crack these vaults, then."

"S'not like us. Leavin' 'em. We're getting old." Grins at me. "Didn't even open one!"

"Actually I did," I say.

"Ehh, what was inside?"

"I forgot to look," I admit.

Daylight past the final arch is framed a lifeless and mute half moon, welcoming after frenzied flames, and hastens my summit as I stare at the things it promises in lucid tranquility. I devour thoughts of minor necessities. Breakfast. A nap. Chill breezes. The sky. And Sik.

Simplicity, when I'm always overthinking. Exhausted Sik who babbles silly stories. Stupid Sik who giggles for no reason. Greedy Sik who eats the last pie. Idiot Sik who dances in delight. Pissy Sik who curses with made-up words. Irresponsible Sik who only watches my back because she knows I have hers.

Outside the shattered entrance, that light doesn't feel so lifeless anymore, the fog has lifted in my heart, and I keep feeling such abiding calm up until the flash of an instant when something darts from my blind spot and bashes my consciousness into the ground.

#

"Relax."

"They'll find a way. The schedule is absolute."

"Over all territory? We're not the Technocracy: ambition and planning aren't synonymous."

"Plus, this winter is dismal, dismal shit."

"Right. See?"

"Gotta be some give for it."

"Exactly. See?"

"Dammit, stop agreeing with him. It's annoying."

"Yeah, yeah." The stranger sighs, pokes at the campfire. It crackles and she sighs again. "Who am I kidding, this whole situation is shit."

Thud.

Sucked in breath.

"Fuck you!" Sik shouts.

"Yeah, fuck me," she repeats. "Be a bunch more fun than uselessly freezing my crotch off out in the wilderness."

I peer out a squinted eyelid. We're still inside the atrium. Still day outside, but afternoon now.

Sik is on the ground, half in the firelight, half in the shadows. She rubs her stomach and moans.

The woman ignores her. Furiously scratches her own disheveled, inky hair, the definition of frustration. Two others sit across from her, one glum as boulders, chin in hands and thinking meticulously, the other trying to sleep.

With a drop on them, I might dispatch one before the others were roused. But there's no weapon at hand. The best I could do is knock one into the fire, and hope the resultant turmoil gave me time to find the pickax or shovel. Sik is in pain, but unbound and pissed off. She just needs a distraction and an excuse to attack.

This'll make a nice change from running.

I shift my position, readying for a sprint. The air is smoky. The floor coarse and grainy under my palms. My lungs tight. I tense. Kick off.

The younger girl with her back turned, lost in a maze of brooding, takes my momentum, pivots imperceptibly, and slams me to the floor. Dazed, it takes a few moments to realize what happened, and then longer to detect her blade held at my throat.

The other woman bucks up, laughs and laughs, clapping her hands. "Fucked if I don't appreciate the feistiness!" But sours right afterwards, lips drawn back in a blank sneer. "Seriously, don't try that again."

The girl grabs me by the collar and jerks me out of her way, then settles back into curled hands and that chiseled mulling look as motionless as silence.

I look at Sik.

She sits up, grimacing, gives a half-hearted wave across the room as if to say, "Tried that too. Didn't work out so well either..."

This group of three, sitting fireside -- and me sitting, stupidly, not so far away...

It hits me harder than the ground did:

I'm not a threat to them at all.

Three relaxed arms, bound with black scarves shot through with a single crimson line each.

"You... diggers." The Executioner with the inky hair. "Always getting in the way at the worst times, the worst times."

The man and younger girl bicker in side conversation.

"There should have been contingency plans," she says.

"There you go on planning again," he says.

"Well, it's true mostly, isn't it," sighs the girl.

"Quiet," the woman snaps at them. They flinch. "I didn't have marching orders until the eleventh hour and I hazard most others too. They wanted us in place. Simple as that."

"And work comes after?" the girl asks.

"Damn right it does! Not much to be done in the weather is there? Emergency action, that's all. That's what I was told."

"Spring can't come quick enough," grumbles the man.

"Cut the whining. This fire ain't going anywhere."

"We are," mumbles the girl.

"And you!" The woman snaps at Sik, who doesn't flinch. *Good girl.*

"Up yours, Execration."

"Stop calling me that already and get your scrawny ass over to the fire! I'm not telling you again!"

Sik sticks out her tongue.

"*You* do something," the woman says to the man, the one closest to the entrance.

"Can't *we*…?" the girl says, hand caressing her hilt.

"Believe me, I wish," the woman replies.

The man leans towards Sik, putting some feigned concern into his voice. "Listen, your fever is dangerously high—"

"Shut up, Execration!"

Sik strikes at him as he approaches -- with a speed that nearly rivals the girl's. Wobbly as she is, she misses though.

"Damn it," the woman snaps again, immediately usurping the delegated role. "I don't care how lucid you *think* you are right now, you stupid girl, and I don't know how long you've been in the cold and worn down to dust, but you need heat for the medicine to work best, so shut the fuck up or I'll box your stupid little ears until you can't tell which way's up and down!"

"I don't listen to stupid Execrations."

Now rising. "I'm not hauling your withered ass halfway over plague's creation! You're gonna walk! On your own damned legs! One after the other until I can bury you my damned self!" Reflexively gripping her blade's hilt.

"H-hey, calm down a bit..." the man says, starting to get as agitated as the other now.

"Yeah? Understand me?" the woman presses into Sik.

Sik reflects the flat gaze. "No."

"Fffffff—" The woman, becoming aware of her hold on her weapon, forcibly yields. Instead of returning to the fire, she stoops down, inches from Sik's pale face. "No one knows you're out here, do they? No. Of course they don't. Who would you tell? Us? The Guards of the Watch? Your friends? Pfffff," she chuckles darkly. "And who are they, huh? Do they dig too? Are they gonna help you? When? In an hour? Right this instant?" Abruptly whips her gaze at the daylight crawling through the fissure. Sik starts. "Hmm, I don't see anyone. Seems kinda quiet, huh? Seems kinda dead, huh? Hey!" A sharp whisper. Sik twitches again. "I don't think anyone's coming."

The Executioner stops talking. Doesn't move. From this angle, I can only see the inky hair obscuring her eyes, the unreadable lips.

"Exe-ex... Exe..." Sik stammers.

"Huh, what was that, sweetie?"

Sik averts her gaze, clutches trembling hands together. "D-don't..."

"Huh?"

"D-don't c-call me..." she says, "*that.*"

"Well, we have a nice agreement there, don't we?"

Not moving, and then...

Sik gives in, nods so slowly I'm not sure she even did.

"Good." The woman turns back to the fire and, soon after, Sik follows. "So, are you trouble too?" she asks me. "Or did you get that outta your system?"

The brooding girl looks at me. "Hmmm."

"Go fix him," says the woman to the man.

He groans, standing again. "Never rest at this rate."

"Yeah, yeah, you were the one insisted on this path," the woman snorts. "Your fault."

The brooding girl looks past me. "Hmmm."

"Lie down," the man tells me.

I squint up at him. "I'm fine, thanks all the same."

He shrugs. "Works for me, not like it'll hurt less." Grabs my shoulder before I can react and then grabs a chunk of my face and tugs.

Pain swells skin-ripping torture.

"Get off!" I shout.

"I'm saving your eye," he explains, though not gently. Peeling back my skin, hot blood streaking, muscles spasming contracting shrinking. I try to fight, but that makes it worse. I can only endure. "Little bastard got you real good, didn't he? Crazy aim, those things. Better than us, can you imagine?"

"You're... pulling my eye out!" I gasp.

"Keep moving like that, I really will too. 'Lie down' I said, but 'no'."

With a final heave, my skin snaps off and I instinctively cover the open wound. Hatred. These Executioners. All Executioners. They should all die, die and be interred the way they adore, no, nothing so respectful, dump them all in a ditch to rot and liquefy into a single, revolting mass!

"Can you see anything?" he asks.

I scowl.

He shrugs again. "If you can, you probably won't go blind." Wads up the sallow paste he tore off me and tosses it into the campfire. It blackens like burnt marshmallow.

I remove my hands to find no blood, only a clear, inert fluid that drips through my fingers, puddles and forms rivulets in the fittings between the stones on the floor.

"We have to go down there," the girl says at length.

Do, I think.

The man returns to his spot. "Have fun."

"Agreed," says the woman, with an audible eyeroll, "I'm not dealing with wormguts today -- or tomorrow."

"But we *have* to go down there," she maintains firmly.

"Yeah, yeah, I hereby declare this very much to *not* be an emergency. Sorry, no asses to be moved."

At that, the girl bristles with the most emotion yet displayed, which amounts to little more than an irritated exhale. "You are so lazy."

"It's rationality! You said it yourself, we have places to be *yesterday* and whoa, look! Two gravediggers to deal with now! Hey, fun times! So, tell me how we're to clear the place out -- which doesn't look inextensive, mind -- while lugging around these blighters?"

"Make them do it," the girl answers plainly. "And that's not a word."

"Oh, a lot of good that did before!" Points at me.

"Hmmm."

"Fine, maybe it's not rationality. I'm mitigating. We can only do so much. Agreed?" the woman asks.

"Hmmm."

"Agreed?" the woman presses.

Reverts to quiet brooding. "For now," says the girl.

"What do you think?" The woman turns her attention.

The man gives up attempting to rest, makes a restrained gesture. He's about to say something, but... "About?"

"You know we can't take them with us."

"Sure."

"Fucking definitely aren't leaving them either."

The brooder stirs. "Are you su—"

"Yes, I am," she snaps at the unmoving girl.

"One option as I figure," he says.

Shaking her head. "That's completely out of the way."

"The Watch are equipped for this..." he continues.

"They're incompetent..."

"… we aren't."

"… why do you think we're out here in the first place!"

"Blast it to hell, Regin, I never said it was good or even best, but it's what's on the barren, bloody table and if you want me to figure it, I've figured it!"

"Fine!"

"There it is!"

They fume with burning eyes and crossed arms.

Tension holding.

The man relaxes first.

"And all this time, thought I was the one meant to keep *you* two from tearing each other apart."

"She quiets easily lately. Enjoy it while you can."

The inanimate girl wakens from reverie and starts rooting through our things. What with our last encounter, I can only assume her morose position and wait this shit out. Sik, either giving up or doped up on whatever they forced on her, is dozing. After nameless horrors, I suppose I should be grateful, but the one called Regin had it right: a shit situation.

"'You' and 'you' won't get me very far," she says to me. "Who are you?"

"Red. Sik."

Eyes rolling straightaway. "Right, didn't think I'd get anything substantial. So. Any cursed down there?"

"Dead people. What do you want?"

"Exactly that," she says. "A lifeless corpse, every one."

"We may have seen something," I offer, "but I never had a good look what it was."

Which is true enough.

If we're luckier than we have been today, they'll investigate. Three Executioners wouldn't fare any better than we did. Though they wouldn't leave us alone to check would they? We'd be drug along.

Shit, that might have been stupid to say.

But if it was, she doesn't rise to the bait. "So. I wonder if that's true."

"I wouldn't bother," the man says, mindful to speak over the girl, in a low voice of gravel.

Regin glares at the entrance. "We can't seal this. Fuck it all to ashes I hate you diggers. Seriously, what is wrong with you? Not even just the *everything*, but antiquated places you break into— fuck, this can't be fixed until summer! It won't be so strong either. You... you... fuck, it's a game, isn't it? Break the shell, eat all the tasty bits inside, and throw it away, yeah? Let someone else pick it up. And look... look at you! Your friend's brains were burning to mush, probably an improvement, and you lost an eye! Some game. It's a penalty game, is what it is. Like, shit, like a bunch of stupid, fucking little children you are. All over! Idiots back at home and now you lot out here. Running around with your pants around your ankles without a sense of what you're screwing with, screwing over, well, everyone I think, your selves included obviously. And for what?"

I try to have a smart-ass quip ready.

But there's none there.

"Stupid kids." Shakes her head again. "And stop chewing your tongue," she tells the girl.

"You're like a mother to everyone, Reg," the man grins.

The woman's dark eyes of warning. "Don't."

"Mom-complex," says the girl.

"That is so disgusting. Hey!" And she raps the girl on the head. "What did I tell you?"

"Not." The girl hands over one of our honey rations. "It's tasty."

"Heh?" Regin bisects it in one bite. Stunned expression, unblinking. Hurriedly slaps the remainder in the man's palm. He gives it a withering glance, but complies -- and with the same immediacy copies her reaction. "I *know*."

"How did they manage to get rations from Apiary?"

"Is it inside? Ungh, I don't want to think about if it's inside," she groans.

"It's probably thieves. They've done it before."

"Yeah, yeah. Even then, they're gonna have fun grilling these two. Sneaky fuckers."

"Found a mausoleum in winter. It's impressive."

"It's disturbing."

"It's ours," the girl interrupts.

"Huh?"

"What?"

Two hands, sticky, slightly golden, each clutching a snack, spread wide the map. The Executioners peer over the contents. I hadn't yet had the chance to view Sik's handiwork, but she can be painstakingly detailed and obsessive when fired up. As trepidation sinks into their faces, the pit in my stomach widens and I start making guesses at how much strife we're going to be plunging into by the end of things.

"Okay. Okay, no fucking around." Regin's eyes become coal. "Where the *fuck* did you get this?"

"Would you believe it's ours?" I try asking.

The coal kindles. "Fuck no."

"It's ours," repeats the girl, nodding to me and stuffing her face innocently like we're all of us picnicking.

The black flames spread. "Where. Did. You. Get. This."

I've been around Sik and Jackal far, far long enough to know I'm not that much of a fool. I see the order of things. I hold back or joke further and it's Sik has the blade caressing the length of a pulsing, ignorant jugular this time. Sorry, Eddy. You're a sweetheart, too kind for a ravenous world like ours and too trusting of two crows perched atop the shoulders of a corpse.

"It's true the map *was* ours…" I begin.

But there's a false narrative being scrawled against the inside of the Executioners' skulls, the ink spills, the scratching is maddening, the ink drowns the brain from the glaring loose-end. Two gravediggers got their hands on an Executioner map and lighted out of Old City before or after the Sovereignty's proclamation -- the timing is irrelevant -- and got to where the digging must be good and undefended.

"And there're always deals to be made with those with information," I continue.

Offhand information is so telling. Break-ins at Apiary? How far can I push the idea that thieves helped us? Minor morsels. Distraction. Distraction. Somewhere Jackal is spinning a twintail around a finger. Over here, over here! Somewhere else Quinn discreetly covers an inaudible laugh. This is the response you wanted. Let me let you in. Let me light the candle. Let me smile you murder.

"We got someone to fill in those blanks," I explain.

I can't do it, though. Would they believe it? I can't out her. Brightly oblivious, almost like Sik, clear vision, powerful lungs and untiring, bare legs untouched by winter's teeth. Her joy.

Regin has stopped blinking. "Who."

I can do it, though. Would they believe it? I can out him. Bleak oblivion, almost like sickness, clouded vision, creaking lungs and tired, barren lives trashed by one wrong turn. His job.

I drop the name. "Bors."

A gamble. He plays both sides of the board, Old Kingdom to Old City, and the Executioners hail primarily from the latter. If we eavesdrop on the pulse of the darker side of life, he jams an ear trumpet straight into the heart and hardly minds the mess or the screaming. After all, he understands as we do the money to be made from a death rattle.

Whatever the effect, they don't let on. The silence is open to interpretation, but the duration has a certain must of plausibility.

"So," she says finally. Folds the map, slips it in a pocket. Passes a second. Click of the tongue. Removes the map and drops it in the campfire.

The man leans forward. "That's evidence."

"I don't like the idea of something like this existing."

"If you say so."

"I don't like this."

He doesn't respond.

"Another." The girl hands over a scrap of paper.

Regin ignores it, intent on nervously pumping her foot up and down. She chews her tongue.

"Give it here." The man studies it and hands it to Regin, but she doesn't notice. Consulting with the girl instead, he lets out a ragged breath. "I don't know this place. Do you?"

"Hmmm."

"Come on, you like maps." Flaps the paper.

The breeze catches fleeting attention.

"I like cartography."

"You know it?" he asks.

"Hmmm. No."

"Is it Executioner?"

"It is, but it isn't, but it most *definitely* is."

He turns back to Regin. "You need to look at this."

I recognize that sketch of the vault in Ensbryng. I had forgotten.

"I really don't like it," Regin mutters, sight roving through the flames. Extends fingers absentmindedly.

The man thinks better of it.

Stows the sketch away safely.

"Reg," he says. "Reg," he presses.

Statuesque. Empty eyes glance at him.

"Let's get on."

"Yeah. Okay." Takes a moment to return to awareness, stands and brushes dust off her ass. "Gather up everything, and... stop— stop screwing with that crap. Let me think.

Yeah. You. *You*," she gestures at me. "Carry your crap, minus the tools. And you, you wake up."

Sik sleeps on in the comforting blanket of drugged unconsciousness.

I expect a tirade of swearing or worse, but Regin doesn't react. Instead, fingertips against forehead, she simply looks exhausted.

#

With everything brought outside and Sik propped against the stairs, I was made to help block the mausoleum entrance. Enough chunks of the broken pillars I had scrounged around the previous night managed well enough. It was a hack job, but the Executioners hammered them into place and were vaguely satisfied with the seal.

"Cursed ain't worming through that," Regin said, unconvincingly.

Leaving the hollow behind and the things that laid beneath it, we made for the tangled forest. The Executioners divided the weight of "Evidence Collection" between themselves -- at least until Sik wakes up. For now, at least, the end of my reprieve is distant and my burden merely the gravedigger drooling in my arms.

We travel north.

I ask where we go, receiving no answer. Begrudging the question, I suspect they have yet to decide. They aren't so talkative anymore. With passions dwindling after the initial encounter, the Executioners devolve into how I have always imagined them: aloof, emotionless, calculating. Running over and over in their minds the scene in the atrium, repeating what was said, what was said to them, searching for a fault, a flaw, a weak construction in the wall, in theirs, in mine, to determine if they spoke too freely, to deconstruct if I didn't speak freely enough.

For my part, I couldn't care.

We have to get away from them.

Last night's fog abides in a sense, a testament to its intensity and why shelter will be crucial from here on out. A sheen of ice covers tree trunks and roots alike, assured to layer thicker with each night that passes. Already footing is treacherous and the sprinkling hoarfrost from upset branches irritates the eyes.

I have heard stories of people being frozen to death, encased until the long thaw begins. How far away the fireplace feels that warmed the chairs around, the voices of the raconteurs, their anecdotes, their warnings, out here where the danger is imminent and the only music the whistle of the wind in the trees, whispering, "Soon... Soon..."

If I had provisions, I could make a break for it. Their speed, I know, it wouldn't work, but still... I *have* Sik. If I could *take* her... instead of pathetically trailing along in the shadow of three Executioners leading me places unknown and none of them good.

"She a narcolept or something?" Regin finally asks an hour later.

"Insomniac," I say. "The hell did you give her?"

She shrugs. "Fever killer."

"Antipyretic," corrects the girl.

"Should be awake by now," Regin mutters, adjusting a shoulder strap. "Tired of lugging your crap."

"Exhaustion amplifies the sedative effect," clarifies the girl, brightly.

"Huh."

"If exhaustion set in."

"Man," Regin groans. "Day keeps on worse and worse."

Another hour on, Sik stirs in dreams. Makes a soft sound, nuzzles closer to my chest.

I smile, in spite of it all. "Waking up, Sik?"

"Mpphmm," the unconscious dreamer breathes.

I stop walking.

The girl halts. Soon, the others too.

"Let us go," I tell them. "You have everything of worth we own. We have no map now. We're not a threat. Probably die out here anyways." Biting my cheek. Shit. Debt to Executioners. Feel like vomiting. "Give us enough food to make for home. Go your own way. You have orders? A schedule? We'll go away. You can make it."

"No, we can't actually," Regin, flat as steel. "We can't actually. We're so entirely screwed up the ass, I don't want to sit down for a year." Fist to forehead. Short inhale. Long exhale. "You're serious, aren't you."

"Half the food. We walk away."

Temptation sucks on her neck.

"No," she states firmly.

"No one will know."

Half-lidded. Lips opening.

"Not happening," she falters.

"Never see each other again."

Teeth clamp down on her tongue.

"I can't do that," she admits, soft and honest.

"Let's do it."

Silence.

Feels real.

It doesn't last.

"No, no, no." Inky hair fluttering. "Not about convenience anymore, this is about punishment. This. All of this is your fault." Accusatory finger rakes the air for me. "I don't want to be here. I'm tired; I want my bed. I'm hungry; I want proper food. I'm cold; I want to go home!" Shaking fists. "And I'm going to have my period in like a fucking week and do you know how annoying it is to have that when you're traveling and it's freezing and you have to keep moving and— and— and you're working!? No, of course you don't! You fuckers don't even fucking have jobs!"

She stamps away, crunching frozen twigs underfoot.

The Executioners follow.

Really thought that might have worked…
For a second, at least.

#

Losing track of time.

Numbness reminds me I haven't slept for a while.

Jealousy reminds me I wish I was in Sik's position.

"Heavier than you look," I grumble.

"Heard that," she says.

Almost laugh, but catch myself so as not to draw attention from our unwanted companions.

"Course you would. You girls are sensitive to that."

Yawns silently. "I don't mind. 'Cept the metabolism bullshit."

"Feeling better?"

"Groggy," she says.

"To be expected. You were gone."

"Yeah. Been trying to wake up for like twenty minutes or something, keep slipping." Yawns again. Then she stiffens. "I hear more than your footsteps."

"You don't remember?"

"… no?"

"How much do you remember?" I ask.

"Bad dreams. Were they true?"

"The short of it: Executioners."

She mouths a resigned 'fuck.'

"Knew it couldn't just be nightmares," she finishes.

"Who says it isn't?" I grumble.

"What should I do? Pretend sleep?"

"Honestly, I don't think it matters," I admit. "We can't run. Can't fight them. I'd rather you were up and alert so we can figure something out on the fly."

She hops down, unsteady, gripping my shoulder.

"Right, I'm up, sorta. Don't count on alert for a while, though. Execrations…" she swears with the next breath. "What rot."

As expected, they notice Sik stumbling beside me without any delay.

"Other one's with us," the man says.

"Finally," Regin sighs. Shrugs off one of our packs. The man starts to do the same, but she stops him with a raised palm. "Ah, don't bother. Look at the way she walks. Barely even there."

"Can we switch out then?" he asks.

"Here." She removes the lantern from his burden, thrusts it at Sik. "Can you manage this?"

Sik, there or not, scowls fiercely enough to melt a frozen tree. "*Thanks*."

"*Sure*." Regin allows a crook of a smile.

The pack she drops at my feet is lighter than it should be. They all watch me stoop down and sling it over my shoulder. Not sure why. Surely nothing of threat to them in here. Sounds like our precious haul isn't inside. Feels like food and food alone.

Ah, so it's that.

They remember the offer. Regin in particular. Still, unless we get explicit sanction, I'm not risking anything. They're Executioners after all. Untrustworthy. Feral. They would only give us a chance to bolt if they saw it as the perfect excuse to murder us and report back to their handlers, faces painted full of convenient truths. Two gravediggers down, two less corpses to bury.

"Where are we going?" Sik pipes up, all piss and vigor after a sleep.

Good medicine.

"If I had my way," Regin says, "take you all the way back to Old City and not stop until I saw you in the gaol myself. But, time and weather as they are, this is clearly not happening."

"I want to inter something…" the girl pouts.

"Inter your tongue and stop opening your mouth, then."

"Where then?" Sik presses. "A new graveyard? We'll trade digging tips?"

"Funny." Mirthless laugh. "Crossroads," Regin answers.

Definitely no surprises there. Where these three are on the Executioner plans... I can't say, but I'm more and more of the opinion it's the fringe. Scouting party? No, she made it out as they had somewhere to be. Sent to secure distant plots? Makes sense why Crossroads would be out of the way, but it's worse for us. All those guards. Chance of escape?

Non-existent.

#

The roots are a coiling mess now. As the Executioners begin to pick their way through, Sik darts to the right. I run left, hoping to draw them off her. A shout. I can't tell from whom. Underfoot the ice is shattering. Are they stuck inside? I feel triumph. And then horror. Sik screams. Wet agony. Bubbling torment frothing out blade-raped lungs. I turn. Regin, remorseless face and raised arm, the last person I see.

The roots are briar patch thick now. Despite the ice, we can climb well enough. The sound alerts them right away. But we climb, and the roots climb higher, and so we climb higher on. Gravity will kill an Executioner as easily as a gravedigger. Will they risk these heights? I feel triumph. But he defies it, hopping up with an impossible lightness. Sik's eyes go wide. He jumps against the side of the tree, seems suspended for a split-second, then springs into Sik. She screams all the way down, stopping when her ribcage has broken his fall. And before I can think, he's already on top of me.

The roots are thinning now. As the Executioners begin to step out, we grab the girl and drag her deeper. Slamming her to the ground -- some poetic payback, grim joy -- and she makes a pathetic noise. Air knocked out, gasping. Sik smiles at that -- shared sadism -- and slits the pink throat.

Are they outside? I feel triumph. But the deva vu relief pivots. Sik doesn't scream this time. The blade, still held tight, now jammed in her own throat. The girl Executioner smiles above a bleeding wound that smiles wider and the two shivering hands which hold Sik's hand rip out -- sickening force -- and stab my remaining—

#

"How's your eye?"

"Huh?"

"Your eye," Sik repeats.

"Right. Sorry."

"Well?"

"Blurry. Hurts a bit. Cold isn't helping."

"Let you know if you're gonna bump into anything sharp," she chuckles.

"Thanks."

"What are we gonna do, Red?"

"I don't know."

"I don't either."

"You heard her, though," I gesture at Regin.

"Yeah. Crossroads. It's rot."

"Tougher going, but we'll be back around nightfall."

"We'll have to do something stupid before we get there," Sik says.

"Can't count on help from the old man."

"Who?"

"Doesn't matter. But you're right. Guards are aplenty in Crossroads. Can't spit without hitting one."

"Ehh, sure, but they're also pretty stupid and tired and unobservant," Sik offers. "Usually."

"Their numbers will make up for that. And the weather might piss them off enough to counteract it altogether."

"… think they'd kill us? Like, outright?"

I don't answer for a second. "Why do you think I wanted to avoid the place entirely?"

"It's true, isn't it? Execrations might not off us, but the Watch sure could." Folds her arms. "Unless the Execrations are already in control of Crossroads."

I hadn't counted on that.

"Bad news."

"Bad news," I agree, staring up at the canopy. No piling snow yet. Only been a day since, why would there be? It'd be perfect though, a snowfall, right now -- a few meters ahead -- breaking through and burying these bastards neck deep. More than enough death in the world to go around, but it's never where you want it when you need it...

#

The girl Executioner reappears after a long absence.

She's an aberration. It isn't the age thing, though it is, but she really lives in her own world. Boredom? Delusion? Mental disability? Each answer feels correct until she disproves them one by one. A defective personality? A random temperament sending her to circle out-of-the-way roots, kick ice until it cracks off of them, or stand alone and space out, placid as any unmoving lake. But then something agitates the waters, usually Regin, and off she goes again doing some other weird thing that the other Executioners are apparently used to.

If this is her quiet mode, I wonder what she's like normally.

"What are you doing?" I ask her during one of her trances.

"Hmmm."

"She's humming," Sik jokingly translates.

"At least someone's enjoying this," I say.

Wherever she mentally wanders, she stays there a while and it isn't until a minute or so later that she catches up to us, running so fast she slams into the man's back. A shout. A scolding. And a return to keeping pace between them and us. The episode forgotten, at least by her.

I nudge Sik. "Try talking to her."

"Ehh? Why?"

"You're both crazy. Maybe it'll make sense."

She gives me a look. "Ehhh."

I shrug.

"You think she's their weakness?" Sik whispers.

"I don't know what I think."

Hands on hips. "Yer hiding something from me."

"Nothing important." Which doesn't convince Sik at all. "Nothing I can verbalize."

"Yeah, 'cause you don't have a mouth or brain or nothing."

"I have an excess of logic. If I'm the one to try—"

"Stop." Holds up a hand. "Enough with insulting Sik today."

And she jogs a bit, then falls into pace with the girl.

"Yo."

No response.

"So, yer all from the City, yeah?"

No response.

"Geez, yer like a friend of mine."

No response.

"Stop making me homesick, jerk."

Nothing.

And now Sik is silent. Shoulders hunched up.

I know that stance.

Depressed brooding.

I sigh. Nothing is going to be easy ever again is it?

But Sik snaps out of it into a breakneck sprint, the way only she can. "So, like, okay, how do you guys deal with the cursed, I've been wondering? Is there only ever one at a time or does it spread so there's lots and that's why you guys are never alone? Or, or is it like a backup plan thingy where if someone gets hurt at least there are others that can help? You're very organized. Or I think so, I wouldn't know, you guys are assholes, I stay away from you as much as I can, but that would explain why there aren't any freelancers."

No response... from Sik, and then:

"Holy shit!"

Regin and the man turn around, see nothing is wrong, and ignore the outburst. Sik runs back to me.

"What if there are fucking freelancers!?" she hisses in my ear.

"We're already screwed," but she's out of earshot before I can finish, "so it wouldn't really matter."

"And how do you stop a cursed? And what does it look like? And how do you know one is? Or isn't? Or do you?" That last freaks Sik out, but soon it slips her mind and the deluge of questions she's always wanted to know about the Executioners, about the cursed, about everything we've tried so hard to avoid all these long years, spills forth, down and down and down, and I'm left guessing when someone will tell her to shut up or if I will.

"There have been murders, of course." The girl's voice is low, passionless, its utterance so sudden that Sik's jaw audibly clacks shut. "That's how it starts unless you find them first. There were a few when we left, but now?" Drums fingers against kneecaps. "If it finally started being contagious, I think I want to go east, keep going east until there's nowhere left to go. That's what I think."

"What, in the City?" I ask.

"Hmmm."

"You mean," Sik asks, "cursed have... they've been out... a-and people died?"

"Murders," the girl repeats. "*Yes.*"

"Who. Who was killed?"

"Names," the girl says. "I don't know them."

"W-well where were they? Down south or up nor—"

"North."

"Eh. The... the outskirts or city prop—"

"City proper," the girl says.

Sik breathes in relief. I'm surprised when I catch myself doing the same, when I don't even believe this cursed rubbish. But my lungs are tight, and I am listening.

That reaction isn't lost on me.

"And the outskirts," the girl continues.

"What." Sik, unbalanced. "B-but you Executioners are supposed to stop that."

The girl halts. Slowly arches her neck, twists her head. The light streaming through the canopy covers her face in shadowy veins. "Outbreaks are scary. Did you know? How they spread. How planning and effort bend to them. And die. Like everything else. Dying... dying..."

"But... but..."

The girl leaves Sik behind, who is lost for words and footing.

"But! What do you mean?" She hurries after. "Y-you said only a few people have been killed, right?"

"Hmmm."

"So does a cursed killing make another cursed?"

"We don't know."

"Is... is this the plague? Is... is it the same thing as a curse?"

"We don't know."

"What the hell do you then!" Her panic-twisted voice.

Dead eyes. Sewn to Sik's. "That we aren't sealing these places to keep gravediggers out." Frowning. "I want to inter something..." Then smiling. "Are you scared?"

Sik's fingers are wrapped together.

"A little," she admits.

The girl dashes off to Regin, excitedly chattering and pointing repeatedly at her backpack. Regin rolls her eyes, but reaches inside and puts food in the girl's outstretched hands. Then, hesitating for a moment, lays her palm atop the girl's head. Something passes between them, I'm not sure affection is the correct word, and the girl marches back into place with a honey-flavored bar in each hand.

"I wanna go home." Sik's voice so dull and lonesome.

She tugs on my sleeve.

"We'll burn that bridge when we cross it," I tell her.

"I'm worried."

Helplessly trapped by Executioners. How to reassure the one stumbling beside me, her mind clouded by drugs and fear? I have no words for that. Only pointless phrases, my cold logic, that I already know before I speak won't comfort.

"Quinn's watchful, she'll keep even Jackal out of trouble. Don't worry."

"But I *am* worried."

I reach over and give her arm a squeeze.

She doesn't recoil.

"I'm sorry," I say.

"Stop that."

"What?"

Tugs harder. "Stop apologizing all the time. You..." she says, "didn't do anything. It's... weird."

She's right.

I haven't done anything. And in this situation, I can't see a way to change that either.

#

"Why aren't we at the road..." the man says to himself.

"Better question," the girl says to the hidden sky. "Where is the sun?"

Full afternoon and, it's true, the sun is completely obscured. Although plenty of light streams through the canopy, the ice that clings to the branches refracts it in random directions. Then the trunks, encased themselves, reflect the light like so many colossal mirrors, further misleading the eye and creating a dazzling, dizzying effect.

Sik whispers my thoughts aloud.

"They've never been out in winter."

While the Executioners stop and argue about which direction we're traveling, we sit and rest on the chilly ground. Sik removes a glove, plucks a frost flower, and watches it melt from the heat of her fingertips. I close my eyes and see Old City, lightly frosted as though trapped in glass, and imagine the groaning of the trees and the stretching of the ice as if the sound of carts rolling down those long, long roads, a destination warmer somewhere at the end.

Frost touches my nose. I sneeze.

Sik pulls the flower back and laughs.

The Executioners can't believe the misdirecting effect of the ice. I can't believe it's happening so early or lasting so long. But my sense of direction, though thrown, sets us curving east. By how many degrees, uncertain, and doubtfully enough to keep Crossroads at a safe distance…

And yet…

Sik puts the mostly-melted flower in her mouth.

Crunch crunch.

She swallows.

"Never taste as good as they look," she laments.

"Fucking climb up there and look, then!" Regin says to the girl.

"Don't actually do it, idiot," the man says, pulling the girl down.

"Ah crap," Sik mutters.

I glance at her.

"You're thinking up another plan."

"I'm that predictable?" I ask.

"More like obvious." Waves two fingers back and forth. "Yer face goes all… not moving when you're working something out. Kinda funny. Well?"

"Wondering if we can keep going east."

"You noticed it too, huh?"

I blink. Rub my bad eye. "Surprised you did."

"Screw you."

123

I grin.

"Oh, you're joking," she says. "Hard to tell sometimes. You get negative real quick."

"Only when things go to rot."

"Yeah, well, they do that a lot lately... Anyways, ah, that's only delaying stuff. Any other point to east? I've already forgotten the map."

"The greater the distance from home and Crossroads, the less guards and Executioners." Shrugging. "I'm delaying for a chance of escape."

"Well, duh."

"So?" I prod.

"Unless you or me are leading... otherwise, why would they listen? And why would they trust that?"

"Think it will snowstorm?" I ask.

She laughs again, less happy this time. "Trusting in weather now? We *are* screwed." Scrunches up her face in thought. Relaxes. "She freaks me out, but I'll try working on the little one. Convince her there's something tasty," she waves, "over that way. Dunno. She seems starved all the time. Reminds me..." She turns to the Executioners. "Hey, we're hungry. Fork something over."

Regin can't be bothered. "Look in his pack." And goes back to grousing at the man.

Sik crawls behind me and reaches in.

Rapid disappointment. "Oh, Execration rations. Figures." Shows me a handful of rabbit jerky, dates and double-baked biscuits. "Always thought they just ate shit," she says before she feasts.

#

It didn't work.

The girl regressed to an unspeaking nature after her snack, despite Sik's entreaties. Absolute ambivalence. And so we all walked on, now edging towards their goal -- not a lot, but enough.

"I have to pee," Sik announced.

Regin didn't turn around. "Behind a tree and no farther."

"Tch," Sik said and didn't bother.

Noble attempt, Sik. But our course remained unaltered.

The light dimmed from then on and the trees started glowing burnt orange. The Executioners hastened our pace, but Sik managed to feign lethargy and keep it from being the light jog they wanted. Were it not for her condition, no doubt we would have been running from the start and been in Crossroads, limbs bound, faces pressed to the dirt, hours by now.

In spite of the final push, the sun set sooner than they had counted on. Orange bled into pink, within minutes pooled into spreading lavender and darkened a shade every other footfall.

Regin stopped. Fist to forehead.

"A few more hours," the girl noted, encouragingly. "Maybe."

"… where is the road…" the man said to himself.

"Maybe," the girl noted further, "two?"

"Fog comes in one," I said.

"I know!" Regin shouts, although from that tone I think she didn't. She kicks an adjacent root, reminding me of me last night at the mausoleum, and the branches above shudder a sprinkling of indigo hoarfrost. Once it settles atop her head and shoulders, she turns to us.

"We'll keep going."

"We are not," the man pushes back.

"We keep going," she presses. "Everyone gather branches for a bonfire along the way. Torches light our path and we stop if we have to."

When we have to.

Man, she's a stubborn, summer-coddled idiot.

Most of the fallen wood we pass is useless. Large pieces too frozen to thaw; smaller bits, melted during the day, too wet to kindle. Eventually we discover a happy medium, thinly-encased that the bastards crack open with *our* tools. Little wonder who will do the carrying.

"That's five," the man's voice calls through the dimness. He pulls out a metallic tube from a pocket, twists the base -- *click* -- and with a crackle like a devil's snicker a searing flame erupts from the other end. We each light our branches from the strange device, the wood sizzling from retained moisture, and journey on.

Firelight reflects off the icy roots, occasionally licking the shadow-smothered canopy until being engulfed itself. Opaque mists rise. I noticed them first, but said nothing except to Sik. They shrink around the trees, seemingly testing the air's temperature with pinpricking tendrils. They hide at the edge of our light, in collaboration with the shadows, for now.

"We oughta stop," Sik advises.

This goes uncommented on.

I glance at her. Glances back. Bites her lip. Winks.

The shadows have solid substance now beyond the trees. The canopy could be hewn from granite for all the lack of starlight. We could have walked back into the guts of the mausoleum, my imagination whispers, and I shiver eye aching. But I understand the shadows as I understand their fog sisters and I know that Sik, for her part, does too. And while the darkness deepens down and the deepness builds and builds around, I know the Executioners do not.

"Hey, we need to stop," Sik repeats later.

She prompts me with a nudge.

"It's too dangerous now," I say automatically.

"Be quiet," Regin says.

Sik nudges me again. Points at the ground. I don't need to look. My twisted grin is a match with hers.

The fog has hidden our feet.

#

We persist in prodding Regin as long as possible. We goad her with false urgency, with desires to stop. It's not entirely untrue, but the risk is worth the reward if what I think Sik is up to works.

When the fog reaches our thighs -- and halfway covers the girl -- Regin finally calls the halt. She gathers all the wood we've carried and throws her torch into the bundle without concealing her disdain. The fog shies away, exposing the ground, but the wood catches too slowly for her. A muttered growl. Shoves annoyed fingers into her pack, produces a cobalt square of... wood? Throws it in.

The fire blazes and fizzles and jumps three feet, nearly singeing her hand, and casts the whole scene into deep blue. The heat contracts, disappears, and I feel the bite of winter gripping my spine and caressing every part of me. Then the unnatural color fades into piercing amber, leaving afterimages of pure yellow that make it more vivid still, and the heat rushes back and envelops. The fog retreats.

The girl's head lolls back and forth. She takes her own cobalt square and raises it high. The man snatches it away from her. Then he turns to Regin.

"Don't waste those," he says.

Ignoring him, she hunkers close to the warmth.

"Don't reproach me."

He doesn't take the bait.

We huddle around the campfire. Three fussy Executioners. Two exhausted gravediggers.

Sik and I start in on the rations. Our friends resolutely refuse to share Darvin's food, even when we offer to exchange. Sik is about to make a row of it, but stops herself short when she finds a container of coffee buried among the biscuits and jerky.

"Don't drink much," I warn her.

"I know."

"You're still sick and you haven't slept."

She hesitates. Painfully. "B-breakfast then," she relents. And then: "Coffee for honey!"

"Fuck a corpse," Regin says to the offer.

"Naw, you don't interest me much," Sik replies.

#

It isn't even a fitful night. I can't sleep at all.

Can't tell of Sik. Probably faking.

The Executioners let the girl nod off first, but she keeps getting up and wandering off into the night. She jams a torch into the earth, somehow, though it's frozen. I hear her undo her pants and pull them down, but nothing happens. After a minute, she returns and lies back down until the ritual restarts anew.

"Close your eyes already," Regin murmurs to the man.

He pokes at the fire. "Not that tired, Reg."

"Hmmm."

"Shhh," Regin says to the girl.

"We don't both of us need to watch," he says.

"Even so."

"Not midnight, not nearly. Sleep, alright?"

She smiles, soft, kind. It feels incongruous to see, but it's undeniably real. "Too agitated. Tomorrow."

"Tomorrow," he agrees.

#

An hour on. The girl rises again, ghostlike. Disappears.

Again, she lowers her pants and squats. Again, nothing. She pulls them back up. Doesn't return.

After a minute, I hear her frantically pulling them down. She strains and strains, and there's a groan that's something more like a sob. But before I can figure out if she's actually crying, I hear two distant thuds and afterwards a softer one from where she is. And then she reappears.

Not lying down now. She sits, bare butt firmly planted against the freezing ground, hugging nakedness and tugging thick, striped socks, the solitary clothing below her waist.

Dozing as they are, it takes her companions a moment to grasp the sight.

"What the hell are you doing!" Regin bolts upright.

The girl mumbles a phrase, kicks the campfire. Ashes fly. She screeches incomprehensively.

"The hell's going on?" the man says.

Holding her stomach. "Won't come out," the girl moans.

"Frostbite won't help that!" Regin says.

Unresponsive as if she had never lashed out, the girl stares at nothing.

"Get her on her feet." Regin wearily stands. "I'll go gather h-rrrrrrn!" She collapses. "Fuck!" And grips her stomach with both hands. "Fuck... ffffff—" She makes as though to stand, leans against the nearest root, but fails.

"What in the hell is wrong with you two?"

While the man's worried face darts between both stricken women, Sik gathers up a handful of ash scattered by the girl's previous outburst and throws it at his eyes.

He blocks, but barely.

In that instant, I'm able to scramble for the shovel and withdraw before either one can unsheathe a blade.

The haze, the heat, of the fire. This turmoil. I don't know what I'm doing, neither do they, but it all comes together -- crashing clarity -- when the Executioner girl screams and blood gushes out of her kneecap and spurts onto Sik's hand that holds a chisel holds a hammer slamming down screaming worse the next and blood splattering the face stained blood stained fire death's demanded chorus and hellish fiend yelling, "Throw your fucking weapons away!" And they don't, and the roused aching eye ignites to hatred's lust and slams shovel against the original screamer and the sound is out and the flames crackle uncaringly at the cracked skull and the limp child, now chisel at jugular and hand raises demanding from grave's depths bell peeling, "I said throw them away fucking now!"

And one does.

The man.

The fire quietens.

The light dulls.

Regin's blade glints, halfway out the sheath, shaking in rage, shaking from tears.

With Sik poised, either terrible sculpture or sculptor, I throw the girl's pack over my shoulder, then the other we were forced to carry. I place the edge of the shovel over the girl's defenseless neck, plant my foot atop and watch them. They want to kill us. I feel the same. Difference is, I don't think we could. But no one moves except for Sik. Now relieved of strangling their weak point, she gathers our lantern, two torches, and no more than Regin's reach, though still restrained, can allow.

Fog and shadows parted for the gravediggers and, though they made way for the seething, hateful torches clutched aloft, embraced the return of two of their own.

#

We pant from the leg-burning sprint, pushing our limits all at once. Sik's eyes are flung wide, shock fatigue insanity, as she waves the torch and forces the fog back. At our pace, it hardly works -- even with my torch swinging in tandem -- being too late, too cold, fog too settled in for the night. So we cover our mouths, try to breathe as shallow as we can.

"St-stop, stop," I tell her when we reach a place where the ground doesn't crunch from ice underfoot.

"S'o... s'okay, I can... keep up!"

I bend down and cough.

My palm is filled with frozen specks.

"Ah crap," she says.

"Caught a bit back there."

"Did you cough blood?"

"Not yet."

"I dunno if we should stop, Red."

130

"We'll have to pace it now. See?" I plunge my torch deep and stir the dense layer at my feet. The white fog disperses, leaving a momentary vision of plowed road.

"Whoa! You knew it was here?"

Silence.

"Sik," I start, "isn't that why you kept egging them on?"

"No?"

"To overshoot this?"

"Uh."

"In the fog?"

"No," and shakes her head, "did it to get them lost."

"That would get us lost too, wouldn't it?" I ask.

Throws her hands high in surrender.

"Well, we were pretty fucked, ya know!" she says.

I root around a pack and hand her the container. "Chug as much as you need. We're not sleeping a while yet."

"Shit, you kidding me? This adrenaline'll have me wired weeks." Throws her head back. "Unnghh."

"Too strong?"

"Coffee tastes like dross."

"In line with what you were thinking, then."

"Pllrghhh," she gurgles between swallows. "Here."

I finish the dregs and just about reflux bile.

Would the Executioners be on our heels? I couldn't know. If they were maladapted to winter, knew of the deepness solely from books and gossip, we may not be so fully fucked as fate always hungered for.

There was one alternative, one final echo.

To Crossroads.

None of our belongings were in either pack, neither food nor equipment. Say nothing of treasure or money, I beg you. Spare pieces of wood, weather-proof quilt, other mundane sundry things, the rations of course, and little else. The girl was, appropriately enough considering, not trusted with anything valuable. So much the worse.

To Crossroads.

"They never checked my pockets," Sik snickered.

Of tools we had lost the pickax.

Newest and most expensive.

That figured too. I only wish Sik had stowed the map as well since that too appears a thing thought overly-sensitive for the young Executioner's hands.

We were heading west, or south-west, it was unclear which, but didn't matter; they went the same place. The road was uneven and each step felt like it had been dug specifically to fit my foot.

To Crossroads.

We'd have to get bearings and that was that. Still... heat and movement would fight off the fog. We were safe en route, but once there? Douse the torches, sure, but I saw what a mirror the fog made of the lantern-light. Could we get around the stationed Watch? And were there more Executioners?

There had to be. There had to be.

My eye stung.

Sik pats my shoulder. "No worries, Red. It'll work out." Grins wide. "And if it doesn't." Grins wider. "I'll fucking kill someone."

The first gravestones loom out of the fog, flanking our passage. We leave the path and work our way through, stomping over the dead, using trees and tombs alike as cover. Sik stubs the torch against a monument an angel crouches over and double-checks the lantern's hinges are tight.

Nods at me, ready.

"Assume they're on our ass," I warn.

"Always assume the worst," she agrees.

"If we can find a map, good. Food? Great. I'm not happy with our stash. But we need to find the road we came in on." I remember the areas the old man and I went through, but Crossroads is spread out and there's plenty we didn't touch. "In and out, no delay."

Fire fills Crossroads.

Braziers rumble and fume.

Blazing torches, as though stars detached from the sky, flow about in languid circuits. It's an impressive display, almost worthy of a festival minus the food-stalls and pounding music. We dart between headstones and trees, pausing when a torch veers too close, then *tamp*, *tamp*, *tamp* it goes, muffled on, and we hurry by.

Though most of the orchard had long since withered, been uprooted and torn out, what existed allowed ephemeral and needed seclusion.

"Wow," Sik said, pointed. "It's creepy, but it's kinda beautiful."

She meant the fog, kept out of the heart of this place by the braziers and passing bodies, how it reared up along the perimeter's edge like enthralled waves desperate to hurl themselves to ground.

I'm reminded of Darrow. Maybe it's the number of tall monuments, maybe simply the lost angels. Whatever it is, it has that same hollow depression. Why do they subject the angels to this? Ripping them out of the clouds, forcing them into stone with no hope to ever fly away from us fools stuck in the dirt. We're supposed to believe they pity us. I'd think they pity that we can't flee our fate.

I peek over a grave. *Shit*!

I hunch down, pulling Sik with me.

The dancing fire stretches the grave's shadow from one side to the other, ultimately fading to black.

I let out my breath and look again.

Finally I spot a familiar landmark. A stumpy tower, two-stories and about as wide as a respectable house. A wooden balcony encloses the upper level. Doesn't look like anyone's up there now. Light pours out of the bottom, burning away the shadows. It's difficult to approach, despite the lack of guards present, but it's so luring a force. The closer we tread, the less cold the air -- and then the balance flips. The temperature isn't comparatively warmer, it's *actually* warm.

Sik sinks against a granite slab. "Ahhhh..."

"Don't go doing that," I say, but sit down next to her anyways.

She stretches. "Nnnnggg! The grave is waaarm. Sooooo waaarm."

A hot breeze, as though bottled straight from summer, rushes past us and out into the graveyard. To see its fires casting such a glow out into the murk of a winter's night... this isn't the time for such bliss, but can it be so wrong to enjoy it?

"We have the shovel," she says.

"Don't even think about it."

"Only verbally sighing, is all."

"Come on, get up." I don't move.

"Yeah yeah." She peers around the stone. "Some kinda shop in there. Not the *welcome! welcome!* kind I mean. The factory kind. Dunno what that's called."

"Like a forge," I say.

"Yeah, I guess."

"Anything in there?"

She comes back. "Not gonna lie. There's equipment and shit in there." Makes a face. "Pretty sure there's a, ah, 'replacement' in there."

"That's a trap waiting to happen."

"Right. Will pretend I never saw."

In the dark, unfortunately, the map in my head of Crossroads is smudged. Nevertheless, there were a few larger structures. Sleeping quarters maybe. Find those and I'll have an accurate position.

"Tristrangulation," Sik agrees, sagely.

"Please stop learning words from Jackal."

"I can wriggle through one of those windows."

"No."

"Seriously! I don't think anyone's inside," she whines.

"Executioners up top I bet…"

"It's *right there*."

"Nothing good ever happens when we split up."

Silence.

I take that as the matter settled, but then she says, "Don't say that kinda thing to me."

"Eh?"

Her lips are drawn into a thin line. The light wavering on her cheeks is pink. She looks away, but doesn't say more.

I shrug and lead on.

Behind a covered hand, she suppresses a laugh and her voice says, "You can be sweet sometimes."

I have some smart response to that, but forget it straightaways.

#

There're Executioners about.

I was only half-serious when I quipped, but two come milling down the path towards the tower right when we reach a thorny copse some short distance away. No torches. They aren't searching for trouble.

Means our Executioners haven't followed us. As nerve-wracking as creeping through a lulled Crossroads is, how would it be when roused to the warning cry of:

'Gravediggers!'

Let's avoid that.

"Better not be bad news," the hollow voice up on the balcony groans.

"Listen to him. Such a negative drinker," says one, nudging her companion's side.

"Thought better of it. Here." A bottle goes careening over the railing and down at the pair.

"Oh! Oh!" The excited woman jumps up at the last second and embraces the bottle's neck. "I can really have this?"

"I want some too," the other says to her.

"Sure," says the now-visible man atop the tower. "Isn't the same with the stars gone all covered. Go on." Beckons with a hand. "What on it?"

"Finally found the blighter. Should we dig it?"

The balcony creaks in the silence.

He taps his chin, staring into the gray, roiling ceiling.

The fog is so low he could touch it.

At length he says, "Wouldn't bother without the cart. Pain to get to?"

The woman lets out a post-quaff breath of ecstasy. "Aha haaa! Nope nope, real simple. He was merely hiding, he was."

"Mark it good."

"Already did," the other says.

The balcony creaks again.

"Well, you know what to do then. Go pass word to the Watch to keep well clear of that area a few days and we'll sort it all out when everyone else comes through."

"And then we party!" the woman giggles.

The man leans at the railing a moment, watching the two amble off, before chuckling to himself and retiring to a reclined seat.

Sik is all unblinking when the tension in the air exhales. "Honest, Red, I didn't think anyone was in there."

"That's why we can't screw around them. As silent as thieves. Hell, they're Quinn's rivals."

"But!" Sik announces. "Now we know there's one there."

"I'm not liking where you're starting this."

"Not starting anything. S'just... one in there, two are securing a grave. This isn't like this morning. *They don't know we're here*."

"You said it," I say. "*This morning*. This has been the worst day of our lives, wedged between that *thing* in the mausoleum and being captured and nearly on our way home *the wrong way* I'm about ready to dig *my own grave* and at least get some rest!"

Has she still not blinked? "I know." Raises a finger. "But don't forget." More shock fatigue insanity. "You're a digger! Have some pride! Some confidence in our abilities!"

I am done thinking, Sik.

Cede this without concession, Red.

I spread my hands. "What do you propose?"

Shrugs. "Do you want to grab that pickax?" she asks. "Or do you want to follow them and learn about the cursed they found?"

"You said you never wanted to see one."

Unflinching. Why isn't she blinking? "Mostly don't care for some reason." At last bowing to some emotion, lowers her gaze. "I think that... that... *that*..." She swallows. "Inured me against fear." Raises her head, looks me square. "Or we can leave. Do you know where we are yet?"

"If that building over there is the one I remember," I point, "then yeah."

"You've never believed in cursed," she says. "This may be the one moment you can face the fact."

The truth matters little to me. Whether the dead really aren't resting and need to be interred doesn't change what I do. I'll still crack open graves. I'll still dig. If it is true, however, we could get well-deserved revenge by waking that cursed up and setting it off to mess up the Executioner's careful planning. The reverberation that shot up my arms when I broke the shovel against that small skull shook my heart, and I loved that terrible harmony, and wanted to hear it again, and other variations.

"And if you're correct and it's all bullshit," she edges in, "that body's got riches with it. Snag that before they appropriate it."

We're broke now. I'm really, really tempted at the suggestion and it'd be a lie to deny I hadn't been thinking that. Still, it's dodgy, even assuming Regin and all don't come limping in until after sunup. The better risk would be that tower and fill our bags with whatever is there. That's the practical choice, practically risk-free compared to recent events. Simple steal.

"Execrations aren't coming for days, ya heard? So," she licks her lips, "it's basically unguarded. Eheh, fuck, we could dispatch that cunt while we're at it."

I jolt out of decision.

"What are you saying?" I ask. "Start up with murder, we're in the shit deeper than digging."

No remorse. "That one," she sneers, "that Regin. You missed what she did before. Kicked me in the stomach."

Gritting my teeth. "No, I saw that."

"Yeah, well, you probably didn't see from your angle, but it was a low kick. Like, kicked my lower stomach low." Bites her tongue. "You have no clue how much that kills and the bitch did it on purpose."

"Even so, that's not Regin up there. We don't have a vendetta against him."

"Same difference. Death to all Execrations." And spits with finality. "So, what did you decide?"

"We're leaving."

"What!" she exclaims, stunned, almost too loud. Hardly lowers volume. "That's your decision, after all that!? We're dusting off our asses and walking?"

"Not risking it."

Shakes her head. "No. No way. I *need* this. I can't leave without doing something to someone. You *owe* me."

And for a moment the memory of last time comes scowling at me from the dark corner I had forced it, what she doesn't remember. That empty gaze then contrasted with this piercing frenzy now, carnivorous and desperate.

"... for what?"

A trickle of drool at the edge of her emotionless grin rolls into a drop of sweat. She brushes it away before it careens down her top.

"I… I don't know why I said that," she admits. "But it feels wrong. I'm not ready to give up. I'm not giving up again. I'm…" Clenching fists. "Not. I'm…" Slaps my hand. "Do-don't touch me!" I force my palm against her forehead again, but she refuses and squirms away. "I-I'm not fevered! I'm… pissed, is all. So pissed at everything… ca-can't think straight. I'm not fevered."

"I feel helpless too, Sik."

"That," she says, "isn't what I feel at all."

I reach out. "Sik."

"That," she says. "That."

"Let's go."

When she does reach out, her arm is trembling and each finger grips painfully. "That's not it at all," she says.

We go.

#

Winter screams.

Comfort is bereft of us.

Roads, maintained or long-left abandoned, are denied. We trudge into the gale winds out over the moors, towards the coming and eventually passing Executioners. We press our bodies together wherever there is a thicket or grouping of trees, faces raw red and shiny, and suffer no relief, the lone difference now the branches that wail unbrokenly.

When the land rises up and gives a glimpse of our original path along the blurry horizon, we can see the carts rolling.

We failed.

I almost feel depression.

But not quite.

Sik is still ill. Keeping warm by moving, but she tires easily; I stoke the fires hot at night, but she slumbers restlessly. Hands uselessly numb, I can't tell if the fever has relapsed or not. Tiptoeing along a knife's edge. How much to push her? How much to pull back? The cold unslackened, the sun's mocking absence of warmth, and no shelter.

We spy the odd shrine, yet she refuses.
Why? I ask. Why?
Executioners. Executioners. Executioners.
But you didn't before. You didn't care before.
I was tired.
Too tired.
Duh.

#

She passes out. Exhaustion.
I do something stupid.
There's another shrine, beckoning. Come to me. I will embrace you. Come to me. Fear not the black and crimson.
No one inside. I want to convince her it's fine. Instead, I rob the cupboard of every rice cake. It's not enough. It won't be enough. I'll put one back. One. One. One.
One could make all the difference.
Sorry, Eddy. Sorry.
I'll apologize to your corpse.
I'll bury your corpse.
You're too good for their dirty hands.
Don't come back.
Old City isn't safe anymore.
Don't follow us.
Life is for the living.
Old Kingdom is dying.
Don't follow us home.
The world is a tomb.
I take the last rice cake.
I'm sorry.

#

Clouds are glowering.
Hateful. Hateful. Hear them moan:
Snows are coming. Hide your head.
Run away run away,
Deepness and dead.

#

I skip meals.
It doesn't help.
The jerky is almost gone.
No more meat. No protein means:
Headaches perch atop her skull.
She slogs, eyes unfocused, black rings circling circling:
She blinks her eyes.
I wonder what—
What?
Huh?
You wonder what?
Oh. Dunno. Forgot.
She holds her head. And walks.

#

Half of the sky is baleful gray. The other -- retreating -- is a clear, harsh, harsh blue. With morning-light, we have an immediate goal: the cover of a distant grove, withered limbs aimlessly reaching in all directions. The winds have died down to a single, drawn-out sigh and Sik has a decent amount of energy for once.

"Fuck winter!" she says.

"Did you sleep?"

"No," she says, raising her arms. "Fuck winter!"

I hand over a biscuit and take one for myself. "Are you getting worse?"

"Don't think I'm sick, actually," she says, but definitely doesn't look it. "Those Execration drugs feel like they're still in my system. Working. Pfff, poisoning me more like. One good sleep and I'll be back to normal, you'll see."

One hour later, she is barely standing. Sitting, panting from meagre exertion. And again that biting air drives us back, the uncaring hand of fate, from home. It meets with the clouds and rushes them onwards, the sky now crammed and the expectant pause is mocking.

Then it snows.

A flurry, swirling, dancing.

Sik tries to hide a cough.

We take too many breaks. We brush each other off, but the snow insists and when we trek on we have to cover our eyes. At noon, the clouds look bubbly and strange and my empty gut urges me to hurry.

But we can't.

By afternoon, a sickly green cast develops on the underbelly of the clouds. Without warning, Sik takes off on a jog and I don't stop her. There are no good options anymore.

I wish we could take it easy.

But that's the hope which prompted this fool undertaking to begin with.

#

Finally some safety.

The grove is dense enough to protect from the brunt of the snowstorm and abate the winds. I light an earlier campfire, then go about gathering up wood. Sik is asleep the instant she lies down and I'm most grateful for that.

If the fever relapses, we're done.

#

"Do you know where we are?" I ask when she wakes in the evening.

"Not particularly, no."

"How soon can we press on?"

"Uhhh," she says. "There any food around?"

"Some berries," I say. "Edible," I add.

Smirks. "'Edible' he says." And then: "Don't we have to? We're gonna get snowed in."

"We've been at this without break since Crossroads. I'm worried about you."

"I know," she says, "and you look terrible." Frowns. "Are you sleeping when I am?"

I don't say anything.

142

"Damn it, Red. Stop shouldering everything. We're fucked, I know we are, but if you don't start taking care too…"

"Don't say that."

"What if they come back?" she asks.

"I know."

"You don't, though, you don't. What are we gonna do if we run into them? I'm a popsicle. I won't be able to help this time. And with you…"

"We'll manage."

"Barely," she says. "Out in the wilderness. Execrations on the roads. No local towns. Mostly lost 'cept to know we need to go west."

"It'll be…" Something.

But she's already fallen back asleep before I think of an appropriate word.

#

When I awaken, it's morning. A dusting of snow covers us and the campfire is basically ashes. I relight it while Sik sleeps and finish my gathering. With the remaining rations dumped in the other pack, we'll be able to take enough wood. I spend the rest of my time picking as many tart purple berries as I can find.

"Time to shog," she announces from behind me.

"We should rest another day or—"

"No," she says. Points at the clouds, still flurrying, but not abnormally-colored. "We got lucky. We need to hit the woods soon or the hail really will come this time. The more we wait, the sooner it'll come. There's no time." And scrutinizing my reluctance, adding: "I'll live."

"One favor." I ask.

"Yeah."

"Don't hide how you're doing. Tell me."

"Constant headache," she reports.

"And only that?"

"For now. And, ah," she mutters, "for what it's worth I think I feel the drugs are…" Grimaces. "Effective."

"That's good, right?"

"Ma-marginally," she admits.

#

Two weeks of grueling travel. Uninterrupted snow of intermittent intensity. Occasional sheltering tree. Firewood runs short. Packing snow, building huts. Raging snowstorms in the night. Wake to deep drifts. Hailstorms in the afternoon. Retire with bruises and bleeding cuts. Firewood runs out. Wake. Sleep. Wake. Can't sleep. Tripping on blanketed undergrowth. Swearing. Ripping up roots. Feasting on the rhizomes. Supplies dwindle. Rations exhaust. Minds exhaust. Eye throbbing. She patches it, makeshift, bandages. Subsides. Tripping. Keep moving anyway. Hail grows in mass. Struck in head. Knocked cold, she later said. It kept falling. Why are we not dead? Her smile is pained. Somehow, she says. We hide. We're tired. We're hungry. We're cold. We're dying we want to say. To make it real, unavoidable, to feel in control of it, invulnerable. And still the headwind, no trees to give it voice, and so it whistles in the ear, no further, no further. How farther on 'till home? The plagued world no longer exists outside the warm solace of home. Does home no longer exist outside the despaired frozen abyss that strangles the horizon? Give up. Walk. Fall down. Walk. Curl up and die. Walk. Sleep forever. Walk. Dissolve to dust. Walk. And be blown away. Stop.

#

"Stop."

One of us said it. I wonder who.

I look up, shaky. I squint, one-eyed. Ah, so that's what that was. It was that all along. It's so strange to behold up close. It's so funny to see this near. The vastness of the evergreen woods in which Ensbryng resides, all rime and ruin, pine scent so cloying after the absence of... I wonder why I'm weeping. Or maybe that was Sik.

#

Our plodding gait had saved us, it seemed. The edges of the woods were so shattered from the storm's devastation, we doubted anything had survived. Yet inside, the great swath of trees stood pridefully against the deepness and shrugged off frightening dents that would have killed the most headstrong person. It was soundless, a scarce wonder considering what wasn't hibernating would have been scared shitless at the pandemonium. Such motionless atmosphere would have brought disquiet, but after the hellish rapidity with which everything followed upon and followed upon from that one day, I felt serene tranquility.

It renewed our fleeting energy to be enclosed by a familiar world. There were harmless plants to munch on that, while they provided no sustenance, calmed the shrieking famine in our guts.

I couldn't be certain where we were.

South of the road I imagined, unless we had veered during the whiteout, but how far south would be impossible to know for now. No matter how distant home lay or how far off course we were...

"Guess we'll survive a bit longer," Sik said.

"Guess so," I said.

#

"I'm telling ya," Sik is saying, while she struggles over a rooty incline. "Angels have to be the laziest, *laziest* people. More than me after eating a whole pie by myself. *Lay-zee.* Flying everywhere, no need to walk or, uhh, climb. Thanks." I heave her up. She doesn't feel very heavy. "And... And! No weather!"

"You can't know that."

"They couldn't possibly have any snow. Fly above it, no problem."

145

"See," I say, "I disagree. You've seen those wispy clouds, you love them."

"Course I do."

"Yes, so, those kinds seem pretty high up. What we have snowing right now is really low. I figure clouds of various height create different weather."

"Ohhh."

"When they migrate, they have to deal with what they've chosen."

"I get it," she says. "What you mean is: we can't see the clouds above *them* because of the clouds above *us*."

I shrug. "It's a theory. More importantly is that clouds continually move. They can't do anything *but* migrate and I have to assume all that flying is tiring."

"No, no," she corrects. "That's the lazy part. They just sit on their resident cloud and it flies for them."

"I don't know."

"It's true. I was there once."

"Really."

"It's true, there was this *biiiig* party and their cooking was *amazing* and everyone was drinking and getting drunk and spilling drinks and then pissing all over just pissing and one girl called out 'bet those earthbound walkers think this is rain!' and everyone was just laughing and laughing. Then I woke up."

"I didn't believe you for a single second. I need you to know that."

"Was kinda disorienting at first," she says, "because whenever I dream of eating I drool all over my pillow every time. Without fail. And I'm, like, wait-did-an-angel-pee-on-my— and jumped outta bed." Cocking her head, finger to lips. "Hey, why is it that I drool when I eat in my dreams, but I don't wet the bed when I pee in my dreams?"

"Life is full of such mysteries."

"What do you dream when you dream?" she asks.

"Weird stuff," I say.

"And when you dream lucid, what is it like?"

"This."

#

"That reminds me," she mutters.

"Where are you going?"

"I'll be back in a minute," and rustles off through the bushes.

So she says, but she isn't.

Did she pass out?

Last time was the first, but with unending physical exertion piling up over malnutrition I could see it happening again.

After a short walk, I find her squatting down with an ugly purple welt on an otherwise white ass.

"Hurry up," I say.

"AH!" Chapped face flushes a darker shade. "I said to wait! Wanted privacy for a change!" To herself, sarcastic. "Always askin' way too much. Geez!"

"You were taking forever."

"I was checking my body over and stuff! Don't you men do that?" Dithers. Rocking back and forth. "Damn it, now it won't come. You're an asshole."

A gentleman would bow out here. Apologize, scurry away, and pretend this hadn't occurred. Wait until his companion started any conversation again, hoped she would, and time would flatten the awkward feeling almost, but never quite, to forgetfulness.

Unfortunately, I'm far too comfortable around her.

My piss streams against the pile of snow, steaming acrid odor, and I let out a boisterous, over-exaggerated:

"*Aaaahhhhhhhhhhhhhhhhhhhhh.*"

She snorts. Tries to ignore it. Quivers. Throws her head back, laughing deeply, pausing at the sound of another trickle, and settles in. She shakes her head. "Idiot," she says, though still laughing.

147

#

Our luck edges towards passable.
The rains of fall already show their bounty.
We forage.
Some meals our stomachs nearly feel half-full.
We gorge.
Days pass. We relax.

Not exactly, as the booming crunch of hail ensures regularly. However, within the heart of the woods, the hoary pines provide complete security and the chunks of ice that clatter down on us are shattered and slowed by their tumble through innumerable branches. I mention they make a good appetite suppression. Sik sucks them like candy.

#

"Mushrooms!" she announces. "Big ones!"

In this secluded area, sunlight barely intrudes beyond the network of ice-glazed limbs overhead and a sizeable colony has taken root: happy caps horning in on whatever unclaimed space has been found wherever it can been found. I take the lantern, mindful of the depleted oil, and angle the light.

"As expected," I say.

Deflated. "Yum. Devilspot cluster," she says. "I'll have the one in the middle, please."

"It's more than that."

Around the colony those poisonous, red-spotted caps rise without any hint of shyness, innocently proclaiming their right to be consumed along with any other. Some hungry animal comes by, or some person, and begins to dine: first the outer perimeter, then the inner, then another, and sooner than later the unknowing diner realizes the mushooms closer to the center are the tastiest, lured closer and closer and finally to the devilspot itself. Is it the most delicious thing in the world? It may well be, but no story will tell you so as no one has ever survived one, being too busy spewing diarrhea out both ends and expiring at an excruciatingly torturous pace.

And why wouldn't it be so?

That's the habitat these mushrooms thrive in best.

As far as I know the abetting mushrooms that sprout up around the devilspot are the only food, the sale and gathering of, which is prohibited by law. I'm not sure what the punishment is, but if it's draconian I can guess.

"Doesn't look as though we can take many," Sik says, arms crossed and counting with a finger. "I think we shouldn't get closer than... two rings. No, three. Three I think. It may have been a late sporing."

The amount we gather bulges in the pack. Gravediggers with a parcel of contraband. The evidence will have to be consumed before we reach home.

Sik looks up, munching away.

"Ah," she says. "My face feels numb."

"That's probably just the cold."

She frowns.

I eat one.

"Well?" she asks.

I don't have an immediate answer.

"Probably."

#

Everything feels so one-step-away on a map. Not that I recall in much detail, but this area always felt compact and manageable -- I understand now because, back then, I could see the boundaries.

"'Along the rim traipsed I, so gradual a degree that, never knowing of the pit I circled, lost sight of the sun,'" quotes Sik.

And so it was, pronouncement of doom or not, and weeks we spent bewildered by the wilderness's labyrinth. Two towns were nestled in here somewhere, one south and one closer to Ensbryng, but we must have bypassed the first entirely, or maybe it was north? We kept the thinning western border of the woods in sight, as weather allowed;

nevertheless that hardly provided much context to our location and instead seeded brooding.

"I guess hitting that final grave in Ensbryng didn't matter after all," I said later.

"Huh? Oh. Ah," she said. "Too frozen to worry about anymore. Ground, I mean. Though, me too."

"Should we have a glance?" I asked later.

"Huh? Oh. Ah," she said. "Execrations are fully in control there. Waste of time."

In my unsettled thoughts, I agreed. This reminded me too closely of *that* dig. Hardly worth the effort, but there was profit. Technically, there was a profit. And then the random fortune of that miserable midnight burial. Where was the random fortune now? The profit? I hated leaving it like this, but she was right and every part of me agreed, but my thoughts remained unsettled. The accounting was impending and every action we took or failed to take, or took and failed at, each tiny flaw I was too exhausted to remember or Sik too oblivious to be aware of, would swell up and engulf us. We dove too deep. Fortune fell. There were hard decisions to make. Yet the cost of them…

Sik made a joke. I forgot to listen.

#

Do you see the sun rises no more or moon, non-light of blunted color from the clouds and a demarcated horizon? He turns the coin. Flat relentless stretch of nothingness surrounded by the sphere above waved in the breeze light breeze dead but going mild and milder. A little smaller every day. A little worse off.

Coal smudge rot and cold embers, never shining not the point. To hide. She gazes, the panic! Embodied in amalgam of corpses vomit the wrong passage and she flees, stabbed him in the kidney chuckling of pebbles tapping away the time. Death came swallowingly.

"Are you like me?"

It was a pleading. Who knew him? He didn't. Not anymore, not after the and she was running always from one comfort to the next and all in her head and none of them healthy or lasting or filling and none of them involving him.

It was a lie, he knew, but he supped of it nonetheless.

River ran on, dimness of perpendicularity crawling on walls spitting wax thick they never used them much, not now, gross and vulgar and not said though understood.

Another lie. It was convenient. She lived in her head.

"Get out of there!"

Didn't ask all afire with the carts up and down east and west going to Dun going to Dun didn't make sense don't explain it didn't ask, coughing leaves autumnal dry breath a makeshift mat leading away to that place unnamed the same season there -- perpetual -- falling falling falling.

Fall, in the sanitarium. But it was longer.

It was longer.

It hasn't ended.

#

Graveduggery

Lula Lucent

Graveduggery

Night fractured

                                                    fractures
                                                        into
                                            ten-thousand
                                              scintillating

        knives were s c i n t i l l a t i n g

                                            a n d f e l l

a n d   f e l l

            a n d   f e l l

#

"Sky cleared up a bit," she says, pushing on my shoulder until I wake.

My stomach squeezes tight. Ugly noise. "Food."

"Threw it away."

"You mean," I rise, "you finished it off."

"Nope. Threw mine out too."

"Why."

"Makes tasty breakfasts better." And getting me to my feet, takes my hand, leads me into a tree. *Kkhnn*! The impact wakes me up. "Sorry!" she says. "Pfff!" she laughs. "No, really. Didn't mean to do that. Are you okay?"

"Not really."

Takes me by the hand again before I can shove it into a pocket and hurries us out of the tree line.

The hell is she doing?

"Sik, would you stop—!"

"Look, Red!"

#

The return.
So many emotions. All of them conflicting.
What to say?
We are home.

#

Streets empty, save for snow.

I haven't been expecting a welcome, but the transient lull in the weather reinforces the disjointed discrepancy between my expectations of the everyday bustle and this strained stillness now.

Lest my overactive mind make much of this, I spot footprints all over the snow. Perhaps it was merely time pausing some scant seconds, drawn out by my relieved exhale to just feel these city streets underfoot once again, but after that moment thawed and I blinked the denizens of Old City, though sparse, began to appear. What few people we met along the way were tense, rushing by with flat expressions.

Something of that repetition becomes infectious as we turn down streets, head towards Darvin's, find it locked tight, and quicken our pace and make for our friends.

Sik vaults up the stairs of their porch, nearly tripping on the final step and barreling over the railing.

She pounds on the door.

"Jackal!" she shouts. "Quinn!"

The windows are dark. Late morning, true, though while Jackal might be snoring 'till noon, at least Quinn would be awake, reading a book or cleaning up around the house.

"It's me," Sik calls. "It's us."

I try to peep inside. Curtains drawn, some windows boarded up. No movement in spite of the incessant knocking at the front door.

"Are you there?" Sik asks.

I come back around from the side.

"I don't think they're in, Sik."

"But wh—" and she stops herself from saying it, wringing hands plaintively. "Red," she quavers. "Tell me they're a-a-al—" Can't finish.

"Jackal and Quinn are fine. They are both okay."

"I don't know..."

"We only now arrived. You threw away our breakfast. Our morning started out differently today, looks like theirs did too." My grin is lopsided, but not faked. "Seriously. Do you really think anything could have dropped on those two other than an empty bottle?"

"A barrel?"

"That was inferred."

Sik laughs gently. "No, I... honest, I don't believe it did. But I need to see them, I really, really do. You understand, right?"

Shrugging. "They're good friends. Four months is a long time. And as such, they won't want to give us a homecoming smelling as we do."

She laughs again, this time genuinely. "Appealing to feminine hygiene. That's low, Red, even for you." Gives the door a final pound. "Right! You two be awake when we get back. I'm getting pissed tonight!"

#

Up our stairs she darts, single-mindedly excited.

Our little gray house.

Looks like a tombstone from a distance, like a monument up close. How could we resist? I slap the waterproofed wood on the climb up. Good condition.

Better check the roof later.

"How you holding up?" I ask.

It regards my arrival with silent acknowledgement.

And past the threshold: the subtle scent of familiarity underneath a layer of mustiness; the window that frames the now-inactive docks; the steel-blue waters beyond, bisected by morning mists; and the creak of floorboards at every step.

And it comes washing over, that wearied relief: we have safely come back to where we belong.

"Wait a little longer," Sik is saying into the bedroom. "I'm too dirty!" And to me: "Me first!" Disrobing en route to the bathroom at once.

I'm about to chide her, but what of it? The floor needs to be cleaned anyway. I pick the clothing up, starting with the hat she never puts on the peg by the door. When I stoop for the discarded panties, she closes the shower curtains.

Bruises are all over her, from shoulders to hips.

"Hell happened to your back?" I ask.

"Huh?" Pokes her head out. "Ohhh. You were physically abusing me in your sleep again."

"That's not funny."

I dump her clothing into the washbasin.

"Fff, yeah it is." Shrugs with her eyes. "Slept on rocks the other night." Disappears. The pipes moan. "Hurts like a bitch."

Then she squeals as the cold droplets assault her.

The pipes shut off. She reappears.

"Ho-o-oly shit! Red, I forgot. Please, *please* go light the water heater."

On my way to the trapdoor, I glance longingly at my chair. So close, it's so close. There's always one more thing to do, always one, one and then another. I refill the lantern to the limit, strike a flame, and descend.

My sock squishes against something spongy. *Unghh.* Am I going to want light to see this? I creep down the staircase, nothing out of the ordinary so far, and...

I burst out laughing. No other response. Laughing, roaring with laughter, every part of me. The sound I make is absorbed, there's no hint of an echo, which makes me double-over further. Sik, baffled as she is, wants to know what's wrong with me. Nothing, nothing, I say, but nothing comes out of my lungs except uproarious hilarity.

"We won't be starving!" I manage in staccato.

"What does that even mean?" she calls down to me.

But I lose it again.

Somewhere in this basement is a mushroom bed, but so overgrown as it has become I cannot say where. The mushrooms on the floor stare up at me, the mushrooms on the walls watch me, and overhead the mushrooms hang down and their inverted caps seem about ready to doff and welcome me, quiet jovially, to their extended family's lair.

#

"My hair's getting long," she says, pinching it, making faces at the mirror. "Longish."

"Need to cut mine too," I say.

Although I don't grow much of a beard and not very fast, what is there is scratchy and annoying. Can't stand the look either.

"Hmm, I wonder," she fusses. "Hmm, yeah, you're frightening like that."

I make what I hope is a frightening face.

"Ahh!" Mock screaming. "Cut it out!"

"You done yet?" I ask.

"Think it looks good like this?" she interrupts.

Darker brown from dampness. Down to her shoulders. A few strands trailing over her eyes. It's different, but it's her.

"Sure," I nod. "It's a good look."

Turning back to the mirror's appraisal. "I see."

#

Heat.

Enveloping, physical heat.

Do campfires make you so forgetful too?

Remember it at the first drop, hissing with a pitch higher than the most fervent rainstorm, there it is: that perfect instant when the body unwinds, snap of the finger, it's bliss, it's persistent, it's the world has stopped and I don't give the slightest damn.

Amplify that for a gravedigger. Washing off the dirt, the smell of rot, the stink of self, crawling out of the grave and clawing at a bar of soap to be born again. From death to life back and forth back and again over and over, a pendulum of opposites of equal pleasure, and I instinctually feel the pull to set back out, shovel over shoulder, without pause.

Sweet obsession.

By the time we've finished cleaning ourselves, it's well after noon. I throw the towel over the rack, slap my face with both hands. Looking back to normal.

I lean against the doorframe.

"Ready?"

Sik ignores me, rocking at the edge of the bed.

"Are you crying?"

"Oh, oh, sorry." Wiping the tears, smiling. "I was talking to Rin."

"Ah," I say. "How is she?"

"Good, good," she says, smiling. "She still smells a little like me. I was worried."

Sik is lovingly squeezing the one-winged angel doll she once told me she 'saved.' Rin's black hair has been done up in twintails. She wears a little white dress. Admittedly, I'm off-put by the face. No nose, no mouth. Black horizontal stitching for eyes and two solitary lines for eyebrows. I... simply can't tell what emotion she's supposed to be exhibiting. Sik says it's eyes shut. She's just sleepy. All the time. "Like me," Sik has said.

I can't help thinking it's a scowl and that Rin is as possessive as Sik.

"Let's go check Darvin's again. Find out what's going on in the city," I say.

"Okay."

Giving Rin one final hug, she hops off the bed and laces up her boots.

#

161

Oddly, Darvin's doors are thrown wide though it's barely afternoon. I wonder if he's rolling new casks in and didn't get around to shutting back up, but no, patrons are already scattered about the tables with drinks aplenty and plates clinking. Our entrance goes unnoticed.

We resolved to double-back on Jackal and Quinn's place after we ate. Sik picked up their key before we left home in case they still weren't in. At least then we could search the place for signs to ease our worries.

Turns out that was unnecessary.

We enter the sightline of one glum face, pivoted against a fist, crimson twintails spread atop the table like the roots of a weed.

"Ah!" Jackal says.

"Jackal!" Sik exclaims.

"Heya, Jackal," I say.

"Ya lesser bastards," she blubbers, weeping with an immediacy that stops Sik mid-chest-dive. "Damn by damn, what is wrong with ya? Leavin' like that, up and off like a thief. I mean, I can appreciate som' like that, but that's a, that's a re-e-eal-ly f-f-foul—" And bawls, unrestrained enough to finally rouse the attention of everyone else.

"Please don't cry," Sik says, tearing up too.

"We're alive," I say and take a seat next to her. "Mostly."

Cheeks reddening, a new emotion cutting through the tears. "I was worried sick ya know!" Sniffs back wet snot in her fury. "And I'm not sayin' that like that phrase. I threw up a couple times!" Exasperatedly wiping away tears, as if she's had enough of sorrow, Jackal dives into pent-up frustrations she can at last indulge in. But with the unstopped waterworks, the effect is comical at best.

Fortunately, I avoid smiling.

"Thought the Executioners rounded ya up or the guards or, or, or *someone*!" she says. "I even went to Bors, thinkin' he mighta had his pinchers in this."

"What'd he have to say?" I ask.

"Nothin'," she sniffs, mumbling, losing track of her anger. "Can never get straight answers talkin' to him, so I…" Sniffs. "I snuck in and went through his ledgers. Wait, that's not the point!" Remembering why she was angry again. "We didn't know where ya two went off to! And winter was comin' quick and, and, and well Quinn said mighta had to do with what the message-runners were all talkin' 'bout, but none of that was good so I didn't know what to think. I was scared. And upset." Takes a meaningful look at us both and shakes her head, lets it hang down to her chest. "We were really, really worried 'bout ya guys."

Sik rubs her on the back.

"I'm real sorry, Jackal. I should've written you a note," she says. "But I told Darv to tell you!"

"You're a lesser bastard too then!" Jackal shouts at Darvin as he places a mug of stout in front of me. "Ya said nothin'!"

His beard stretches wide.

"Oh didn't I?" And setting down a glass of milk before Sik, says conspiratorially, "Now we are even, my girl."

"But I apologized!" she protests.

"Is that what that was?" Chiding click of the tongue. "You lit off on adventure and I had to clean that up."

"I did too apologize," she grouses.

"And now we're even."

Sik protectively embraces Jackal.

"Hurt me next time, not her!" she demands.

"Confessing to the next time already," Darvin laughs. "Good to see you lot haven't changed."

We shake hands.

"Red."

"Darvin."

"Be out with grub in a moment," he says.

"Thanks for the food." I jerk my head. "Before."

He places a finger to his lips, but nods. "Worked out well, everything?"

"Not really," I mutter. "But it did save our asses once, so we're in your debt."

His smile stretches wider. "Course you aren't. That was the favor, wasn't it? And, well, should be said, little miss included." He looks between us. Sik watches him hesitantly, still guarding Jackal, but extends her attention. "Welcome back."

"Yeah," Jackal repeats. "Welcome back, ya two." Kisses Sik on the cheek and hits my shoulder affectionately. "Oi, what a day," she sighs. "Lessons for everyone. Ya to be more transparent and me to not trust that fell wanker when my tab's runnin'."

"I'm glad you're okay," Sik says, "and Quinn? She's okay?"

Jackal blinks. "Um, she's okay, yeah, no, she's good. Why ya askin' all anxious like that?"

"We heard about what happened," I say, "and couldn't be certain if either of you girls were hurt."

"Or killed," Sik says solemnly.

"Ha! Us? It's the tricky poxxer what can get a drop on us. Like to see anyone that skilled, could make money off on that angle. Hmm..." Rubs her chin. "Errr, wait, what happened?"

"Cursed broke out or something like that," Sik explains. "People were murdered by 'em."

"What load of crap is that?" Jackal quirks up her nose. "Cursed? I haven't heard of that. Not here, leastwise. Maybe out in the wilds, out there, but not here, definitely not in the city, that'd be a panic and no way I wouldn't have heard that. Sure ya got that right?"

"Executioners told us that," I explain. "Cursed in the city had killed people."

Silence.

Unblinking eyes. "Oi," she utters. "Oi oi oi, ya had a run-in with…" Dithers. "*Them*?"

"It wasn't good." I catch myself unconsciously reaching to scratch my eye.

"Oi, that's screwed up," she says. "I know I thought likewise, but to hear ya say it. Just… whoa." Shakes herself, but the tension in the air hangs on. "In… in any event, Red, I, uh, think they were messin' with ya. Nothin' like that has happened. Not at all."

Sik's fingernails are digging into years-old scratches atop the table. "Those fucking Execrations. I can't believe they made that shit up." She stares shame at me. "And I believed her. She terrified me and I fucking believed it."

Gritting my teeth. "It's like I say, every time. Untrustworthy opportunists. There's no curse. There's no reburial of the dead." If there was any wavering in my belief at the outset of our journey, it had hardened to the bone, cold and inviolable, with Jackal's correction. Disgusting. The Executioners had the city worked up into frenzy, gilded our apprehensive lives with a new and needless nightmare. Perhaps we diggers should be digging for evidence to prove that fact to the masses, instead of selfishly pursuing gains. Sik took it personally. Whether the revelation shook her theories isn't showing, but I'll bring that idea up later.

"Oi, calm down, guys. Let's eat and forget 'bout heavy matters, yeah?"

"That's right," I say, pleased for the change of topic. "Place is busy for the time. Did Darvin change hours?"

"Ah, that's right you wouldn't have known," Darvin says, overhearing. He fills the table such that the wood beneath is no longer visible. Two savory cabbage pies, a hearty heaping of smoked bacon, fried sweet potatoes, and a moon-melon with cleaver prominently jutting out of a fragrant wound.

"Known what?" I ask.

"Curfew's on," he says, leaving Jackal to pick up there.

She nods, munching on a strip of bacon. "Yep, curfew. Fog's been gettin' into the city all over, down Old Kingdom way too. Now, ya wanna talk 'bout deaths, been a good dozen alone. I figured," she chews, swallows, licks her lips, "I figured we might hit some places what with people nowhere on the streets, moreover guards wouldn't be out neither, but that fog seeps into any mask in short order. Too risky. Eventually, we had to hole up and board up the windows that weren't so tight." Gives a sleepy smile. "But it's fine! The winter's so frigid this year, I want to curl up with a blanket in front of the fireplace until it's aaaall over.

"But everyone's so edgy," she sighs. "Ya noticed it, I bet: the strained air. The city's frazzled. It isn't the weather alone, ya know: it was a miserable harvest. Technocracy, for their part, have been working up winter-bearing crops, though nothin' yet circulated to us *commoners*," she chuckles. "You'd havta ask Quinn. I don't know if they worked or no." Squints at a thought. "Some have been accusin' each other of being cursed." Shakes a finger at me. "So that Executioner may have been half-truthin' with that, though it's still crap."

"Well, I bet the city feels secure under their administering watch," I snark.

"Sounds like we're not the only ones in the biscuit crunch," Sik says.

"Basically." Jackal stretches. "Old City is stressed and needs to vent, and drinkin' and amusements only take that so far so long."

"Sounds kinda boring when you put it like that," Sik says.

Jackal shrugs.

"Sure, if ya like. Normal is normal, mostly," she replies. Then, starting to get worked up: "But the fes—" And claps a hand over the word.

"Ah." Sik gapes at Jackal.

"Ah." Jackal gapes back.

The subtext is palpable, even to me.

"Festival," Sik blurts out.

Jackal shakes hands, arms, head back and forth.

"No, it—" she tries to say.

"You were gonna say *festival*."

"No, I, uh, no it, I, was, ehh."

Sullen. "We missed Pumpkin Fest." So sullen. "I even forgot about it." Sik stares grief at me.

"It wasn't... it wasn't that great, and..." Jackal tries lying.

"My favorite time of the year too..."

"We... we'll all go next year. This, this year I mean!" Jackal says. "Okay?"

"Okay," Sik repeats, not feeling it at all. "Was there a new Pumpkin Cat King?"

"Ah, no..."

"Aww."

"... there were two," Jackal stupidly finishes. Sik scowls at her, unable to find any words to express her rage. "I only read *one*. I promise I left the other for us to read together. I'm sorry. I had to read one, I told ya, I was upset and all, and readin' one helped. So... so ya aren't allowed to be mad at Big Sis anymore, okay?"

"What *else* did we miss?" Sik manages to get out.

Jackal grimaces. "Ya aren't gonna let this go, huh?"

"She enjoys brooding," I offer. "You can't really deny her that."

Jackal takes Sik by the hands. Sik is receptive, but suspicious. "Ya know Big Sis loves ya, right? Would never lie to—"

"You just tried to."

"It, uh, um," Jackal blithers. "Rottin'..." she begins to swear. "*Fine*. There was fireworks."

"What's a fireworks?"

"Some invention of the Technocrats. Accidental offshoot of their... tek-no-krass-olo-jee tree? Um. Yeah. That's what they called it." Now explaining animatedly with hands. "This post gets lit ablaze and fizzles and *sshhhriiiii!* it zooms into the sky so quick-like ya can't even watch, kinda anticlimactic I thought at first, and then *POM!* a colorful flower that's bigger than, uh, bigger than, um, your house? Yeah, prob'ly, and it's huge and explodes *pom! pom!* into all these colors."

"It's a flower?" Sik asks, confused.

"Yeah! Well, no, it looks like one."

"'*Pom*'?"

"Uh huh, uh huh. It's super-loud when it explodes. Pissed off the Executioners pretty fierce and they made them shut it down altogether. And then that pissed *me* off, 'cause Quinn was really diggin' it."

"Huh," Sik says, not sure how to respond. "That sounds weird, but pretty interesting."

"Next harvest festival we'll watch them. Everyone liked it so I bet even the Executioners can't stop that. It could be a new tradition!"

"Any good business deals going down?" I ask, steering the conversation to my primary concern.

"Not really. Like I said, we're done for the winter."

"So nothing from Killjoy?"

Her eyes spark. "That's right! He knows whatcha did!"

"Knows what?"

"Fine, doesn't know, but he suspects, yeah?"

"Which is…?"

"Disappearin' without word of that chalice in hopes to drive the price up," she finally gets around to explaining.

The man's astute.

"Did it work?"

"Eh? You mean ya really were doin' that?" she asks. "I covered for ya, said ya were lightin' out for somethin' big that he'd be interested in. Seemed to work, calmed him down at least." Half of her face frowns. "Oi, Red, I gave him assurances with ya. Don't go messin' with a good relationship."

"Mine or yours?" I laugh. We all know this is a selfish business at the end of things.

"Both!" she says. "I still think we can all rake in massive profits with him, though, it's true, it's been sluggish." The rest of her face frowns. "That's what Quinn told me to do: be patient. So I will. Only…" Tugging on a twintail. "Part of me feels that we've gotten as close to Killjoy as he'll let us."

"Is that my fault?" I ask.

"Naw, naw," and waves the comment away. "Hidin' somethin', he is. Nothin' horrible, don't get me wrong, it's his manner, I don't mind him that. Killjoy's got Killjoy's angle, yeah? Dunno what's the what of it, don't need to. I don't think it'll get in the way of our ventures, so…"

She trails off, that topic apparently done.

"Well, I'd be glad for a meeting with him. If you can."

"Can't. Man's pulled your trick too. Shut the auction house down, for the season I'm guessin', makes sense, and I can't find that assistant of his either. We're on our own. 'Deepness and dearth', huh?" Polishes off her mug of cider. "Ain't that the truth."

"Maybe we can find another buyer, Red," Sik suggests. "Things calmed down after the proclamation, didn't they?"

Jackal juts out her lower lip in thought. Nods. "Yeah. Yeah. Most fences are up to the usual fix." Then twists in her seat and confronts me. "Ya hid that piece real good. I'm impressed. Quinn was too."

Is she admitting what I think she's—

"Didn't go for the mantelpiece plan, huh?" she asks pointedly. "I looked there first…"

"We're fine with you using our house," I start, "but can you not pinch our loot?"

She's hurt. Deeply too. "Safekeeping, ya trustless snot! Geez!" Leans in, Picker and Stealer voiced. "What if the black and crimson had nabbed you? What if they had nothin' on ya and went trawlin' for evidence? It felt like the right thing to do. So I won't apologize for tryin' to help. And I know Quinn wouldn't for her part." Sits back, gruff. "Never found it anyways, is what I said. Hence ya needn't worry 'bout your precious loot."

"That was real sweet of you, Jackal," Sik says.

Jackal nods rapidly. "Exactly what I said."

I raise my hands in defeat. "Alright, alright, I'm sorry. I didn't mean that as accusatory as it came out. Thank you for the thought."

"Feh. Small recompense." She resists a bit, then uncoils her arms. "You… you're welcome."

A waitress checks on us. Our drinks are refilled. In the lull, the obvious question expands until Jackal, clearing her throat, gives it weight.

"What exactly happened, you two?"

I reach for my stout.

And I start from the last time we saw her.

#

We alternated in the telling.

Sik ran with it and let excitement tow her to whatever embellishments felt natural, but she kept it straight for the most part. I pulled her back to fill in any gaps she had the tendency to vault over, and halted the story to input my perspective on the times we split up. From length alone it was an epic and I began wondering what audience we would draw to speak openly before the central fireplace, the raconteurs' favorite dramatic backdrop, were the substance of the material not taboo -- let alone illegal.

Jackal sat with uncharacteristic silence.

She listened intently, not joking, asking pertinent questions for clarification or expansion and then falling quiet once more. Sik did the same when we hit Crossroads, having not entirely heard the details before. She made the occasional comment -- with the corollary that she hadn't wholly been in her right mind at the time. I paused at the exposed punchline;

Jackal simply watched me with a sober face and said nothing.

Upon reaching the mausoleum, Jackal stopped talking altogether. She absorbed the same seriousness that encumbered each word. Her mouth did not open. Her face did not move. The drink, inches from clasped fingers, untouched. She stopped smiling at Sik's enthusiasm.

By the end, that blank expression slackened into one that was likewise unreadable. The chair creaked when she shifted against the backrest.

A pause.

She leaned towards the barely-emptied mug of cider at first, then withdrew her hand and folded it in her lap. The chair creaked again.

"Fuck me," she breathed at last.

And the singer crooned, "*Look for me underground.*"

Jackal didn't lift her gaze from the floor until the song was finished and the clapping had subsided.

#

The air moves beside me and the chair, which I can't recall being there before and likely wasn't, is now occupied with a woman dressed in shadows -- the only discernible color a deep violet ribbon that ties up a long, equally shadow-black ponytail.

"Been a while, Quinn," I say with a broad grin.

"Mm," she says with a faint smile.

"Oh, flirtin' already," Jackal sniggers.

"Heya Quinn!" Sik says.

Quinn says our names in turn and dips her head in politeness.

"Ya don't havta always call them that," Jackal playfully chides.

Quinn blushes.

"Habit," she says.

"How much of the story did you hear?" Sik asks.

171

Quinn shakes her head no. Then, holding up a finger to stop Sik from starting at the beginning a second time, hails Darvin. She removes an arm-length glove, places fingertips atop his arm and whispers. He beams and leaves for the cellar. Quinn then gestures for Sik to go ahead and picks at our leftovers while the story is recounted.

Jackal has regained her energy and chimes in with her own peppered commentary. The instant we are sealed into Ensbryng's vault, a waitress brings Quinn a bowl of potato-mushroom stew and a tumbler of apple brandy.

The buzz in the room grows in pitch, exhorted by the singer in the corner and her band. At times we have to shut up and wait it out, our loudest voices bent towards Quinn not enough to cut through the booming vocals. At length we finish, though mostly due to the respite between sets. But no sooner have we done so and given Quinn time to mull our tale over, while she swishes the brandy round and round, than the band blasts the air again and the crowd revels in the wash of music.

"*Oohhhh, ohhh the Bleeding Hours pile up upon my head. Every time I flee away from, each time I thought I went into, your cold embrace I suffered fever dreams and empty cracks running through the halls I ran to find you,*" she sings. "*Hollow veins scratch at my insides emptied of their meaning and the meanness of the sun enveloped and one of us was living. I wept when it was you,*" she sways. "*Oohhhh, ohhh the Bleeding Hours, the only time that's left. Bereft of midnight stillness and mornings come too fast and rising like a shadow of your grace I drifted in and out of any bottle the streaking sun shone through,*" she sighs. "*Bleeding out the nothing that my heart beats.*"

The singer's voice is hoarse, but not from belting out the lyrics in a constant wringing of passion. It's a natural scratchiness, uniquely captivating and yet sad, desperate, and inevitable. A diagonal scar is gashed across her otherwise attractive features, though whether the slightly crooked nose it intersects is related, who knows, though I wouldn't be surprised. Its redness is fresh and dripping sweat reveals it beneath concealing, flesh-tone makeup. But she doesn't care. That smirk at the end of that final sustained note is real and the applause responds from our table as well.

Someone hurries through the door and, blind of all else, aims for her. The smirk slips. They have a rushed conversation at the side of the stage. An instrumental song has already begun, so no one notices. The singer bolts a glass of water, stamps a foot, hardly wants to listen. The man gestures forcibly. She looks away, still stamping. He points at the door. She scowls. Suddenly, she jumps back on the stage, avoiding the narrow hand about to hold her back.

"One more!" she cries out and everyone cheers.

It could have been a shantey. That's what Sik said immediately, convinced she was a digger too. She may have been. "*Not Yet a Corpse*" she sang, about a baby born into a grave, left there to live, the dirt slowly filling up as it grew into an adult, fearing to die; it was bleak, it was darkly hopeful, she cried for it, she sang for it, unwinding the night that was falling outside and wrapping herself in the heat of the moment before the plunge.

But just a little longer, she meant. Just a little longer.

During the middle, Darvin came out with a special pie. Red wine apple pie, Quinn told us later, lifting the remnants of the bottle he had handed her and tipping it back, no glass necessary. Swallowing, swallowing, flushing.

The song was ending.

The song was over.

She was gone.

The atmosphere settled down. Some patrons drifted out, some more drifted in. The motes of dust shook up by pounding heels floated in the candlelight of each table, dancing about our dizzy, drunken heads, disappearing, reappearing, always there. It had been roughly four months since we had been with Jackal, probably half-a-year since we had last seen Quinn. But after everything that had happened, we all sat together, encircling the delicious pie, within arm's reach of one another, laughing, drinking, touching.

And now we can feel it.

A joyous lament.

#

"I'm looking forward to simple things," Sik says. "Like sitting down to crap."

"Yeah. Ya needa fatten up. And ya too, Red, though I'm surprised to say," Jackal presses. "If I didn't think ya already knew... well, I'd say it anyway, heh, but ya guys look like hell."

"Unghh." Sik slams her hands on the table. The plates shudder. "I have had a permanent headache for *a week*! I am eating the world now that I'm home."

"Healthy appetite," Quinn approves.

"But you... your..." Jackal points at me. "Your eye is all... screwy and bloodshot."

"The wormgut," I clarify.

"No, yeah, I get that." Peering closer. "Maybe it's the lighting. Seems... worse?" she asks Quinn.

Without any polite delay, Quinn takes my face in her hands. "Hm," she says, then holds the candle close, squinting. She twists my head, nearly imperceptible but apparently important angles. Prompts me to follow the small flame with my eyes.

Colorless wax, dribbling over her hand, slinks down her wrist.

"Doesn't that hurt?" I ask.

She follows my gaze. "Mmnn." Shakes her head no. Replaces the candle, wipes the wax from herself on a napkin, then presses a fingertip against my upper eyelid.

I recoil.

She scowls, but not at me.

Next she presses my lower eyelid.

No pain.

"Pus," she declares. Starts heating a needle over the candle's flame.

"Ahh, Quinn, you've been drinking," I say. "Nonstop."

Though I say so, I observe how disturbingly motionless the needle is.

She ignores me. "Risk of blindness," she says.

Sik leans over. "Thought the Execration crap fixed that."

Quinn shrugs. "Wholly, no." She closes my eye tight and pinches the lid. "Don't move." I press my head atop the table, squeezing both eyes shut. The drunkard is going to stab me. What the hell am I doing. But without hesitation, she plunges the needle in and pinches tighter. The pain shoots through my face, so intense that I think the needle is still driving in and I reflexively jerk away, but her hand clasps down on the side of my head so unexpectedly and so forcefully that I don't move.

She sits me up, presses a cloth pad against my eye.

"Oh hoh, ya survived," Jackal says.

I open the other eye. Quinn removes a roll of bandages from her coat and begins winding it firmly around my head.

"What's with all this preparedness?" I ask.

Quinn smiles.

Jackal scratches herself, embarrassed. "I get scrapes on the job sometimes…" Quinn's lips part delightedly. 'Sometimes' must have been an understatement.

"Am I finally alright?" I ask, dull pain throbbing.

Quinn nods.

"What would have happened?"

"Swelling," Quinn says. "Violent eruption."

"Wait!" Sik panics. "You mean *that* could have shot us in the eye and—" Points at the yellow-gray fluid on the napkin.

Quinn nods again.

Graveduggery

"Warn me next time! You were aiming right at us!"

"Oi oi, whatcha worried for? Quinn has everythin' under control." Jackal puffs out her chest. "Right?"

Quinn blushes. "Mm."

#

We drink well into the evening.

"A toast to the dearly departed." I raise my glass towards Sik, smashed as she is.

"Don't kill me off so quick!" she snaps.

#

"And he knew the Pumpkin Cat King!" Sik exclaims.

"That's… that's, like, super-impressive!" Jackal exclaims back.

"I know, right!?"

"I wanna meet him!!"

"We'll all go tomorrow!!!"

"Yeah!!!!"

#

"I'm never sure if it's, if it's 'devil-spot' or 'devils-pot,'" Sik says.

"Yeah, yeah," Jackal says. "And I always read 'under-fed' as 'un-derfed.'"

"What's a derf?"

"Dunno."

They look at Quinn who, rosy-faced, fails to shrug.

#

"Whoa!" Jackal clenches and unclenches fists.

"Wha?"

"I think I drank myself sober."

Sik giggles. "Weirdo."

"It's true though. Oi, Quinn?"

"She fucked herself fixed!" Sik giggles hysterically.

Quinn hugs a bottle, fast asleep.

#

"No, no, no," Sik protests.

"It's true. Admit it."

"No!"

"I see the way ya look at him."

"I do not. You're making things up."

"Come on."

"*The Haberdashing Pumpkin Pumpkin Cat King.*"

"It is not!"

"Is so."

"Ya clearly love *Pumpkin Dashers* best. Ya always laugh the most."

"It's hilarious, but my favorite is *The Haberdashing Pumpkin Pumpkin Cat King*. It's written better. It's deeper. It's the best issue."

"But the Pumpkin Dasher is *cute*."

"You wouldn't understand. I'm faithful to the Pumpkin Cat King."

Arms crossed, they stop speaking for many long minutes.

#

"You went to the festival without me," Sik is crying.

"I didn't want to," Jackal embraces her.

"I missed your boobs," Sik wails.

"My boobs missed ya too."

Sik starts laughing uncontrollably, but now Jackal starts bawling.

I flag the waitress down for water all around.

#

"Sounds like the festival kept the city's spirits up, at least," I note.

Jackal cradles the snoozing Sik. "Somethin' has to. Camaraderie and art. We havta indulge."

"The Sovereignty wants us to indulge."

"Course they do." She gently strokes Sik's hair. "We were all of us here twelve years ago when they froze the economy."

177

"And we're all still looking for those twelve-year old corpses. Find some, you'll be pissing money 'till death."

"I wonder why it's so impossible for ya to find one. Aren't there records?" she asks.

"Archives may have had info, but whenever I ask Quinn she says it isn't worth the bother. It was only when the Executioners came that burials became more organized, but were the deaths dated...?"

"Strange."

"Now we have what we have: Sovereignty painstakingly doling out money in certain quarters. It's spread around, but too thin. Everything is running, but..." I strain for the word. "Haltingly?"

"No, I get whatcha mean," she says. "I don't really understand these things, but Quinn, she says they did that so it... so... um, so the somethin' wouldn't destabilize. Because we had money reintroduced, ya know, how we didn't have it for a while there."

"I guess," I say. "It's tenuous. Everything."

"It's true. When I'm depressed, I wonder how much of it's an illusion. It feels like society is back, but not really? S'like... if we poked our heads behind the curtain, we'd see no one backstage. It's scary."

"And now," I lean forward. "Now we have the Technocracy. Who the hell are they? *Is* there even a Sovereignty anymore? Ceding control, abdicating decisions. Everything's in flux."

"Twelve years..." Jackal peers off into the distance. "State of emergency has never officially been declared to be over."

Silence.

"What does Quinn think?" I ask.

"She doesn't really have an opinion. She's an observer. Prob'ly the best line of thought on any of this."

"Does she know if voting rights will be abolished?"

"'Indeterminate' is what she said. The Technocracy is bu… bu… burdenin'."

"Huh?"

"Bu… bludgeonin'?"

"Burgeoning," I say.

"Yeah, that. But it's in its infancy. I don't know. We don't know."

"That's what I hate," I mutter.

"Not knowin'? Dunno. I find that comfortin'."

"You shouldn't."

"You're right. But, ya know, I think I feel that way because I let Quinn do all the thinkin'. I'm an ass."

"That's fine," I say. "I'm a thinker and an ass myself. Quinn probably is too."

"My ass?" Quinn yawns.

"Hey you," Jackal says with a smile.

#

Darvin claps his broad, calloused hands together.

"Down your drinks, pay your tabs, and shuffle off!" he shouts so that the drunks in the upper level can hear. "In that order, mind!"

"So early," I groan, head pounding audibly.

"Can't be helped. Fog's comin'," Jackal says, getting Sik to her unsteady feet.

Quinn settles up with Darvin, absolutely refusing my insistence to repay her, then grips Sik around the waist and helps haul her home. I follow after, stumbling too, when I feel a hand on my shoulder and instantly find myself crashing into the wall. Jackal holds me there.

"I'm really mad at ya," she states flatly.

"For what?"

"What do you think? Your damnable diggin'."

"What, not her?" I jerk a thumb at Sik as she's half-carried over the threshold.

"Course not! Ya know she'll shadow ya anywhere!"

179

"You heard her what she said."

"Yeah, so I did. Red came up and saved her. Now, what 'bout that one time somethin' horrible happens to her and ya don't? Or when I can't? Or Quinn. Whatcha gonna do then, huh? Make myself not give ya crap over this all the time, I know I'm playin' with knives too, so I can't, but I won't shut myself up every time, Red, and like I told ya before: take some fuckin' responsibility." Letting go. Tugs on a twintail. "That's it." And leaves.

#

Sik stirs in the middle of the night.

I should be trying to shrug off the burden of consciousness and slip recent memories into impermanent oblivion, instead of turning it all over endlessly -- no matter how much it piles further weariness atop the weariness already steeped into my bones. The fog outside glows from the streetlights, casting false warmth through the curtains. If not sleep, I should at least watch over Sik, but as I see her shoulders rise up and fall, instead I see tomorrow.

"Why am I awake," Sik whispers.

"A soft bed feels strange, doesn't it?"

"You too, huh."

She clutches Rin to her chest and begins methodically stroking her black hair.

"Should I light the fireplace?"

"Naw, s'ok," she says. "I feel fine. I'm," she yawns, "so glad to be home."

She drifts away.

#

The week drags by and we're pleased for the languid pace. We laze. We clean. I inspect the hail's damage to the roof and Sik tosses up replacement shingles and, later, lunch. I cook dinner; she patches the holes in the basement that were letting in wisps of fog. She makes breakfast; I clean out the chimney and take a needed shower -- she yells at me and when I step into the living room she is on her knees, scrubbing soot off the floor. I make her tea; she calms down.

We take trips to the local distribution center for the bags of rice they hand out. I feel a little embarrassed, but it's nice to know it's there when you need it.

We spend time with Jackal and Quinn. Sometimes they come over, but usually we visit them and lounge around and hang out and sleep over. Quinn is jealous of the basement and won't let me down there, blushing when I press. And Jackal is true to her word, spending whole days under a patchy blanket.

We talk.

We listen to their stories. Sik is either curled on the floor, or lying flat on her back and staring through the ceiling at Jackal's words made real. Quinn leans against me, an empty wine bottle slipping through her fingers.

I imagine this is how most people pass the deepness, holed up 'till spring or, at the very least, waiting for it to thin.

\#

"There's a new Scriber," Jackal is saying.

"Where?" Sik asks.

"The new theatre. It uses an 'arena stage' apparently, rather than thrust."

Sik makes a face. "What's that mean?"

"Seatin' around all four sides," Jackal explains.

"Interesting," I say.

"Is it a comedy?" Sik asks.

Jackal ugly-laughs. "Definitely not."

Sik cocks her head. "Huh, I wonder if it's good."

"Quinn could tell ya. She saw it four times, to see it from each of the sides."

"What was that like?" I ask Quinn.

"Different perspectives," she replies.

\#

Sik returns home long after breakfast is cold. Before I can inquire, she flashes two tickets. I wasn't sure she'd do that since Quinn hadn't been keen on a fifth go and Jackal wasn't interested.

"I can't handle that genre," she had stated.

Sik had seemed deflated and over the idea completely, but now she was fired up.

"This'll be fun!" she announces.

And I had been planning for us to talk about serious matters this afternoon...

The theatre is situated in the heart of Old City, far enough to feel like going to Old Kingdom. We set off after a sizeable lunch, our first time walking long distance for what feels like a complete season.

Puff melaleuca trees parallel the gray streets, gusts of wind blowing their ivory blossoms about like snowflakes. Most that land in piles of snow will sprout by spring, and with them—

Sik bemoans the absence of rabbits.

Perhaps Rabbit King convenes with them for now.

Crowds are gathering for the play. Every street adjacent to the theatre is a wildfire of color, pastel paper lanterns adorn boughs and the puffs that fly between them flash lavender, pink, yellow and green. Here was an echo of the festival we had missed.

I remember extensive lines wrapping the block at Killjoy's place when it was still a theatre. Food carts would roll by, their speed determined by the size of the audience that waited, and often stalls would be erected when the line wasn't moving at all.

It became a pre-show event in itself.

Here was efficiency. Three lines, each to their own door, fed into the lobby and snaked up three separate staircases along the wall. Presumably for whatever tier the seats were actually on.

I checked the ticket, but it didn't say much besides production information, location and time.

"*Boundaries of Sorrow*" the larger font announced.

"What tier are we?" I ask, reading over the ticket again.

"Whichever. Whaddaya want to pick?"

"I don't really mind."

"Alright, let's do… this one."

And she picks the middle door.

#

Still and silent. The auditorium welcomes us, grimly.

Dimly lit, the stage is filled with corpses. Or so is my initial impression. Yours might have been different.

Chalk-faced, a group of actors are assembled in unnatural poses reminiscent of a hedge of thorns, splitting the stage into two triangles. Elevated on one side is an old man, his gnarly beard pouring from his chin and coiling around the pedestal, many meters down, before tying up his ankles on the other side. Face obscured, he reaches towards the audience. On the opposite side in a ditch is a young girl, her dirty hair streaming down around her, exactly as long as the man's beard, and binding her hands in a painfully plaintive gesture. She is visibly screaming at me. Off to the edge, outside the stage entirely, a figure stands in shadows, a single beam of constant light illuminating a single hand writing in a held book: the only movement.

"Excuse me," I whisper at Sik, "I must be in the wrong place. I was looking for the charnel house."

She chuckles quietly. "Afraid the Execrations banned those years ago, good sir." Tugs my sleeve. "Let's sit on the far side."

I try to get a good look at the figure outside the tableau, however, no details readily offer themselves. Sik is extremely intent on finding out, darting down to the railing for a better look.

"I wonder if that's Scriber," she says when she returns.

"Would he really do something like that?" I ask.

Taking a seat. "*She* would. Maybe."

"Whatever he is, it wouldn't be the original."

Sik shrugs. "She could be hundreds of years old."

"Come on."

"What," she nudges me with an elbow, "we've seen plenty of people that age."

I enjoy this time when the patrons file in. There is always a hush, now pronounced by the harrowing scene below, but it is always there and somewhat sacrosanct. Why theatres always possess us of such a mood is curious. Graveyards, tombs, what have you, carry the same weightiness of air, but only gravediggers, Executioners and the rare thief would know. And so inwards they shuffle, taking care in the low light, clothing rustling and whispers whispering.

After half-an-hour more, the ordeal of the old man and the young girl ceases. The lights fade out. Blackness. Stillness and silence. The play begins.

#

It could have been any city -- and it probably was.

The writing on the wall was chaotic. Everyone read it, but it didn't make sense. Advertisements ran into missing persons reports, the rough sketches and their angular smiles unwillingly marketing a new bakery or a paste to stop up drafts or a cheap apartment space. But the dates were jumbled too. The bakery might have 'just opened' last week or five years ago. The paste was X'd out, did it not work? That apartment complex was condemned, bricked-up -- though the passerby couldn't be sure.

Her arms were delicate. They hesitated when they nailed up a sketch of a woman: late thirties, thatch of hair like the bristles of a broom. Once done, her resolve strengthened and she hurried to the other side to nail up another one.

She made to leave.

But another person began nailing up some paper, nothing legible from a distance.

"Stop!" the young girl begged.

"I'm in a hurry, lass."

"Anywhere else," she said. "Please."

"Someone's has to be covered up," he replied. "Never no stopping that."

And he really did hurry, up with it and off with him.

She thought of tearing it down. The people around her were milling back and forth. A handful read, a few talked, more passed.

Though confined, the stage was broad enough to allow the actors' movements to replicate a busy street. In the bustle, many took up different roles and positions about both sides of the wall. I tried watching one, but eventually lost sight and became convinced people were leaving the stage and new additions were taking their place. If this effect was achieved from blocking and careful lighting alone, it must have taken forever to perfect.

So while these people swelled around her, she felt invisible, and truly came close to tearing that paper down. But while her heart was angry, her arms were delicate, and her hands gentle.

She left, dragging her heels, but at the stage's edge she had an idea.

"Fool," she called herself, "you can move it!"

But the crowd condensed as she returned. The closer she came, the tighter they wound. She tried to squeeze through, but they pressed her back out. She tried to plead with them, but the sound of their footfalls was thunderous and their idle chitchatting gagged her voice. Desperately, she tried to pry them apart -- one by one, one by one -- but they rejoined the mass and half of them pushed the wall off the stage and half of them pulled the wall off the stage and they were gone and she was alone.

She was always alone, even in crowds. Worse in crowds. Loneliness was magnified with each new arrival. She hid in the corner of the stage where she had been left by the oblivious crowd. When she turned, full of shame, a cerulean light shone over a slumped figure far off the stage. He sat in a chair. The air around him glittered, likely from dust used for effect, and it looked magical.

"Father," she said, not shocked. This was familiar. It was expected, but it wounded her already scarred heart.

The old man said nothing to her, though he mumbled to himself.

"Father!" she called, rushing over to the edge of the stage. She knelt down, going no farther. "Father, please come in. It's freezing."

"Come," the old man requested. "There is no time like this moment. The frost, the way the stars strike it, it's lovely, you know. Like you." And he looks at her for the first time now, and it's a kind smile, the kind only those in the wintering of their years are capable of showing. Why is it only they can be tender?

"Don't worry me," she said.

"You worry when I'm in," he said, creaking as he stood.

"It's not the same."

"No, which is why I don't understand."

"But even so."

"Even so," he acquiesced, taking her hand and climbing to the stage.

"Did you eat?" she asked.

"What?"

"Food."

"There is none."

"No, no," she corrected. "I filled the pantry as much as I could this morning."

"There's no food," he said. "Simply survival. Terrible survival."

"But even so," she pressed.

"Even so," he acquiesced.

"We must live on, you know."

He shrugged. "Perhaps."

"Someone must live on."

He shrugged again. "Why us?"

A pause.

"I don't know that," she admitted.

Of course she didn't. None of us did. Dig up a corpse, see those clouded sickly white eyes, if the corpse is so lucky to have them, and ask: *why aren't you looking down at me looking up at you wondering why you're so damned lucky to still have eyes, liquid blood, and warmth*? I never did figure that out. I was too busy scrambling for the next certain meal and trying to enjoy the spaces of calm in between.

Their world was small, confined to a modest home. When she left, she hurried everywhere she went, afraid of being lost, afraid of the wide plazas, always afraid. Hopelessly. Cripplingly. She sat on her bed, hugged a pillow, her only real possession. Her father slept on his bed or maybe he had died, so stationary as he was.

The world in her head was bigger.

It faded in and out of perception, as though she were flipping through a book to find a specific page. Outside the stage random figures appeared and disappeared. A man and a woman huddled in the dark, gripping a sputtering torch between them. When the flame died, they reappeared on opposite sides of the stage. They lifted each other's lifeless bodies into vaults and began interring each other. Their tears were so bitter. Then, another man stood with his back to a woman whose hands were covered in blood; she implored him, he shunned her and left. When they reappeared, she was smiling, she was smiling as she was held in his arms so tightly, she was smiling as she was held in his arms so tightly that she threw up blood, and he wept. Then, someone with a flaming brand dragged a young girl by the wrist while she wailed, her body cried black blood, leaving a horrid trail behind them. In moonlight she reappeared, naked, leathery wings sprouting from her forearms, and keening so hollowly. Then, there was a group of three wanderers who had tumbled to the ground, and the older woman placed the younger woman's hands to her own breasts and simply asked 'please,' but the younger woman apologized, and the man who watched on said nothing. They reappeared in candlelight, lying in a bed together, cold and frightened, and the man leaned towards the candle, hesitated, sighed heavily, and blew it out.

The angel stood before her, gripping the edge of the stage.

"You found me," she said.

"I found you," the girl replied, setting the pillow down.

"Do you want me to hide again?"

"Not yet."

"Are you learning?"

"Yes."

"Have you made friends?"

"Yes."

"Are you happy?"

"Yes."

"You're a good girl."

"Thank you."

"Do you want your reward?"

"Yes."

The girl crawls off the bed and snuggles up against the angel.

"Where shall I touch you tonight?" the angel asks.

The girl stiffens.

"You don't know?" the angel asks.

The girl points at her hair.

"Are you sure?" the angel asks.

The girl nods.

The angel reaches out and runs her fingers through the girl's trembling hair.

"Good girl. Good girl," the angel says.

"Th-thank... y-you..." the girl shudders.

When she raises her head, eyes wet with joy, the angel is gone. Her father is sleeping. She goes to bed.

I don't understand why Scriber never names his characters. It's true I haven't seen all of his works, but I venture that this pattern's the same. When characters are called something it's their role. Father. Daughter. Girl. Angel. Why never names? Sik thinks it's because, to Scriber, the relationships are more important than the individual. It couldn't be that, could it? We don't go to the theatre to be invested in what ties two archetypes together, but people. I think Scriber intends for each character to be a vessel we can project ourselves into, but if that's the case the characters onstage will never be anyone, always be *someone else*.

And in the end I still don't get it.

The broom was brittle. She swept, but each time a straw snapped off. When she knelt to pick it up, excruciating pain shot through her knee. She managed to stay standing by leaning on the broom, but then all the bristles snapped off. She panted, hobbling towards a table to lean on, trying not to bend her hurt leg any further.

Always counting the passage of time by new pains. Each month was a pain. She almost had a calendar. First, the wrists. Second, the elbows. Third, the shoulders. Fourth, the neck. Fifth, headaches. Sixth, the feet. Seventh, the butt. Eighth, the back. Ninth, the stomach. Tenth, the knee. If she were very lucky, next month would be the other knee. Four weeks nursing this pain until the next arrived. Always taking pains to count, her favored form of self-pity.

She prayed the new year would be happier.

Leg straight, she eased down upon the chair and hid a pained expression within a pillow of folded arms.

The desks appeared all around, denying respite instantly. Bolting up, agitated, she covered her mouth. There was a blank piece of paper under her arms. She scrutinized it, more and more lost. She looked up. Every desk was filled with a shadow person and the stage was full.

"Excuse me," she said aloud.

A warbling, muted voice sounded through a metal pipe in the ceiling, speaking too low and garbled to decipher. When it was finished, the shadow persons stared at the paper they each had atop their own desks.

"I'm sorry," she said. "I don't understand this."

But everyone ignored her.

"If you could, if you would only help me," she said, "I think I might understand it a little bit better."

No one would help.

She tried reading the paper once more, failing to hide embarrassment as the seconds ran away and were replaced by a constant swelling of anxiety. She shivered. She rubbed warmth into her arms, but it was simply an excuse to put the paper back down.

But nothing changed, nothing ever changed.

She became fixated: this time on the adjacent shadow person. Reaching out, she laid a hand on its shoulder. She smiled. It turned to her. The smile disappeared.

"Can you please help?" she offered the paper. "I really, really don't understand."

It spoke in the same muted voice, though this time it came from a metal pipe in the floor. The girl listened to every word and comprehended nothing. When it finished, the shadow person turned away and she was entirely defeated.

The desks pressed in, slamming into her. She cried out in fright, in pain, trapped in the seat, tormented by the incomprehensible warbling. She slapped the paper up and down on the tabletop.

"Please! I want to understand! Tell me what it means! I want to learn! I will learn I will make friends I will be happy!"

Perhaps she was as unintelligible to the shadow persons as they were to her. Every desk pushed harder and harder against hers and those that were too far away pushed harder and harder against what desks were, and the stage was grating and screeching, and the wood of them sounded about ready to snap. Not talking, nor listening, she was having the breath crushed out of her and she clawed for a way out, couldn't push anyone back, and the repulsive purple light that fell on her horrified face made it look one second away from asphyxiation. Her body tipping to the side, tipping…

She began to faint as the lights blinked out.

And when they came on a short moment later, she was on the ground and the desks were gone including her own. She clutched at her other knee and grimaced.

The month was far from over.

Crawling, grunting, in the middle of the road, fleeing the inescapable trample. Shadow persons flowed around. She would make progress towards one edge, but then a dense cluster would impede her way and she was forced to go elsewhere. Eventually, strength faded and she just lay there, waiting to be stamped into dust.

When Jackal had said the seating surrounded the stage, it sounded like another of her mistakes. But now seeing the use of negative space around that elevated platform -- or rather sensing it as the actors, dressed in black from face to foot, were effectively invisible -- I was struck by how practical it allowed actors to enter and exit, without need of wings, or for stagehands to rapidly change sets. In fact, these probably were stagehands walking down the busy street.

An older woman, the only color in the scene, drags the fallen girl to the edge of the stage and leaves. One after another the shadow persons disappear and regular, mundane characters replace them. They gather round a message-runner, exhausted as he is, ostensibly finished with his official capacity. I've heard that runners tend to be accosted for news of everything when they arrive in distant cities and while it is said to be against their organization's rules to dawdle or make personal deliveries, most overlook that.

He accepts what little he can, refuses overtures to tarry. They are insistent, but polite. He is clearly about to leave.

The girl realizes that fact at the same time I do and scrapes at the ground, frantic to reach her broom. With the improvised crutch, she rises, unable to suppress the pain, forcing it on herself, forcing it through herself, and the bristles snap again and again with each strained step she manages. Tears streaming halfway across the street, but she endures because his departure is imminent and her weak voice won't carry. He leaves. Everyone disperses. She stops.

"Wait!" But it's barely a whisper.

Darkness falls again, save the solitary illumination that shrinks, contracting with each exhale.

"Yes?"

The light returns, clear sunlight, basking yellow and the message-runner stands before the girl, and waits.

She's flustered.

"I have there's a if you could and also more."

"Excuse me," he says. "I'm sorry, I don't understand that."

She hands him a piece of paper with a sketch of the woman from the first scene. "Please. The biggest city. Let her know I'm here."

He takes the paper, carefully folding it and placing it in his satchel. About to leave again.

"Please," she says, offering her hands.

He hesitates, unsure of the meaning, then extends his palm. She clasps it, a wide smile, teeth gleaming, pure joy, and she skips away as though a little girl having gathered the prettiest flowers on the knoll, and hurries home. Woodwinds pipe in reflection of the swelling mood, coming from both ceiling and floor, adding a reverberation that is at once surreal and as if out of a memory.

The sound slackens with her pace, in time the lighting dims, grayness, she is sluggish, and the hurting resumes so mercilessly, the crutch is the only support in all the world, and everything is so deep in its vapidity.

"Let me help you," the old man says.

"Father! Father!"

He takes the broom out of her hands and begins to gather the scattered straw at her feet. "I can mend this."

"There was a message-runner, father! And he took my sketch and said he would take it to the biggest city, the one which has the rains!"

He chuckles. "What a kind lad he was to do so."

"My body is very weak."

"I can help you," he repeats, beginning to dip each straw in paste and gluing it to the broom.

"No, no," she says. "I'm not very strong. I'm not. I wish I could become a runner too. But he took my sketch and even if I can't go to New City and feel the rains, he can take it for me and if she sees it I know my feelings will reach her!"

"A kind lad to make such a long, long journey."

"I wish I could see her face. I wish I could touch her smile. I already love her." She lays down in bed. "I miss sister so much."

"You have no sister," the old man says.

"She's in New City," the girl recites. "With the rains."

"Such a kind lad." He finishes fixing the broom. "I can mend you."

"All this degeneration has come to pass because I had the hubris to try. I wish I could be punished for some true iniquity: my sadness, if that can be called a thing wicked.

But I'll keep trying. And I'm alive. That's something, isn't it?"

The old man said nothing and set down the broom.

"It's something," she repeats.

The old man left.

"I wonder…" but she drifts away.

She dreams underwater, rising in exhausted and lethargic movement. The seagrass tickles her feet with each step away from bed. With half-lidded eyes she regards the blue-green light, filtered through a moving gobo, that covers her skin. She feels weight lifting, rising with a current's upswell and suddenly she awakens to the glory: low echoing noises from the deep and bubbles streaming through the blood within her ears, forests of seaweed sweeping high and out of sight.

The burden of living is lost.

Bending knees to feel no pain, touching outstretched and beckoning fronds with outstretched and welcoming hands to feel no pain, walking to feel no pain, breathing to feel no pain, being conscious to feel no pain!

And she dances, laughing freely, twirling and jumping.

And she dances, crying openly, springing and tumbling.

And she dances! She dances! She dances!

Salty scent bathes us in the audience too, cleansing and clean. The encompassing release, long-awaited, devoutly-yearned, finally arrives in waves and the crashing churning violence is rapture.

"How much rain must fall to fill such a world?" she wonders. "Is this New City too? Can I really make it there myself?"

Peering into the beams of wavering light.

Could it be there? Above the surface?

She makes as if to swim, but languishes, rooted to the seafloor like the anchored plants themselves. She stares upwards again and waits. A light passes over her eyes. She makes a joyful shout.

"I see! Towers of metal and glass rising into the clouds, sun reflecting off every angle. This is where they can make the rain. Where they need not wait for it. And sister. Sister!" she yells. "Sister, can you hear me?!"

Frantically, she climbs the nearest stalk, but after a few feet it becomes too slippery. She gives up. Head hanging. Hair drifts in the current.

"Freed of my body," she says, "am I to be confined here, now, too?"

She gives the seaweed one more look, climbing it in her mind.

"Oh," she says and plucks a strange purple fruit from it. She tastes it. She devours it, sucking on each finger to sup up all the juices. It dulls the pang of disappointment. It nourishes encouragement. She finds another to consume, then another. She finishes the meal, contented at last until she begins clutching at her throat.

Dark froth pours out of her open mouth and in the desperation to breathe she collapses flat on her back, staring up at the mocking lights that are so close, while she is expelling the choking spume.

This would have horrified me had I not seen Sik stupidly gargling milk to find out what would happen once, but I imagine we may be the only two in the audience to know how this effect was achieved.

Sunlight intensifies.

The seaweed hisses and wilts. The seagrass melts into rock. The light is so blinding that I have to look away and cover my eyes. It passes. When I look again, afterimages of yellow paint the stark scene and cast the wasteland in a pitiful color.

The girl lays on the ground, laboriously pushing herself up, and spitting out the residual fluid. So the final month had come. Weakness afflicted her body, every movement was agony. She soon gave up entirely.

"The agricultural district is off-limits!" someone shouted off-stage.

She struggled to see if that was true. "Oh," her brittle voice, "how strange... to wander..." and didn't finish.

People came to view her. Always from a distance, never setting foot onstage. You could see them plainly enough -- these were no shadow persons -- and yet so furtive did they scowl at her limp form, darting in and out of low lighting, that they were hard to remember.

First came the farmers.

As a massive breach to protocol and a potential danger to the city's food supply, they sent for aid.

"Luck alone that she didn't find the supply stores," one said. They all agreed.

Second came the guards.

They set up a cordon at the stairs on all four sides of the stage, then gave instructions on where to find the closest message-runner. Someone ran off with the missive.

"Always some idiot has to ruin everything for everyone," one grumbled. They said that was so.

Third came the message-runner.

He let everyone know that the city officials had received the message and asked patience until they arrived.

"Acting impetuously tends to make a matter worse," he noted. They were silent, but knew he was right.

Fourth came another message-runner.

She explained that the officials wouldn't be coming after all, but that they had provided a message.

"Throw her out if she's a risk to public safety," she read.

"She's a nuisance, but I can't reckon much more," said the farmer.

"We'll charge her with trespassing, but it seems like she's ill," said the guard.

"Wait, I delivered a message to a doctor who described this once," said the first runner.

The second runner understood that and gazed at everyone assembled with tremendous gravity.

And then she said *it*.

"She has the plague."

Over the course of a month, they attempted to get rid of the girl. They ordered her to reach the gate; she wouldn't listen. When they threatened not to feed her anymore, she complied. Scant progress could be made each day. She asked where her father was each day. They gave her bread and water each day. The only relief was not to move.

Finally, one month later, the gate was in sight. The guards had masks, blunted pitchforks and prodded her on. Halfway there, she stopped. She spread her hands, those hands now awash in the noontime sun as they had once been in calming blue, and yet... the atmosphere was the same.

"My body," she said.

"Yes," someone said, "you have to leave. One plaguer can destroy a city."

She spun. "But my body," she said, "no longer is painful!"

The new year dawned in that instant.

After endless suffering, at the threshold of losing what scraps of a life -- her life -- remained, she was reborn.

She exulted.

"Every day was a pinprick on my sole such that I wished to stop walking and sleep... because at least there I could soar. My dreams were salvation and now... I don't have to dream to live." She smiles at them. "You don't need to have me walk any further."

They hesitated, but a voice boomed.

"No," it said. "Suffer not a plaguer."

The guards breathed mercy no more. She pled. She begged. She made promises no one could keep and said them loud and passionate and without pause. And, at the brink, they shoved her out of the gate and she toppled over the stairs, off the stage.

Even that wasn't enough to break the newly-roused spirit she possessed, until she looked up to see her father.

"Don't turn away," she says.

He said nothing.

"Don't leave me," she says.

He said nothing.

"Don't reject me," she says.

He said nothing.

"Father!" she screams.

He slammed the doors shut and the auditorium shook.

"Please…" wept the voice out of the darkness, the voice that no one listened to except us in the audience.

She didn't speak much as she walked. Broken sentences, half-started words that trailed off and slipped from memory before she could remember them. She had never been outside. No one really had, except the runners. She had been healed of normal ailments, but had inherited the plague.

Where could she go?

At least it was summer. The nights were warm and there was food, though she had little appetite. She walked on, aimless, but always around the darkened stage, circling the same area in a daze.

Then stopped. Stared into the audience, so bleak.

"Why am I walking."

And a flash of visions came, up on the stage and out in the emptiness where she had walked where she would walk: a man and a woman dancing spirals arm in arm, then another man and woman stargazing, then a young girl gleefully throwing something at someone else, lastly an older woman and a younger woman pointing and laughing at an embarrassed man. But each image winked out the moment she looked at it and they alternated with each jerk of her head and ridiculed her slowness and she covered her ears shut her eyes moaning, "Stop, stop, stop."

They did.

The angel knelt at the edge of the stage, gazing down at the slumped form she had curled into.

"I found you," the angel said.

"Did you?" the girl asked.

"Do you want to hide again?"

Terrified. "No!"

"Are you learning?"

She hesitates. But she must answer.

She knows. She must always answer.

"N-no."

"Have you made friends?"

She doesn't want to say it, but she is compelled.

"I... haven't."

"Are you happy?"

Unless she speaks the words, the angel won't reappear.

Ever. Again.

"I'm so... lonely."

The angel frowns.

"That's a problem," the angel says.

"I'm a... good girl!" Approaching the stage, quaking.

The angel said nothing.

"I'm... a good girl!" Reaching out hands, quaking.

"I can't give you your reward."

"Pl-eeease."

"I want you to try harder," the angel says.

"I don't... know how anymore!"

"You can't expect people to do everything for you."

"That isn't what I mean," the girl pleads.

"You mustn't expect people to do anything for you."

"I understand, I understand, but I need help. If you would only help me a little bit, I know I can do it myself. Only, my heart hurts so badly and I don't want to have to do everything for myself. I'm so isolated. I want someone to talk to me walk next to me to to to," she cries, "to hold my hand."

"Poor girl."

Defiant, she wipes away tears, pushes the emotion back. "Isn't that fine!? That's enough for me. It's more than enough!"

"Show me that you can do better."

"I can't!"

"You will."

"I don't want to!"

"You must."

"Pity me."

"No."

The angel left.

The girl walked on.

She came to a village, scarcely more than a few huts. It's possible to find such a place on a journey where a small family has lived generations, although every one that Sik and I have found has been deserted. They're a relic of history now.

A child watched the girl approach.

"Hello!" it shouted.

"Ah, hello," she responded in a reedy voice.

The child's mother exited a hut, regarded the girl's torn clothing. "Do you bring trouble with you, girl?"

"I promise not to approach you. In truth, I have the plague."

"Mama, is she going to die?" the child asked.

"Why are you here?" the mother inquired.

"I…"

It struck the girl that she had no purpose, had been eating and sleeping. Mere existence. Perhaps it was the angel's admonishment or one of those sparks of inspiration you get in a pinch, but she announced, "I am traveling to New City."

"I wish you luck in that, girl," the mother said, "for that is a story."

"It's real, mama!" cried the child.

"Yes, it's real," the girl agreed.

The mother sighs. "Let me find you some food."

"No," the girl says, "I have to do this alone."

"How will you get there?"

"I will search."

"Where will you?"

"Everywhere."

"You'll die."

"Yes."

"You'll die."

"Yes, one day I will."

"You'll die."

"Today I will not," says the girl.

The mother sighs again.

"Then, sit. I will tell you a story."

And she tells the girl of Green Valley, prefacing that it's simply a tale she had heard. Maybe the idea of New City spawned from it? Maybe there was some truth to it, though which parts were or weren't she didn't know. It was a sad, beautiful place.

A commune for cursed, shunned from society.

There was a woman whose eyes would turn those who made eye contact to stone. Ignorant of this curse, the woman watched her city paralyze until it was a tomb of statues. She realized the origin was herself too late. Self-loathing. Despair. She flirted with tearing her eyes out, but was too scared of blindness. Instead, she wrapped her face with bandages that cut so deeply into her skin it seemed she cried tears of blood. Perhaps she did. She went away. And while she avoided people, eventually loneliness blunted self-punishment and the temptation of kindness lured her into a loud, busy settlement.

She met and made a lover. She learned to live blind. She felt protected in that ironic darkness she feared to make permanent.

The two were happy for a time.

In these stories, it is always 'for a time.'

A great fire broke out. Their home was among the engulfed and the winds of autumn fanned the conflagration. Her lover was stricken and the cursed woman struggled to save her and escape inferno. She succeeded and fell to the ground, grateful for the caresses of the cold night air. Her lover, however, was unresponsive and not breathing.

She administered aid as she could, breathing for her lover who, after a terribly long moment, coughed and began to breathe on her own. In fear, the girl tore off the bandages from her eyes to confirm that her lover was indeed alive. She was. But, while embracing, their eyes met and the lover was changed to stone. The cursed woman wailed so stridently that the winds were afraid and fled, and she wept so much that the deluge doused the flames. She entwined herself further around the statue of her lover, reached for a broken fragment of glass, and gazed upon her own reflection.

She was immune.

Or maybe -- in that act -- the curse had been lifted.

When the citizens offered to break the arms of the statue that bound her, she cursed at them and threatened to make statues of them as well. In solitude, in the darkness that was perhaps a birthright, she finally tore her eyes out and threw them away, bleeding tears of blood.

When the mother finished the story, she added:

"The name of that city is unknown, but maybe the name of that vale which surrounds it can lead you. I do not know if cursed are immune to the plague, but they may welcome you as they are able."

The girl thanked the mother and, bidding her and her child farewell, hurried on.

Around the circuit of the stage she went, and found another impoverished village. Although the same scenery, underlighting made it appear unique and more ramshackle. A feeble old woman sat upon a bench, barely raising her head when the girl approached.

"Are you death, come for me at last?" the elderly woman asked of her.

"I may well be," the girl responded, "but I do not think so. I have the plague."

"My daughter is lost. Did you see her? Did you take her away too?"

"I haven't. I didn't."

"Where did you take her!" she moaned. "She was the last person left."

"I'm sorry," the girl says.

"Why is it that we go on and the young perish?"

"I don't know that."

"Has spring finally ended?"

"That may well be so."

"Then, where do you travel, child lost to summer?"

"New City and the Green Valley," says the girl.

The old woman leans back.

"Stay a while and I will tell a tale."

And she tells the girl of White Falls. It was a turbulent, pristine place. An area of high crags with a city down by the banks of the churning waters.

A man traveled there with a commission to detail the surroundings as both an artist and cartographer. Being accustomed to the plains, he was fascinated by the lofty peaks and spent many of his days climbing and sketching the panorama. Each day he ascended higher until he found a cavern. Within, there was a magnificent frieze along the wall depicting a harvest scene in what he assumed were the fields out past the city.

He was obsessed.

He spent days in the cavern, returning to the city when his supplies were exhausted -- always reluctantly. Sketching the frieze, over and over to perfection. And once he could close his eyes and remember the location of every blade of grass, each subtle crease upon the exuberant faces, then he slept.

When he awoke, a naked woman knelt before him.

He knew her: the one that laughed as an autumnal gust scattered the wheat she had reaped. The one who, had the frieze been painted, would have worn clothing of dun colors and sunset scarlets. But now a broken shell of stone and a hole -- third figure from the right -- were all that remained of her former presence.

They went to the city. The seasons passed, all filled with laughter. The woman was ignorant of many matters, but he took pains to teach the most common knowledge. She was enchanted by all things.

Autumn came, brisk and golden. Each day she ran to the fields and helped reap and tie bushels. Each day she smiled a little less. When winter was perched on the horizon, she said she was going home. She missed her family.

He was stunned by this.

He had been planning to start his own family with the woman. But now he remembered his commission and how he too must hurry home before the fall ended. He entreated her to come, but she refused. He begged more time to convince her, and she cautiously agreed. Yet, when that time ended, she still refused and began the ascent.

Silently, he followed. In the cavern, she screamed.

Every figure on the frieze was missing, some parts had been smashed, limbs and heads and torsos strewn like fallen leaves. He explained that craftsmen had removed the people and transported them to his home, that now everyone could be together and that, for the ones accidentally broken, he would task a sculptor to repair what could be repaired and recreate what could not.

But she screamed through ceaseless tears. She ran to the top of the waterfall, with him ineffectually imploring right behind, and reverted to stone. One arm was wrapped around her stomach, the other cradled her face.

In her shadow, he knelt and moved no more.

"Only the passing ages and the weathering of time will change her now," the girl envied. "She is immutable."

"Yes, and forever sorrowful," the old woman stated. "But perhaps she can teach you perseverance in your own condition."

She thanked the old woman and again continued around the stage.

Next she found a decrepit village, barely lit save for the campfire in the center. Eerie illumination shined through various cracks in the walls and roofs of the buildings, visible now that light sources inside had been turned on.

A malnourished, sickly girl poked at campfire embers and hummed when the wood sparked.

"Hum hum hummm," she sang.

The girl tried to get her attention. "Excuse me?"

"Hummm hummm, hum hum, hee hee," she sang.

"Excuse me?"

"Ah." The sickly girl turned. "Ahh! Visitor! Waiwait, I taught this, see look." She scurried into the nearest house and brought out a shabby futon. "Isis warm in summer, okay? Sleeps outsides!"

"Thank you, but I cannot stay."

The sickly girl thought about that with much difficulty.

"Ah. Ah. Oh!" She had trouble understanding, but she smiled brightly despite what she said next. "You don't want to be my friend, I see okay!"

That disarmed the girl.

Weary from travel as she was, it was not the soles of her bare feet that hurt most. She almost didn't understand that statement though it struck so suddenly deeply sincerely.

"You... want to be friends... with me?"

Clarification she asked for. Despair she expected. There was silence when the words were gone. So resigned to putting foot in front of foot for so long, she had no idea what to do with herself now.

"Friends?" the sickly girl asked, mulling the question over far longer than would be necessary, but answered so brightly suddenly deeply sincerely. "Okay oh, yes okay!" And then: "Ah ha ha!"

The girl was moved, labored to respond or determine how to respond, but the sickly girl kept talking for her.

"Soso, we sleeps outsides, okay?"

"I'm... sorry," the girl choked out, "I... can't."

"Hummm, butbut... friends?"

"Yes, we... we're *friends*," she choked again and the sickly girl begins to read the mood, unconsciously if nothing else, listening attentively. "I'm a plaguer. Do... do you understand what that means? I have the plague, so I can't get anywhere near you or you'll catch it too."

"Ohhhhhhh," the sickly girl says. Her faces never stops moving as she thinks. She reaches a conclusion. "Ah! Plague too plague too! I have, yes okay?"

"You have it too?"

"Uh huh uh huh, sleeps too, okay yes? Friends!"

"It felt like I was the only one who had it." Drooping at the edge of the stairs, she wants to climb them, but stops short. Does she feel like the hope will be torn from her hands the instant she closes her fingers?

But the sickly girl energetically runs down the stairs and clutches her by the hands. "Ah ha ha! Together plagues, yes, and now beds. Come upup." And pulls the girl back onto the stage in open invitation. She hurries into her own futon and pats the one next to her until the girl lies down too.

They stare up at the stars.

"Pri-tty," the sickly girl says.

"I had forgotten."

"Hee hee."

The sickly girl turns away from the fire, facing the girl, and closes her eyes. They rest. The campfire crackles away, reminding me of the comfort of home, of memories hunched over our own campfires out in the wild. These small moments of suspended calm. The girl tries to fall asleep, but fails each time. I smile. That was us not so long ago too.

"Can't sleeps?" the sickly girl asks, concerned.

"I really want to."

"Bedbedtime story."

"You want a story?"

"Okay, listens, okay okay."

And she tells the girl of Night Woods. It was a perilous, frightening place. An eldritch uncharted forest, filled with exciting mysteries for adventurers.

Two friends had been exploring it for weeks, yet every foray ended in disappointment since they never found a true mystery. Their families had long since told them to give up on fame or riches or whatever idiocy drove them to risk their lives so. They found that these letters made decent kindling. Not good. But decent.

Out of boredom, they got themselves lost and slept until midnight before trying to find a way out of the tangle of roots and prickly weeds and star-snuffing boughs. Fear pounded inside them and they exhilarated in it.

On their way out, a glint from the torchlight caught their attention. They found it was a blade stuck into the side of a tree trunk with a carving that read: "This be our pact, sons and daughters of night: whosoever would unsheathe this blade will receive my everlasting curse and I shall decimate the countryside until it is returned to me."

The friends were thrilled by their discovery and ripped the blade from its heart. Black ichor swelled to a bursting bubble from the wound, then began sputtering down like putrid sap into the roots.

They celebrated at their success and, upon returning to their city, promptly fell asleep from exhaustion. In the late afternoon, one woke the other with shouting. The friend rose to see the other pointing outside in horror.

The walls at the entrance to the city had melted into a repellant mass, the fences along the road were slag, and far out in the forest the trees had turned a nauseous purple. Corpses, limbs twisted all the wrong ways, carpeted the road from their very doorstep to the maw of the forest.

But the friend who had awoken second glorified in the sight, saw nothing but a horrible beauty and an excitement unending. And so one tried to run the blade back to its fell sheath, the other tried to use it to paint a grotesque landscape. They fought in one direction then the next, making no headway. Finally, the one who hated the other's bloodlust stabbed that friend and ran back to the cursed tree, leaving them in a puddle of blood.

In the end, however, they caught up and found that the other friend was wounded and could not reach the tree. Black sap gushed out like a waterspout and their friend wept and clawed and swam and climbed and failed failed failed to stop it. Both were overcome with guilt, and pushed each other onwards, despite bleeding all the while, and struggled to the tree. But the wounded friend had swallowed sap by accident and weakened, and the other that was stabbed weakened, and they fell to the ground -- the blade unsheathed -- and died.

The girl is quiet when her sickly friend finishes.

"These places," she muses. "There's a repetition of cities and water. They must be, in part, stories of New City."

"Didid you likes? Good stories, okay oh! I made upup. My friend likes, uh huh?"

"I think we can find New City together with your stories."

"Me makes more upup? Thinking thems fun."

The girl yawns. "Yes. Tomorrow we'll make up more stories and discover New City."

The sickly girl crawls over. "Goodnightnights." She kisses her friend on the forehead and, before the girl can process that, hugs her and falls asleep on her chest.

The girl smiles.

A true smile. Maybe the first in a life of grief. Those tears are happy. I swallow the lump in my throat. Sik is covering her mouth with a hand.

Morning dawns, the first natural transition of the play. The friends rise and greet each other, eat, and set out on their expedition. They chat, almost shallowly, no hint of subtext or greater meaning. And why should there be? They are getting to know one another. Asking questions. Listening. Teasing. Laughing. One of the sweetest, most ephemeral periods of a relationship.

Good night. Good morning.

It was their nightly promise, their daily wish.

Did they believe it? Neither said, but the girl's smile was resigned. I've seen Sik give me those looks before and I never like them. One day, the girl gave it voice.

"Happiness is always transient in the stories."

"Isee Isee."

"But we don't need to worry about that, I think."

"You think soso, hmmm, I think soso too."

"We're plaguers. We always knew how we would end, so there are no surprises."

"Our ends?"

"Yes."

"I hope isis happy!" the sickly girl exclaimed innocently. "Ah ha ha!"

The girl was morose after that exchange, but her friend did not notice as she plucked dandelions to share. They breathed deep the barley-scented afternoon breeze, puffed up their cheeks, and blew. The little seeds twirled and danced over the stage, some drifting out into the audience and one landed on Sik's hair.

Summer bled into fall. Fields of wild grain whispered *sii sii sii* in the wind and *kutsu kutsu kutsu* as they brushed by. The friends continually found clues that marked their way.

A forest with discolored, rotting treetops. Abandoned cities. Weather-stripped bones. Sun-bleached bones. Marrow-sucked bones. Always bones, as numerous as salt in a salt box. Atop a mountain they found a dry waterfall and a derelict city some miles away. When they found a miniscule stream on the other side, they excitedly knew they had come upon a trail. But that was when the sickly girl started to drag feet when walking, smile only partway when laughing -- and those laughs were raspy and more like faint chuckles. They rested often. The girl rolled an apple for the sickly girl to catch and eat, making mealtimes a game. She told stories of her sister. Those were her friend's favorite. The sickly girl slept in frequently. The girl brushed strands of hair out of her friend's sleeping face.

"I wanna meet your sisis," the sickly girl whispered.

"Me too," she whispered back.

Upon awakening, the sickly girl had a burst of energy. She spoke of a wondrous dream in perplexed terms and hyper language. The girl couldn't follow, but gathered that they were both in it and that something new was over the next hill. They ran up it, but the liveliness of the sickly girl diminished so soon. She stood, about to swoon, and then coughed blood.

The girl caught her and laid her down.

"Whatsis happen to me?" the sickly girl asks.

"It's the plague."

"Ohhhhhhh. That's... plague, huh, okay oh?"

"It's not okay," the girl says.

"Ah?" The sickly girl is confused. "Ohh." Then she smiles. "I'm sorries."

"Why?"

"Not smarts."

"Me?"

"Mmmnnn." The sickly girl tries to shake her head. "Me me."

"But you make such lovely stories."

"Stupid. Me. I don't understands very well. Ah ha ha. I don't... really... understands very well."

The sickly girl, for the first time, is at a loss to emotion, unsure what to show. This is probably a confession she had always held in, now -- finally -- finding the right person in which to confide.

"I don't either, you know. I never understood what people were teaching me."

"You too?"

"I was sad. Were you sad too?"

"Sad," the sickly girl agrees.

"But I liked pictures, so I drew instead."

"Hee. I do thats too."

"Want to see one?"

"Uh huh uh huh."

The girl gently set her friend's head down, began to claw up the grass underneath them. Clumps scattered. The grass was ripped apart. And when the soft earth lay exposed, she drew with her fingers. Desperate strokes, pleading arcs, anguished curves, tearing lines. It was a perfect copy.

She lifted her friend up to see.

"Pri-tty," the sickly girl says.

"Yes," the girl says, stroking the sickly girl's cheek. "She's so very pretty."

Her friend stares back into her eyes. "She look justis like you," her friend breathed, smiling, she was always smiling, and as she returned her friend's embrace her death rattle said: "ah ha ha."

I expected crying or screaming or anything, but the girl's silence was the most terrible sound I never heard.

Fall sloughed into winter, but nothing was white.

She clutched her friend as the landscape wilted into dreary colors, as her friend wilted into asphyxiation blues and lividity purples. She was haggard, broken. With each day that the girl knelt, moving only her head when she thought she heard something that wasn't there, her skin's color seeped away and her eyes sunk.

In weariness her grip slackened, her friend fell from her arms and disappeared through the ground. And in weariness she hardly noticed.

She stood.

Tramped up the rest of the hill and looked out at Green Valley. Light raised on the area that surrounded the stage: stunted bushes, tangible shadows, a garden of ash.

"New City is beyond?" she asked, spite rolling off her tongue. "What's the point. Refuge for cursed? There's no welcome in the world for a plaguer. No one is immune. Is sister cursed then? That's why she is there? I'd kill her. I'd murder my sister by embracing her and she'd hate me, hate me, hate me... At least if I could see her face if only from a distance, I... This is all over, isn't it? I'm dying too."

Bass violin played in the approximation of wind, echoing with slow melancholy out of the pipes in the ceiling. Light contracted around her.

"You aren't there to help me anymore are you? You told me to try harder and this is where I stand, overlooking a dead world. I came so far and I have to try harder? What did you ever do? Flying down from your cloud and for what? To mock me that I can't soar? All I can do is kill. Where can I go? I won't kill my sister!!"

And it comes to her with such disturbing ease.

She laughs, twisted delicious corruption.

"Ah, ah, so that's it. The stories always ended with a city dying didn't they? Didn't they!? Ha ha ha!" She turned in the direction of her sister. "Goodbye then! Goodbye! I love you! But I have to go... ha ha ha... go... Going home."

And she leaves the long way she came.

In darkness she walks and each day -- the sun rising and setting in the span of a few seconds -- she looks worse.

It appears impossible for her to go on and after a week she doesn't. She wavers. Collapses.

Scratch scratch scratch.

The noise comes from opposite sides of the stage.

Scratch scratch scratch.

Silence.

And then a new sound returns with disturbing intensity, as if someone's limbs were seizuring within a confined space. Then silence again and...

Scratch scratch scratch.

A man and woman, covered in blood, dig a grave in center stage. A young girl with leathery wings walks a funeral procession around the edge. An older woman, younger woman and man are wrapping the unconscious girl in a blanket like a shroud. And then the two vaults on opposite sides of the stage break open and another man and woman, both missing their eyes, begin climbing out and walking up the stairs.

Once they are all arrived at the center and the grave is dug, they lower the shroud into the pit and refill the gaping wound. Underground the entombed girl screams. They leave, save the young girl with wings who takes up a position at the foot of the grave. At a drawn-out pace, she wraps one arm across her stomach and with the other covers her face. The smothered screaming crescendos and -- when the gargoyle-like girl ceases her movement and is illuminated in dappled gray -- peaks feverishly, then stops.

She wakes up in the exact spot she had fallen. Shadow persons drift around off-stage. She scrutinizes them.

"I know you're there," she says, getting to her feet. She hunts each side until she finds the angel hiding among them. "I found you." And grabs the angel's wrist and hauls her, protesting, up on to the stage. "Aren't you happy to see me? I'm learning so much about what I can do."

"Please, let me go."

"We have a journey to make, come on."

"You're hurting me."

"Then fly away! You can do that much, can't you?"

"I don't like this."

"Be quiet."

The angel hangs her head.

"We're going," says the girl.

The angel doesn't move.

Angered, the girl pushes her to the ground and straddles her. "This will be fun. Hee hee. Come on, get up. What's wrong?" She runs her fingers through the angel's hair, caresses her face and kisses her cheek. "You were with me all along, weren't you, sister?"

The angel is horrified. "What?"

"I love you so much, sister. So much."

The angel tries to force the girl off, but seems to have no corporeal strength. The girl sits her up into an embrace she doesn't want. The girl kisses her again, methodically begins to stroke each soft wing from shoulder blade to very tip.

"St-stop!" the angel says. "Don't touch me there."

"Hee hee hee."

"Don't... touch me like that..."

"Hmm? Don't you like it? Doesn't it feel good, sister?" She hugs the angel tight. "This feels good doesn't it? I like making you feel good, sister. Do you love me too?"

"I... I..." The angel is scared. I can't tell if she means what she says next or not. "I love you too."

The girl pets her head.

"Good girl. Good girl."

"Good girl..." the angel repeats mechanically.

The girl jumps up and offers her hands.

The angel takes them reluctantly, and is pulled up.

"Are you ready now?"

"Where are we going?" the angel asks.

"Home."

"Home?"

"We'll hold hands, okay?" the girl asks.

"N... no."

"Sister! We'll hold hands, right? Because we love each other so much."

"Y... yes."

"You're such a good girl."

"Th-thank you... I... I..." the angel says.

"You?"

"I..." Anguish flooding. "I love you too, sister."

They go. The girl is happy. The angel's wings droop.

They go. The girl is singing. The angel's feet shuffle.

They go. The girl is dying. The angel plummets, unnoticed.

"Time to say goodbye," the girl says to no one. She coughs blood, watches it dribble to the floor. "My turn, sister." She stoops to pick up a broom with its bristles cut off and hobbles towards the gates of the city with the crutch. The closer she draws, the more painful each step. She had forgotten this sensation.

"It doesn't matter," she says. "They have forgotten me. Father was old. Father is dead. Now everyone can die together, clinging. Finally I'll be free of pain. Finally..."

The gates open wide, the arms she always wanted, and her face reflects the light beyond, such rapture. She hurries, but it's useless. She has barely enough energy to stand.

There is so little distance left, but she won't move on.

"St-stop. They threw you away for the good of the city." She coughs blood again. "So stop hesitating." But she does. Her next footfall stops halfway. Her face screws up and the tears are endless. Suddenly, she struggles to turn away and hasten back to nowhere, but the light is eclipsed:

He totters out.

The elderly father's beard is so much longer than before and his body so thin, so infirm, as if the beard had sucked the life from him.

And then he begins to chase her.

For both, one footstep is horrendous labor. She flees desperately. He follows desperately. She is so weak. He is so old. It's so pathetic.

"Turn away," she begs.

He takes a step.

"Leave me," she begs.

He takes a step.

"Reject me," she begs.

He takes a step.

"Father!"

"My daughter!"

To hear these words, to be called such after all this time at last, that remaining vestige of strength wastes away and she crumbles, a lifeless doll. Despair. Hope. Wrapped into one overwhelming, unnameable feeling. And she weeps.

"Shhh," he says.

"Don't look at me. Don't touch me. Don't love me." And yet when he falls to his knees and holds her to his chest that is what he does.

"Shhh."

"Please…"

"Shhh."

They cling together, as we do, beneath the constellations in their eternal dance unaware of our existence and uncaring of our oblivion.

The old man's shoulders are heaving, his tears dripping onto her face.

"Papa…"

"Can you feel that, dearest?" he asks. "New City."

She reaches up and feels the water.

A clarity. The girl's mouth opens at a tragically slow pace into a bright and beaming smile, and holds. The old man slumps forward, obscuring her face.

One by one the pinprick starlight winks out until a single shaft illuminates them. It dims, but does not vanish.

And so the end is written in the beginning. Like the ancient before the show, like the waif after, these are the faces we never see. The Executioners bury them. We gravediggers dig them back up. Emotionless? It's business. Our stories are our own, we weave in and out of those of others, and after that ultimate instant the tapestry goes on like the ones down in that nameless mausoleum: frayed, faded, moldering.

The lights of the auditorium are unshuttered.

We do not move.

#

"Plays about the plaguelands sure are popular." Sik cranes her neck over the railing in the lobby.

It's packed tight down there, same as up here.

"We really are morbidly curious, aren't we?" I ask.

"Duh."

"No, I mean 'everyone' we. You'd figure we'd leave it alone, pretend it's not there and smile."

She shrugs.

"It's the pallor of consciousness. What are ya gonna do?"

"Catharsis and sleep," I say.

"Fair enough. Hey, quit it!" Sik fusses as I push her aside and look over the railing too.

"Show wasn't sold out was it?" I ask.

"Naw, there were a good handful of seats around us. I didn't see if otherwise on the other sides, though."

"No one's leaving," I notice.

"I'm glad no one clapped," she says. "I'd've gutted the first dolt did that."

"Not proper form, right? Clapping's for comedy, silence for tragedy."

"Naw, naw. Some fools clapped once when I saw this great epic one and the bittersweet moment at the end was sooo perfect, I was teetering on bawling like a li'l girl and this fucking... gah, he just up and *slap slap slap* like... dunno what, but it was... look, it just ruined the moment alright?"

"I hear ya, I hear ya."

"Did you cry?"

"Yeah."

"Really? I didn't hear you."

"Real men don't sob. They sigh."

"That's the stupidest shit I've heard for a while." Then turns to look me square, half the side of her face upturned. "Is that really true?"

I laugh, relieving some of the lingering heartache. "Not really. Some, hell most, would tell you so. It's crap. Denial of your own emotions isn't a strength, leastways not as I figure."

"Course not. You know how pissy I am when I'm upset? That's when I get the most murderous."

"Please don't say strange things in public," I say.

The crowd below is beginning to shift around.

I tap Sik's shoulder and point.

"Looks like we're moving finally."

But the press of people at the entrance parts to let in a newcomer. The guard calls a hush and shouts out. His voice is earsplitting, the acoustics impeccably designed even here, and annoying in the ambiance's afterglow.

"Right. So," he says.

"Fuck if I don't love the ones that never know how to talk to people," Sik mutters.

"Fog rolling in early. Sit tight. We're setting up escorts."

"Unexpected inconvenience," I say.

"Thanks, Quinn," Sik says.

"What time is it?"

"Not dinnertime even."

"Weird."

"Better here than outside."

Another guard calls out from the streets. "We'll stagger this until more of us get here," she explains, "so I'll be leading the first batch. Alright! Everyone who lives in Lower Quarter gather up with me. Upper Quarter and Artisan Way over there, and over there." People begin squeezing through the entrances while the rest of us swarm down into the lobby to take their place. "It'll take a while, so gather up with your nearest neighbors. We're going by district after this, Inner to Outer."

"Oh you are kidding—" Sik is about to say.

"If you're in the Outskirts, better find a comfy spot to wait."

"Rot!" Sik cusses.

I gesture. "They brought some carts in for snacks. You'll be fine."

I buy her a baked sweet potato.

And let her have most of it.

#

A group of girls in the lobby's corner are tittering, young enough to not understand the full effect of the deepness but old enough to be troubled by it. Give it a few more years, I think, and then: how depressing that they have to. They're playing with some sort of stones that look like black hail.

"What is that?" I ask them.

They stare up at me and giggle.

A bolder one says, "The tech-heads are givin' 'em out."

"Tech-heads?"

But then she giggles too and they ignore me. And I feel kinda old and stupid for a second.

"Oh I saw those," Sik says, sucking her orange-stained fingers. "Wanna go get some? They're free."

"Yeah, but what are they?"

Pulls on my sleeve. "S'over here." She takes me to a stall nestled under the stairways. A tired woman with sandy braids dozes behind the desk. The boy next to her is discreetly cracking open one of the many crates piled up behind them. "Technowhatsis said anyone who bought a ticket can have one, so we can get one each."

"I'll pass."

"Unghhh," she groans. "Are you lumping *them* into your conspiracy theories now? Give it a frickin' rest already, Red." And then pipes: "Two please!"

"It's one apiece," the boy says.

"It's for him too."

"Don't want it," I tell the kid.

"Two apiece," Sik says, extending her palms.

The boy dithers, considers waking his associate up. "I'm not suppos—"

"It's fine," I tell him. "Just give her the one."

"Bloody hell," she mopes.

"Here."

"Stingy," Sik says, taking the black stone. "GA-GAN!" she shouts. "Holy shit! It exploded and killed us all!"

Everyone in the lobby and everyone outside gapes at her. And by 'her' I mean 'us.' I look away in embarrassment. The girls in the corner start giggling again. And the poor exhausted woman behind the counter shrieks and whips her head about in wide-eyed terror.

"Oh look," Sik says to me, "*nothing happened.*"

"You're an ass," I say.

"Sure am!" She grins.

#

"It's called a sunstone," Sik is explaining -- mostly to herself -- while we sit outside. The fog blankets everything. Can't see the top of the theatre or the main road. Only the regularly-spaced paper lanterns show it's a street at all.

"Can it burn off the fog?" I ask, barely listening.

"When it works, maybe."

"When does it work?"

"After the sun shines on it."

"That helps."

She spins the stone. Looks the same from every angle...

"I think it's pretty," she declares.

"You would."

220

"Red, the Execrations and the Techs aren't the same thing."

"I wonder," I say. Regin and lot certainly had some equipment I'd never seen before and I highly doubt it was of their own invention.

A hole in the fog appears and with it five guards agitating the air with their torches. The tunnel closes up shortly after they enter the courtyard. We're in the final group and ready to get on. They assemble us and take positions encircling us, leaving one guard in the center. The leader describes the general route we'll take and requests people call out when their homes are reached.

And off we go into the icy, would-be impenetrable mists.

#

Our group tapers after an hour of walk, the guard in the middle leading the departers through the fog whenever they shout out a stop. When he returns, we move on. We're a small party. Not many in the outskirts would spend time or money on a play -- or not in this weather at any rate. Maybe they knew better than us, but I don't recognize anyone. We generally keep to ourselves, better that way for everything, so it's no surprise.

"What was the water anyways?" Sik asks.

"Knee-jerk answer? Hope," I say. "But that feels too simplistic."

"It felt like fear," she says, "to me."

"But she embraced it as a... means to reach what she wanted. Towards the end when they found the channel or when she realized it was a clue to New City. For her it was never a metaphor."

"Yeah, but," Sik says, "I felt like something lurked in the water, something bad. It never satisfied her, ya know? S'like... that stuff called 'dry water' where you drink and drink and drink and die of dehydration."

"What was so bad about it? It kept her going."

"But it always rebuked her sooner or later. When she couldn't climb the seaweed and, like you say, when she found a road to travel. Her only friend died and she lost all direction. Like the angel. She was there, but never helped or never helped in a way the girl understood or in a way that was practical."

"Fear, huh?" I mull that over. "Surrounded and drowned in it. Underwater. Tears. Her sadness that crushed her. That's pretty insightful of you."

"Thanks." She thinks. "Uhh, are you insulting me?"

"I'm complimenting you."

"Oh," she says. "Thanks."

"'No relief in tears.' Maybe that was the meaning of it. What's the line you like?"

"*I write what I see. If you read no hope within the lines of each page, then it follows,*" she recites by heart.

Nodding. "No relief. No rest."

"This is us," Sik says.

The guard guides us out, fanning his torch, and clomps up the stairs before ensuring we make it safely inside. "Goodnight, miss, sir," he says. "Keep your home secure then." And with a curt yet polite enough bob of his head, he hurries back down the stairs.

Sik can't help making fun of him a bit.

"But it's not *night*," she says, latching the door.

"It's convincing enough," I say from my armchair.

"Kinda wish it was, though. I'm a little drained."

She goes into the bathroom. After a second comes that familiar noise of brushing teeth.

"Say, Red," she manages with a mouthful of foam, spits. "I know we're always around each other, and I enjoyed seeing the play with you, but this silence you've been carrying lately... I feel real lonely around you."

I give the side of her face, half-hidden by the doorframe, a bemused squint. "I'm hardly being silent."

"Isn't what you're sayin' what's bothering me."

"What is it then?"

"That's my line." Gargles, spits. Leans against the wall, back to me. "At Jackal's, I felt you were ignoring me. Or… avoiding me? Were you?"

"We were all catching up. Doesn't it make sense to chat with Quinn or Jackal instead?"

"Sure."

"So what's the problem with that?"

"Nothing."

Silence.

"See, there it is again," she says. "I noticed it when we were in the theatre. You not talking during the performance. You talking to me since our return to the city." Long pause. "They felt the same. Exact same."

And silence.

I let out a breath through my nose slowly. That only makes the silence more protracted and uncomfortable.

"Let's talk," I say.

"Yeah," she says. "Yeah." Sits in front of me, no smile, no frown. Placid. "Okay," she starts. "What's up?"

"We're broke."

"Duh."

"That doesn't worry you?" I ask.

"Not the first time," she says.

"Never this bad."

"We have the cup," she reasons.

"We can't rely on that," I tell her.

"Don't have to. We'll figure something out."

"Exactly. And we need to, right now."

She looks towards the basement.

Then, she looks back at me.

"The mushrooms will last us, you told me so."

"Can we not joke through this?" I plead.

"I wasn't," she says. "They're nutritious."

"They're equivalent to the goblet. Yes, they're good at the moment, but if they don't get us anywhere, we haven't got a thing. So again: we can't rely on it."

"We use them as a means. It's not reliance at all."

"No, but you think because we have them we're fine."

"No. I think because we have them we should use 'em."

"I'm not debating that," I say.

"Well, so, okay, what's the issue. You're confusing me."

I don't understand why she doesn't get it...

"What I'm talking about is how we use the goblet and the mushrooms."

"Right. They're both of them tools."

I put my finger up. "There. 'Tools.' What about the equipment we lost? That's going to cost us."

She scratches herself. "We can rely on Jackal and Quinn if we need to." Groans. "And don't use me saying 'rely' against me, you know what I mean."

"But that's also what I'm saying. If we force ourselves on them too much it'll tarnish our relationship."

"Holy hell, man!" she says. "They're our *friends*. They're happy to help!" Cuts me off from responding. "Fuck no, I'm not conceding that point. You're *supposed* to rely on your friends. This isn't that Killjoy or Darvin or, shit, even Bors. Not. Business. What if there was a... a fire? Their place *foom*! burnt to cinders. Quinn sidles up to you, tears in her eyes, and pleads for help. You think for a second that you'd look down on her for that?"

"Of course not."

"Because I'd hate you for that, Red, I seriously would. That's not the you I know at all."

"You know I wouldn't do that."

"Then," she struggles, "why are you talking like this?"

I sigh. "I don't know, Sik. I... Don't you feel like we should be self-sufficient?"

"I guess?"

"Isn't it good to be in a position where we can pick up their tab or not be in debt to anyone?" I ask.

"We can do that."

"Not now."

She's about to object, but remembers something.

I can guess.

"How much money do you have?" I press.

"Spent it on the tickets," she admits.

"That's more or less what I'm getting at."

"Wanted to spend some time with you…"

"Sure, and well, and I liked it, you know," I tell her.

"But you're saying I shouldn't have?"

"Not exactly."

"*Not exactly* means *yeah kinda*," she grumbles. "Geez, it was a fun time and you're reducing it to boring financial whatevers-we-can-afford. Isn't that screwed up?"

"It seems pragmatic to me."

"Look, I'm not a brainless cunt, Red. I've been stressed to shit for months. And stinky. I was totally stinky and so were you if you never noticed. I thought we could *afford* a minor luxury."

"There's that word again," I say.

"It's fine," she says. "Isn't it?"

"Maybe you're right and we'll be fine. Maybe Killjoy's buying now and we'll make a fortune, but we don't know that. We don't know. So if we're completely screwed, what will we do? Sell the house? But is there even a buyer? We have to talk about this."

She crosses her arms.

"We are *not* selling our home."

"What if it comes to that?" I ask.

"It won't."

"What if it did?"

"It *won't*."

"Sik, if you aren't going to look at the 'ifs', we—"

"That you'd even *consider* selling this place, after all the time it took to save up for it…"

"I'm not," I say. "I'm making an example. If we're up against a wall, we need to know which directions we can run, right? You know well enough that getting lost down endless corridors is terrifying."

Blanching. "I…" Flushing. "The fuck you bring that up for."

"That's…" I stop. "What I meant was… you know, when we *met*."

She doesn't reply.

"We were broke then too and had even less."

"But," she carefully comes around, "we have everything now."

"So let's not lose it, okay?"

She's silent again. Tapping fingers together.

"It's like in the play," I explain. "We have to focus on survival because nothing we've been doing has done us anything. We have no security."

"That's not what it was about!" she snaps. "It was about holding on to your loved ones and being happy!"

"And in the end that got her nowhere."

"She got to meet her dad again!" Voice rising. "He got to atone!"

"And now the Executioners will bury them. Some end."

"That's fucking cold!"

"I will grant you that the tragedy was inevitable," I say, "but plague notwithstanding, that's a pretense. Replace 'plague' with 'destitution' or 'disability' or 'depression' and the result is the same if the situation is untenable."

"She did the best that she could!"

"We have to do the same. And get out from under any weakness that could crush us. That's life."

"But it isn't living," she says.

"I don't see a distinction."

"What was that you just said?" she asks. "We haven't done anything of anything lately?"

"Our digging," I say. "Nothing was gained. We were almost killed, captured, almost killed again. We've profited nothing. Hell!" I swipe at the air. "Pickax and the rest of it, we're back with less than we left with!"

"That's wrong."

"Useless venture."

"You're *wrong*."

"Wish I was, but that's *a fact*. Sure, we'll deal with it, but it's crap," I say.

"Things aren't useless. *Dying's* useless, but I don't think the stuff what comes before is. It can suck, but it's not... *invalidated* because some *arbitrary* scale in your head weighs our pack and finds it light."

"Living isn't doing random crap to fill the day, then sleep."

"I didn't say it was," she protests.

"You're saying things aren't pointless, but then... what? We earn some coin, walk down to the gutter, and drop them in, that's okay because... it has some meaning? What meaning?"

"That's not what I'm saying!"

"There's nothing sanguine about where we're at. We tried something. We failed fucking amazingly," I tell her. "It was all masturbation."

Her expression drops, mouth sagging open, enough to show a line of freshly-cleaned teeth. Then she gets up and goes to the bedroom.

And nothing was resolved.

Great.

But she returns immediately afterwards, clutching her pillow and begins to unlatch the door.

"Sik, what the hell?"

"I'm leaving," she says.

"Where?"

227

"Who cares."

"I do, moron."

"Can I do this without it having anything to do with you?" she asks.

"The fog is out, idiot!"

"Stop fucking calling me that!" she yells.

The silence returns.

But now it has a weight.

I move across the room. "Why are you doing this?"

Looking at her feet. "What are ya gonna say next, Red?" Looks up, two streams of tears. "Damn, didn't think I had any left." Her brow twitches. She swallows. "'Digging's useless, Sik. I don't want to dig with you anymore, Sik. Let's find a safer way to live, Sik. Waking up alive tomorrow's more important, Sik.'"

"Sik…"

"Shut up," she sniffs. A trickle of liquid snot creeps onto her lips. Brushes it away, but it trickles down again. "I don't ever want to hear you say… such sad things." Forces back a sob. Another takes its place and pries its way out. "Damn it," she cries. "Damn it!"

"I wouldn't—"

"I told you!" she sobs. "T-told you this didn't… it's not…" she sobs. "It's not about…" but she can't finish.

I could reach out and take her hand. Would she flinch? Would she accept? She's so close.

She's always so close to me.

"You know what!" she blurts out. "I broke my promise." Cheeks, lips, wet, spasming. "When we were… down in the… mausoleum… and that thing… and that thing…" Her whole body is shaking. She hugs her pillow and the impression of Rin stuffed behind the casing sticks out. "I wasn't… hiding… in the vault," she sobs. "I wasn't hiding!" she screams. "You understand that… right!?" she screams at me. "I wasn't hiding! I wasn't *hiding*!"

But if the moment was there, it slipped away when her wrist slipped through my fingers. She leaves the door wide open as she runs away.

And the curtain of fog doesn't rise.

It presses in.

Mutely.

#

I couldn't find her.

It was a second's delay before I took off, but the fog swallowed her so completely that I couldn't follow the clatter of her heels. I coughed ice crystals and narrowly felt my way back home, leaning on the buildings and trying not to suffocate. With towel smashed against my mouth, I set out yet again.

There was no other place she would go.

None that I knew of.

I hoped that was true.

But when I finally reached their home, after getting lost twice, I hadn't tripped over her slumped body. I tried not to think how wide the streets were and how I could, at any moment, have passed by and never heard a cry for help, let alone the struggle to breathe.

I hesitated at the door.

Only Jackal's voice was audible. Soft, reassuring.

The other wasn't speaking much. What I did hear was indistinct, but I could tell it wasn't Quinn.

I turned away without knocking.

It would have made things worse.

#

Dawn was blurry through unsleeping eyes. I watched the daylight burn off the fog that tarried beyond its hour and stood to feel a crook in my neck. Reflexively, I glanced into the bedroom on my way to the front door. And when I opened it and found no one standing there, it was hollowly as expected.

I lied down, noting the absence of one pillow, and knew I wouldn't sleep.

#

I woke in the afternoon. Groggy, unrested.

Stumbling down the stairs, picking a few of the plumper mushrooms. I didn't bother taking them back up. Sat on the lower steps. Ate. They were bland. No taste. Strange. All the previous ones were pungent and earthy, whether cooked or not. I picked another off the railing. Chewing. Watching the mushroom bed.

My hand dived into the colony. Feeling around. *There.*

So here was the cup again. Dry and warm and safe. Worthless? It felt worthless. I put it back and went upstairs and outside.

#

It was true, the fences were still buying. *Any edicts against improperly acquired items?*

"You do know what I do, right?" she joked.

I checked with others anyways. Been a while. Had to make rounds. *Anyone shaking you down?*

"What you'd imagine. Nothing new as the phrase goes," he shrugged.

I appreciate straightness. So do they. *That proclamation, the Executioners, what happened?*

"They aren't touching us," they said. "Yet."

Then, it's expected, oversight or not, it's expected they'll pull something?

"I can respect the guards. They have the angles and can trigger up a clever raid, but the Executioners? Imbeciles. They muscle up and that's all they do."

But that said...

"Haven't much in the way of leads anymore," she said.

But that said...

"I can only buy smaller items for a while," he said.

But that said...

"But that said," they all told me, "I can't deal in anything that's obviously been dug up."

#

Could I pry out the stones?

Spread them around?

What was the going rate of silver?

How much would melting it down cut the price?

I thought this over as I waited at the distribution center. Vaguely registered the shutters being lowered when I was fifth from the front. Everyone left without a word. I read the sign. Supplies exhausted. No additional shipments until spring. Blame the harvest. Blame poor crop yield.

Blame yourself.

#

Days piled into days, compressing me somewhere underneath.

I spent hours regarding her forgotten hat on the peg by the door.

I hovered at the entrance to Darvin's. Wondered if they were in there. What would I do? I couldn't join them. And sitting there, not joining them, at the bar, back turned, or in the upper level, back turned, and knowing they saw me sitting there and...

I left.

I walked halfway to their place again, turned back, went there again, but turned back, and went back, and stopped, wondered what the fuck I was doing and why I was acting like a stupid lost child. I turned the corner, full of instantaneous confidence, but when I saw the house my first thought was *what if they see me*.

And Quinn did. Exiting a lane and entering the courtyard, ambling along in that attentive yet spacey way of hers. Gave a little wave, closed the distance and came up to me. I looked behind her at the windows, but those were the ones boarded up. I felt pathetic for my relief.

"Ah, hi, Quinn."

She gave a smile and nodded.

"Is Sik here?"

She glanced off to the side, thought, and nodded again.

"Ah, good," I said for some reason. "Good."

She waved and gestured for me to come in.

"No, that's okay," I said. "Thanks."

"Finished cleaning," she explained, pointed at the broom lounging against the railing.

"No, it's alright. I have to get on."

She blinked, but otherwise didn't answer.

"See ya, Quinn."

"Mm," she said and left for home.

"Hey, Quinn," I called after.

She turned full around, smiling once more, hands clasped together.

"Can you not tell Sik I was here?"

Puzzled. Glances off to the side. But nods.

"Thanks," I say.

With a final nod, she leaves and so do I.

#

She was knocking on the door half-an-hour after I got home.

Not Sik.

She would've just come in.

"Yeah, it's open," I called.

Nothing.

"I said it's op—" I twisted in my chair. Quinn, already inside, flashed one of her halfway smiles.

"From Darvin," she stated, handing me a small parcel.

"What for?"

She blushed and placed fingertips against her stomach.

I couldn't tell if this was another generous gift from her or truly as she said. Rapport aside, I couldn't see service from him unless it was weighing down a hefty bill. So it was

232

Quinn feeling bad for me then... I mumbled thanks and unwrapped the paper.

One of his rare pastries. Powdered sugar sat atop. Shameful and smuggled.

"Since when was there a sugar shipment?" I asked the air where Quinn was. I saw her at the door, adjusting a bag's strap over her black coat. She shrugged innocently, then covered up an inaudible laugh.

I wanted her to stay, but I waved instead. She waved back and let herself out.

My eyes strayed to the hat.

#

Weeks dwindled.

Spring woke up, but she was chilled to the core, shivering in the obstinate grip of winter.

One evening I decided to go through the spoils of our adventure, bitterly left untouched until then. There wasn't anything of real value and certainly nothing that offset the losses. I suppose I was merely scavenging for a reason why events had turned out so abysmally. Upturning the contents on the floor before the fireplace, I hunched over, chin on one hand while the other riffled through the odds and ends.

It wasn't much to speak of and I felt like tossing it into the flames to scatter ashes.

That girl Executioner was an oddball. She had a sewing set, a collection of ugly rocks, dead and almost powdery flowers, and a cloth purse. Of the latter, weight and texture alone told me what wasn't in it.

I snuffed the flames and went to bed.

The sunstone glowed blue on the windowsill. The kind of blue that the moon, during the coldest nights, appears about to attain but doesn't. I put it there last week. Didn't think it would work. It did. But it didn't.

I roll to the other side and close my eyes.

#

Ridden in the willowing spikes, ripping chaff from brain and nothing left blood puddle and swept away. The broom tumbles from skinny fingers, but doesn't fall. Another day, non-season, everything gray without within and winnow?

He didn't know. Wasn't ready. Hard to check.

Gray.

He was stuck on that, the lack of colors. Turpid rains wash the streets with filth.

Fill up the basins, fill up the mugs, there's your fill now spin you drunks at night, petrified statues of ice for the heat despite the weather you decided to or not I wouldn't mind but I wish you would.

"Honestly, I wished I wouldn't have to," she said.

Couldn't be helped.

Shoveling for a season, no, that was confused: there were no seasons here. But digging! Dirt to dirt to dirt and the ribcage cracked and the sanity snapped and there was I and you and I waving at me? Not possible. But they were, they were, were where none aught at both instances be and grinning remembered from illusion? Or fantasy?

The bell rings. Thin. High-pitched.

Remember the fading of all things.

And suddenly: there! We, the remembered.

Recalcitrant we. The harbingers.

"That can't be right," I say.

But their smiles are crescent moons and can pierce a jugular with a simple kiss.

#

"That can't be right," I repeat, disoriented, slipping out of bed, the floor made of squishy meat, fumbling for the sunstone and, almost tripping three times, reaching the purse.

I loosen the drawstring.

Similar to rice, but smaller and irregular.

Unobtrusive, unnatural seeds.

"You beautiful weirdo," I breathe.

#

With no patience for daybreak, I pace from the front door to the window. Too nervous to swear at the fog that's out there. I pace. I pace. I pace thinking it over. I pace fully assuming this is another failure. But I can feel it welling up, a bit of hope. I hate that feeling, especially lately, but when I have nothing it isn't folly to allow such foolishness.

When the sun is up and those damnable wisps are disappearing, I hurry over the bending, twisting streets that lead out of the outskirts and over to a little graveyard along one of Crypt Dun's many corpse roads.

The Executioner, cross-legged on the low stone wall, eats breakfast. The plate is filled with potatoes, fried eggs and toast. *Fucking eats better than me*, I think, but more in self-deprecation than spite because now... now...

"Morning," she says to me. "Where you off to? You don't have business here, do you?"

Be casual.

"Morning," I reply. "Is that a problem?"

"No." Takes a big mouthful of toast. Wipes away the crumbs. Swallows. "It's really early, that's all."

Be sincere.

"I was going to visit an old friend before I get on with the day."

She plays with the eggs, then starts slicing them. "I'm obligated to tell you your acquaintance may not be residing here. Not a whole lot are lately, to be honest."

"If I could at least pay respects."

"I'm okay with that. Go on."

"By the way," I say, "how do I know if he's been, ah, 'interred' is it?"

"Sure, sure, yeah, 'interred' is correct. Sorry if that's the case, mate. But you... you'll see if there's a marking on... on the headstone. It should be an X. Unless the marker got lazy, but it would be an X."

No other Executioner is around the plot. Probably in the little house with the smoking stovepipe. I wend as deeply as I can, mindful of the windows and the watchwoman, and reach the other side of the wall.

The ground is different. On graves left blank or marked with the telltale X, the soil is frozen solid. But the ones marked with a single line are soft and pliable. I kneel before the grave of some poor sod interred by the Executioners.

I bow my head, fold my hands.

Let's begin.

I don't know how potent these seeds are so I spread a frugal pinch. They dissolve almost instantly. I poke at the dirt. Frowning. Still frozen. Does it need more? I poke around. Through lowered lids, I peek at the woman. How long does one take to pay respects anyway? Overthinking leads to uneasiness. Calm down. You're a citizen. Not a digger. She gets suspicious, she asks you to leave. There are no inquisitions.

Shit.

Are there inquisitions?

I look at her again, but she continues to feast. Merrily.

After waiting a few minutes, I think the ground is softening up. After one more minute, it's as if seasonal warmth was always here. I pull out the hidden trowel and strike. It digs in. The dirt sprinkles over the sides.

"Bloody hell," under a breath, "it works. It actually bloody works."

I'm dazed. I think the Executioner wishes me a good day and apologizes for something. What did she apologize for? What did she do wrong again? We did one thing right. It was an accident and yet... it worked? And it works? I dizzy my return to the outskirts, losing myself in one unknown corner or another and find myself staring back at myself in the window of some store that's been out of business who knows how long.

And he's grinning. Same one from the dream.

Deadly. Deathly.

What was that?

An apology?

Ah, that's right.

I forgot.

That's what this is all about.

Time to apologize.

#

My fist hesitated at the door again.

Then knocked before I could change my mind.

Someone yelped. Something crashed. Halting footsteps. Jackal opened up, wincing at the sunlight.

"Morning, Jackal."

"Hey, man," she yawns.

"Sorry for the early call."

"Ya kinda freaked me out." Rubs her butt.

"Sorry about that."

"What's goin' on?"

"Can I talk to Sik?"

Yawns again.

"Quinn and her are out shoppin' at the market."

"Can I wait for her?"

Picks sleep-dust out of the corner of her eye.

"Can," she says, then gives me a stern look. "But isn't this more comfortable if ya do it at home?"

"That's... true," I say.

"Right?"

"Right, well, let her know then." Stupidly nervous. These are my friends and yet...? I hate this feeling. Being detached. Feeling like I'm made to be aloof when this is my fault for being aloof to begin with. "Tell her I'll be waiting."

"Okay." Begins to close the door, then juts her face out. Eyes a little bloodshot. "Ya have an answer for that question I gave ya?"

"Yeah," I tell her, confidence rising in my voice. "Yeah, I do."

She thought that over a moment before she said, "I'll let Sik know."

#

My heart is twisted up, each beat binding the knots tighter. I don't know what I'm planning to say. I try to think the proper things and every one is contrived and if any are good I forget them straightaway. Do I stand? Do I sit? Do I wait or make it look as if I'm busy with something? I could be holding the sunstone. That would make a worthwhile topic. She likes it. Ah. I was against it before. That's too negative then. I could make lunch? Ah. Only mushrooms. Are there bad memories attached to mushrooms? Then… Then… Alright, what about. What about?

Nothing comes. I stare at the door.

Hurry across the room and open it.

I don't expect her yet and she isn't but… but…

With the doorstop in place, I feel an odd relief looking outside at the city. Maybe it's because she left it open last time or maybe because I don't want her to come home and see a shut door. Either way, it calms me.

It's afternoon now. The breeze puffs in and ruffles the curtains. I throw open the window. It feels clean. Pouring in from the mountains, filtering through our living room and out towards the lake.

When I turn, Sik is standing in the doorway.

She kept growing out her hair. It wafts around her shoulders. She's wearing her favorite spring shirt: big floppy collar, short sleeves, nearly long enough to cover shorts were she wearing them. Instead, her only pair of pants. It's a good outfit and one I can attribute to nothing but happy times. Spring tends to be like that.

"Hi, Sik."

"Hi, Red."

238

"How've you been?"

"Okay," she says. "You?"

"Same," I say. "How are the girls?"

"Okay. Jackal's been a little fussy."

"A little?"

"Caught a cold."

"She seemed a tad out of it," I say.

"I think it's an excuse to sleep in."

"And Quinn?"

"Quinn is Quinn."

"I won't argue that," I say.

"But she likes pampering Jackal, so whaddaya gonna do?"

"Are you still pissed at me?" I ask.

"Yes."

"It wasn't only the name calling. I really insulted you. And us. What we are. How we work. That wasn't what I was trying to say. But that's what I did… and I said it wrong. I never… I never meant to attack you. Or make it seem like I wanted to attack you."

Quiet.

Pensive.

Then she says, "Let me ask you this. Did you mean it?"

I pause.

"Which part?"

"Well, since you mentioned first, how about the names? This isn't the first time you've called me stupid. You do that," she says.

"I don't think you're an idiot. And I'm not parsing words to say, but you can be a little idiotic. And so that's what comes out of me, sometimes, when I'm frustrated."

"If what I'm doing is unsafe or really, really dumb, I *do* want you to call me on that. That's fine. But not the angry stuff. Never that."

"You're capable, if distractible. I respect you."

"You don't show that well. Piss poorly at times, turns out," she says. "But thanks." Quiet again. Then, "What did it all mean to you?"

"What did it all mean?"

She nods.

"Was it all useless?" she asks.

"I think so."

"Everything?" she asks.

"No, that's what I need to talk to you about. When I was going through the Executioner girl's crap, I—"

Shaking her head. Long hair whips left and right and left and right. "No, Red, no. That isn't it at all. Our adventure. What did it mean to you?"

"Well, it was a long dig."

"Right."

"We found stuff. We lost stuff."

"Go on."

"It started well enough, but soured quick."

"No."

"Lots of bad luck."

"Red, no, you're not listening."

"I am trying. What part do you want me to focus on?"

Spreads her arms. "How about here? Me?"

"I made bad calls and hurt you."

"But?"

"And in the end I didn't accomplish much that would keep you safe."

"Okay, fine, yes, I get it. You try to protect me, that's fine, I try to do that with you too, but, okay, listen, Red," she says. "Did you even enjoy digging with me?"

"Not if it hurts you."

"Okay, fuck whether I get hurt or not. Do you enjoy it?"

"Of course I do."

"Years pass. We look back. What do you see? The pain? Or the stories?"

"Bo—" I stop myself, but then continue. "Both," I say. "Is that... That's the wrong answer, isn't it?"

"It's your answer. Not mine," she says. "You know, I was talking to Quinn about it, and it made more sense to me. I have this tendency to concentrate on only one thing at a time, but you... you burden yourself to see all things all the time. I... I don't think that's healthy, Red. If you are gonna feel pressured every day and not be able to be happy with happy things, right?"

"I'm always overthinking."

"See? That's the problem. You think everything up and then end up missing it all anyways. Or get lost. Or confuse me. And then we argue..."

"Yeah..." I say.

"Yeah..." she says.

I think the breeze stopped or I can't feel it or Sik standing in the doorframe is blocking it. The silence feels like the one she pointed out before. It has physical presence. Dividing us. Pushing us apart despite the fact we're only a few scant feet away.

Tell her.

"Hey, Sik."

"Yeah?"

"You know that little cemetery north of the Dun? Taking the road to the second right turn. The one that has that house over on the left side. When you're looking at it."

Brushes long hair over her ear. "Sure," she says. "It's miniscule, but nice."

"I was there this morning checking something out. When I put the trowel into the dirt, I... I wanted to keep digging. Needed to know what was down there. Executioners had probably emptied the whole place, but *still*. I wanted to dig, you know?"

"I..." That flash across her cheeks. She looks like I'm about to stab her again. "I understand that."

241

"But it didn't matter," I say. "Could have been a twelve-year. Or some meagre change. Or, hell, one of those cursed they go on about, I don't know, but, look, that isn't what I mean."

"What you mean," Sik says at the ground.

I can barely get it out. There's nothing else I need to say. Nothing I could want to. Or would think of, overthinking bedamned, it's just... it's just... I can't get it out because my throat won't stop swallowing.

"But it wasn't right," I choke. "'Cause Sik's supposed to be next to me. Holding the lantern. Or with a shantey. Joking. Complaining. Digging with me." I force it all out. The end of winter. The start of spring. All the thoughts bookending me into this squalid shitty existence where she isn't there where she isn't talking to me where she isn't laughing where she isn't smiling at me. "If that weren't the case then I wish the guards had found me in the catacombs and hung me right on the spot since that wouldn't be so excruciating."

"Don't say that," she says, "if you hadn't stumbled on me then, I wouldn't be here today either."

"Fuck." I wipe my eyes. "Did it again. I didn't mean it like that."

But her smile is reassuring. "What did you mean?"

"You're more important than the digging. I'm okay to lose everything like we did if it means I don't have to lose you," I say. "I miss you."

It happens in one instant. When I'm blinking. Between an inhale and an exhale. Between the beats of my heart, that scarcely countable time when I unconsciously affirm my will to keep going. And I think it's the wind rushing in a scent of apples and soap and sweat, but it's Sik: head pressed against my chest, hair tickling my nose, willowy arms wrapping me, spindly fingers digging into my clothes, embracing me for the very first time.

"Yeah, well, I missed you too, s-so," she says, "you aren't all that sp-special after all."

"Sorry I hurt you."

"Me too. Sorry."

"In the end, it really was simple. 'Life isn't simply living,'" I say. "You were right."

"I can be at times."

"You are."

She steps back.

"And what's that losing me crap?" Points at her hat on the peg by the door. "I was coming back."

"I thought that meant you weren't."

"Red. Geez..." Rolls her eyes facetiously. "Why are ya always overthinking?"

"Well, you aren't, so one of us has to pick up the slack."

"Heh. Jerk."

I lightly rap her on the head. "Next time you wanna leave, kick me loud enough instead or something."

"Make sure there isn't a next time."

Seriousness passes between us in silence.

This time it's comfortable.

"I promise," I say.

"Yeah?" she asks.

"Okay?"

Beaming at me. "Yeah!"

#

"You're shitting me," she says.

"Nope."

"Not even a little?" she asks.

"They work."

"But they're so... pissant."

"Thoughts?" I ask.

"Haven't got any. Too floored if it's true."

"Telling you. It is," I say.

"Then you know who we gotta tell."

#

"I'm back!" Sik doesn't wait. Plows straight through their front door without a knock.

"Jackal was sick wasn't she?" I ask.

"Ah," she says. "I forgot."

"Why won't ya two let me sleep," groans the voice under the blanket on the sofa.

Quinn, legs crossed and reading on the other cushion, pats the heap until its oath-making subsides and places a finger to her lips. She ushers us into the kitchen and removes the lid from a pot of steaming water.

"Take a look at this, Quinn." I toss over the bag of seeds.

Sik explains it.

The frozen ground. Its sudden thaw. From eagerness alone, she acts as if she was the one who made the discovery. Quinn listens voraciously, rolling a seed in one hand.

"Ever heard of anything like that?" I ask.

Wide-eyed, she shakes her head no.

Then pops the seed into her mouth.

"Um. Quinn?" Sik edges in with apprehension.

Were this Jackal, she'd make a show of being in the manic throes of poisoning. For Quinn's part, she spits the seed back into her hand without a cringe or acknowledgement that it had ever left. Pokes at it. Rolls it through thin saliva.

It appears unchanged.

"What do you think?" I ask.

But I should know better. The scientist obsessions in her are entirely piqued. She tries it on a stone from the street that's been exposed to winter. Nothing. She drops it in a cup of chilled water. No change. She pulls a snow bunny from the icebox and pushes it inside.

"But I made that one," Sik whines, petting its leaf ears and gazing deeply into its berry eyes. Fortunately for Sik -- and the bunny -- nothing happens.

"Put it in my heart," Jackal chuckles, blanket-swathed.

Quinn rushes over, momentarily oblivious to her myriad experimentations, and places a hand to Jackal's forehead and then her cheeks.

"I'm only tired," Jackal says.

Quinn folds her arms and gives a stern look.

"Fine." Jackal, about to return to the sofa, frowns. "Can ya make me puddin'?"

Quinn smiles. "Mm."

"Okay then." The blanket shambles away.

Back at the countertop, Quinn takes the understandable next step: chips a hunk of ice out of the icebox and sticks the seed inside a drilled hole. Within a few minutes the seed has dissolved, leaving a puddle of water spreading out in every direction.

"Interesting," Quinn notes.

"We have a good amount here, but I was wondering—" I start to ask.

"Replication," she nods.

"You know someone?"

Shaking head no. "Inquiries," she says.

Then, with a dark wooden spoon, she takes powdered tea from a little vessel and drops it in an imperfectly-painted bowl. Dips a long scoop in the pot of water, taps the side -- *tong* -- and adds the piping liquid before, finally, mixing the tea with a wiry whisk.

Shrih shrih shrih shrih shrih.

"Quinn's fancy," Sik says. "I just use a kettle."

Shrih shrih shrih shrih shrih.

Blushing. "Woman of tea," she admits, placing the bowl before me.

"I want honey," the blanket says.

"That's illegal," I say.

"Ohh, that's right. Quinn, can you show him?"

Quinn nods, bringing a waterproof pouch out from a cupboard. Opening it, she shows me the snowy-colored sand.

"That is *definitely* illegal," I say, "and you have to tell me the story." She takes the sugar away. "Hey, hey! None for the tea?"

The blanket fumes. "Short-sighted much? Oi."

Sik nods sagely. "We've decided to give it to the old man who ran the dumpling stall."

"Is he opening again?" I ask.

"Once the Sovereignty releases the shipment, yeah."

"You actually *hit* that... I thought it was the tacit promise of your kind not to touch foodstuffs."

Jackal's face appears, encircled in blanket.

"This is a girl thing, Red."

"You wouldn't understand," Sik says.

Quinn blushes again. "Sweets."

#

During lunch, I ask if they have a map.

"Ya think we're mere random burglars? Feh."

Jackal's energy is back. She sits at the table with us. Quinn retrieves the cloth scroll and unrolls it while we clear plates to one side.

"I barely saw the Executioner map. Sik, do you remember anything at all?"

"Gahhhhh," she protests. "When I say it's fuzzy, it really is. I can't see much 'cept vague imagery. If you introduced me to Eddy, doubt I'd recognize her."

"Can we commission you two to steal our things back? Better yet, cudgel the nearest Executioner and check their pockets."

Jackal frowns. "Ehh, that's above our pay..."

Sik is concentrating so intensely she may pass out. "Fuckfuckfuck I-know-somewhere-somewhere."

"Don't strain yourself. If you don't know it, you don't know it."

"No! Fuck it! I'm pretty sure there were two places."

"Around Old City?" I ask.

"No, no. *Inside.*" She lights up. "It was totally inside!"

"Two inside the city?"

"Or Old Kingdom. I… can't get at it…" Presses fists to head, but no new information is squeezed out."

"So something is here. We can eliminate graveyards. That would be known. And mausoleums, too prominent to hide. What do you figure? Catacombs? That's possible. You sure it wasn't the Sovereignty's that was marked?"

"No, it wasn't that far south."

"Positive?" I ask.

"Totally positive. I'd've remembered that." Sticks her tongue out playfully.

"Some type of burial space. Could be anything else. In Old City. Where could it be…?"

"Old City?" Jackal's head rocks on her chin as she thinks. "Residential… shoppin'… artisan… trades… Mostly business-oriented, apart from on the Old Kingdom side of things."

"Which is more of the same," I start, "but storage facilities, farming, foundries. Origin of establishment. The government. Technocracy now, if that means anything."

"We'd've known if it was Old City," Sik says.

"Not necessarily," I say. "Think about that mausoleum. The structure went deep. Could be something huge under us we don't realize."

"Royal Catacombs don't stretch that far."

"Not saying it does. Could be something else."

"Prob'ly is," Jackal mutters.

"Old blood," Quinn states.

"Meanin'?"

"Old money."

"Would the rich really do that?" Jackal is skeptical.

"Hm," Quinn wonders.

"Family crypt?" I look at Sik.

"Yeah," she says. "Yeah, that's possible."

"But it'd have to be old. No one does that anymore."

"Told ya once: never seen it," Jackal says.

"Quinn, can you look into that? Specifically, old families that might have, at least once, managed the interment of their own."

She nods.

"Favor Old Kingdom," I tell her.

She nods again.

"Oiiiiii." The lusting Jackal licks her lips. "Wanted to take on one of those bloated places a while…"

"Spring's technically here. We won't need the seeds soon, but guards don't patrol as fervently in the winter. If we're going to make a go of this, we have to do it within the week. Agreed?" I ask them.

"Agreed!" Sik bounces.

"Hell yes." Jackal hits the table.

Quinn has already slipped out to search for information.

#

It took a few days.

But we now have some leads.

Quinn herself has been casing whatever spacious joints down Old Kingdom way fit our criteria. Unfortunately, it couldn't be as straightforward as pop a head over the wall and look for tombstones. Single building residences were right out. Too unlikely. What she came up with was a fair grouping of dwellings with at least two buildings, attached or multi-leveled or both, that may hold our target.

I shouldn't have been surprised when Jackal produced rolls upon rolls of sketches of these buildings. Apparently, they really had been eyeing many of these places for years. The drawings were literally pieced together and illustrated both their meticulous preparations and what limited areas were safe to actually scout at a given time.

This was the best we were going to do without actually stepping inside.

Luckily, the nighttime fogs were finally thinning out. Beforehand, I had had one hazardous yet brilliantly blithering idea to use the fog to mask our transit. Sik slapped that one down without pause.

"I ran here, basically smothering myself with my pillow, and I was still choking. And didn't Jackal say they tried that already?"

"A towel clamped tight worked," I countered.

"We need both hands for digging. Plus, what's gonna keep it on our face so good?"

"Jiggering up something shouldn't be that difficult..."

"Liability," Quinn agreed with Sik.

"Denied!" cackled a recovered Jackal who now had far too much energy.

Their place has become our unofficial headquarters, though I tend to think that has more to do with their variety of food and drink. Shameful? Yes, but as the shameless Sik says: "Diggers are the most practical and wickedest wights!"

Besides, the girls have been cooped up the season.

They're itching for a trick.

We regard the map spread atop the table. Quinn, only now returned as afternoon wanes towards long shadows and longer hours, perches next to it with a bottle of port in one hand and a glass in the other.

"Would any of the walls be scalable?" I ask.

"Nope," Jackal says. "They're ablaze for the fog and guards patrol up there. Now, there is this one." Passes over to me the layout of the 'smallest' location. "No walkway flankin' the walls. Ehhhh, I'm not feelin' it though." Taps the paper. "Ain't that just a stupid shed?"

"What we're after is underground," I reason. "Could be an entrance. Could be."

Sik, across the room, gives a thumbs-up.

"Guess you'd know, still..." Jackal twirls a twintail. "How deep?"

"If it's simply a grave, you're looking six feet." I raise and lower a hand. "Beyond that the center of the world's the limit."

"That would be the ultimate duggery!" Sik announces.

"Quinn taught me that gems are made in the earth because of prescience. Your Big Sis would *definitely* stoop to manual labor to help ya!"

"We'll be rich!" Sik cheers.

"I will eat only dumplin's for a year," Jackal sighs.

"I'll filch half of yours and eat them."

"We can commission *our own* Pumpkin Cat Kings."

"Ooooohhhhh!" Sik is entranced.

"Hey, Quinn, what's the lowest point we can reach in the city without diggin' first? The sewers?"

"My own Pumpkin Cat King…"

"I swear you girls tend to grow stupider the longer you think at each other," I say.

"Unfortunate spiral," Quinn teases.

"But sewers, Jackal, that's good. Quinn, do you have an overview of the sewers too? We could layer the two maps. Eliminate the homes with pipes running under, rather than around."

"Improbable method."

"We haven't got anythin' like that."

"Red, please don't tell me you're gonna ask us next to wade through poo and dig down there."

I'll avoid mentioning that idea.

Quinn shrugs apologetically.

"Farewell to that then," I say.

"I like this one." Sik taps the map.

"Why?"

"I feel drawn to it."

"What's more compelling about it? Are you remembering somethi— Oh hell."

Sik gives me a funny look. "What?"

"That better not have been a pun."

"What? No. It feels right. Even though I don't recall."

"Alright. Mark that one. Let's go through the rest."

#

Nothing is overtly burial on any map. But Sik did finally pop one bit of information she's sure is correct: the two places were a good distance from each other. Not much, but that lets us bypass the Watch-crowded core of Old Kingdom -- and that can only be beneficial. We've whittled the selection to three, including Sik's previous flash of inspiration.

"You know which my vote has," she says.

"I'm inclined to agree."

"The two open gardens worry me," Jackal states.

"Plenty of trees and broad shrubs, though."

"You'd think so, right? And it is, givin' ya that, but guards... they like to... cuh... cluster. Benches and all that."

"Hm." Quinn sets the unused glass down.

I step away for her. "Please."

"Shattertree." Points out the map positioned farthest from Sik's choice, then pulls forth some sketches.

"What, it's called that?" I ask.

But her finger makes a circle of a large tree planted on the grounds.

"Potential distraction." Nods at me. "If necessary."

Sik and I are both horrified.

"They have a fucking shattertree *in their lawn*?"

"Wh... why!?" I ask.

"Oh that guy," Jackal says nonchalantly. "Big eccentric. Big. Most rich prune flowers. Not this one. Nurses that hulkin' thing and takes erection, excuse me, 'pride' in the fact that the winter comes in the winter goes out and hail doesn't smash it to gravel. Or..." Makes a searching gesture that ends in defeat. "Whatever the equivalent is."

"No way."

"No."

"Let's pick this other one."

"Yes."

"Guys!" Jackal claps. "Oi! Winter is over, stop freakin' out on it! We'll avoid the damn thing. Not like this undertakin' is gonna be bloodless, yeah? But there's another good reason—"

"Another doesn't count if the first was fuck-all retarded!"

Jackal hugs Sik. "Big Sis will protect! Raaaaaahhhh!!!"

They start giggling.

I think we've gone as far with this as we can today…

Quinn massages my shoulder. "Hm."

"Let's hammer this out, Quinn."

"Mm."

"What else is noteworthy?"

"Trellises."

"Where?"

She draws on two adjacent sides with a finger.

"Good cover from above?"

"Mm."

"Are they lined with hedges?"

"Some."

"Continuous like a hallway?"

"Mmnn."

"But that's why you favor this joint?"

She nods, folds her arms.

There is a warmth to this air quite unlike any I've enjoyed and the roaring fireplace and their body heat and my quickening pulse are only a scrap of it.

"We should have done this a long time ago," I say.

Jackal and Sik stop play-fighting. Quinn cocks her head. I run through everything one more time, a single flash of multi-storied opulence, impeccable landscaping, and idle imaginations on lazy bastards who rode out near economic collapse on whatever fine foods and spices and liquor were left while everyone else in the city looked to barter looked to desperation looked inwards each to each -- and we looked to the dead.

It's like she says.

It feels right.

"Ladies, I think we're decided."

#

Sik and I rush home to gather what supplies we actually have. I mourn the lack of pickax, though Sik assures me that Jackal said she'd try to lift one for us en route. We'll pay for it later when we have money. In the meantime, the girls are making their own arrangements and gathering what we'll need. This is exciting. We've never broken into a home of the living before.

Everything's piled together at the door.

Sik, leaning against the chair, is playing with her hair.

"Hat?" I offer, about to fling it.

She stands profile, pulling it all up.

"You like ponytails, right?" she asks.

"They're alright."

"Eh?" Drops it. "Thought you had, like, a thing for them." Sees my expression. "Ya know, because of Quinn."

"Not especially." Shrugging. "It suits her."

"Thought I was being left out. Only tailless woman," she jokes.

"Are you tying it up then?"

"Ahhhh… That *would* be convenient." Dithers. Jumps up and snatches the hat out of my hands. "On second thought, it's not me."

"This is a new you too, you understand."

Her long hair cascades with each laugh. "I think so too!"

#

It's well into dusk when we find them loitering in an alleyway. Jackal must have met with success because she starts hopping from one foot to the other, presenting an incompetently-wrapped package.

"Ta-de-da!" she cheers.

"Thanks, Jackal," I say, pulling out the tool. "Oh, you bloody imbecile."

"Oi! What gives?"

"This is a mattock." I shake it under her nose. "Mat-tock."

"It's a pickax!"

"My ass it is."

"What's…" Shoots Sik a depressed grimace. "What's the difference?"

"One's for digging. One's for walls," Sik explains.

"Which did I pilfer?"

"Digging."

"But that's what we're doin'! Diggin'!" Gives me a fierce look, wrinkled and huffy, acting as if she'd been vindicated.

"The *shovel* can cover that. A pickax is for any walls we need to crack through."

"Walls!" Jackal throws arms high. "How much noise are ya plannin' to make? Listen, Red, this is quiet work we do and we must be as wraiths."

"Vault, wall, whatever. If we're underground or enclosed enough, it shouldn't matter. But this will make the dig go faster, so it's not a total loss."

I stow it out of sight and Quinn leads us through the streets. Jackal, still steamed, takes up the rear. We weave our way through what shortcuts they know and away from the main roads.

Night is descending and curfew is on. Tendrils of vapor are rising. They'll meet somewhere in the middle, one a regular companion and the other a temporary enemy.

After a few hours, we arrive. The sconces atop the walls are well-lit and the fog, safely-thinned by a breeze, twists about below. Guards pace. The main road is quiet. The residence is enclosed by a park, free of any watchful eyes, and appears to sleep.

It's time to begin.

#

According to the sketches, one of the trellises extends almost to the rear wall. That'll cut down on our chance of exposure, so that's where we set up. The torchlight above is bright enough to illuminate our dig yet dulled by the mists, so we should be blocked from the view of anyone peeking over.

The seeds are sown.

Jackal tosses a hefty rock absentmindedly from hand to hand -- in case anyone atop the wall gets too curious. Quinn is up in a tree with the lantern, opening the shutter to inform us when a patrol nears.

Still slightly unconvinced, Sik stamps on the seeded dirt. But when she steps on the shovel and the blade digs in... Mouth wide open. Exhalation. Eyes shut. Pure ecstasy.

We work together, shovel and mattock.

Sik hums a shantey.

Jackal starts tossing the rock in time to the rhythm.

#

"See anything?"

Jackal shushes me.

"What did I tell ya 'bout noise? Sshh!"

She crawls back into the tunnel, poking her head out the other side. After another few minutes of surveillance:

"I'm not seein' anyone on the grounds. Widen it quick-like, yeah?"

I break up the dirt with the mattock and Sik shovels it out. When the hole is broad enough to allow us easy access, Jackal signals Quinn.

"Now, listen to Jackal," she instructs. "That shattertree is on the other side."

"And long may it remain so."

"*Listen to Jackal*," she fumes at me. "I'm gonna go set some stones within throw's reach of the thing. I'll get a better view of the interior while I'm at it. When I'm back, ya guys stay behind us a good distance. If we get separated, come back here and we'll bring ya back in. Point is: no bunchin' up! I know ya work together, but lotsa times Quinn and me solo. When a guard is about, easiest to find a hidin' spot for one instead of two."

I nod at our group. "Let alone four."

"Ya got it, yeah?" Twintails bobbing appreciatively. "Back soon."

#

When Jackal returns on all fours, Quinn extends a hand to assist. She dives right into description before standing up, mostly speaking to Quinn.

"Pretty busy in there. Music on the second floor. Party, maybe."

"Ending?"

"Impression's it's a nighttime thing."

"Troublesome."

They were both Picker and Stealer voiced now, such sudden and callous disparity to their previous affection making the exchange far more unsettling. This was their side of the night and it was uncompromisingly self-interested, pitiless and sucked of color.

"Higher stakes, both ways of it."

"Indeed."

In the same instant, their eyes flicker at us, then away.

A shudder rips up the blades of my spine.

"All first floor windows locked tight. No apparent extra security."

"No Sovereignty presence."

Jackal doesn't respond.

Quinn says her name.

"Dunno. Feels odd. Atmosphere."

"Treacherous?"

"Not makin' me nervous."

"Very well."

"Are we ready?" Sik prompts.

"Wanted to stow ya in the kitchen, but that's not possible," Jackal admits.

"Because of this party?"

Nodding. "Too many servants'll be scuttlin' to and fro."

"Too bad it's not a costume party," I say.

Disturbing grin. "Too bad," Jackal echoes.

"Entrances?" Quinn inquires.

"Four," she says. "Main. Garden. Servant: for kitchen, most like. Will need pickin'. Last on the storehouse is different. Strange lockin' mechanism."

"Can we get in that?" I ask.

Eyes darting again, then away.

"Might need some persuasion."

"Come," Quinn says to us.

#

A few guards had begun making circuits outside. Their torches and movement kept the fog from growing any thicker -- and made for some tense moments as we hurried from hedge to hedge along the trellis walkway. Between them and the watchmen on the walls, it felt like being back in the graveyard.

Jackal and Quinn shot off towards the storehouse, running low to the ground. The guards divided us, but Sik and I hunched down, breaths held, and ran once the girls signaled it was all clear on their side too.

"Place is waking up," I note.

"Naw, prob'ly caught them during a shift change. Or they were screwin' around while the master of the house was indespised."

"Indisposed," Quinn corrects.

"Right. But forget 'bout that," Jackal says. "This is that lock I mentioned."

Metallic veins angle through the wood of the door like immobilized lightning, intersect at the keyhole, then pierce the earth. It's clear that a normal key wouldn't work here. Quinn fiddles and probes with a lockpick anyways before yielding.

"Eeshh," Sik says. "So complex…"

I heft the mattock.

"I'm not seeing any working persuasion."

Jackal's face conceals a knowing wink. "Check out that bush."

I move the foliage, half-expecting this a practical joke, when I see half-a-hole at the bottom corner of the wood right where a burrow is.

"A rabbit couldn't gnaw through this." I knock the wood to confirm its thickness.

"Whatever it was, no one told it that. Yeah, I'd wager they thought someone was nickin' things and installed this weird contraption, never noticin'."

I brush my hands off.

"Not sure we can do it. Bushes like these drop their roots way down to survive the deepness."

"The mattock…" Jackal starts, a little embarrassment creeping in.

"Nope," Sik says. "Need a saw or nothin' doin'."

"Got any backup plans?" I ask.

Quinn nods. "Mm."

Jackal smiles. "Always."

"Gimme a sec." Sik is fooling with the hole. Sprinkles some seeds and tries digging beside the bush while I force it down. She gets roughly a square foot out, but it's pretty pointless. "Hand me the mattock. Got some leverage, I think." Now aiming the spiked-end of the blade towards the door, she jerks upwards -- and it sticks in. Then she wrests it out, taking with it a few paltry splinters.

Once more the mattock bites in. She pulls out a hammer from a pocket, lies down on the frozen ground and starts knocking it in. I transfer the bush to my foot and pull upwards until the hammering knocks it clear in place. I wave Jackal and Quinn over and switch out with Sik.

While the three strain to pull up, I hold the base as a kind of fulcrum, and the wood splits off. Fortunately the sound doesn't travel far, though it freaks Jackal out all the same. We repeat this at a few other angles until there's room for Sik to wriggle through.

"Pitch black," she reports, but I'm already unshuttering the lantern. "Ahh, yeah, storage place alright. There's sacks of grain. Beans too. Smells like shit, guys, they have some rotting corpses stacked in the corner. That's so disgusting!"

"Rottin'!?" Jackal looks ill.

"Corpses are like ice. Poorer people use them, but this party-thrower of ours must be a frugal, sadistic fuck. These were the unproductive servants." Her voice heaves a little. "Oh shit, that one woman has her face ripped off." Gasping. "It's been *eaten off*!"

"Sweetie, get out of there!" Jackal implores.

Quinn, biting her lip, scans the area. Nothing is amiss.

After a moment, we hear the dull turning of a crank and the metallic spears, firmly entrenched, now rise. The hinges groan. Sik stops opening the door until that sound dies, then pushes slower.

She's all devil-grins on the outside.

"I'm kidding. You're so gullible."

"You!" But Jackal, the woman with a thousand oaths readily available, can't find a single word.

It amuses Quinn though.

The storage comment, at least, was accurate. If there's time, we'll take some of the contents along home. For now we search the area, until Jackal finds a staircase leading downwards. I hoist the lantern and take us into the shadows.

Each underground room houses a certain supply, some edible, some not. Dried, preserved fruits. Stacks of split wood. At least two wells, but then we find another.

"Is this how ya normally go?" Jackal asks.

"Meaning?"

"You're too abrupt," she chides. "Take your time. Stop lookin' for loot. Look for hidin' spots first."

"That's your method?"

"Of course! Only amateurs pop into a bedroom and start rootin' through the drawers."

"Jackal, don't steal people's panties," Sik scolds.

"*Desk* drawers, ya little… and I'm still peeved with ya, so watch it, yeah?"

Sik's laugh echoes off the narrow hallways a malicious waterdrop.

"Hu hu hu."

We're under the main complex now, this area crammed to the brim with enormous casks each the size of a small room. Shorthand markings tell what they are, though I can't understand it. For all the variety, I assume the odd assortment of whiskey, brandy and wine. Could be they're the same drink except aged in different types of wood.

Not my area of expertise.

Sik beckons at the bottom of the staircase, ready to sneak into the residence itself.

"That's not where we're bound," I tell her.

"Come on, let's have a peek!"

We're about to go up, but we're missing one.

"Knew… Knew…"

I turn around.

"Knew it. Knew they…"

More than slightly astounded.

"Knew they were like this. Didn't seem possible, no way to get them in here, they build them here, I see, I see, but still, it's, it's. Mm. Yes. Beautiful."

And there's Quinn, reverently hovering from barrel to barrel, stringing together more words at once than I'd ever heard come out of that reticent lush of a woman before.

"Damn by damn," Jackal says, stomping back down the stairs. "Hold on, this'll take a..." Doesn't finish. Carefully lays hands on Quinn's arm.

Quinn slaps the tawny barrel at hand and declares:

"This one."

"Ahhh, Quinn?"

"Mine."

"Quinnzy?"

She caresses the barrel. Fingers the bunghole. "Mm."

Jackal tries to pull Quinn away, but she refuses to budge, entranced, in awe. They start whispering, although I'm not sure Quinn is talking to anyone in particular. Jackal keeps pulling, assuring that we'll return and take it later, just not now, the job and all, but we'll make sure, okay, let it age a bit longer, a few hours, and then it'll be perfect just for ya, Quinn, okay?

But it's really only the pulling that takes Quinn away. Even when her eyes are turned -- physically turned -- to the stairs and gaze into mine, she isn't completely there.

Drunk already on fantasies.

"Should we slap her?" Sik asks in all seriousness.

"She's fine. Quinnzy? Right?" Jackal nudges. "Time to work?"

Silent nod.

"We have a plan here? I was figuring Sik and I would stay underground."

"Thought to hit the second floor and up," Jackal confesses, "while ya two were at it. Only... Could show ya the way we work, if ya like?"

Sik cheers. "Yeah yeah, it's fun!"

"You act like you've already..." I scowl at her recognition. "You were in on the sugar run."

"I have no idea of what you speak," Sik says, haltingly, poorly lied.

"Shit. I don't want to hear it," I say.

261

"Interested?" Jackal insists. "We've been wantin' to switch it up long time now. Go diggin' with ya, come thievin' with us."

"Can't say I'm not interested if it's safe."

"Yeah?" Jackal glows. "Not safe. We're breakin' into some fool's home, yeah?" Entertained snort. "With a party on, expect traffic up and down what staircase is convenient between kitchen and guests. Avoid bathrooms. Pissin' and parties go together like... um... well, they go together. I want to screw around the ground level. Quinn, didn't ya want to scale the eaves?"

"Mm."

"Me, I like slinkin' into a place from below, but Quinn prefers a roof entrance. Likes to climb, this one."

Quinn smiles.

"So?" Jackal puts hands to hips. "Who's with who?"

Sik snuggles with Jackal's breasts. "Eeehee."

"N-not here, you twit!"

Quinn wraps herself around my arm, pressing her own small breasts, smile widening.

Actually... *is* she drunk?

"Oh hoh. We'll leave ya two lovers alone then," Jackal taunts.

She and Sik mount the landing and carefully push the door ajar. "Ahh, see? This is why rich homes are advantageous. Look at all that plush carpeting!"

"Quiet traverse," Quinn says.

"Let me wipe your soles clean," Jackal says, kneeling down in front of Sik.

Quinn tugs on my arm and we exit out the way we came.

\#

I jump. She grabs my wrist and heaves.

The wooden shingles squeak underfoot. We sneak from window to window, avoiding the light and sticking to what shadows are dark enough to keep ignorant the guards upon the walls. If we can get out of this without rousing a single person, it'll be pretty damn remarkable.

I'm lighter on my feet, having stashed our gear behind the bushes of the storehouse. Quinn said any dusty corner underground would do. But what if things go wrong fast tonight?

Can't risk losing what else we have left.

Quinn checks the windows, finding everything thus far locked, and rounds the corner.

I follow.

Torches almost appear to shine through the shattertree, lit at cunning angles and reflecting off mirrored surfaces. It's a behemoth. I could expect to find one soaring like that in a forest of unfathomable magnitude. Not here. Not in the city. Not in a garden. Fucked insanity. To shatter, straight drop: a mess of detritus to clean. But if it pitches at the base and keels over onto the house?

People not worried about money certainly thought things differently.

Quinn kicks off a winged statue, reaches the upper eave and pulls herself up. She reaches down and helps me ascend, leaving me thankful I don't have a problem with heights.

She's getting frustrated.

I can read it in her pinned back shoulders, the dismissive movement of her hands.

Everything is latched. She doesn't say so, in fact she continues to say nothing, but I'd figure the higher we climb the more lax the security. Do they fear prowlers? The fog? Or simply a chilly draft?

It's more than that. Quinn has had a lockpick between restless fingers for a while. Spins it almost as a nervous tick.

I lean in to whisper.

"Windows can normally be picked from outside?"

She ignores me.

What a ridiculous question. That was embarrassing.

Her shoulders loosen up. Side-long glance, a partial smile. "Observant," she compliments. "Come."

And upwards we go, climbing the overhanging vines.

The rooftop is cut steeply to drain rainwater. We proceed with care, each step a deliberate decision lest we fall. Towards the front of the building, finally: a door.

Quinn sticks an ear to it.

Five long seconds pass.

And her hands shoot out, starving, unrestrained, skewering the lock with the pick and probing and turning and forcing and stabbing the tumblers and seducing them, so very quietly, clinking and scratching and then -- *clack* -- gives a simple nod, replacing the lockpick in a pocket, and holds the door open for me.

The attic is a home of dust.

Boxes and castoff bits sequestered to the dim parts of memory and ultimately, fated, forgotten.

The floor moans of our passing. Quinn urges me to step where beams hold up the roof. The floor quietens, lulled back into torpor.

She checks a few crates. Nothing of much worth to us. Under linen covers, I discover old paintings. Is it worth anything? She shrugs, but diligently examines them, then turns away.

Guess she was appreciating the art.

At the bottom of a small set of steps, Quinn stops me. She gazes back up at the boxes and points.

"Interment?" she asks.

"No. Even long after a rot, the smell would be distinct enough to seep into the lower floor. Our man might be an eccentric, but he can't be that perverse. If it *is* here, it's in those tunnels."

She nods, but ineptly works on the next locked door. Is she flustered? If Quinn is capable of that. Possibly embarrassed by the question the way I was with mine.

"Peculiar as it is," I continue, "there's nothing saying he couldn't have built stone coffins and placed them somewhere. Unlikely. But we'll keep an eye out anyways, okay?"

"Mm."

From the hallway alone, this is evidently an affluent dwelling. I can see Quinn, Jackal and Sik going a little crazy at the splendor and forgetting our original purpose down in the dark and the earth. I might too, broke as I am. Digging is getting overshadowed. And yet if things go to shit, I think I feel alright with that tonight. If not for our friends, we wouldn't have been able to do this, nor would we have considered it. If not for Jackal berating me or Quinn's kindness, it may have taken additional weeks to make up with Sik. If that's true, I'd like tonight to be a 'thank you' to them.

Indigo carpets, thick and soft, turn our footsteps into murmurs. Which means anyone else bumbling around, guard or guest, could slip upon us without warning.

Quinn's ears are as active as my eyes. Picking up the slightest noise, change in atmosphere. Determining if someone is coming towards us or away.

Eventually someone does come. She hides us behind a statue in an alcove until this stray guest passes, whose heavy eyelids regard the statue unnervingly too long.

"No guests on the third floor!"

The guard's voice calls from down the hall.

"Ah, you there!" he says to the guard, stumbles, rights himself on the statue.

I unconsciously lean into Quinn.

She covers me with her long black coat.

"I say, I really like this one!" Patting the statue. "Know you who carved it? I wonder if he'd sell it, the sly bast— ah! You *are* a tall one."

"Thank you, sir," she says to him, "but I'll need you downstairs now."

"Ah," he says, uncomprehendingly. And then at last: "Ah!" Comprehending now that the guard has a grip of his shoulder. "Are you escorting me, dear?"

"Yes, sir," she says, "I'll be your escort."

"Always wanted an escort!" he exclaims wildly. "That's fabulous, that really is."

"Very much so, sir. Please come this way."

He fawns over every artistic piece. The paintings, the vases, the figurines, the wallpaper. He fawns over the guard -- who keeps him at bay with a professional demeanor.

Quinn creeps out, peeks around the bend, and waves to me. We take the advantage and reach the end of the corridor. She unlatches the window.

"Always multiple exits," she counsels me.

Good advice.

Regrettably, the way out of a grave is usually one way...

She opens the window, urges me outside.

Confused. "Quinn, are we leaving?"

Shakes her head no.

Points at the door of the adjacent room. "Empty?"

I sidle up to the window nearby. The bedroom is lit, but unoccupied.

"It's empty," I confirm, but my exit is shut and Quinn is gone. Heartbeat fluttering. "Crap... Quinn?"

Then the bedroom window opens.

Quinn waves at me and smiles.

With the festivities below us, it's the guards we have to worry about primarily. No other roamers have found their way up. We skip from room to room. Hiding spots first, then loot as Jackal noted. Quinn explains that it's best to take trifles, though with an eye for quality. That explains why we give the pricey pieces in the hallways a miss.

"Revisitation," she says.

That's the same as digging. One-year-out dredgers will dig up everything in sight and leave the graves gaping when they leave. Professionals leave no trace. Keep the guards snoozing. Besides, once you learn the trick for getting in, there's typically no one to block you from then on. The one difference is: pillage anything of value at the time. No telling if another digger will hit a crypt you've cracked wide or if the Executioners'll seal them permanently -- as I imagine is going to be the case everywhere from now on.

Three flights of stairs lead below.

Guards at every one.

"We could pretend to be lost," I say, half-serious.

Dropping down to the second level from outside would be the most prudent course, however, Quinn expects it's shut and secure like everywhere else. Aside from the balcony near the front that's flung fearlessly open to spite the fog, it's pointless. There might be one unbolted window somewhere, but considering how thorough our initial inspection?

Waste of time.

There's one guard at the stairway farthest from the party. He mutters to himself from the landing halfway down.

"Should we jump him?"

Quinn is surprised with me. "Reckless," she says.

"I thought you two sapped people when you had to."

"Last resort."

"Well, we need to descend here, don't we?"

"Mm."

In her hand is a glass orb, the size of a marble, and she hurls it against the ceiling five windows away. I'm about to call *her* reckless as it shatters, except the sound it produces is minute. *Tink. Tak tak tak.* Localized and diffuse.

We duck behind a potted plant. When the guard leaves to investigate the noise, grumbling about the lack of food for the Watch and the bothersome 'accidental' intrusions of the visitors…

"Don't touch!" I hiss at Quinn.

It's a dwarfed shattertree in the pot.

She hadn't noticed. Nods appreciatively in my direction and signals me to follow.

We soundlessly reach the staircase only to hear someone coming back up.

"Hey, told you—"

Quinn seizes my arm and flings me over her shoulder before I can object before I can figure out what she's *shit!* I'm tumbling at the fucking shattertree!

"—not to wander—"

It's luck. It's aim. I can't tell. I roll to the side of it, back towards where we were.

"—off while I—"

She unlatches the window by the staircase, flies outside, closes it up: one perfect, seamless movement.

"—get the stew," the new guard complains.

I stop myself from slamming into the wall full force.

Thud.

Suck in a breath. Instinctively reach for the shovel not slung over my back.

"Thought I heard another one," replies the other guard.

Sounds like they didn't detect us.

Damn it, that was too close.

"Can't be too careful. Boss'll have our asses if they walk off with so much as lint."

"Hey, hey, that lint's paying your salary."

"Ha. Don't I know it."

"Winter's done with so I can't say as I'd mind the boot. Thought I'd get something with the crafters up in Old City."

"Can't see that being cushy."

"Naw, naw, hear they're pretty good."

"Really? Huh. Well. Let me know if that turns out that way. I'm having trouble making ends meet myself."

"Sure."

"Here, down this. Your sweetheart gave you an extra roll."

"Ha. Thanks."

"And don't spill it this time or you definitely will be hunting jobs rather than overly-inquisitive guests."

"That weren't me. Benny, that was."

"Sure, sure."

A pebble hits my head.

I look around to see Quinn in the window frame, gesturing at the glass marble resting next to me. I pick it up and climb back outside.

"I thought this thing broke on hard surfaces," I say.

She covers a laugh. "Exception."

#

With the third floor cleaned out as much as Quinn wanted, we checked the rest of the second story windows. Same thing. The master of the house was taking all precautions. For the security outside, it didn't seem likely anyone had been here before, but I'm a simple digger.

Quinn takes us for a closer look at the gathering. The balcony has seven guests, unwinding out in the chill while liquor and pipe-smoking heat them from within. Leaning against the railing. Chatting. Laughing. Quietly enjoying the music from the room.

Recognizable atmosphere.

Still, too subdued for me. I'd prefer Darvin's.

"Rafters," Quinn remarks, a little excited.

"That's a good idea *how*?"

Climbs upwards again, takes me by the hand and refuses to let go. Her fingers a tender, snug vice. Crouches at the edge, ducks her head under. Satisfied. Lets go of me and says:

"Come."

Quinn drops off the roof.

We're so close to the guests, I don't dare protest verbally. I give as fierce a glare as I can. She smiles. Shrugs. Offers a hand to steady my unarguable pursuit.

While the lights below lick at us, leaving sharp-edged shadows gnawing at the ceiling, the rafters are hidden enough

269

to allay my worries of being seen. Those have been replaced now by an intense dread of plunging into their midst.

Good thing we're both sure-footed.

Now we can get a good look at the party.

And it's not exactly what I expected. I'm not accustomed to the rich. I imagined fancy dresses and garb, multi-layered everything, frills, shiny flare, an assortment of outward showiness. It's true, the cut of their clothing is noticeably better than mine, yet… where's the outlandishness?

I have to ask.

"Quinn," I whisper, "are they rich?"

Nodding. "Mm."

"Is what rich looks like in my head a cliche, or…?"

Thinking. Puts palms together. "Businesspeople."

That clicks.

So it's a gathering of the economic movers. Now that she says so, I sense the undercurrent to this ostensibly gala celebration: an agitated, unvoiced constraint.

Jokes are told.

Clapping hands and chuckling voices never rise above a certain pitch.

Statements are made.

Nodding heads and shaking fingers never move at any kind of extreme.

No one is truly relaxed. Crossed legs. Crossed arms. A hand positioned against the lower lip. No sitting or standing still. Always some movement. A twitch. A shifting of weight. Eating. Drinking. It's delicious. It's wonderful. It's *mechanical*. Occupying, occupied, filling the gap, any gap. Trying to find peace within a chaotic jumble of a score of people, each one doing something else.

I look for the musicians and find no one. I think back to the music in the theatre, how it was piped in, and before I can nudge Quinn and speak up, there it is: an unassuming chest off to one corner, propped on an end table, popped open and eliciting a crisp, complex tune from its strange innards.

I can make out at least four separate instruments, but how have they been compressed into a space no larger than a sack of rice?

Quinn is watching it too, spellbound in her own Quinn-like way.

"Kinda bizarre, huh?"

"… beautiful."

"We're not going to perch up here all night, correct?"

"… no."

Reluctantly, she goes.

There are plenty of pockets to be picked on that floor and that's not all. The spread is a mouth-watering sight, the sprawling table surely dipping in the center as laden as it is. Pungent aromas, sweet and spicy, pervade the air, a kind of invisible, inviting fog. I'm glad Sik isn't here. Between that and Quinn's newly-claimed casks in the cellar, we'd never leave.

Where the rafters penetrate the wall on the other end, a crawlspace leads out. Our overhead walkway splits off left and right; however, it ends abruptly down both corridors. We'll have to risk the carpeted hallways one more time.

She charges me with jumping down and opening one window while she gets the other. When the hallway perpendicular to this one is clear, I shoot her a thumbs-up.

She holds up three fingers.

Then two.

Then one.

We drop. I crack the window open and dart outside.

Squinting back through the frosted glass, but I can't see Quinn. She never said what came next, so I decide to wait for her. I lean against the wall. It's a strange kind of run, screwing around someone's home. In practice, it's not all that different from a dig. Not substantially.

But, shit, if it isn't grinding my nerves to pulp…

Plenty of hiding spots in a cemetery. Hardly anything down these hallways for the living that stretch near enough forever. Better than a catacomb. If not for the windows, I'm unsure how Quinn and Jackal would deal with it. The side of a bed? Under a table? In a closet? It works. Slapdash though it may seem to me, the uninitiated.

Hell. When someone lights upon us and we're both of us in a grave, Sik and I cover the excavation with the tarp and keep ourselves as silent as the corpse we stand atop.

That's probably the equivalent of the girls holding up a sheaf of wallpaper and not moving when someone enters the room.

"Ah, damn," I growl.

"Hm?"

"We have to get a new tarp too."

Quinn's lips move to the side in thought. She pats the satchel hanging across her chest.

Stifled clank of coins.

"A fair response. You win," I say, raising my hand.

She pulls me up, nods. Opens her mouth, eyes sparkling, then changes her mind and says nothing. Nods to herself, places a hand on the window.

Back to work.

#

This floor was hectic. The majority of the rooms were set in the middle, so our window-reliance was no longer an easy out. Also, the servants came clattering back and forth, new dishes and bottles replaced by dirty plates and empty containers, tableware jangling and chiming at each step. Keeping tabs on them wasn't difficult. It was the not-so-chatty guards whose strides were drowned out in that clamor we had to be paranoid for.

Quinn started using a pocket mirror to glance around corners, or out doorways, before we fled.

In the roomy library that descended to the first floor, we found breathing space. And in good time too. Its entrance was visible down three hallways and we couldn't be sure when or where anyone would appear, so when the lock turned out more difficult than first glance, sweat started streaking down my back in torrents. We threw ourselves inside right when someone came out a nearby room we had yet to ransack.

Our lungs screamed to pant.

We forced the breaths to be slow, unfulfilling. Pushed against the doorway out of fear, even though Quinn relocked the doors the moment they were shut.

Now, in the lull between frantic heartbeats, we dally with the shelves and flip through the books.

Quinn pockets one occasionally.

"Worth anything?" I ask.

"Mmnn." Shakes her head no.

And again. "Worth anything?"

"Mm." Runs a finger down the spine.

"I have this feeling you'll be spending a lot of time rummaging this room."

Her smile of pleasure…

"*Stop, thief!*"

… disappears.

Quinn whirls. Hand clutching a secreted weapon. And—

Relents. Ponytail drooping. Arms slack.

The fallen book slaps the floor.

"Gotcha!" Jackal jeers.

"Ur… urnnnn…" or something like that strains Quinn's throat.

"Oi oi oi," Jackal bites her lip, "such a hot look ya gave me, yeah?"

"Told you," Quinn whispers, no louder than the pages turning at her feet, "not to do that."

"Aww, but I like it."

"I told you."

Jackal's eyes flash around at everything in the room except Quinn. That vacant and shifting expression searching for another stupid crack, mouth forming a smile somewhere in between mirth and pain as she casts about for the proper words. It settles on a weird, fake grin, twitching in the cheeks, a melted mask, plastered.

Finally, she tries to lock gazes with Quinn -- whose averted face refuses.

"Oi…"

"Useless dross," Quinn swears at the book.

Silence.

Jackal dashes to Quinn and enfolds her in a tight hug.

"Quinn, please don't be mad with me. It was a joke. Ya know I forget. I'm sorry. I'm sorry. Don't be angry, Quinnzy. I'm sorry."

Quinn hasn't moved.

But after a lengthy pause, she slowly raises her arms in an embrace. Reserved yet forgiving. She gently pushes Jackal back and reaches up to wipe away the tears leaking from the corners of her remorseful eyes. Jackal hangs her head a little, then bends down to pick up the book. Returns it, then places her hands over Quinn's. They look into each other's eyes, a complicated emotion.

I clear the awkward atmosphere with my throat.

"Is Sik down there?"

Glancing over the balustrade.

"Nope, she's underground," Jackal says, finding her pep again. "Ah, ha ha…" Tugs on a twintail. "That sounded real bad, huh? Naw, naw, Sik got a headache so she went back for a snack break."

"I better head back too then."

"Okay, man. Prob'ly best if ya go through the storehouse again. We're like on the opposite side from here to the cellar and damn! it's busy downstairs."

I wave at the tall windows. "Can I get out from these?"

"Ya guys window-hoppin'? We weren't so lucky. Y'know, the outside patrols. Nope, I can't figure out the windows in here. Gonna havta backtrack."

Quinn listens at the door, opens each side a crack and checks with a mirror. Nods.

"You're good, Red." Jackal shoves my shoulder. "Don't get caught!"

"You too," I say.

I hasten to the closest unlocked window and start working my way over the eaves. I'm sure Jackal and Quinn are planning their attack of the second floor and, unquestioningly, that expensive box containing music.

Wonder what kind of profit a thing like that would turn…

#

The grounds are a bit more active now; nevertheless, I reach the tunnels without much hassle. Only when I stand at the staircase and its unseen landing that I realize I didn't remember I'd need the lantern.

And Sik isn't with our gear.

"Ah, hell."

I think about staying put, but why? She finds something, she'll be likely enough to simply hang out there.

I gather everything up, hopefully not missing anything, and start looking for her. Feel my way along the walls… floors all even, so no fear of tripping, though… damn fool neglecting the obvious. I think of the sunstone I once scorned.

Rusty brain already.

Should have thought of that.

This is no catacomb though, so it isn't long until I spot a hint of lantern-light swinging merrily side to side.

"'Bricked up stone to stone, bury bodies low. Sealing all the crevices with nowhere left to go. Stop the eyes, bind the hands, words unsaid: sing we now the names of the dead,'" she recites.

I think about pulling Jackal's feint. Bad idea in the dark. She'd freak and wouldn't stay a hand at the last second as Quinn did.

"Pumpkin King," I say.

She snorts. "The hell's that?"

"Didn't know what to say to not make you jump."

"Pumpkin *Cat* King, Red."

Rolls eyes, hands me the lantern.

"What is a cat anyway?" I ask.

"I dunno. Some little animal the author invented. Think rabbit with short ears and longer tail."

"Strange."

She shrugs. "It's funny."

"So you tell me."

"But the plot thickens when you apply enough heat… like porridge."

"I get it, but that's a weird example," I say. "Anything yet?"

"Actually, yes!" Claps hands. "Found a *my-steeeer-i-ous* doorway."

"How mysterious?"

"Very!"

I glance around. "What, and you left it?"

Knocks on her own head. "I'm practicing mental mapping. To be like you."

"So you can take wrong turns and get sealed in Ensbryng too?"

"Eh heh, that was *different* and you normally don't do that."

"Well, thanks for the confidence. Anyways, good work."

"Proactive!" she cheers. Changes tone right after. "I think I'm lost."

"Oh."

"I did say I was practicing."

"Well, keep at it," I tell her.

She responds by puffing up her cheeks at me.

Despite a minor relapse to obliviousness, she notes a few familiar areas and we find ourselves in the cellar yet again. I mention my forgetting the lantern.

"Should we wait here or at that storeroom? Jackal said it was busy on ground floor."

"Yeah, it was. Pretty exciting! Did you like it? You guys climbed the roof? Was it fun?"

"Umm..." I'm thrown off by the overexcited chatter. "I guess so. Different, but fun in its own way."

Sik takes a handful of something out of a pocket. "I stole a silverware set," she says. "From a platter that was going upstairs!" Cackling. "Caught a whiff of the food from the kitchen. Holy shit, it smelled glorious. Let's have fish soon?"

"Ah. We could do that."

"Yeah! That's great. Fuck, it made me so starved. Wanna lick those plates." Curls her tongue around the dull side of a dinner knife. "Oh, right, these weren't used. Damn."

"Sik, are you okay?"

"Huh?" Blinks a few times. "Oh, no, I'm... kinda hyper. Is all."

"I can see that," I say. "So, wait where?"

"We know what Quinn will insist on. Do you think Jackal can dissuade her?"

If Quinn is still a little upset with Jackal then...

"Not tonight."

"Here's good then," she says.

We kill time.

I tell Sik of my adventure. How we were almost caught a couple of times. How Quinn's quickness saved our asses. Well, my ass at any rate. I'm sure it would have been much smoother without having to keep track of me lumbering about. Still, we pulled it off.

Then Sik narrates her own tale. How she used a mirror to peek around corners while Jackal picked locks. How

Jackal pieced the sound of a coming guard out from among servants' blather. Sik, a bit panicked, slammed into the doorframe before it closed shut. Jackal hid in the closet; Sik under the bed. The guard poked his head in, but left believing it was nothing.

We pause a time or two when a servant shuffles downstairs and hunts an exceptionally elusive vintage.

Party doesn't seem to be winding down…

After the last search, causing us to play an inadvertent game of hide-and-seek between the casks, Sik says, "For the amount of guests, you don't think they're after a pickpocket?"

"*There was no need!*"

So Jackal declares, scaring the shit out of us both.

"Did you not learn your lesson!?" I ask.

"Shiiiiii— cut that out!" Sik yelps.

"We want to, but a crowd? Sheesh, ya havta be *inside* for that. Like I said, pity it's no costume thing."

"Mm."

"Ready to go?" Jackal asks.

"But we gotta have the main course," Sik says.

"Told ya, if we can't pick their pockets, there is no way you're gettin' at the grub."

"She means she found a locked passageway," I translate. "Maybe burial."

"You're kiddin'. I thought we'd have to pull every book in the library or som'."

"I think that's only in stories, Jackal."

"I did it once!" she claims.

"Is that true?" I ask Quinn.

"Mmnn."

"Feh, spoilsport."

Sik shutters and unshutters the lantern repeatedly until she has our attention.

"Less talk more walk!"

#

She leads us through a recess at the back of a room packed with barrels. Beyond the brick and stone architecture, a shaft dolven into the umber bedrock corkscrews deeper underground. At the base, there is a single metal door.

Jackal squints into the keyhole, jams her tools inside and sets to work.

Clammy, stale air kills our desire to chat.

If anything, that's a sign we've found something.

We settle in.

Jackal concedes the lock to Quinn without a word.

Soon, it's apparent Quinn herself finds it unworkable.

If we had a proper pickax, we might be able to widen the seal around the door...

Sik steps up.

"Hey, Sik, if Quinn couldn't—"

The lock clicks instantly.

She thrusts the heavy, groaning metal wide.

"I..." Jackal, stupefied.

Quinn applauds quietly, smiling.

"I loosened it for ya!" Jackal says.

"Thought this looked important," Sik notes. Shakes an old key, rusty at the handle.

I rub my temples.

"Not surprised," I say. "I'm not."

"When did you find that?" Jackal demands.

"Under that pompous-looking desk." Sik grins victory. "Did good, didn't I? The neophyte becomes the virtuoso!"

"Careful ya don't cut yourself on those big words," Jackal mutters.

"You're one to talk," I say.

"Oi! This Pick-On-Jackal Day? 'Cause I didn't hear the message-runners announce nothin'!"

Quinn playfully pulls on her twintails. "Not listening?" she teases.

"You too, Quinn? Geez."

I step inside and the unmistakable hint of old death worms its way into my nostrils. This is it. The passage extends to an unlit brazier, then splits off into three hallways with alternating vaults and alcoves.

"Creepy," Jackal breathes.

"This your first?"

"It is. Wow. Are there cursed down here?"

"Don't even say that." Sik elbows her.

"Ow! I'm only askin'."

Voice hushed for fear of waking one.

"Do you get lost, Jackal?" I ask.

"I can't do hedge mazes without cheatin' if that's what ya mean."

"Remember where you are and how you came in. That's the first and last rule needed for a crypt or the like."

"Okay, yeah, I mean that's what I do for a job, right? Still... do I have to worry 'bout... *them*, Red?"

"I don't know about that."

"Red thinks it's a huge conspiracy that everyone in the Sovereignty is in on."

Jackal sighs in relief. "Oh okay."

"But that doesn't mean he's correct. Means he and me haven't bumped into one yet."

"Big Sis really isn't good with this kind of thing, sweetie, so..."

"If I'm frightening you," Sik states matter-of-factly, "it's to have you keep your wits alert. See something scary? Run. We'll be right with you."

Jackal swallows. "Will a..." Swallows again. "Will one of *those* be... too?"

"Dunno. Let's all be careful and not find out, agreed?"

"Will do..."

"Mm."

"End of the line." I give Jackal the lantern. Having a task should calm her nerves. "Crack this one?"

"Sounds good, Red." Sik chisels the antiquated mortar.

I give the corners a good whack with the sharper end of the mattock to loosen the covering. We grip the makeshift handholds and wrench it off. Dust plumes and grains fall as abrasive stone grates against abrasive stone.

"Good thing we robbed the place before makin' that noise," Jackal says.

"They shouldn't hear anything," I say.

Sik shrugs. "Servants milling around the cellar might."

"Shit!"

We both turn to Jackal.

"What is it?" we say.

"Q-Q-Q-Quinn?" Jackal spins, finds no one else in the shadows but us.

"Relax. She probably left to shut the door a little."

"But what if somethin' else is down here? Or the door gets stuck? Or or," she says, "seriously *please* do not play tricks on me, ya two!"

I put my arm around her. "Jackal, calm down already. We'd take the piss with you, but we're not interested in giving you a heart attack. We'll wait until Quinn's back."

Though I say so, I hardly need to. Quinn pops back into the light without a word, discovers us waiting for her and gives a polite nod. Jackal is fine now. Then she moans, "We waited with our backs turned to the grave…"

"A little death never hurt no one!" Sik says.

"Also, it's a vault," I explain. "Graves are—"

"Gah! I don't care anymore! Just dig or whatever and let's get outta here and back home!"

The corpse inside takes no heed of our conversation, its ears having thoroughly rotted off.

"That reminds me," Sik says as she lifts up the shroud, "would you give offerings to your family if you're burying them at home?"

"If you liked them, I can't see it being any different."

"Yeah, but it may be a '*wellll*, they're only downstairs… I can offer something *tomorrow*' and then you forget about it during dinnertime and later you're like 'but it's kinda *collllld* and they aren't *going anywhere*, so *mayyyyyybe* next week' and so on."

"That is the laziest burial ever."

"This guy's coming up empty, Red."

"There has to be at least one generation gave a crap."

"More light, Jackal."

"I haven't seen a corpse before," Jackal admits, leaning in with the light. "This is gross."

Sik perks up. "Ah! Here's some stuff."

Jackal takes a cautious sniff of the vault.

"Do ya guys smell after this?"

"You get used to it," Sik says merrily.

"Unnghh."

"Okay that's this one," I say.

We get into the groove of things and crack open the next vaults in succession. The bodies are comparatively fresher the more we approach the brazier. Sik and I are thinking the same thing, but refuse to voice it.

Don't jinx it.

Never during a job.

"Your turn," I say after closing up the vault.

"Pass!" Jackal says.

"Which do you want?" I gesture at the nearest two.

"You're not even listenin' are ya…"

Quinn covers her mouth in thought, clearly interested in doing the dirty work if Jackal won't.

Jackal appropriates the mattock before she can decide.

"Down for keeps, then," she says. "In case I have to smack somethin' in the face." Frowns. "Or what's left of one."

Complain as she might, Jackal clearly enjoys the carnage. I keep charging her with standing still until Quinn breaks the seal properly with the chisel, but she won't listen.

"Look." Finally fed up. "If you're going to steal the wrong tool, you're damn well gonna learn how to use it right. It is not made for getting through the mortar!"

"Too much waitin'! Let me strike it a few times and it'll save time. Ah!" She stops, beholding an epiphany.

"What now."

"So that's why ya needed the pickax. Then ya could break the cover in one blow!"

Some epiphany. "That isn't it at all."

Once inside, she isn't so enthusiastic.

"I don't want to smell like that. Unngh! His face is... flappy."

"Get in there with the light."

"Bully..."

If Quinn is ill at ease too, she doesn't show it. She feels around the limbs, looking into the shroud just as Sik did. Occasionally, she turns back to me and I nod in approval. She smiles. Other times, when her hands pause, I lean in and give a hint or explain how to do it better.

"How do you hide your trace?" she asks me afterwards.

I smile.

"You already were. Careful, deliberate movements. Don't stir up the dust."

"I see."

"The shroud mostly holds the corpse together once all the connective tissue decomposes. If you have to move parts, put them back how you found them and rewrap the body."

"Like this."

"Exactly."

"Oh, nice!" Sik says.

"You're a natural, Quinn," I say.

She blushes. "Mm."

"Admittedly, this is perfectionist. No one will bother checking the vault unless it's distinctly been tampered with. Evidence that you've broken *in* is the main thing to avoid."

"Actually, that would be 'being caught'," Sik corrects.

"You're talking to Quinn, Sik."

Quinn backhands my chest.

It's that uncharacteristic bashfulness that comes out once in a while that I find so amusingly cute.

"That mortar stuff isn't evidence enough?" Jackal asks, scratching her head and then immediately making a sickened face. "M… my hair…"

"No, it is."

"I like gathering it up at the end and hiding it behind the stiff," Sik says.

"But ya haven't been doin' that."

Sik sticks out her tongue. "Didn't feel like it."

"Get to it," I tell Jackal.

"But she—!"

"Fine fine, I'll go get it and put it with yours. Deal?"

"I don't understand what I'm gettin' out of such a deal," Jackal gripes.

I oversee the hiding of the mortar and the resealing of the vault. Cross my arms pompously, assume the haughty stature of an Executioner. "Seal it as permanent as death itself, lasses! No diggers getting through this rock!"

"Aye aye!" Sik salutes.

Quinn salutes me too.

Jackal rolls her eyes.

"We used to go so far as reapplying a fake mortar, but that wastes time. Best to simply take a pouch of baking flour with a sieve attached and sprinkle it on your footprints or anywhere else you've disturbed the dust," I explain. "And we'll be skipping that bit."

"What, more laziness?" Jackal asks.

I shrug. "Nothing for it. Executioners have ours."

Quinn lifts the chisel and hammer, smiles.

Jackal cocks her head. "What is it?"

"More," she requests.

#

The family that settled its roots here surely must have expected the world to last a while longer than it did. Scarcely more than half of the chambers have been filled. I can't say I have a decent guess on how many further will be occupied before the end, but I'm curious what yours is.

Thanks to Jackal's lack of focus, we chanced upon a chest in one of the empty vaults. Trust a thief to reflexively check for false walls. At the back, there was a compartment that stored the hidden box.

"Heavy," Quinn notes, though nothing inside jangles from the shaking.

"See, now this is the kind of diggin' I can get into," Jackal says. "No bodies, just loot. Much cleaner."

"Why don't you try this one, Red."

Sik hands me a lockpick.

It's definitely a complex lock. After that storehouse's entrance it's to be expected. I close my eyes and try to see the tumblers in my head, but it's too complicated to keep sense of. I lean in, prodding the thing and getting so close my nose—

The mattock slices through the air and slams against the lock.

"WHAT THE FUCK ARE YOU DOING, CRAZY WOMAN!?" I shout.

Sik laughs and runs away before I can land a hit.

I almost had it too.

I pierce the lock again and find the spot I was in. There, yes. It's a screwy one. Almost… almost… No. There's a trick to this one I'm not… feeling… out… Maybe it's one of those counterfeits: impossible locks that frustrate you to the point that you'll never think to check the other side for a secret way to—

Clang!

"PLEASE STOP DOING THAT!" I roar.

But Sik just laughs and laughs.

I leave the intricate labor to Quinn and Jackal while I grind my fists against the pressure points on Sik's head.

"Ahhhh! Aagghhh!! Give! Give! Give! Stop!"

"I already nearly lost my eye once! Apologize!"

"If-if-if it means much, I feel bad about not feeling bad."

"You little..."

"Agggh! I don't mean to be a bitch, I'm gruuua-*owww*! I'm just good at it!"

"I'm going to make porridge out of your brains for breakfast!"

"Eno-*owww*-ugh! Apologizing! I apologize! I'm sorry!"

I let go.

"You take your jokes way, way too far sometimes, Sik."

"*Owowow*, I know. I can't help it. It's just funny in my head and I... urrr-*oww*, wanna make everyone laugh."

"Har."

"Also, I wanted to teach you the lesson I've learned."

"And that is?"

Holds a finger up.

"A gravedigger should always keep her eyes open!"

"I had you girls to watch over me. I didn't have to worry about being snuck up on. So don't pull that crap again."

"Sorry, Red."

"It's fine."

"I really did think it was funny."

"I might too tomorrow," I say. "But don't ask."

#

Jackal has given up. "It's no use."

"Neither of you can get it?" I ask.

Quinn is sulking in the corner.

"Let's take it home and worry about it later," Sik says.

"Once we do that, he'll know someone's been down here. Whether he checks the vaults or not is immaterial at that point," I say.

"Not like we're coming back," Sik counters. "Least, not until one of his family members snuffs it."

"Maybe for ya two, yeah?" Jackal leans against the winged, headless statue in the alcove. "We like to squeeze a place a bit at a time. And this place? Oi, it's an opened bank vault." Sighs. "With all the guests, we thought to take one bigger piece too."

"That box that made music," I say.

Quinn looks over her shoulder at me, then hides again. Jackal chews the inside of her cheek.

"So... we take this!" Sik says. "A guest will be suspected. Same difference."

"Wrong." Jackal's humor plummets. "Got a glance at the shindig. Everyone knows everyone, *him* most of all. Sure, there were wanderers. That happens. Unlock the door and find the box? Wouldn't happen. Oh, and find the key and smuggle this thing out? Unseen? Were I that good, I tell ya I'd retire tomorrow."

Sik thinks. "Could be his life savings in there..."

Jackal nods. "Or a wad of cotton."

"But it's heavy."

"Heavy cotton then."

"Try for both targets," I suggest.

"Getting' late, Red," Jackal says. "And we havta put the key back and get ya two outta here. And ya havta fill that hole, right? I don't see us havin' time to do all that and get home safe."

"A fetus," Sik says.

"Ehh?"

"In that box. His bastard stillborn is in there."

"That's... oi, that's foul!"

"It's a family crypt and we don't know what's in it." Sik shrugs. "It fits, doesn't it?"

"The inference or the kid?" I ask.

"Both?"

"Guys," Jackal brushes away the banter. "We gotta decide."

"I say we leave it and hide our tracks. We can always return another day," I say.

"Take it. Plant the key. Frame a guest. Or a guard," Sik says.

"I don't like chance." Jackal kicks the chest. "I wanna swipe the music-box. That's unique enough to be priceless," she says.

"Quinn?" I glance over at her.

Quinn is unresponsive.

"Right," I say, "so we each have different plans."

"Impasse," she finally says.

"I'm lost on this one, Quinn," Jackal says.

"Hm."

"Should we take what's in our pockets and run?" I ask.

Quinn shakes her head no. Points at the steel box that looms between us, the physical manifestation of our indecision. "This."

"He'll find out," Jackal presses. "That music-box might be off to the bank by mornin'. If he doubles security, that cellar will be impenetrable too."

Quinn frowns.

"There might not be a next time."

"I know."

Jackal cradles the chest, bending backwards ever so slightly to counterbalance. "Changin' vote, then."

I step forward. "I'll carry that."

"Thanks, Red," Jackal smirks, "but every woman's gotta carry her own burden. This one's mine tonight. So ya better be worth more than the placenta what spat ya out," she tells the contents.

Quinn extends her hand to Sik who, not being entirely well-versed in Quinn's silent language, takes a handful of long seconds herself to figure out what she wants.

Quinn flashes the key at us, stuffs a pocket with a scoopful of dust, urges us out, locks the door and runs off.

"Guess she liked my idea too," Sik says.

"Ya go first," Jackal tells her. "If ya wanna help, Red, catch me if I fall. Time to go home and sleep!"

#

Quinn never told us how it went, but assured us she wasn't caught. Upset over choosing the unpickable lock to the music, I bet. She came waddling to the hole under the wall where we waited -- two bottles held in each hand, precariously clutched with fingers -- while hiccupping. A bittersweet scent emanated from her.

She went straight to bed.

"Ya can stay over again." Jackal rubs puffy eyelids, scowls at the false dawn rising behind us.

"I wanna take a shower before I sleep," Sik says.

Jackal wakes up at that. "I forgot!" Makes a disappointed face at the bedroom and the bathroom beyond.

"Come take a shower," Sik offers.

"Can I? Okay."

"Quinn didn't, did she?" I ask.

"Huh?" Then she catches my meaning. "Oh balls." Disappointment becomes revulsion. "Tomorrow is laundry day…"

#

One minute after the steamy water strikes the basin, they're both giggling. Then the sexual harassment really begins and Jackal soon starts telling Sik off and ordering her to wash her own damn by damn back. When they're out, Sik's a little dazed.

"Jackal with hair down," I remark. "That's a first."

"It's really that odd?" she asks, drying it with a towel.

I shrug. "Different."

"Never seen Quinn that way have ya?"

"Nope."

Jackal smiles softly. "Super-beautiful and long. It combs so perfectly too. I'm always jealous. Mine goes all tangly."

"And then you accidentally tear some out," Sik says.

Jackal laughs, sheepish. "So true. I hate that."

#

Spring blossomed.

The box remained locked.

We hit a few other residences over the weeks, attempting to nail down that second dig. Varying success. More loot, sure. A couple of run-ins with the law. Jackal skinned her knees but good, Quinn sprained an ankle, and I have a new scar to proudly display if I wasn't a little shamed by its location. Sik was fine, of course. Still, we never did find that final crypt or whatever it was. It's possible we stumbled upon it or walked over it at some point, but if it was there it must have been moved or filled in.

Quinn said the Executioners probably got to it and I was inclined to agree.

As it was, the weather had grown temperate and with it the guards were now attentive and looked at every shadow, whether it contained us or not, with suspicion. People get greedy and although we may have had the run of things when the fog and remnants of winter were present, we weren't the only ones out now. A little desperation breeds much competition.

Now was the lull.

Picker and Stealer are stuffed, monetarily speaking. The fences were like famished boars -- too delirious to remember their last meal -- being thrown slop, except we were lobbing them pecan pies and baskets of truffles. There was much goodwill. Though not enough for me to sneak that blasted cup into the mix…

But it hardly matters now. The buzz on a few pieces is circling around and even if they don't sell, we're stable on money through next winter. I kick my feet up, that tends to be my preferred position these days, and enjoy the balmy breeze whistling through the windows.

It's a good feeling.

#

Sik is napping. Jackal and Quinn are running at the water's edge, throwing a ball back and forth. The rolling hills are green on this side of the water and farther south I can just make out the terraced rice fields.

Some perennials, mostly to the north, died during winter and the patches of brown and gray are an eyesore. The Sovereignty used to expend an alarming portion of tax revenue to recultivate such plots of land, but it never worked. That's how it is now: certain bits of earth waste away and never regrow. Eventually, they planted evergreens to block the view instead. As you can see, those have been disfigured into trees of unwillingly deciduous natures. I can see them reviewing how draping the bare, tortured limbs with ivy and covering the ground with open planters teeming with bracken might work next.

We may lack things once plentiful decades past, but there's no shortage of existentialism.

Grass tickles Sik's nose.

She flinches and, in stages, wakes up.

"Where…" she slurs a minute later.

I smile. "Hey."

"Huh…"

"What's wrong?" I ask.

"A… Urnnnmm…"

"What's that mean?"

"Had a dream…"

"Any good?"

"Sky was… so blue…" Rubs her eyes. "I've never seen it… so blue…"

"It's pretty blue right now," I say.

Not a cloud in sight.

She squints upwards. "No it's… not. It's not… the same."
Closes her eyes again.

"Are you going back to sleep?"

"No."

"Oh."

"I can't."

"Want to go play with the girls?"

Doesn't answer. Turns away and covers her face.

"Sik?"

"Nothing's fine," she whispers.

#

City rabbits finally reappear.

Where they burrow or how they survive the deepness is one of those urban legends. Jackal and Sik are cuddling one with a spotty rump and a half-white-half-tan face.

"We must champion the bunny," they agree.

"Why?" I ask. "They are everywhere. I can't walk for fear of flattening the little buggers. Hardly need any help from us doing whatever it is they do."

"So heartless, Red!" Jackal hugs the rabbit, cheek-to-cheek, pulling it out of Sik's grip.

"All they do is flop around," I say.

"As if they need do more!"

"And yes, they keep the streets weeded, but… Leave them alone and stop picking them up all the time!" But Sik ignores me and scoops up another one anyways.

I turn to Quinn for help.

"Qui— Nnah! Even you!" I cry out.

A little black bunny with a single lop finishes a crunchy sprig. It and Quinn look back at me. One of them blushes.

"Precious creature," she says.

#

With the commencement of spring's markets, we invest heavily in the most expensive, nutritious mushroom cultures available. Sik is crazy. Okay. *Crazier* than normal. From stall to stall she flies, haggling and dealing and somehow getting discounts usually reserved for wholesale.

"If yer able to go down to fifty for the bunch, why not throw in the other for less?" she probes.

"The thing is—" the seller starts.

"Say ya do that, I'll go ahead and drop thirty for that dozen, twenty-five for the tubers, and another for the basket. I can't carry with only hands, ya know!"

Though she says so, I'm the one exerting the effort.

And it works.

Her mind is incredibly adept for finances, calculations worked out between the time her sharp tongue starts waggling and her teeth click shut. She hates it though. *Boring fucking numbers*, she'll say. Yet sometimes I'll wake in the morning and see her slumped over a paper crammed with scrawled formulae and arrows I don't understand. Apparently it isn't gibberish. *Gets stuck in my head and won't come out unless I do something*, she'll say. That's a thing I think I understand: my thoughts feedback loop when engrossed in novel architecture and I can't really explain why or what I'm even thinking.

Definitely her oddest quirk though.

And definitely one that helped whenever Bors was short-changing us.

"Please come again!" the pretty shop girl calls.

The sun is bright.

Colorful banners crack in the wind.

Depression of winter no longer has the heart of the city in its vice, and people are so preoccupied with living that none acknowledge the guards thronging the plaza -- no matter how much they press in or look over the shoulders and at the hands of each and every shopper. Not that thieves don't come here. We see Jackal and Quinn across the hubbub purchasing bread and wheels of cheese. They simply come here legally.

It's a hopeful time for Old City.

Message-runners, most freed of official duties for the season, are nipping every which way on errands for common citizens, delivering correspondence, carrying parcels, some barking out the scripts the local shopkeepers and stall-owners have given, and each one adds a new pastel color to the gaiety.

One woman with spiky hair and about nine pastel scarves at her hip, a dizzying rainbow whipped about by a lively gust, actually shimmied up an unused flagpole and cupped her mouth.

"Fer the best *dregs*, jaunt yer keisters through Tunnel Street and visit Gavergam!" she advertises. Rereads the paper. "*Eggs!*" she shouts. And to herself: "Does no one practice penmanship!?"

The crowd attracted by her display laughs and a good few probably listen.

I keep my eyes open for a runner with flaxen-colored hair, but don't see anyone. Sik comments that it's nice to find them without *You-Know-Who's* livery. She juggles one potato. It's fine, I tell myself; it's an expansive city.

But it vividly brings to mind the deepness.

And a stolen rice cake.

#

"Let's expand our house," she said.

Such an offhand, effortless comment.

She can say so and run off to invite the girls to dinner, but I'm the one that has to stay here and fixate on it over and over, stirring the stew she prepared running through so many potential blueprints wonder how much the cost if I can construct it myself and add a little extra salt, that's what she likes Quinn's favorite staple after all, dash of pepper, where would we even knock it through without invoking the eye of the city planner and her architects and—!

"Is it ready yet?" she calls. "I put it on early enough I thought."

Six boots clomping clomping, shuffle, pulled off.

Thomp thomp.

"About what you mentioned," I tell her when she takes the bowls from the cabinet.

"Huh?"

She already forgot!

#

If building upwards… If we knocked a doorway between the fireplace and the window, we could install a balcony with a stairway leading to the roof. A sundeck would be nice for summer… could eat outside, have some drinks… watch the candles being lit from here out to the docks, stars popping into existence one after another.

Or we could build a raised planter up there. Potatoes? Being a little more self-reliant would be good.

Potatoes would work…

I pull out a stack of papers and try to find wherever it is that Sik stashed the inkstone.

#

When I'm finished she isn't there to ask, so I wander over to Jackal and Quinn's.

No one answers when I knock. I let myself in.

"Hey, is Sik—"

Sik wheels around, arms spread.

"The baby was dead when I got here!" she yelps.

"The— what?"

"Oh, it's you, Red. You scared me."

"Who did you think it'd be?"

"Guards or Execrations or anyone else."

"Why?"

Jerks a thumb. "We cracked the box."

"Seriously?"

"Very seriously."

"What's in it?" I'm all but salivating on my way over.

"I was waiting for Jackal to come back before looking."

"Thought we'd have to resort to melting the damn thing," I say.

"Yeah, I know, right? Quinn was all set on returning to the scene of the crime to scrounge the key. Kept feeling we were almost there, ya know?"

"Sure. I thought I had it back in the crypt."

"Right, so, Jackal, so Jackal has the thought—"

"That's a first."

She hits me. "*Has the thought* of commissioning special, extra-thin lockpicks. Thought we could caaaarefully work them in alongside the normal ones and get at the more difficult tumblers."

"Or snap and jam the lock so it can never be opened again."

"Not like it was doing much different otherwise!"

Quinn yawns from the bedroom.

"Ah, we were too loud," Sik notices.

"'We' she says."

"Anyways, to paraphrase."

"Oh, this will be good."

"I dug around the side on impulse and found secret tumblers! Or, okay, more like switches. That turned. Turn-switches. So, okay, so like the key would be a normal key and yet it would be unusual with... prongs? *on the side*. But! See how wide the lock is and convex? It's faking a style! That throws ya off to the fact it's more complicated than simply tumblers. So by turning those switches with the rest of it in the right way, crack, open we go! Hey, Quinn! Sorry I was loud."

She yawns again, then sleepy eyes catch the open lid.

"Oh."

"Should we peek?" I ask her.

"Wait for Jackal!" Sik demands.

Roughly fifteen minutes pass before we hear her bounding up the steps. "I~ am~ home~" she sings.

Quinn claps excitedly.

"Oi, throwin' a party without me in my own house. Invite me next time, yeah?"

Quinn points at the box.

"Oooh!" Jackal cheers. "I am kissin' whoever did that. Now! Who is the lucky lockpicker?" Licks her lips, arches her fingers to attack.

Quinn gestures to herself.

"There was never any doubt." The predatory Jackal tiptoes closer. "Come here come here!"

Sik jumps in the way. "But I did it."

"Nevermind that. Ya can't escape yer Jackal~!"

Sik pushes Jackal back from her goal. "But-I-was-the-one-did-it!"

"Ehh." She relents, disenchanted. "Quinn, ya were lyin'?"

Quinn nods.

"The truth is—" I say, hands to hips.

"Ya wish, Red," Jackal says. "Ya got it, huh? Well done, sweetie, that was a tough one."

"Everyone helped a little."

Modesty doesn't dampen those proud, shining teeth.

"Mmmmmmm," Jackal kisses her cheek long enough that Sik starts giggling and squirming to get away.

"Let's look!" Sik pulls Jackal towards the chest, takes my hand and pulls me too.

Quinn removes the velvet cloth on top and reveals nothing but another question.

"The hell's that?" Sik asks.

"Um."

Quinn removes the brass cylinder from its snug fit.

I check the interior. There's nothing else inside, no room for hidden compartments, simply the plush covering and skillfully-molded cushions.

"So it's fragile?" I offer. "Fragile's... usually expensive?"

"Hmm, hmm." Sik nods. "No doubt."

"Is it a weapon?" Jackal suggests.

Suddenly, the apparatus elongates. *Thhhk!*

"Don't... don't use it in here, Quinnzy..."

But Quinn merely spins it in random directions. Collapses it. Lengthens it. And it makes a strange sound when she does either. Maybe it's another musical device. She looks through the hole on one end, then—

"Fuck! Don't point that at me!" I dodge away.

She persists.

Before I can tell Jackal to stop her, I see through it: Quinn's eye framed. Nothing happens. I stick my finger inside the other end. Appears harmless enough. She collapses the device once more, then drops one of those glass marbles in. It falls out the other side and into her hand.

"If I'm being honest," Jackal says, "it's kinda..."

She and Sik trade looks.

"Benign."

"Useless."

"Boring."

"It's worth something to someone," I say, "to go to all the trouble to hide it."

"Seems like rot to me," Sik says.

"I... guess we can give Killjoy a gander."

Quinn shrugs at Jackal, puts the thing away.

"Is he in?" I ask.

"Didn't I say?" Raises an eyebrow at me. "Was checkin' if he was back yet. He turned me away. Assistant hadn't arrived yet, he said, and was workin' on projects in the meanwhile. Said I'd pop by next week. Wanna come?"

"Thought I'd pay a visit, but actually..." Scratching my head. "After our last haul, I'm not sure I care anymore."

"Don't go sittin' on that chalice 'till it's not worth scrap, Red."

"Wasn't worth much the first time around," Sik says.

"Yeah, yeah, ya said no one else is touchin' it. And Killjoy, he was pretty piqued, ya recall."

I laugh. "I don't know. Maybe I... simply want someone to lust after what I can do for *them* for a change. Kinda sick of being under the heel of the affluent. Well. What passes for affluent these days. You know what I mean."

"Suit yourself," Jackal says. "Lemme know if ya change your mind, yeah?" Heads towards the cellar. "I'm a little annoyed with what turned out to be in the chest, Quinn, I'm gettin' a drink. Want me to get ya som'?"

Quinn blocks her way and goes into the cellar herself, practically shoving Jackal to keep her from following.

"Really? Still? That girl..." she says.

"So, Sik, about the whole expanding our house thing you brought up before..."

"I did?"

"You did and I was thinking it over."

I hand her the folded paper, explain my ideas and the main one I settled on. She takes it all in with the periodic nod or glance, turns the paper for another point of view, bites her lip, glances again, and nods with understanding at the proposal.

"Ah," she says when I'm done.

"Do you like it? We could drop this off at the local administration's office on the way home."

Makes a funny look. "Red, I just meant, ya know... add some window boxes..."

"Ehh."

"For flowers."

"..."

"Our one at the door died while we were away."

"..."

"It was kinda sad."

"You specifically said 'expand'."

"Thought you'd get what I meant."

299

I take the design back from her.

"We could add window boxes to it…"

She starts nodding. "Yeah, let's do it."

"Yeah?"

"Yeah, I want dahlias."

"Dahlias."

"Yeah, they're cute," she says.

"Right. Dahlias."

"And sunflowers."

"Those are kinda big."

"What are?"

"Sunflowers."

"Are they? Aren't they like this?" She draws an imaginary outline of some small thing in the air. I have no idea what it is, nor can I remember where her fingers traced.

"They're taller than I am."

"Fuck! That's amazing! I want some!"

"Let's see how the dahlias grow first," I hesitate.

"Alright." Taps fingertips together lightly, somewhere between being deep in thought and clapping. "I think it'll be fun."

She smiles.

#

A week later the message-runner knocked at the door.

My proposal was rejected.

'Unapproved' was the official designation.

Still, there was a vaguely encouraging note scribbled on the back that read:

Ladder access to roof would probably be approved. Records show additional weight within building parameters (no metal!). Top of new structure must be angled for rain (resistant to hail (special glass? that's expensive (just cover with removable plywood!)!)!). Cannot be higher than seven feet (even that might be pushing it!). Good luck. :3

And lower: *P.S. window boxes a-ok.*

Which was a good thing.

Since we had already built those.

#

Summer and heat come in waves. The dahlias are doing fine. The potato planter on the roof is all set up. Sik particularly likes that the ladder, situated between fireplace and window, goes up into the... 'greenhouse' is the wrong term, but I refuse to say 'potato room' as Sik refers to it.

She places the vegetable soup and boar steak before me.

"And I didn't burn it this time," she says proudly.

"But is it grunting?"

"I cannot deny that," she says, sitting down. "Be thankful that means it's fresh." Passes a basket of barely-risen rolls.

"You're getting decent at baking, you know."

"Yeah, thanks. I befriended this bakery girl in the market. Gave me some pointers after work."

"I was wondering where you kept running off to."

"Yep."

"Is she a good instructor?" I ask.

"Here." Gives me a spoon and fork. "You get the bigger ones."

"Thanks. So, the lessons are good?"

"Yep. Good stuff," she says.

"You forgot the knife?"

"Huh?"

"The knife."

"Oh yeah, thought," she says, "thought you said something else. Almost done." Finishes slicing a piece of meat. "Here."

"We're sharing?"

"It's fine, isn't it?"

"What happened to the other knife?"

Chewing.

"Mmmm, savory," she notes.

Swallows.

"This is our special set," she explains.

"Didn't know we had one," I mention.

It's shinier than I remember.

Then I recognize it.

"I thought you hawked this?"

It's the silverware set she took during our thieving run.

"Was gonna. Before I did, thought: 'we could use some nice things' and kept it. It's fine?"

"Sure, only I'm surprised."

"Bringing it out for special meals is fun." Sips a spoonful of soup noisily. "Right?"

"Why not?" I say. "On second thought, let's not for visitors. It'll get complicated."

"It'll get hilarious," she laughs. "Let's do that too."

\#

Some nights are balmy, some are chilled. Everyone finds a reason to enjoy it and those that toil under the sun doze where they are able, most of them down by the water where the moon ripples in transit across its twinkling surface. We've never truly had that luxury. Summer is prime digging time and while I prefer the transition seasons best, I can't deny the efficacy.

Searing sunbeams beating down?

Humidity blooming within the forests?

Whether in cover or not, your afternoon-shift guard will be groggy an hour after gloaming.

Dig then.

Actually, I hadn't thought this way before, but it might be the most important time of the year for everyone in the City. They live for the spring, to plant. They await the autumn, to harvest. To store to hope to endure until they reach the new year, and so it goes down the generations in a world where it may be humanly possible to conceive though may no longer be humane. Now comes the rest. Brief yet so needed. So, in that way, that makes this time the most transitory of all.

Sik has been taking me for walks for a change.

I feel like she's scraping for things to fill the normally busy evenings with. I'm not complaining. It's as pleasant as the cool air.

"You've been enjoying these walks," I say.

We're skirting the water, staying on the edge of the city and passing through the docks.

"Yeah, I think so."

"I'm almost too relaxed."

"Really?"

I stretch, grin at her. "Not really."

"Oh."

"You want me to be tense?" I ask.

"No, of course not. Why would I?"

"It was like you were disappointed."

"I want you to have fun, is all."

"I am."

"Me too!" she says rapidly.

I nudge her.

She hits me.

We walk. The water splashes against a nearby watercraft. Another has been hauled up onto rigging of sorts to scour off all the crap that accumulates underwater. Always wondered what was out there on the lake.

Perhaps we'll explore that in a few days.

Rice fields come into view, spiny sprouts impaling the paddies' surfaces like the underside of nailed boards.

Damn. That building project did take way too long…

"How far are we going?"

"How far you wanna go?" she asks.

"I don't mind."

"Have something better to do?"

"Nope."

"Okay."

She sings a shantey and steps, balancing perilously, along a low stone wall. I catch her twice.

"Eh heh, harder than it looks."

I jump up and step along it too, picking up on the note where she fell, but with a sonorous and overdramatic tone.

"—*to olden shores. Ei! Sound the horn, string the bow, drum the drums fathoms low. Play the bones and bid them dance, round about 'till all collapse, dug up, dug up, dug up away!*"

"*And the sea will catch the metal rain that falls to ground away away, merry merry dance we rings, and in the Springtime whispering—*"

"*Sail on, sail on!*" we shout. "*Sail until the tides are gone, float until the rocks have won, and diggers dig with trowel and curse the spate what burials break, sing the wake that drowns all lords: dig them deep on olden shores.*"

The diggers sang without care. The guards ignored their revelry. The Executioners were stuck up in their duns. Still the diggers sang on -- through the bleeding hours, through the flooded fields -- of the sea, of death, of dirt, of dearth, of dreams, of home, of journeys back and journeys on, and ever the clomp of boot, the clap of hand, beat the heart of the music over the streets of Old City and -- pulsing into moonlit shadows -- trailed away as the winds rose up and fell.

#

"Where are you going?" I ask.

"Wanna show you something," she says.

"Something?"

"Somewhere."

"What is it?" I ask.

"Secret."

"Is it going to end with my arm in a sling again?"

"No!"

"I've heard that before."

"When did that even happen?" she wonders.

"It didn't. Just wanted to see what you'd say."

"Red, you're more a jerk than me, I think."

"Is this why we keep going out?" I ask.

"No. Yes."

"Well, which is it?"

"Yes."

"Do I get any hints?"

"Nope."

"Why?"

"Secret."

"Is it really that secret?" I press.

"Secret!"

"This is a lie, isn't it?"

Silence.

She kicks me.

"Ow, fuck! I'm teasing. You don't have to draw blood."

"Sik's surprise... is secret."

"Can anything be *that* secret?"

She balls up her hands and I'm thinking I need to get ready for one of our rare fistfights.

"Fine! W-we're... goin' home, then!" she announces.

"Hey, hey, come back, don't take this so severely, I'm sorry, alright?"

Folding arms. "... really?"

"Bury me with a fish if I'm not."

Suspicious. "A... fish?"

"Then I won't feel so rotten about my stink."

"That's so stupid." But she snorts a laugh and has to cover her mouth to hide the unwelcome smile. Clears her throat. "Okay, fishmonger. You said we'd have fish back in spring. I think it's time you made good on that offer."

"I'll cook it."

"Damn right you will, boy."

"Forgiven?"

"Fuck no!" Scrunching face tight and angry. Relaxes. "Do you want to see it?"

"Yeah. I do."

"Well…" Dithers with a loose stone, kicks it.
Clack,

    cli-clack.

"It's that way," she mumbles.

She follows the noise.

But not before taking me by the hand.

And folding spindly fingers between mine.

Off on a run, no warning, before I can comprehend the warmth.

#

We went out nightly like that, spiraling around the city, dipping into Old Kingdom or so I assumed, stopping for snacks at those hole-in-the-wall shops that stay open forsakenly late throughout summertime, the ones you usually stumble across halfway down an endless road or towards the end of one going nowhere at all, when I'd kick feet up, soak in the atmosphere of a thin yet invigorating drink while Sik stuffed honey-tobacco in the pipe that had escaped Executioner confiscation, lit up, the scene moved slow, *puh puh*, white-gray mists out her nostrils, and I felt in a hazy dream.

She only held my hand that first night.

Constantly lost, she didn't find that special spot either.

Puh, went the smoke.

Dispersing in the breeze instantly, barely hanging there.

Puh.

    Puh.

#

It happens one morning, before Sik rises, when I decide to purchase fresh coldstones for our icebox. They haven't absorbed much chill for over a year; when they do, they hardly last a week and their inconsistency is wasting leftovers. As it is, Sik can't help lift the bloody things.

Should probably leave money for that poor wight who lost a perfectly good mattock time back too…

"It's gone."

306

I think it's a joke. The company we keep. I turn, almost expect to see three smirks, floating disembodied.

Instead, the failing coldstones prop open the door and not even Sik is there.

Snores quietly. Curled up.

I should wake her.

She'll kill anyone does that.

I sit at the edge of the bed.

Waiting.

Hours crawl out the front door, struggling against the wind, trundling over the stairs.

It's inaudible the way they strike the ground.

\#

"Mmmorning," she rasps. "Urrrr, my throat... water..." Fumbles at the glass on the nightstand, knocks it over. "Shi... do that every time," she moans. Sits up. "Whhhy so silent. I'll clean it and..." Yawns. "Cup's indestru... uh... uhhhh." Yawns again, collapsing into the pillow.

I yank the sheet off she's about to rewrap herself in.

"Sik, our money's gone."

"Rrrred?"

"Did you move it somewhere? When I was sawing... or... or when we were cleaning, or anything like that?"

"Stop talk... ing so fast. I'm barely here." Moves to my side and pushes herself up. "What happened?"

"I was going shopping. Went to get money, nothing there. It was underneath that brick under the fireplace, right? You didn't move it?"

"Yeah, yeah, that's where I hid it."

"Fuck."

"What, nothing's there?" she asks.

"What was storing it is, and that's all. Fuck."

"Okay. Okay."

"When did we last go to market?" I ask.

"Uhh... uhh, three days ago? Four?"

307

"I can see that. We were out then, we *have* been."

"Calm down, Red. We're not gonna starve."

"Of all things! Sik, we were right there, we were... we *had* it."

"I know, but that's not gonna help." Rubs my back. "Come on. You're gonna get me all freaked out and upset you keep that up."

"Sorry, sorry... it's... fuck, that was *everything*!"

"No, no, it's okay."

"It's not, it's—"

"It's okay, Red, look." Bounces off the bed and shakes the curtains next to the dresser.

"What am I looking at?" I ask.

"Listen."

"What?"

She shakes it again.

"If this is another joke, I'm fucking telling you—"

"Oh for fuck's..." She shakes it now with such a violence that her face is pink when finished. I heard coins, though hardly at all: silenced by stuffed cloth. "I always hide a little for emergencies."

"That's..." ...*what is it?* "Good, I gue— Wish you told me that."

"Hoped we wouldn't need it," she says.

"Sometimes we have."

She plays with the dark fabric.

"That's not something should be done. Use it and it's gone. It *really* has to be an emergency."

"How much is there?"

"A week's worth. I think. I dunno. Never counted just... dropped one in now and then when I had a spare. I'm sorry for not having more. But it..." Hesitates, gripping the curtain. Bottom-weighted, it sways.

I let my breath out. "Hadn't... been an issue before."

"We were digging before."

"That's what we do," I say.

"Y-yeah, well…"

"… well?"

"Well, we haven't been doing that, doing digging, have we, Red? I'll answer," she says. "We haven't."

"After the job with Picker and Stealer we were set for a while."

"Why can't we dig if we have money?" she asks.

"Don't you want a rest?"

"Yes? No. I… I don't know."

Silence.

"It's not coming back is it," I say.

"Nope."

"Won't be found either, huh."

"Nope."

"At least we can hide our tools upstairs. That'll be more convenient. When we go out…"

"Potato room…"

"I'm…" I take the coldstones. "I'm gonna scrap these worthless things. Make a stop, see if anyone heard anything about anybody in the area. With luck… Well…" Trailing off.

"Yeah," she says, brushing hair back, "I'll go hit the run of them too and see if they got any juicy tips."

"Always someone dying," I say to the city outside the door closing behind me.

A half-hearted laugh comes from the other side.

"Everyone a corpse," she says, and it shuts.

#

Didn't know if it'd be insulting, but on our way out I informed Quinn, who was genuinely appreciative. She hadn't heard of a thief in our end of the outskirts, said she could investigate the scene if we liked. I shook my head.

"What's gone is done. Just cast around for the culprit. If we're screwed, at least you can edge the bastard to the gaol and push him off your territory."

She hides a smile. "Freelancers."

When I laugh, I realize how much tension has been knotting me up inside.

"Tell Killjoy I'd like a meeting."

She blinks.

"Is he pissed at me?"

Blinks again. Shrugs.

"Fuck, I hope he—"

"Jackal."

"— isn't— ehh?"

"I'll ask," she says.

"She gone?"

Nods. Then adds, "Two days now."

"Should I be concerned?"

Half-a-shrug. "Happens," she says. "Time to time."

#

I don't like to dig in the city limits, including what's along the tangle of corpse roads to the north. When that's all the fences have to throw at us, I get to feeling like it's going to be a long night and a longer morning, to say nothing of the week to come. Close to home, do you figure it's easy?

You're an idiot.

And, being that we were gone as long as we were and not knowing, I'd take that bit further.

You're a fucking idiot.

I had thought the final whisper of that echo that rang through the streets of the city that brisk morning of the fall had brushed over me on our return to Crossroads. Fuck it, Red, you fucking reject. Sik's the oblivious one and you're the one forgets this. And so here it comes back again, rebounding off the ends of the horizons we trampled and the pits we blindly dove into then clawed our way out of -- bleeding out both ends -- and, finally, striking into me full force like a bell of myself, resonating inwards at my seething core, and I feel each echo resound trippingly and the self-loathing mounts and refuses to recede even when that echo, that fucked forsaken echo, is now and truly ended.

The Executioners control everything.

Absolutely everything.

Did they spread themselves thin, as Regin insinuated?

Had they been preparing for this from the beginning?

How many years ago *did* the Executioners found themselves?

I couldn't care. This is it.

They're everywhere.

We are ardently and unerringly fucked. And it's my fault, my own damn fault for lollygagging. And and… and I had the gall to tell Sik *that* was masturbation? The hell have I been doing! We're a pick short, a tarp missing, and the fucking Executioners have the trappings of the Technocracy at their beck. What do we have then? Tell me, what do we even fucking have!?

"This is gonna be complicated," Sik says.

"You fucking think?" I snap. "Idiot."

"He… hey, Red, that's not…"

"I know. I wasn't talking to you."

"Wasn't…?"

"I know, shit. Sik, I'm sorry. I'm not mad at you. This is all my fault for being so complacent. I'll apologize to you properly once we've done this."

Pain lances through her features. "N-no, Red, it's…" she starts to say, strained, stopping short, mostly by me ignoring her words.

"Should've known when I tested the seeds. Executioners at that cemetery in the morning? She was eating breakfast damn it all. Breakfast! Have you ever seen such a comfy scene?"

"N-no, I…"

"Whatever. How many here?" I ask.

"One here. The next one over has three."

So here we are, digging where I'd never have chosen to dig. Unlike guards, these Executioners aren't on patrol. They're spaced relatively evenly. Rotating clockwise to a colleague's vacant position every few minutes. Their vigilant eyes peer out into the night for those that would get at their precious corpses: burrowers and us. That'll be a blessing if we can manage to sneak in. That low wall is an impediment to a burrower; would make a hell of a racket trying to squirm over or, in the case of a stone-burrower, gnaw straight through.

"Tell me it's in the middle," I say.

"It is." Pointing. "Around that memorial I'd guess."

"How do you want to do this?"

"For style? Climb that tree and inch along the branch, right there, and drop down before the statue."

"Out of sight. Still… lantern makes that stupid to try."

"Figure we might not need it," she says. "This place is lit up enough."

"Trust me, that's probably my biggest worry."

"Otherwise, I say circle until we find something to dart behind the moment they move."

I nod. "Sounds good. Meet you back here."

"Yep."

After half-an-hour, no good. Sik isn't back yet. I could have sworn there was a larger structure on at least one of the sides of this graveyard. Thinking back to my last time here, I can't find it in my memory either. Did they purposefully remove it? Expand the wall outwards? Not inconceivable given the amount of deaths per year. I remember it was flat, diagonal due to the weight of itself on the soft earth. Some kind of plaque mounted in front. If it's farther in, I can't make it out.

That familiar footstep in the dirt breaks my thoughts.

"Anything?" I ask Sik.

"If I were this tight, I'd have a second asshole."

"Want to skip it?"

"Your call. It's only one."

I scowl. "Which is all it takes. Let's try."

"Okay."

"Think you can shimmy along that branch then?"

"Not the problem." Cocks her head. "Can you?"

"Take the shovel and I can."

She grins. "Hide our crap at the trunk. I'll go first."

It's a prominent drearwood. Despite its myriad leaves, its fat limbs are almost half as thick as its trunk and should make for mostly-quiet movement. They're strange things, drearwoods. Smell of dryness -- if that has a scent -- is the best way to describe. Squat, as if a gargantuan being stepped on it and the treetop split straight down the middle, splaying in all directions.

Sik crosses the branch without pause as easily as though she'd practiced. The leaves rustle at her passing in the imitation of a breeze. No Executioner knows. I scramble up the knotty roots with less grace, but no less quiet. The branch itself is touchy. In the dark, I keep brushing into crisscrossing branches and stirring up more than a natural-sounding gust. My heart is pounding when I step onto the stone slab and drop down next to her.

"Never a stir, Red, well done!"

"Praise me once we've found something."

"Only after you praise me. I got the lead, ya know!"

The grave is two long strides from the sheltering cover of the memorial and two strides too far away for comfort. Each time the Executioners move, this area is awash in angry torchlight.

"Here." I squeeze the trowel into her hand. "Crawl over there on your belly and give us a good hole."

She responds by doing as I instruct. When the Executioners shift locations, I signal by tossing a bit of gravel at her. She hurries back and we wait it out. Awkward yet deliberate, that's the way of it. Seldom happens, but sometimes this is the only dependable technique.

At a depth of three feet, I switch and dig. She signals me the same way every few minutes. I duck into the grave until gravel rains down. Each time, she throws in a little bit more, trying to bury me, and I swear I can make out a suppressed snicker.

The shovel clinks.

I set it aside, dig in, and lift up a few coins.

Normally I'd be smiling.

It's so small compared to what we had.

After pocketing the lot, I refill the grave and we steal back over the drearwood path.

#

The next dig doesn't go well.

Spacious cemetery, plenty of hiding spots, but the Executioners actively patrol here. Once I memorized their paths perfectly, I realized too late -- knee-deep in it -- that they changed it up. I forgot we had no tarp to cover the dig with, and one of them spotted the hole.

"Watch out for a burrower!" he called.

"Or a bloody digger you mean!" shouted another off a ways.

"Either way!" he responded.

We lit out of there, leaving two graves undug.

"Never leave a grave undug," Sik complained. "S'bad luck."

"The curse of Ensbryng," I said, meaning it jokingly though it came out sopping in bile.

#

"Fuck…" I breathed.

"Wow."

"Is that a *dun*?"

"Dunno, but I think it's clear we aren't touching this one," she said.

I knew this graveyard. It was among the first she and I hit as partners. From end to end it was three times the length of a standard plot, although radically narrower. Gradually it wound up a sloping hill, enclosing the gentle summit where a lone weeping willow slumped upon a crooked trunk. We came here many times, most of them not to dig at all but to picnic beneath that eternally-sighing willow which never could appreciate the weather.

Now the whole thing was enclosed in depressing stone.

I couldn't find an entrance.

Not until we literally stumbled into a staircase built into the megastructure. A group of Executioners were chatting away the night up there, sounded like playing a board game too. Or maybe something with cards.

I wasn't paying attention.

Ghosted away.

Sik was trying to say something.

Actually, she was.

For one reason or another, I couldn't make out her words either.

#

With dawn's approach, we can only strike at one extra place from her list.

"Which one has the most?" I ask.

"Last on the trail."

"Jog with me."

"H-hey," she calls after, huffing and hurrying. "Th-thought we'd save that for a single night."

"We'll go now."

"I… I don't think there's time, it's spread out."

"What is?" I ask.

"The… graveyard," she says, awkwardly.

"Let's get what we can."

"A-alright."

Here was a grand plot, teeming with lights and every one of them an Executioner. It might have been an entire quarter of the city itself and, given time, I'm sure it will be.

Sik whistles.

I'm at a bit of a loss given the sight. "I wouldn't even know where to begin in this warren."

"The fences didn't either."

"Have to do this a blind run," I say.

"Figures."

"Eyes peeled, Sik."

"Like grapes."

#

Stress stabs me in the back with each step I take.

Walking forward, yet my head is always turned over my shoulder. Then the other. Again. Again. *No respite.*

Executioners everywhere, down the paths, over at a campfire, loading up a cart.

I haven't seen that before. I'm transfixed.

Two stoop into the grave and pull a corpse out. The third stands aside, hand to hilt. They are careful. So, so systematic. Disciplined. Scrupulous. None of the bark of Regin. Deathly silent. They load the cart up, refill the grave, and move on.

Sik was right.

We shouldn't be here when they're working.

Our sliver of lantern-light is a trail leading back to us.

Before I think better of this stupidity, I spot a heap of earth above a nearby grave.

"There!" I tell Sik.

She shuts the lantern.

We dig quietly so they won't notice us.

They walk quietly so we won't notice them.

That's the game we play.

#

Graves are clustered off the main path so we needn't worry about stragglers. The tombstones are near enough to dump the displaced dirt between them without alerting even the most paranoid Executioner. Sometimes piling atop another grave works, but there have been those scarily observant few

-- a couple of guards too -- who remember no one was buried there lately.

The wooden wheels of the cart squeak and we can hear it from where we are. While Sik digs, I watch the spectacle of Executioners trying to find a speed at which the sound subsides. They don't find one and I'm happy to enjoy their buffoonery. Makes this aggravation somewhat worth it.

When I finish up, add the offerings to loot collection, and start shoveling dirt back in, Sik taps me.

"Found a few more," she whispers in my ear.

"A few?"

Good news.

"Clumped together. Done here?" she asks.

"Give me a second. Little bit left. And... got it. Which way?"

"Over here."

Overgrowing nettles face the center, though the opposite side is completely exposed to the wall. There's definitely an Executioner out there. Have to keep an eye on him since he's not patrolling.

Could be lazing.

That type tends to be unpredictable.

"Risk some light. Which ones?" I whisper.

"Here. Here. There. And that one."

"Right. These two and those marked ones. Got it."

Sik watches the patrols, straddling a gravestone, and studying that loner for changes. I feel secluded enough to have her dig too. If I start on those other ones, I can keep an eye on him at the same time.

"Sik, finish this one up for me and watch for anyone behind me. I'll get your back."

"No Execrations sneaking up on these diggers!"

I left her a foot or two. With the trowel, it'll be less efficient, but hopefully she'll get at the goods by striking straight down. After many long minutes, the careful rejoicing

I hear from her grave means that it must have worked just as planned.

I'm nearly to the bottom of mine when she comes over.

"That one stunk," she whines.

"Was it a twelve-year vintage?"

"Yuck. No."

"We can probably dig a— Hello." I hit something.

"Ehh?"

I drop to my haunches and feel around.

As hoped, coins aplenty.

"Hit that earlier than I expected."

"Good stuff!" Sik rubs her hands together. "So, 'we can probably dig a' what now?"

"One more," I say.

"Ahh. Ya know, if I started on the fourth like before, we can totally get that too."

"Let's do it."

"Okay!"

False dawn is coming sooner than a digger can ever like. I fill the grave, Sik tears into hers, and that Executioner is sitting still, the immobile sod. If light didn't flicker from him every so often, I swear I'd take him for a statue. Practically is for all the good he's doing not discovering us.

"Hey, trade with me," I tell Sik.

"Why?" she asks.

"I can't see that bastard so good where I'm at."

"Okay. Got a decent foot for you."

"Thanks."

She hops over and kneels before the tombstone, stabbing the earth with gleeful over-the-head plunges.

#

The Executioner gets up and walks away the instant I reach my goal, as if he had our night choreographed just so.

I shiver mentally.

This isn't right.

Is this a trap?

The offering was at four feet.

The offering is *never* at four feet.

A latecomer screams, "Wait! Wait! Don't bury her yet! I didn't say goodbye!" He flings the coins high and they land, gently flopping as though on a fluffy bed, in the uncovered dirt between shovelfuls that bury the dead.

I could see that in a comedy. A dreadful comedy.

My smile is grim. No joy in this.

We're running low on time.

The hint of a hint of false dawn is rising.

I have to know.

I don't want to know.

I have to know.

#

Arms throbbing from exertion. Seven feet down. Just in case? No. No. I kept digging because I didn't want to stop. If I stopped, it would mean I was right and I don't want that, I can't mistrust yet I do and I'm blank filled with darkness that deepens as night begins to tenderly lift.

Seven feet.

Be mistaken.

Using the tombstone for support.

Please be mistaken.

Climbing out.

Just please be mistaken.

Running my fingers along its face.

Only just please be mistaken.

It's smooth. It's coarse. It's smooth. It's coarse. It's—

If only just, please be mistaken.

It's a line.

It's two lines.

It's an X.

#

"Why did you bury our money."

"H-huh?"

I shove Sik down into the pit she's been digging.

"Why in the fuck did you bury our money!?"

"What are you on about, Red?"

"You can't bullshit your way out of this one, you twisted fucking—!"

Slaps her hands over my mouth. "Execrations will hear! Shut up! Shut up before you say something you'll regret!"

But I made too much commotion. Or at least ample. That Executioner from the wall is coming this way along a path I hadn't previously noted which led, though not directly to us, exceedingly close.

"Don't move!" I pin her down.

If we're very lucky my back will give the grave the illusion of being full, provided the torch isn't bright enough or the Executioner curious enough. Given the gaping hole a few feet away, it's probably shit.

Our hearts are slamming against each other. Sik attempts to force her breaths to slow, every one as loud as wind in my ear, shuddering and hot. The air escaping my nose is trembling, strained. Sik grips my shirt with one hand, pulls the trowel against her chest with the other, and watches in the direction of the approaching footsteps.

"I said don't move!" I force her into a painful embrace.

"But!"

"You aren't fast enough!"

She relents, barely, clutching the shaking trowel.

Gravel crunches beneath the Executioner. Grass rustles when he tramps off the path. He sucks in a breath. Exhales. Silence and the smell of tobacco. My single act of bravery is to look backwards.

He stands stock-still.

Does he see us?

If he doesn't, shouldn't we attack?

This can't end well…

He walks on, deeper into the foliage, and it isn't until I hear him gone that it feels vaguely safe.

Sik is the first to react.

"Get the fuck off me." Knees my stomach, edges away, her back against the side of the grave.

"Where is it."

"Everywhere," she admits. "Just about."

"Why!"

"Keep your voice down!"

"Why would you do that?"

"I couldn't deal with it. I can't sleep. I tried finding other things, I really did, but I couldn't frickin'… settle down. I tried to be domestic-like, but… but it didn't work, never worked."

"Deal with what?" I demand. "Things are good."

"I want to dig, Red!" Vehement, too loud. Then hushing. "I want to dig."

Branches crack underfoot.

The Executioner is heading this way again.

I manage to grab the shovel and hide it with us.

He picks around.

We hunker low, clutching our worthless weaponry.

Then he returns to his spot by the wall, sits down, gets up, leaves for another area out of sight but within earshot. He begins chiseling on a tombstone.

I turn my fury back on Sik.

"Why then! Why wouldn't you—" I can barely keep my voice level, let alone undetectable. "Why wouldn't you just *say something*? Say anything!"

"I-I… I th-thought you wouldn't want—"

"I would have gone out that instant!"

"Since when?"

"Always! When did that change?"

"B-but you were… relaxing. Only relaxing."

"We can do that sometimes," I say. "We *do* do that after long digs."

"It wasn't long. That guy's place was one night. One night!"

"Then I took it too far. I'm sorry!"

"You should be! I really wanted to dig!" she says.

"Tell me these things!"

"You should know them!" she says.

"Then I'm sorry for that too!"

"Stop apologizing and *do them then*!"

"We'll plan them from now on."

"It doesn't… Fuck damn it, Red, it doesn't have to be *all planned out*. Life is spontaneity!"

"My brain doesn't work like yours. I reflex to thinking things out. We talked about that."

"Good! You're self-aware! Congratu-fucking-lations. Maybe if you spend a little of that energy put towards *doing something with that knowledge*, I might pat you on the fucking back!"

"Don't you throw that on me when you started this bullshit," I say.

"Oh, oh! We're going for the origin of the shitstorm, fine, I can plough that!"

"Do it. I want to see you grind the two sides of that empty-headed gap inside there together and come up with a logical, coherent thought for once. Impress me!"

"You fucking git," she spits.

"What? Was that it or are you warming up?"

"Why are you averse to going out with me?"

"I'm not."

"Lately?"

"I like spending time with you!"

"You make it seem like a chore!"

"Right now it is! I'm digging up my own money!"

"I'm enjoying it!"

"Why!"

"Because I get to spend time with you," she says.

"We're *always* together."

"You aren't *listening*."

"No, it's that I don't follow," I say.

"I didn't want to argue about money like we did before—"

"Oh, well, well done on that."

"— so I tried taking care of it different."

"Taking care of it stupidly, *idiot*."

"Hey!"

"You told me to call you on it when I needed to and I'm telling you: this is the stupidest fucking thing you've ever done! That alone is praiseworthy."

"The hell we need all that money for?" she asks.

"Food? Taxes? Equipment? Dry spells? What do you think money is for?"

"Great. Back to this shit again."

"Yeah, apparently you didn't listen the first time through."

"You either, asshole!"

The Executioner makes a move and we shut up. When it's clear he went to chisel elsewhere, we dive back in.

"Sik, what you don't—"

"No, shut up," she interrupts. "We've been drooling over a twelve-year forever now, right?"

"What of it? Anyone would like one."

"Never thought much of it. Thought we'd get one. Eventually. That's all I figured. It wasn't 'till the gig with Jackal and with Quinn. But just... just what would we even do with all that? What... what would we spend it on? And more important, having it, why can't we dig!"

"You deserved a break," I say.

"I didn't want one."

"You said you did."

"I didn't know, don't know what I want." Takes handfuls of gravedirt. "Except this."

"What do you want from me?" I ask.

"Less seriousness. I think."

"I can't help that."

"Pay attention to my feelings."

"You seemed happy," I say.

"I wasn't!"

"*Red, come dig with me!* How hard was it to say that instead of doing all *this*?"

"Admit it, you were avoiding it!" she barks.

"If you said *let's dig*, we'd dig."

"Bullshit!"

"How is what we've always done been bullshit!? Typically, who finds the leads? Makes the plans? It's *you*!"

"We both do the leads," she says. "*I* just happen to have a feel for weather and the right time to go. *You* plan where and how and how long."

"So we're arguing over semantics?"

"We're arguing that you're an insensitive shit who wants to isolate me," she says.

"Would you *stop* accusing me of this baseless tripe?"

"Summer is *prime digging time*. Who said that?"

"Sik, if—"

"Answer the fucking question!" she demands.

"I did!"

"Exactly! Look how you never brought it up once, not once!"

"I already said—"

"Don't want to hear it, it's crap, utter swill! And look how coy you've been tonight. There's no swearing at the Execrations or thinking aloud how to screw with them or any of your normal stuff. You see them and boom! Freakin'... pissing yourself nearly."

"I am not."

"It's close enough. You aren't like normal Red. You're being a wuss!"

"Yeah, yeah, not as much bravado, I'll grant that. I've felt more restrained since the mausoleum shit. What of it?"

"You got over what they did to you, right?" she asks.

"Mostly."

"But not me, huh?"

"What is this leading up towards?"

"Tonight, you have never looked at them without glancing at me right after. You're worried *obsessively* about me. You don't want to take me out around them. Is that true, Red? Or is it not? I'm asking."

"That's not it."

"You haven't taken me out 'cause you're thinking they'll get me!"

"That isn't it."

"Stop lying."

"Alright! Fuck it. Yes, I'm scared! I was worried before, but now after walking around? Seeing that... that stone dun or whatever the fuck, I am terrified, Sik. We are not as strong or as fast and here we are in a city infested with them, okay? I don't know how to pick through that yet or if we can at all and I want to keep you safe!"

"You don't fucking get to fucking decide that for me!"

She punches me in the nose, missing a direct strike solely from the lack of light. But she follows it up with another to the jaw before I manage to slam my fist into her gut.

"Ha! I like it," she says, kneeing me in the groin. "Going for my stomach first thing. Unlike you, I learn from my— hrnnff!"

I strike her throat and she falls back.

"But still aren't too observant," I counter.

I stomp at her ankle which she twists away, pulling my leg with the same movement. As I fall, she throws a punch way off the mark, unbalanced, grabs my shirt and headbutts me on our way to the ground.

"You're so selfish!" she cries out, then misses again.

I manage to find her face and hit her cheekbone as hard as possible. She's knocked off me, wincing audibly.

"Selfish for thinking of you, that's funny."

I step on her foot. It sinks into the dirt enough to hold her there and I swing. It would have been her face, but she dodges, and when I try again she twists out of my grasp and it smashes into her breast instead.

"This was about how *you* felt. Not me!" she says. "You never even asked me!"

And she jumps on me and we tumble into the grave again, hitting each other back and forth like a violent pendulum carved from flesh, swearing at each other, most of the words slurred and indecipherable, over and over. When the angle is right, I slug her untightened stomach. She starts wheezing for knocked-out air that refuses to reenter her lungs, and I think it's over, but all it does is piss her off the way kneeing me in the groin did.

"Hey! Someone over there?" the Executioner calls.

I answer him by yanking Sik's hair.

Sik answers him by biting my forearm.

"Great, another burrower. Never get this place secure…"

Instinctively I know the approach of his footsteps should stop me. Instead, I find myself letting her punches land so I can hit her without being blocked or evaded.

He's almost here. We keep fighting.

The bushes are smarter. They part for him.

And the torchlight flickers upon two fool diggers, rolling around and snarling.

"What the—"

He doesn't get the chance to finish the question.

Or the thought.

"Stop underestimating us!" Sik howls, spraying spittle and flecks of blood on me.

She boots my thigh, elbows my ear and flings her hate-filled frame straight at the Executioner. Metal glints in the

326

fire blood streams a memory of the screwy girl bloodlust handicapped and grinning Sik's severed jugular and I'm rooted staring through a hollow lens Quinn holds up, a hole going nowhere except to ground and grave.

Is it blood? Was it the torch's flare?

It's over.

Her shoulders heave. The Executioner crumples into the nettles, unconscious from the blow -- if not dead. She looks back at me and throws the shovel.

"That's what we can do, you piece of shit!"

And she's back on top before my arms have moved away from my face.

"They're fucking people! Like us!"

Battering me in the nose.

"Diggers can be better than 'em!"

Boxing my ears.

"We can be stronger!"

The pummeling stops hurting.

"You're stronger than me, so why...?"

The fists fall without force. Weak. Exhausted.

"Why can't you have confidence too?"

I can't move anymore either. Blood seems to pool within me, dragging me down with more burden than gravity, more finality than the pit in which we lie.

She collapses against my chest.

It takes all my fleeting, remaining strength just to lift my hand. Where did that energy go? Seconds before, I could have beat the shit out of her through the day and on into the next night. And yet now, this simple movement...?

I drop my hand atop her head.

"I can take it," I say. "I can get beaten up. I can lose my eye. But I can't take them doing whatever they want to you."

"I won't get caught. I'm better than them. Better than... a fucking Execration."

"They saved us, Sik."

She says nothing.

"They *saved* us, Sik."

She shakes. Fighting back shameful tears.

"I can't forgive them for that, but worst of all is I can't forgive myself."

"You didn't do anything wrong," she says.

"Didn't do much right either."

"You're wrong," she maintains.

"Am I?"

Struggles to rise, enough to face me. "They only *helped* us. Okay? *You* saved me. Wasn't a guard, wasn't an Execration, wasn't anyone bad that was there when I heard someone next to me and looked up, scared to shit," she says. "It was you. It was Red." She smiles, bruised and bleeding. "It was my precious friend."

I sigh. "What the hell were we even fighting about."

She lies back down on me.

"Fucked if I remember."

We laugh, though it can scarcely be called that being no more powerful than a whisper.

As a gray false dawn spreads through the floor of the sky I stare up at, I feel lighter myself as if, given a few more moments, I'll tip over the world and dive straight down into a brand new color -- and Sik would be there too, like she always has been since the day I rounded that corner in the Royal Catacombs and stood next to her, looking down at the frightened girl with the soot-covered face who, for all her idiocy and rashness, would save me too.

In a partially-dug grave, we hold each other until the morning sky is an ocean of gold and the islands of clouds are washed away.

#

"Hey, ya guys here?" Jackal pops in. "He— oi! What happened to ya?"

"We had a heated conversation," I explain.

"It was a tie," Sik says from the bathroom, then walks out with a proudly-displayed black-eye.

"Ah, ah, sweetie, ah, that looks real painful."

"Yeah, it really hurts!" she says cheerfully. "And look here, I got this bruise on my boob. It's green!"

"Bruise on your... oi, Sik, you're like bruised everywhere, ya know."

"Yeah?"

"Uhhh..."

I interject myself into the mix. "Jackal, we haven't slept. Are you saying 'hi' or...?" I gesture at the bedroom.

Her face is a little blank. More so than usual. Finally she says, "I... I feel like I should be angry with someone. So... should I be angry with someone?"

"No worries," Sik says. "We were bonding."

"I don't think that's how you're supposed to..."

Her voice trails off into a faint moan.

"Jackal. Stop zoning. I want to sleep," I say.

"Oh, umm... oi, you're really wantin' me to accept this as normal, Red..."

"We dig corpses for a living. When were we normal?"

"That's... okay, that's fair enough. Um... Yeah, okay."

"Goodnight!" Sik rounds the corner, dives into bed. "Ah shit, Rin, be careful! Almost bled on you..."

"This has all kinda confused me. Why was I here again?"

"Why were you? Quinn said you were off?"

Dazed. "Um..." Jolts. "Ah! Right, Killjoy, ya wanted a meetin' she said. Thought I'd take ya along if ya were up for it, was gonna drop by today, but... ya definitely aren't up for it."

I shrug, then wince at the pain in my shoulders.

"We've kept the man waiting long enough. I'll go. Let her sleep."

"Want me to," Sik yawns, "meet up with you when I wake?"

"Sik, it'll be tomorrow when you do."

"Just a couple'a… hours… and I…"

"Should I grab the goods? Are we making a deal?"

Jackal's face has an unreadable expression. "No clue, but it wouldn't hurt, yeah? Honestly not sure his mood on this. You're good at talkin' your way outta things, so be ready for anythin'. Don't worry, he's not the physical type."

"Good. I can't take much more. Hurts to walk."

"Yeah, well, it's a long way there…"

"And I'll remember every step," I mutter.

#

Blazing afternoon sun beats down as we hurry from shade to shade. My legs are relieved when the vine-choked and mossy old theatre comes into view.

The alcove is cool and brighter than I remember.

Jackal knocks.

"Speaking?" asks Killjoy's strange assistant.

"It's me."

The girl opens the door. "Hey, miss Jack— ah." And then closes the door to a sliver, nearly smacking Jackal's nose, and peeks at me with suspicion.

"Oi. What's wrong? We had a meetin'… uh, didn't we?" Jackal bites her lip, starts counting on her fingers.

"Hmmm, who is that?"

"It's Red."

The girl consults her ledger for a full minute.

Jackal, good-humored, leans against the doorframe. Viridian eyes glance up at me, then down, then back, and shutting the ledger and stuffing it in her dress, she says, "Welcome, mister Red."

"Red's fine."

"Good. I have no teas for that."

"I'm sorry?"

The door opens fully and Jackal slips through. "I've gotten the girl to loosen up somewhat," she tells me. "If I'm lucky,

330

I can get a paragraph out of her." And then she asks the girl, "We did have that meetin', yeah?"

"Yes. It's us until evening though we'll have to crack the crate open at some point. Hmmm."

"You don't happen to have a sister, do you?" I ask her.

She stops dead in her tracks. Cocks her head. "No."

"That was random," Jackal says.

The girl turns and stares at me for long seconds before replying, "Do I?"

"If you don't know, I wouldn't."

She mulls that over and without another word leads us through a dark passageway and into the untidy workshop. Someone moves behind a partition, Killjoy I presume, and Jackal goes to meet him. I look around, about to thank the girl, but she's gone.

Killjoy's greeting is a chuckle upon seeing my colorful face. "Heard you were busy," he opens, "though I confess I understood it to be something more financial in nature."

"Technically, it was," I say.

Jackal plays with her hair. "Anythin' yet?"

Spreads his arms. "Deep apologies, my dear. I'm afraid she wasn't in the mood, but try not to let it dissuade you."

"Damn by damn, thought I had a lock this time."

"A finicky disposition, regrettably borne of passion -- one of those incalculable things -- is often impossible to reason with. I was such in my youth and, well, here I stand." His face splits into a smile. "Give me the word and I'll give it a number. If it comes to that, seeing it with a tag and with bids other than her own, she may be so moved as to be inclined."

"Known her for years, ya reckon it much a shot?"

"Not in the slightest."

Jackal shakes her head. "When's the cut-off?"

"None yet, as it happens. At earliest?" Retrieves his leather coat from the back of a chair. "Three weeks. I can push it out six, seven, but no further: autumn follows harshly and I'd like two by the end of it." Frowns, slipping his arms through the sleeves. "Merely one last year as you know, quite a shame. Absolute. Ah!" He catches me studying two paintings on separate easels. One is wet. "Pardon the talking of shop, my boy, it happens with me."

I point. "It's a forgery."

"But it's a very good forgery: an original Killjoy."

"I think I'm beginning to see how this works."

"Not at all." Hand against my back, he leads me towards his closed office. If he leaves evidence like that lying about, it makes me wonder what exactly he has to keep shut in.

It's a cramped office.

Entirely organized. Lit by a single window of beveled glass. When I catch sight of the grouping of leather-bound ledgers on the desk, the image comes to mind that this is more his assistant's room than his own.

I unwrap the goblet and place it on the desk between us. The lines on his face crease, though which direction isn't easy to determine. Jackal leans against the wall, one foot kicked up behind her.

"Learned to be blunter over the seasons, I see."

"The deepness can change the nature of a man. Ever been out there?" I ask.

"Perish the thought."

"What's your price?"

"I'm afraid things have gone a bit more complicated in that regard," he admits.

"The price has gone up. How much?"

He laughs without humor. "You're astute, of that you can be assured, but not the way you consider."

"The fences are functioning as normal. They won't touch this piece. You had a hand in that, didn't you?"

"Again, my previous compliment, though you ascribe more deviousness than I deserve. I... simply suggested it not to be in their best interests to get involved in this item. The curse and all."

Now I laugh. "Damn thing probably is cursed, but I don't believe that and neither, I'll wager, do you."

"I haven't been vacationing the winter over while the demand grew," he says, then raises a hand. "I apologize. Auctioneer's joke."

"It was hardly a vacation."

"Settle down, settle down, my boy." He leans back. "Did you have your reasons?"

I keep my voice even. "We couldn't wait."

"Dare I ask if you brought back," tapping the goblet, "anything else?"

"Would that I could say that, and one time I could, but no. Not much I saw I could get back to, unless you have a market for ancient tapestries that haven't withstood any decade with much grace."

"I see, well. Perhaps you could describe them to me."

"Landscapes, maybe. Gray... hell, it was all grayish, and I couldn't make out more than a random pattern. Sik said: fields of something, hills of some color, people of an angular design, a square symbol on the corners -- but she was fevered at the time, so she may have imagined it. Sound like an artist you know?"

Thinks, folds his hands, fingers flicking. Each nail is so pared down to the quick that even were they deep in the dirt all day, no speck would ever remain to hint at it.

"Not as such. Viable with however much you can recall? Possible, but we can work that out at a later date," he says with casual dismissal. "'Has the city settled?' That's the question I have asked myself over and over. Has the city settled? Perhaps enough? If so, not enough." Shrugging. "When I say it's more complicated I mean for me, personally. I am leery of the Executioners."

"Baselessly," Jackal says.

"That may well be the case; I'm taking no premature chances."

"What's the issue?" I ask.

"I've been researching your piece -- our pieces, if you will -- and have all but confirmed it. Six goblets were the accounting. *This* won't be enough."

"So we're missing one again. What's changed?"

"Everything," he says. "I was shattered when I discovered who had it."

"Who?"

"You wouldn't know the gentleman. Adwin Guiney. No? As I said. Few had in the trade, least ways, until he cracked the vaults of First Trust wide and his sister croaked in the process."

"You know this guy?" I ask Jackal.

"Naw. Not by name, anyways."

"But you've heard of this."

"Rumors, way waaay back." Chews the inside of her cheek. "Ya never hear 'bout the big ones, not really. If they go right, no one knows. If they go wrong, it's hushed up, yeah?"

"Unless the Executioners are involved that is."

"Got that right," Jackal says to me.

In the uncomfortable silence, Killjoy leans forward.

"Vicious person, Adwin, no getting around that with the description, he wouldn't part with a fig should you give one. Thrown in the gaol he was, couldn't attend the funeral -- and wouldn't have is my opinion -- and his chums, *her* chums too I should mention, sent her off to Dun goblet in hand."

Now I'm leaning forward. "Why?"

"Why does anyone bestow a corpse a piece of worth?"

"'Well-wishes're wasted on the dead,'" Jackal quotes.

"We're sentimental fools who find something rabidly romantic about our own absurdities, contrary to rationality --

or perhaps because of it. Don't mind me," Killjoy chuckles, "waxing philosophical."

"Surely we can get at his part of the pair." I'm almost telling it to Jackal directly.

"I have *tried* that," Killjoy puts a stop to it. "We do this in partnership with him or I'm afraid it's bust."

"Aside from the obvious, what do the Executioners have to do with this?" I ask him.

"I'm beginning to edge towards the mind that they're snooping the dealers for… misappropriated goods."

I frown. "That's difficult to prove."

"And I'm tellin' ya," Jackal says testily, "we haven't seen anythin' of the sort. Ya assert without proof."

Killjoy spreads his hands. "A moderate helping of paranoia keeps the world turning, if only a while longer. And now comes the rub is this: we have to prove to the man that we have the set, minus his."

"I'm not breaking into Crypt Dun," I state.

"Nor am I helpin' som' so stupid as that."

Killjoy isn't pleased, though clearly unsurprised. "Then precisely nowhere is where we stand." He gets to his feet and hands me the goblet. I guess negotiations are over already and this bloody thing's value remains what Sik said of it. "You do know they've begun the construction of a new dun, yes? Time will, unfalteringly, be seeing you and your partner companions interred once upon a tomorrow." I can't help giving him a look at that comment. "Oh, don't misunderstand, I shan't be that far behind. The Executioners are set on making of this world a dun." He stares into the shadows of the room. "What depressing poetry."

He holds the door open and we take our leave.

Once we're across the workshop, it finally latches shut.

#

"Why doesn't he throw a lump of money at me and be done with it?" I growl at Jackal once we're outside.

She shields her eyes from the sudden change in brightness. "Ahh, I can't get him, Red. I wanted him to take somethin' off my hands too, but he refuses. It may be the Executioners really do got him spooked." She stops me in the middle of the street, holding my shoulder even after I face her. Bodies pass us on every side. Busy afternoon for the heat. "Red, I saw ya restrainin' yourself. Did ya learn that from Quinn or som'?"

An analytical Jackal. The day is full of surprises.

"What do you mean?" I ask.

"Really want him to take it off your hands, don't ya?"

"I do."

"Are ya hard up, Red? Did you spend so much on that, um, potato room?"

I keep myself from laughing.

She'd probably take it the wrong way...

"You and Sik really have to stop learning from each other."

"Oi?"

"But we are a bit fucked on money."

"Oh." Her twintails sag. "Well, I mean, we'll help ya out if ya need help."

"Thanks, Jackal, but it wouldn't work."

Furrowed brow and sisterly frown. "Oi... I'm not lettin' ya guys starve..."

"We're fine for food for now, but even if you helped, what about equipment we need?"

"We'll steal it."

"And medicines for when we're sick?"

"Quinn, she can make a little."

"Really sick."

"Steal that too."

"And taxes?"

"Uhhh..."

"See?"

"We... we can help there too!" she exclaims.

"More than once?" I prod.

"Urr…" Groaning a little. "Quinn can figure… somethin' out…" Wilting like a neglected flower. I take a twintail in each hand and tug. "Owowow, stop that! What was that for?" Rubs her hair protectively.

"We aren't very close, are we?" I ask.

"Now what are ya sayin'?"

"You and I don't spend much time together."

She warily follows the turn of conversation and my footsteps. "I don't get it. Are ya hittin' on me or somethin'?"

"Out of our group, we're both furthest from each other. It felt weird to embrace you."

"And so ya yank my hair? Damn by damn ya show your affection strange." Scowling askance. "Ya realize if ya had no scars on ya this mornin', I'd'a made a few."

"Is that a challenge, Jackal?"

"That's a promise! Been long time since I've been in a scrap, but I could teach ya some stuff 'bout fightin' unfair!"

We walk in silence for a bit.

Then I ask, in low tones: "Is there really another dun?"

"You're askin' me?"

"I haven't heard a thing. Was he lying?"

"Should I look into it?"

"Hell, we all should."

"Hey! There you are! Hey, over here!" Sik is slumped in the shade, waving her arms overhead.

"Weren't you asleep?" I call out.

"I woke up achy and that was that. Told you I'd come down, just… thought I'd make it there in time. But you're done? Geh, I shouldn't've unngh…"

"Here, here, Big Sis will be your crutch!"

"Don't need a crutch, but if it's you, heh heh heh…" Despite leering, Sik's lecherous hands stay around Jackal's shoulders. "Wasted effort," she says.

"Mostly," I agree.

"We're still broke. Hurray!"

"I wanna know this story," Jackal hesitates, "but do ya want me to ask?"

My side-eye is blistering. "No."

"It'll be funny one day," Sik explains. "Only not before we've recovered."

"I swear ya lot are a handful and a half."

#

"I want to hit the Dun," I tell Sik.

"You're fucking daft," she says.

"I know I am."

"We don't need the money that bad."

"I don't think it's about the money anymore."

"Think I'm glad you're bringing this up today. Any other time, not so exhausted, I'd be screaming at you."

I sit down. "Hear me out."

She stays standing. "Red, I am crazy, but I'm not insane. The Dun? Fuck, that's just mental!"

"Oi, is this another 'heated conversation'?" Jackal asks behind the closed bathroom door.

"No, but hurry up in there," Sik insists, "Red's talking shit."

"Level with me. How much money did you save up?"

"None. The curtain thing was a ruse," she says without hesitation. Outrage-clouded, it's only when I don't reply that she understands what she just revealed. "S-sorry..."

"Doesn't change anything so don't worry about me getting mad again," I reassure her.

"Okay, but... I don't like lying to you."

"I know and... thanks, for what that's worth."

"Ah," she looks up, mimicking my voice. "There's that word again."

"And our money's really that scattered?" I ask.

"I went everywhere I could. Digging it will take forever what with increased Execration presence, won't lie about that. I mean, you were there. It's like that. I divided as widely as I could over the weeks. Forgotten quite a bit of where I went too… that was… kinda the point…"

I shrug. "I holed us up 'till winter. You made us busy for the same period."

"P-pretty much…" she says.

"To do what Killjoy's insinuating would give us the breathing room to recover everything. It would set us up for a year and then some, honestly, time to study the Executioners more closely, pick at their weaknesses, and let us dig wherever we want whenever we want."

"Yeah, I can see where you're coming from, but it's fuck-all stupid as hell. Look, Red, just sell the fucking thing already!"

"He blocked us there. The fences aren't taking it 'cause he's got them thinking it'll curse them and the Executioners will come bashing down their doors."

Rolls her eyes. "You have to be dead to be cursed."

"The distinction is starting to blur, at least on the rumormongers' tongues. And with the Executioners cavorting unchallenged I don't suspect anyone is inclined to disagree."

"Either way, even Jackal knows the difference between confidence and temerity."

"No I don't." Jackal throws a towel over the sink's rim. "Okay, so what're we talkin' 'bout?"

"You tell her," Sik says curtly. "I'll start beating myself if I hear me saying the words."

"And what's temerity?" Jackal asks.

"Reckless boldness," I say.

"Oi, that's me!" she laughs.

"Crypt Dun."

"What 'bout it?"

"I'm considering making a run of it."

"I backed ya up when ya said ya wouldn't!"

"Wanted to see how he'd respond," I admit, "though I didn't guess he'd shut me down so quickly."

Tosses her head. "Yeah, well, he's like that."

"I think we should look into it."

"Why?"

"Call it the reverse of your mantelpiece. Looking at what we're suppose to be avoiding as the prize itself."

"I won't help ya in somethin' so foolhardy. Quinn wouldn't neither. Oi! You think I'll let ya risk my Sik for that? Last tossers tried that... who knows what the Executioners done to 'em!"

"Nothing says we can't see how possible it is. If we pool our skills—" I start to explain.

"No way. I'm not listenin' to this."

"Jackal," Sik says, "you don't have to leave. I'm not keen, but Red's not stupid. I respect his thoughts."

"To me, there are things ya simply don't do, stuff ya never do," Jackal says. "Like pilfer from the Sovereignty or even *try* to break into their stronghold. Could Quinn and me do that?" Throws her hands up. "Does it matter? No profit outweighs that risk and Crypt Dun is *your* stronghold. Stay away from it, ya guys."

Sik plays with the items on the table.

"What's that?" Jackal asks.

"Souvenirs," Sik says of them: an Executioner's blade and sheath, black and crimson scarf, a metallic torch, and three cobalt chips of wood.

"This is kinda what I'm talkin' 'bout..." Jackal says.

"You should've seen it!" Sik cackles. "We buried the Execration neck deep, just his head popping out. Ha ha ha! Bet he pissed himself when he woke up! Oh oh! Maybe they interred him!"

Jackal fidgets and dithers, unsure how to respond.

"Ever since ya made me crack those vaults, this has seemed... heavier... to me. These Executioners aren't held back anymore. I'd be tellin' ya even without that story of yours and it's true. I'm worried. I think..." Looks straight at Sik.

"I think I can't condone this anymore, sweetie, as your friend. Ya go along with Red too much on this..."

"I'm a grown woman, Jackal," she says.

"So am I, yeah? And so is Quinn too. We might only have a few extra years on ya, but I don't think you're bein' objective 'bout diggin'. Maybe not my place to say, but I've said it, huh? That's it."

She leaves a silence with us when the front door closes.

I lean back into my chair.

Sik sits down across from me.

"I'm not saying we do this to do this," I tell her.

"I'm listening," she says.

"You told me last night we could be better than them."

"Damn right!"

"Is it more important to prove that to ourselves," I ask, "or to them?"

"What's that mean?"

"There's a lot we can do with a successful job," I say. "One, the goblet and Killjoy's auction. Two, we can determine if that cursed bullshit is bullshit or no. Three, embarrassment for the Executioners, show the public what they really are. All this authority poured into their lap and none of us got to vote on it?"

She unsheathes the sharp, glinting blade.

"Disbanding them would be delicious..."

I smirk. "Lowering their esteem in the Sovereignty's eyes is probably all we could do."

"That's better than what's gone on this past year." Her fingernail makes the blade's tip sing. "Go on."

"They're an organization funded by the Sovereignty, backed by this Technocracy." I tap the metallic torch. "How many diggers are there?"

"Us. Couple of acquaintances. We keep to ourselves, don't we? Can't be too many. Several dozen? Can't be a hundred, no way."

"We have to be smart about how we attack them. Since we're so few, they probably don't even see us as a threat. Hell, I know they don't. We're ancillary to their ultimate objective, whatever that is."

Her lips curl.

"Do it 'for revenge' is what you're getting at, isn't it?"

"Won't deny that. Though there is a stronger reason."

"Oh?"

I place my hand over hers. "Because it's fun."

The devil-grin deepens.

It's beautiful malevolence.

"You say a good thing, Red."

"But it's your call."

The grin slips. "Ehh?"

"I'm not forcing these decisions anymore. I did that in Crossroads and swore I wouldn't do it again, then I did it again and I can feel it coming now too. I'm not digging that grave. I want to do what you want to do. We're partners and I forget that too often, Sik, because of how comfortable I feel around you."

Face blank, stunned.

Embarrassed myself, I look away to give her time for composure.

I'm not sure when I should look back… but I realize at some point, when I was pretending to study a dust-bunny in the fireplace, she placed a hand atop mine.

An angelic smile spreads.

It's beautiful radiance.

"You say a good thing, Red," she repeats.

#

I can think of only one place to start.

The stone lanterns light our path up the stairs to the shrine, more than a few blown out by Sik who, for some reason, regards that as rebellious. She fusses when I jerk her away and tell her to stop drawing attention.

342

"What? Shadows gonna see us?" she whines.

They might at that, I think when Crypt Dun rises out of the darkness something blacker.

Torches are aflame at the entrance, along the corpse road and out of sight to the countryside beyond, an inexorable vein linking every graveyard, every person who's died.

An austere oaken gate provides solitary access in and out of the crypt, an entrance guarded by battlements on either side which extend out in a half-circle to ensure no one can sneak in at any angle.

Simple construction hence its impenetrable nature.

The facade's more to scare off any idiot straying too close, though if I recall it's considered trespassing to be on this corpse road to begin with. Not that there are many who would willingly wish to travel over one while alive.

We sit on a bank of whispergrass behind the shrine and overlook the coming and going of the carts. Sik reminds me often how boring this is, but shuts up whenever a cart rolls into view. We pass a container of coffee and sandwiches as the hours dwindle.

It's a tight operation they have.

The main door never stays open longer than is necessary to get the cart clear of the swinging gate. Most average four Executioners to a cart, but never less than three. I'm guessing it depends how far they are going or how many corpses they expect to dig up. This is partially confirmed when I count the bodies coming back compared to those pushing them along.

They look like normal corpses to me...

"How do you wake a cursed up?" I whisper to Sik.

"Disturb them."

"How?"

"Dunno. Like... make loud noises or manhandle them, I suppose. Execrations do things quiet and careful, right?"

"Think one would wake if I chucked a rock at its face?"

"Fuck! Don't even try!"

"Why not? I'd like to see the Executioners scrambling for safety at those walls."

"We are *not* doing that. Told you I never want to see one. You wanna satisfy your disbelief, do it when one's interred or do it by yourself."

"Alright, alright."

"And don't do it by yourself either..." she mutters.

"Thought I'd find ya here," says a shadow from behind the shrine's fence.

"That you, Jackal?" I ask.

"Who knows," it says. "Got some info for ya."

"What?"

"Found two new duns."

"Two?" Sik holds the coffee between her legs and looks at me expectantly.

"Executioners took over the hill in Parkside," it reports. "Area's quarantined."

"Actually *in* the city?" Sik gapes. "Bloody hell, that's suicidal! Or homicidal at least. What the fuck!"

"Isn't dug yet, they merely claimed the land, so maybe that don't count. Other one is right outside Pauper's Pit. Settin' that one up right quick. Pile of crap they've ripped outta its guts is almost a dun itself."

"Execrations are completely unchecked..." Sik says.

"Thanks for the heads-up," I say.

"Yeah, well... I was bluffin' too, wasn't I?" it says and leaves, as silently as it came.

By the time night is nearly gone, we've learned nothing new. I get up, stretch. Sik doesn't move, chin propped in her hands and elbows propped on her knees.

"I want to try digging the other side," she says to me. "Wondering how thick it is. The hillside."

"Enough that that would take months."

"Are we in a rush?" she asks in all honesty.

"You think they're faking security?"

Shakes her head emphatically. "I'm not thinking anything. That's gotta be the sole weakpoint. They wouldn't risk a cursed getting out as much as a digger getting in." Lets out a long breath. "But if you're right, we could tunnel in undetected. *Shit*."

"What?"

Looks at me. "This really is a fearsome undertaking."

"It'd take a plan dimwitted or brilliant," I say, "and someone's already tried the first."

"Pity. I'd be good at coming up with one of those…"

She grunts when she stands, cracks her neck.

Someone walks away from the shrine.

I turn around, seeing no one. Only when we start down the steps do I spot another shadow at the bottom. It halts, regards us, then merges with other shadows -- and I wonder if having friends willing to help on such an endeavor means I should be finding a way to put a stop to it entirely.

"Should we really be doing this?"

I ask no one in particular.

Sik chuckles. "Getting freaked out now?"

"Somewhat."

"Good. That means you still have sense."

"Heh. What do you have then?" I joke.

"A goal."

"Which is?"

She thinks for a long moment. "Something fragile. It feels like this is the correct path to walk, so I'm… I'm gonna keep walking it as long as I can."

"Fancy that, Sik being poetic."

"I'm not always matter-of-fact."

"Just mostly."

Bumps into me. "Would it give you peace of mind if I were only one way?"

"Now *that* would freak me out. Especially if it was your hyper side."

Sik laughs lightly. "It's true, isn't it? The two of us are on a journey. We never stay the same person we are. At times, I like to guess who you were when you were a boy."

"Shorter. Angrier."

"Jackal and Quinn too. I bet they have real interesting stories about when they were girls."

I nod sagely. "Jackal was a failed student and ran away. Quinn was birthed from a book."

Hits a lump on my head. "Asshole," she laughs. "Don't make fun of them!"

"Ahhh, no more hitting!" I recoil.

"Shit, I forgot!"

I wave away her concerned, probing hands. "It's alright."

"Rot. Sorry, Red."

"Little Picker and Stealer, huh?" I try to imagine that.

"The littlest tails bobbing from their tiny heads. So cute," she giggles, then sighs. "I think it's kinda sad," she says, "things changing."

"Everything does," I say. "Everything must."

"That's what scares me. Right now."

"More than the Dun?" I ask.

"Yep."

"Huh."

"Hmm."

"Smile," I tell her.

"Smile?"

"You're not a corpse yet."

"Nope, not yet," she agrees.

"Means you have time to figure it out."

"Do you think I'll figure it out?"

I keep descending. She doesn't follow. I stop.

"Is it that difficult?" I ask.

"Horribly."

"Is it something I can help with?"

"Uh uh."

"I don't know. Try your best, Sik."

"Do you believe in me?"

"Okay, now you're being sappy."

She scrunches up her face. "Am not. I'm scared, is all. What if I die before I figure it out?"

"You wouldn't. You succeed when you try. So try your skinny ass off."

"That was a weird compliment."

"You're a weird girl, so it fits."

"Says the weird boy."

"Say the infinitely *smarter* boy."

"Oh bull! He's barely smarter than a turd."

"Okay, I'm getting you for that one."

"Nyah! Nyah! Turd-brain-boy, turd-brain-boy!"

"Get back here, skinny-ass-girl!"

"Nnnn-yaaaa-aaahh!"

And we chased each other down the steps, spiraling around in overacted mischief that was surely far more truthful than we'd have admitted to ourselves. Through the streets, unconscientiously unmindful of the early hour in our antics. Just a stupid girl. Just a stupid boy.

#

The vigil ends when the festival begins in the middle of autumn. I thought we would have finished by now. Apparently not. I try to remember what we planned, what was the plan? I see carts. Carts, corpses, and a gate that won't open until we're dead too.

There isn't time to be playing around.

But Sik dashes to my side and says:

"They're waiting for us!"

Who?

But the paper lanterns are shivering on their lines and heat from the festival-goers is hotter than the stoves in the stalls. Sizzling. Dripping meat. Caramelized. Sugary.

Quinn brushes up against me.

She isn't wearing black tonight. Hands me a stick of dumplings, then hides behind Jackal. I can't tell what color she's in.

Jackal, however, is in a white summer dress and her hair is down for once, a little wet and dripping. I ask if she's cold.

"Oi, what's that supposed to mean?"

The alcohol is clear as fresh water and goes down smooth, celebratory. What were we celebrating again?

Is this the harvest?

Sshhhriiiii!

Sparkling raindrops drizzle upwards into the dark sky.

POM! POM POM POM!

Flowers bloom pink and cobalt and gold and silver and—

"Red! It's so pretty."

It is. So much so that I can't agree with the lump in my throat that drinking doesn't drown, though now I can see that Quinn is wrapped in every color I've ever seen and her cheeks are flushing crimson beneath black eyes.

The shrine would be the best place to watch this vivid show.

I climb.

The hilltop is so tall.

I fall to my hands and knees and climb not moving, climb not climbing.

Sik, Jackal and Quinn go on without me.

I don't have the strength to call after them.

Focusing on raising a hand, then down it drops, burdened by weight that isn't there.

The ground will open and swallow me up, digesting my exhaustion and spitted back up an empty husk to be loaded in a cart and burrowed off to Dun, saying it's a sedative, knowing no I am truly dead.

When I raise my head, the shrine is there and a young maiden with a broom cleaning the pathway of fallen leaves that are desiccated fingers that point at me until she sweeps them away.

Fall in the sky, burning flowers.

Fall in the city, burning shrine.

Smoke rising and smothering the fireworks exploding in dull thuds, unseen unsatisfying.

The maiden regards the shrine, now a gigantic inferno that scorches a hole in the cloud of smoke and a hole in the sky above and the stars snap like sparks and wither into a hole that gapes into nothingness, and she shrugs at the inconvenience.

"Dunno why I even bother to clean," she groans.

Where did my friends go?

"Where do any of us go, I wonder," she says.

I have to find them.

"Suit yourself, fella."

Please, help me stand.

"Fine fine. I can do that much."

She yanks me up, one-handed, and leans on the broom.

"What a mess," she says of the city.

It's on fire too...

"Don't joke about that," she snaps. Roughly turns my head around to see.

The city is alive, alight only of paper lanterns, a distinct happy din.

"And you better hope it stays that way. I am *not* cleaning that too. This is enough for me."

Can I help? I ask Sik.

"That's sweet, but— Oh. You aren't talking to me."

I don't feel dizzy, but everything is blurring together I feel if I shut my spinning eyes now they'll never see this again.

"Well. Whatever!" She grins. "I'll leave it to you lot to clean up after yourselves."

Sik? Jackal? Quinn?

Gravedeuggery

"Are those your friends?"
You look like Quinn.
"Do I? I dunno a Quinn and I never had children, so she isn't mine." She laughs. Her teeth shine.
I don't know you.
"Really? That's okay, I guess." Picks a finger lodged deep in the broom's bristles and flicks it away. "Gross. Ah, where was I? Oh right. Yeah, don't mind, I don't know myself either."
Who are you?
"Huh? Told you I didn't know, right? Don't even know my own name. Kinda lame, isn't it?"
"Red!" A call over her shoulder.
She turns. Three panting shadows are scrambling up the steep hillside behind the shrine.
"Ah, those must be your friends."
I hurry towards them falling invisibly weighted hands striving to crawl not moving and when I blink the scene disappears further into the back of my mind where I can't reach them.
"You're lucky you have that festival to look forward to," she tells me over her shoulder. "I seriously get sick of cleaning when everyone's busy having fun without me!"
But though she says so, she laughs.

#

From a distance, there wasn't any indication what -- if anything -- was going on at Pauper's Pit. As Jackal said of Parkside, as Regin had said of faraway eastern plots, the Executioners seemed of the intent to secure everything possible and carefully manage decisions from that omnipresent foundation. That they didn't have the funding to do whatever they wanted simultaneously was a boon, though a mediocre one.
The new dun was for the Pit.
Proximity made that indisputable.

At first light they cored out the depths of a hill that was flatter than Crypt Dun, heaping their carts with rocks instead of bodies. And when the light grew dim, streaking dying and ruddy colors across the dilute cirrus, the piles of rock stood like monolithic pyres. Torchlight began appearing around Pauper's Pit and even from a distance, once night had fully fallen, we could spy an unearthly blue glow from the center, pulsing at the rim.

"Let's pop inside for a look," Sik suggests.

The entrance was sealed by the last workers, but there isn't anyone standing guard. Tufts of dry grass mar the dirt road, most squished flat under the burden of relentless wheels.

This place has already assumed the hush of a cemetery.

"Feels like wood," I say of the seal.

"We can bust that down."

"Recon, Sik, recon."

"Ah, right."

I sink my shovel into the dirt by the base. "Let's tunnel in and fill it up when we leave."

"Haven't dug into a tomb so huge before," Sik observes, offering an inconspicuous sliver of lantern-light.

\#

She whistles in appreciation, a note that ricochets back at us thinly from down the corridor. After the entrance hall, the room expanded quickly. This answered for me where the carts get stored when not in use. At the rear, the room tapered again to a hallway that was cloven into the bedrock, angling downwards. From end-to-end, it was a straight-shot for wheeling a cart.

I nudge Sik and point around.

"I always imagined it… narrower."

"Me too."

In my mind, the corridors of Crypt Dun always press in on me. There's something distinctly claustrophobic about my imaginings. Never realized they might have planned to bring carts the whole way through. Or perhaps they did things differently now, having had years of experience to know where they screwed up the first time.

"No vaults," I say.

"Does that mean they aren't near finished?"

"Depends when this all started."

The manpower necessary for tunneling and carting this must have been drastic. Were they solely Executioners or were they hired help? Again, my ignorance digs at me.

How many Executioners *are* there?

Sik shines the lantern down the corridor.

"Long way down, Red. Maybe they only now started?"

"Could be they're digging the levels first?"

"Any other place would've branched. To say nothing of vaults along both sides aaaaall the way down. *This*," she gestures, shadow of her hand scratching at the walls, "is such wasted space."

I can't figure it either.

"Executioners have their own screwy logic," I offer.

"I'll say. If I were them, I'd slap a cover atop Pauper's Pit, just leave and call it."

"They did that in the city already."

"And they're putting a dun there too." She swallows once, noisily. "What the fuck's happening to our city, Red?"

"Killjoy probably wasn't that far off: they're planning the interment of everyone."

Sik shivers. "That's fucked up."

"I'm half-serious, but it's not likely incorrect is it?" I ask. "'End of the world...' that phrase has to mean something and damned if I can guess what's going on elsewhere. But even if we still had messages coming from other provinces, would you want to read them?"

Silence answers.

Not a whisper of air, not a hollow drop of water.

Two gravediggers, thinking on the oblivion of all things.

"I have dreams in the deep night," Sik says finally, walking onwards. "Nightmares. Not always, but sometimes."

"We all do."

"No, it's different," she says in a low tone. "Usually I like nightmares too. Get to run like hell. Get to climb all frantic. See weird, impossible stuff. Kill shit too. Sheer terror. No, scratch that." She trembles at the memory. "*Manageable* terror. Part of me likes the excitement, but these nightmares sometimes... they're just disgusting."

"What happens?"

"Nothing. I... They're just images. And yet, they stick with me. These disgusting images I can't even explain to you now. I don't have the words." Swallowing again. "I get the feeling... the feeling this is what plague looks like past the Gap."

"I don't think you have to worry about seeing that here."

"Hope so. The plague probably would have reached us by now if it was gonna, huh? But we have our own horrible things to grapple with, I guess."

I stare into the shadows. "A world alive with death."

"Is that Scriber?"

"No, it just came to mind."

"It's good."

"Thanks."

"And scary."

#

The corridor branches at the deepest point. One incline. One decline. Two new passageways shooting off perpendicular to us. Sik makes the sensible judgment call.

"Let's split up!"

I laugh.

When the echo recoils, my voice is vacant and strained and dark, exactly like these hallways.

More endless, unbranching corridors extend down both the level above and below us. We decide to follow the right-hand passage on the first floor. It extends almost as far, then turns right, and continues to wrap in on itself with smaller and smaller distances until it reaches a final dead-end.

"I think we can guess the layout of the rest," I say.

"Strange."

"Yeah, poor plan for delving. Pain in the ass to push a cart all the way here and back."

"No, I mean, how are they gonna check up on the vaults?"

"For what?" I ask.

"Make sure no cursed are breaking out."

"R… right."

"So they send some bastard to walk down *all that* and risk waking them all up in the go? That's *strange*."

"Yes, yes that is."

#

One path was as good as another. We poked our noses briefly down others, but it was all the same. Hurried on out, filled the hole back in, and lighted on home. We had spent longer than I had expected and the decision of whether we were using this information to a purpose or not had neither been raised nor settled.

Sik's summertime lapse from bluntness ended there.

"Whaddaya think?" she asked me directly.

As did my lapse from being concerned.

"I'm unnerved by the idea of cracking Crypt Dun, assuming it's possible. Here are the bones." I wave at the hill we had only just scouted, now lost behind the woods used to hide it from Old City's sight. "But to work our way into the sinew, the entrails…"

We had lost our way. Our normal character.

Sik stares into my eyes. "Do you want to do it?"

And all the lusty yearning stupidity bubbled up in our hearts that had been dormant so long.

"I really, really do."

It wasn't about the money anymore.

Only for that ephemeral thing I habitually overshadowed nearly a year long.

Sik smiles her own answer.

#

Viridian eyes were black in the darkness.

The girl wobbled a little at the door. Hands reaching for a ledger that wasn't in her pajamas. She frowned at me. I think her nightcap did too.

"It's past bedtime," she told me as if I wasn't aware.

Her hands didn't know what to hold, so she scrunched up a section of pajama and looked like she might go back to sleep on the spot.

"Tell Killjoy we have a business proposition. We'll return around lunch."

"I don't know the schedule," she mumbled.

"We can wait. Either way, I think he'll make time."

When we left, Sik waving goodbye, the girl merely stood there. Trying to recall our names or perhaps she really had fallen asleep.

#

The air is so dry it cracks like skin.

Sik finishes her sandwich when I'm knocking at the door. Sweat trickles down her face. Wipes it away.

"Between the heat and the walking, I think I already burned this off," she complains, swallowing the last bit of crust.

"Impose on his assistant."

She opens up when I say that, as though it was a summons.

Her ledger is waiting.

Pen poised.

She is ready.

"You've been added to the schedule," she informs me.

"I'm hungry!" Sik announces.

"Me too," the girl says, opening the door for us and taking us to see the man himself.

#

Killjoy sits upon the edge of the apron stage, pretending to survey the setup of the auction hall. In reality, he's watching us out of the corner of his eye the entire time.

I nod at him.

"Killjoy."

He spreads his arms wide.

"Welcome," he says. "Or should I say 'welcome back'?"

"Whichever is friendlier."

His face splits into a smile.

"I take it you've reconsidered?" he asks.

"Nothing may come of this, you know."

"I can only apologize for not reconsidering my position," he says, pulling out a pipe, then thinking better of it. "Really, though, my hands are bound on this. Were it not for the unpleasantness of last autumn, I suspect I truly could have taken it off your hands, as it were. As it is, timing is the crux."

"Say everything goes well, do you have a buyer?"

"Again, the timing. I might. I might not. These matters are more difficult to predict with, well, time."

"We're all a bit fucked," Sik says. "You can understand we'll need at least some assurances that this effort won't be for rot."

"I can give what I can give: Guiney has expressed interest. I took the liberty to test the topic in case you changed your minds. The theory is there, the execution...?" At that, he does take out his pipe and begins to stuff it. "An exceedingly poor choice in words. Forgive it." He lights up, waves out the fire and at us in the same movement. "Walk with me."

He takes us into what used to be the wings of the stage, still filled with counterweight bags for the flies. Sik kicks one and winces in pain.

"I'm invested in this city. That may be an odd phrase these days as nobody living here has any other choice. We are, each and every one, invested in Old Kingdom, Old City, and where their fates go so do ours. That is our condition."

He yanks a lever behind one of the broken projection lamps laying around and a trapdoor drops open at his feet. "Make no misapprehension about this," he continues, leading us down old, dusty steps, "these fates are now navigated by the Executioners. Though I hardly need tell either of you that."

"You're real freaked out by them," Sik mutters, running a hand along the wall for support in the waning light.

"If you found your goblet where you found it and I'm telling you where the last is, from where do you think the others I've come by originated? I never asked, but I knew. No, I unquestioningly knew." He lights a lamp and leads us to a room under the stage, hung with thick black curtains like the ones a floor above us, dampening our voices.

"If how we live is changing," I say, "the way we do business must too."

Fingers snap. "Precisely that, my boy."

"Is that why you sat on them so long?" Sik asks.

"Never knew which way the plague was blowing and thus I waited. For what? I hadn't known. Now it would seem it was you."

"Crypt Dun is worse than a fortress," Sik dramatically describes, "because at least that you could scale. Here, it's: one way in, one way out."

"And being dead mostly the way, although that's been tried unsuccessfully," I remark.

"Yes, I had heard. Rather clever." Killjoy breathes smoke deeply, leaning against the table -- the only piece of furniture. When he lets it out through his nostrils, his face is momentarily clouded before it dissipates. "Are you familiar with the concept of change blindness?"

"That wouldn't be much different, would it?"

"If we could know how the Executioners have altered their security, it would help to know if it might be an option." He goes to a grouping of copper pipes by the wall and speaks into them. "Where are you?"

A few seconds go by, then behind me comes: "I'm making sandwiches without bread."

I turn around and see no assistant, only the mouth of another conical pipe.

"So you are," Killjoy says into the pipe as if that's the most natural thing. "Can you bring the model down when you finish?"

Another second goes by. "Yes, I can do that."

He taps the pipe and turns to us.

"Kills a bit of the magic to see this, doesn't it?"

We discuss what few concrete observations we made of both duns. Their schedules, their patterns, what we surmise, what we can logically trust. He listens, all the while smoking. Eventually, Sik lights up too and the assistant arrives with a plate of lettuce-wrapped 'sandwiches' and later carries in a disturbingly unappetizing green cake.

It's a model of Crypt Dun.

Killjoy pops off the lid and reveals a blank circle inside. He takes a cloth sack from his assistant and dumps the contents next to it: sections of wall, representations of carts, and little figures painted black and crimson.

"Looks like a game," Sik says.

"The most deadly game of all," Killjoy corrects.

#

Jackal waylays us in the street almost immediately.

"Oi, you're really gonna do this."

"Certainly trying to," I say.

"Do it or don't start," she snaps at me. "Tryin' will get ya in the gaol. Or dead. Likely both."

"Have some faith," Sik say cheerily.

Jackal has more than an oath held back by tight lips, but an emotionless "Did ya mention us?" is what comes out.

"Only that you have your reservations," I reply.

"Heh," she sneers. "That's one way to say it. Got a plan drawn up?"

"We have no idea what the layout of the Dun is."

"We can guess," Sik says.

"But more is impossible right now. It might look exactly like the one over by Pauper's Pit. They share the design of a single entrance. Beyond that, who knows?"

"Red, do ya know what Quinn and me do when we run across a place like that?"

"One goes in while the other watches?" I guess.

"We leave it."

"What if you see an expensive bowl filled with rare foods on the mantelpiece?" Sik drools audibly.

"Then we *definitely* leave it."

"It was a joke, Jackal," I say.

"I feel like ya aren't takin' this serious." Thumps Sik on the nose. "Ya included, missy."

"Don't take that out on my nose, Jackal!" she fumes. "And I am. Very, very seriously. If I wasn't... I don't think I could make fun of it."

Jackal folds her arms. "So? You're doin' this blind?"

"Two problems," I say. "Have to find the corpse's vault."

"We got a name," Sik says, "but she could be anywhere."

"And we need a viable way to break inside."

"Execrations may've got lazy since the last time. Even so, they know one method to watch out for."

Jackal holds up three rigid fingers.

"You're forgettin' 'bout gettin' out alive."

"That was assumed," I say.

"That's the least assumed, fool!"

And she strikes me this time.

I try to calm her down. "We aren't forcing you to—"

"Be quiet." Socks me in the shoulder, this time with actual force. "If you're determined to commit suicide, I won't help that, but at least we can give ya fools the best chance to make it. So if anyone's gettin' dragged into this ridiculousness, it's us. And that means riskin' Quinn too."

Teeth grinding. "If the worst goes down, I'll never forgive ya, Red, and if ya don't die I'll murder ya my damn self."

"Stop attacking him." Sik interjects her skinny body between us in case Jackal raises a fist.

"What in the hell is wrong with ya?" Jackal shakes Sik by the shoulders, expression spasming near-frantic. "We'll give ya money! We'll give ya food! What is it that ya even want!?"

"Plague's coming, Sis…"

"Ehh?"

"Sure, it stopped around the Gap. And yet… Do you know what's down there? I don't. Maybe it really has stopped. Maybe only us were saved." A self-deprecating click of the tongue meant not only for herself but the remains of a civilization hanging on. "'Saved'? Ha. That's the real joke. Cursed. Execrations. What are we doing? City's just hunkering down for a storm it thinks is coming. I know the truth of it. That's why I'm doing this, Jackal. S'why I gotta."

Jackal's arms drop slack.

"… what truth?"

"Storm isn't coming. Already came. Fucked the world, though we don't know when or what. It's a new kind of deepness, wrapping us up tighter year 'round, choking us. We're sitting on our wealth. Dunno what to use it for. Help other cities? Can't. What if we need it? It's fucked."

"… but why this?"

"I dunno when that plague gets here. I wanna live now," Sik affirms, then says it louder. "I need to live now. 'Cause tomorrow I'm dying." She trembles. "What does the day matter more than the hour? That's what I think. I'm still scared, but… I don't want to be scared anymore."

When Sik glances back at me I see that at least in this solitary moment it isn't fear coursing through her veins, but passion.

"That's how it is," I say.

"That's how it is," Quinn repeats, who had apparently been tailing us three in secret the whole time.

#

We debate throughout the night. Quinn keeps the coffee coming, jittery as Sik is after the fifth cup, and ignores the cellar door entirely. She was unsurprised by Killjoy's model or his preparations; perhaps she knew him as resourceful or they had used a model with him on one of their own heists.

"Carts as a weakness," she states succinctly.

"But hooowww," Sik groans, longing for bed, the perpetual hater of all-nighters.

"Could we go under them?" I ask.

"That's stupid, Red. We'd fall off."

"We wouldn't be hanging there," I say. "We could build something to support our weight."

Jackal questions that. "Wouldn't that be obvious? I mean, more so than an extra or... or a replaced corpse?"

"Test runs," Quinn suggests.

"No, I thought of that," I say. "If we do something weird to one cart beforehand, I can see that getting around to the rest. 'Double-check the carts, someone tampered with ours!' and *who* would tamper?"

"One go," Sik says.

"A perfect run," Jackal notes. "Which never happens."

"But I'm liking this idea, underneath." Sik nods, a little twitchy.

"You shot it down, like, right now you shot it down," I rebuff.

"It answers *how* we leave! That's why those two diggers were dredgers! Great way to bust in, otherwise clueless! Oh, yeah, 'cause they're gonna wheel out two strange bodies straightaway."

"Fair point," Quinn says.

"Chancy too." Jackal meets her eyes.

"Distraction needed."

"Visual?" Jackal asks.

"No. Triggers alertness."

"Aural?"

"Mm."

"I scream good," Jackal says.

"True." Quinn covers a smile.

"What else?"

"Confusion."

That excites Jackal. "Ohh."

"Executioners' worst fear," Quinn says, leadingly.

Sik raises a hand. "I know that."

Quinn points at her.

"A breach," Sik replies simply.

Quinn claps her hands and smiles.

"If we could breach the place, I'd much prefer that," I say. "It's unfeasible though, isn't it?"

Sik shrugs. "We won't know 'till we dig."

"Assume that doesn't work. Can we use that with a distraction? If you grab their attention -- diggers are at the *back* -- they aren't likely to check the front as quickly, and by that time—"

"We'll be inside and off the cart," Sik finishes.

"Crypt Dun's pretty broad, Red." Jackal plays with a twintail in thought. "To lure them over there... I can figure them findin' that obvious. Plus, I can't think of an in... in-sih-den-tuhl? sound a person could make to reach that gate on the other side. Mmm."

That stumped us.

Half-an-hour later, Jackal hesitantly spoke.

"If we uprooted that shattertree..."

"NO."

"FUCK NO."

And still we were stumped.

And shuddering.

Which, annoyingly, Quinn found delightful.

"Say…" Sik starts on an idea, forming it with the care of an adroit lockpicker.

"At least this will be better," I mutter under my breath, "than fuck-bedamned shattertrees."

"Oi, I'm sorry, okay? But genius and insanity walk a thin line, ya know!"

"Yeah, and let us know when you find it."

Jackal scowled at me so fiercely for saying that.

A shade darker than her hair.

Which Quinn found utterly delightful.

"What about those firestick things?" Sik wonders.

"Firestick?"

We look at each other, but no one understands.

"You know." Animated with hands. "Shhhriiiii, ga-gan!"

"Oh!" Jackal lights up. "The *fireworks*!"

Sik nods excitedly. "Them!"

"But that's an even *more* obvious distraction, I think, sweetie."

"What if we aim them down? At a hole in Dun? Would that explode a hole?" Suddenly, the idea grips her in totality and hyperness eclipses the coffee like one of those firework explosions must. "Whether it worked or not, Execrations would *totally* think we were trying to get in. And and… shit! And *if* it worked, they'd be searching the rear while we fucked around the front! *That's fucking brilliant I'm so smart!*"

"Oi, not bad."

"What if where the vault is *is* in the rear?"

"Oh! Red said a dirty!" Sik cackles.

"I— wait, what?"

"Listen, Red, this is amazing! This is our distraction and way in. I got it! Dun's broad, Jackal's right on that, but it's also high and it's deep. Like me right now!" Devolves into a giggle-fit, then springs back into onrushing thoughts unfazed. "Okay! We'll have time to screw up and down, wherever…

wherever we need! They come, we go. Up down up down! Hide under the cart once we got the loot!"

"There are a load of conjectures you've tucked inside there," I tell her.

Silence.

It's almost deflating.

Until I say, "Sik, you're the gravedigger the Executioners are going to learn to hate."

Grinning devil girl.

#

Killjoy could push the auction back three or four weeks until the cusp of autumn.

"This is my inviolate exception," he proclaimed. "Grant you, it horns in on next season further than I and my associates would prefer, not to mention the surplus of annoyed sellers it will rattle *this* season... However!" Clapped his hands. "A tidy profit loosens tension all around! And I'm sure I can find some way to make it up to them..."

We sorely needed the time too.

#

Quinn and I worked out plans for a design that would latch to the underside of an Executioner cart. Their organized nature screwed them in this instance: every unattended cart Quinn measured was an exact copy, well within an infinitesimal margin of error -- despite her insistence it *had* to be within the millimeter. I promised to cut the wood as perfectly as my hands would allow.

But this provided a new workaround.

It had earlier occurred to me that we couldn't be sure how long the cart we piggybacked, or whatever the inverse was, would actually be in the Dun. If they took it back out, which was absolutely plausible, we'd be pretty well fucked. Add to *that* the fact they'd be wheeling us off to whatever empty vault the corpses were bound for... I hadn't the heart to douse Sik's inflamed passions by mentioning it.

But with a clever design, I found, we might make this clandestine undercarriage portable.

... but how?

Anyways, I'm glad to have the time. Jackal and Quinn still need to determine if there are anymore fireworks laying around, where they are, let alone the actual retrieval of them.

I'd add 'safely' to that...

But the more I crush failed ideas, their remnants sifting like irritating sand through the folds of my brain, the more it feels like a word and not a real concept.

Sovereignty. Executioners. Technocracy.

Effectively, we're pissing on everyone.

Wonder how that'll turn out...

#

Sik was quiet.

I worked at the desk. She cooked meals.

I ate at the desk. She tidied up.

Out of the corner of my eye, I noticed her resting in my chair -- something lost in thought.

She took naps. She yawned. She pissed. She bathed.

Every so often, she'd open the door and window for some fresh air.

Every time, the wind blew my papers all over and she fretted back and forth, closing the door, grabbing at them, shutting the window, dropping them, cussing under a vehement breath, straightening the pile, and putting them back on the desk where she thought they went and every page out of order.

Days were counted in the stubble on my cheeks.

Finally I said, "I'm sorry this is so boring."

"I'm cool."

"Really?"

"Do you mind the noise?" she asks.

Lifting the broom she was using.

"Thought you got over the domestic thing."

"It relaxes me." Frowning. "Look, I have nothing to do yet. Worried to shit for them too. This is dicey."

"Gonna get a whole lot more that way too."

"Let me support you. It makes me feel useful."

"You are."

Smiling. "Okay."

And, humming, she swept.

#

I'm scrapping the collapsible design. Isn't working.

Once I get *something* working, I can go back.

Simple is best.

I nick myself with the razor.

There's something symbolic about that.

#

How in the fuck can we get this piece of shit hanging there without nails?

#

"Eat," she demands.

"Fuck off for a sec."

"Eeeeeat," she insists.

"Sik, I'm on to something."

"You've been on to something for two days now."

"And I'm going to be on to something two weeks more if you don't—"

"Oh hoh?" Smirking at me.

"Sorry."

"That's right." She takes the pen out of my hand, replaces it with a spoon.

"Thanks."

"Yep."

#

Oh. Of course it's this obvious.

#

Sik brings up a good question. It stops me drawing.

"Why is he delaying the auction at all?"

I think that over. "Making time for this run, isn't he?"

"This isn't the biscuit crunch. Couldn't we auction it next time around?"

"Well… I suppose he might have a buyer lined up."

Crosses her arms. "Okay."

"And this gives him time to spread rumors to drum up a buzz beforehand."

Shakes her head. "But that's the same thing whether it's this time or the one after."

"Huh." Now I'm wondering.

"Yeah, I know, right? What's his rush?" she asks.

I finish up drawing the section that will secure our feet to the cart before answering. "He's not the suspicious sort."

"Which makes him all the more suspicious."

"If a betrayal was in the offing, Jackal would steal the cup from us and throw it in a gutter."

Sik nods. "And gut the man himself."

This design is on the right track.

Accounts for the difference in our heights too…

"It's poor comparison for me, not knowing him, to say he's different from *now* as he was from *then*, still… the Executioners have him on edge, that's clear."

Then she asks it: "Could he be in league with them?"

I could draw a straighter line with my lips than this ruler right now.

#

That's it. Satisfactory.

I'll run it by Quinn and get a prototype cobbled together.

#

"Let's take Killjoy out of the equation," I say.

"I hate math," she says, "but I like that."

"He doesn't need to know our plan specifically," I reason. "Let's claim a fake day we'll go, see if anything transpires. If it doesn't, I think any mistrust can be settled."

"And then we do it for real?"

"He doesn't need to know an exact date. But, yeah, then we'll go."

#

Sik found a note hiding in one of the flowerboxes when she watered them after breakfast.

It was Jackal's angular script. Read simply:
Got em.

#

We relayed our plan to Killjoy.

A branch will have "broken" from one of the fragile trees around the bend right outside Crypt Dun. When the Executioners leave to haul it away, we'll crawl under the piled corpses in the cart and wait 'till we are inside.

I led him along with a probing "and you'll announce the auction's date once you've verified the authenticity?"

"Absolutely!" He replied, then added, "Worry not about the provenance. She never penned any."

When night fell and a distant cart approached, the four of us dropped the prepared limb in the middle of the corpse road. We retreated, Quinn staying nearer to the road than us, and watched.

As you probably expect, the Executioners reacted normally from there and on into the Dun.

"It's possible," Sik says when the great oaken gate shuts, "that they are currently slitting our throats and pissing directly into the holes."

But doubtful.

Killjoy was trustworthy.

Picker and Stealer take the opportunity to run their own observations while Sik and I sit on the shrine's walkway, eating salted riceballs and drinking pulp-slush.

#

"Are we done yet?" Jackal prods.

"What are you whining about?" I ask, somewhat confused. "You love this stuff."

"Quinn said she had a surprise for us after."

"No matter how strong it may be, Quinn," Sik says soberly, "alcohol won't exactly be surprising."

Quinn arches her neck in a silent laugh, then presents that strange metallic tube we made off with.

Sik is puzzled as all hell. "Okay, so... now what?"

Quinn extends the second section.

Then she holds it up to Sik's eyeball.

"I'm glad you aren't testing this on me," I say reflexively.

"It's pretty," Sik says, "but what am I seeing?"

Quinn smiles. "Old Kingdom."

"... huh."

Sik lowers the device, squints south

Then looks back through it.

"What in the fuck..." she says softly.

I grab the thing from her hands. "Let me see."

"Hey!"

Curiosity buries caution. I peer into the tube.

"I wasn't done yet..." she complains.

And there it is.

Old Kingdom, gleaming.

Rooftops appearing closer than Old City below us.

I breathe some word. Whatever it is makes Quinn chuckle and Jackal snort.

Is that a *person* climbing that balcony?

"Oi, me now!" Jackal snatches it away and is instantly dazzled. "Wow... Quinnzy, is that where ya kept going?"

"Mm."

"How is it possible?" I ask her.

She raises her hands. "Special glass."

"That simple?"

Fingers wiggling. "Explanation?"

"Not tonight. I'm vertigoed enough..." I say.

We pass the tube around, staring at various things. The forests out east, the sparkling water to the west, the mountains north. At night, if this is how things look… magnified, how better would this be during the day? We're already running out of things to marvel at.

A tear trails from the eye that Sik presses against the thing. "Red…" Husky and quiet. "Look…" Holds it to my eye and tilts up at the moon.

None of us have words after that.

Passing the device back and forth, everyone without it staring upwards anyways. I can't name this emotion.

I feel big.

I feel small.

I feel young.

For a short spell, Crypt Dun fades away…

… and there is only *this*.

This feeling.

This connectedness.

This wonder.

This moment.

#

The girls see us home.

"Soon, then?" Jackal asks.

"We'll let you know," I say.

Sik smirks. "Get some rest."

"On call, huh? Oi, this is gonna be a heart-pounder."

Quinn nods.

I wave. "Goodnight, guys."

"Yeah, 'night."

"Mm."

"See you soooon," Sik giggles.

#

Days blend into one continuous stretch of night as we reset our schedules. Sunset becomes our dawn, the pans and plates clattering in the kitchen drown out the chirruping fiddlebugs outside, and with the heralding sunrise we stop up our ears against the wakening city and sleep.

We dream of dirt.

#

"Not yet?" I ask.

"Not yet," she says.

"You're making a good call."

She doesn't turn away from the window. A night breeze brushes the curtains beside her. "Am I?"

"There's no hurry. We've waited this long."

"Just a little longer then, huh..."

I glance over. "Second thoughts?"

"No." Errant strands of her hair stir. She says it firmly, but wraps her arms around her stomach.

"Sure?"

"Red."

"Yeah."

"Why am I still waiting?" she wonders.

"You want this perfect, don't you?"

"Is that it?"

"It's the hardest thing we'll ever do. Makes sense, right?"

"But it'll never be perfect. I'm too stupid to know what perfect is anyways. It'll be messed up, like me."

I rise in the chair. "Sik, that's bullshit."

"Is it?" Grips the windowsill, as if she might fall. "I want you to be right about this. Not sure... not sure if every part of *me* can be right about it."

"We can practice," I offer.

"Huh?"

"If we practice, there's more chance it will go smoothly."

"That's kinda... weird, Red. Do it or not, practice just seems... I mean..." A strong breeze blows by. She shivers. "I practice. In... in my head and my... and I practice."

"Good, me too." I clear my throat. "Thing is, I thought of this before, but I wasn't sure if it would... ah, get us overworked?"

"What do you mean?"

"Like if we practiced too much, we'd overthink and choke when we actually did it."

"Choke...?"

"Either way, Quinn and I can jury-rig a fake cart we can work on."

She stiffens. Covers her face and talks into her hands.

"Oh rot f-fucking..." she says.

"What? It'd work."

"Do you know *how embarrassing* this was?"

"For what?"

"For me, you freaking—" Stops short, then starts laughing. "Ah, I'm an idiot. Nevermind. I get it. Blunt Sik. It's harder to be her lately."

"I feel like I missed something."

Sidelong glance, rolls eyes. Leans out into the night.

Breathes deep. "Good morning, Old City."

#

Sik avoided me a little for the next week.

Or at least that's how it felt.

I was getting anxious. When would we go?

Were Quinn and Jackal feeling the same?

If we were to check on them, I felt it would be like breaching the fourth-wall.

But the anxiety.

I hate that I love it.

#

Another night, our only day.

Sik pulls up the covers. "Red?"

"Mrmm?" I ask the pillow.

"Kinda cold. Light the fire?"

"Mrmm." I tell the pillow.

#

Same night, our only day.

Sik pushes the covers away. "Red?"

"Nnrphh," I tell the pillow.

"It's hot. Open the window?"

"Nnrphh?" I ask the pillow, but comply.

\#

When I turn, Sik has kicked the covers to the floor. She sits, bare-chested.

"Do you need another nightshirt?" I ask her.

"Uh uh."

"You're not sick are you?"

Only the tousled hair moves.

Huh. Doesn't feel febrile.

She removes my hand from her forehead and places it between her breasts.

Ba-bump. Th-thump.

Over and over.

Ta-tump. Bu-bump.

Again and again.

"Are you that worried about the Dun?"

"Fuck me, you're dense," she swears. But the gaze that rushes into mine and the eyes that glisten like her pale skin are soft, frightened and determined. "Fuck me," she repeats.

She runs a hand over my chest, drawing close, gently kissing my neck. Pulling back, looking, searching, unsure. I stroke her face. She flinches away. I try again and she forces herself not to move, though averted eyes show the effort that takes. Then I run my fingers through the long hair that has become so natural to see flowing over a rising and falling shoulder whenever she slumbers.

Lying back on the pillow.

As our quickening breaths rush against each other, lips brushing, I hesitate -- and then kiss Sik.

And she returns it.

Each time I feel a new part of her body, she jumps, but settles back into my lips with a shuddering, moaned exhalation. I lick her ears, neck, chest. Suck on her nipple while kneading her breasts.

"Ow, not so hard."

"Sorry."

"It's okay," she laughs lightly, playing with my hair.

She tenses up when I part her knees.

Gasps when I begin lapping at her soft, moistened mound.

"Nnnghh!"

Back arching, frenetically reaching for gripping at pulling on shaking anything.

"Haah, haah!"

Sheets. Pillow. My head.

"Aaahnnnghh!"

I pleasure her. Listening to the change in breathing, enjoying what I can do for her, all the while feeling myself harden against the mattress. She moves. I move with her. She moans. Breathing rapidly. Is she close?

I lick faster. Caress her thighs.

Her breathing is sharp.

She sucks in, lets it out, thin, almost shrill, with an intensity that shakes her entire body. Again. Again. I skirt the edge of her climax. My hips push forward unconsciously.

Did I learn such patience from her?

Her body tenses and quakes. Again. Again. Her breathing so loud. "Mmm. Mmm." The sound she makes, rising louder with every second.

I slow down, but it bubbles out of her throat almost uncontrollably.

And I stop, stick my thumbs around the sides of her soaking panties, and slide them off.

Up, over knees.

Down shins.

Hanging a final instant at her skinny ankles.

I smile at her face.

But she's hidden by a little black-haired angel who is missing a wing, and she is still making the same noise again and again while her body shakes with each wracking sob.

Tearful eyes peer over the angel at me. She holds back her crying -- and begins to spread her legs wider.

"No, Sik, no," I tell her immediately, pulling the panties back on and closing her legs. "It's okay, you don't have to."

She clutches Rin.

Turns away from me, weeping bitterly.

I brush her arm.

She kicks her leg, misses, and sobs horribly.

Helpless, I hover over her, as unsure now as she was at the start.

I slump at the edge of the bed.

Aching above and below.

Inner thigh clammy.

Cover my burning face, stare through splayed fingers, stare stingingly, sitting in the light of a failing blue orb we forgot to lay in the sun.

And she cries.

She cries.

She cries.

#

I sleep dead through the day and wake sometime beyond sunset.

Sik is cross-legged. Wrapped in a blanket. Holding Rin.

"Good morning," she croaks with a voice that sounds like it's never been used before.

Rin crawls over my chest and stares at me.

"Good morning," she repeats from Sik's mouth, cracking, higher-pitched. "Good morning…"

"Hey."

I get up.

"Did you put my shirt back on for me?" she asks.

"Yeah."

"Thanks."

"I thought your underwear would be… so I thought… but…" My voice trails off, awkwardly.

"No. Yeah. Thanks."

I sit cross-legged across from her.

"Yeah," she continues, "they feel pretty disgusting," she says, "like me."

"Sik, don't say that."

"Will you listen to me, Red?"

"Never doubt that."

Swallows. "You know how I have problems with... How I have problems." Swallows again.

"Sure. I understand that," I say, "even if I don't understand them."

She plays with Rin. Quiet, upsetting seconds.

"Is it about the sanitarium?" I ask.

She nods. "Y-yeah."

"You want to talk about it?"

"Yes."

"Okay."

"No."

"Okay."

"Really?" she asks.

I nod.

"How much have I... told you?"

"Just that you were there," I admit.

She nods repeatedly, until I realize she's actually rocking herself.

"Quinn and Sis, they don't... I never mentioned the place. Got a..." Smiles without joy. "Got a fake backstory, me..."

I listen.

"I need you," she says, urgency flashing behind puffy eyelids, "to know... t-to..." swallowing twice, "to know... *that*... didn't happen. Okay?"

I nod.

"It was... it was only... sad. I was so... sad. So lonely. And sad... and and... and then... when I went to sani... sani... and when I was in sani... tarium... I... and..."

"You found Rin there, right?"

"Y-yeah, that too… that too… Rin…" Squeezing tight. "I saved her."

"Is that what this is about?"

"No, n-no… different… it's…"

I listen.

"Nothing… bad happened," she says finally. "Only… only… it's…" Stops. Doesn't know where to start. Doesn't want to, but doesn't want to stop either. Casting around, eyes, faltered words, eyes, broken sentences.

In the darkness, with nightshirt on, with hair done up, she and Rin would be indistinguishable. Both as silent as stone. As unmoving.

One of them sighs.

"Like I thought," she says, "I can't do this at all."

I reach for her, and halt. Ask if it's okay.

"I don't know," she says despairingly, then plaintively, "but you can try."

I stroke her hair the way she strokes Rin's.

Ask if it feels good.

"I don't know," she says despairingly, then plaintively, "but you can try here."

Lets go of Rin, offering her hand.

I take it.

"So warm…"

I ask if this is too much.

"It was hard doing this when we were running… singing… so hard…"

You don't have to push yourself.

"Sometimes I want to."

But you don't have to.

"So kind…"

It's enough.

"I want to be more than I am."

It's alright.

"No. It's all rot."

Sik…

"Red…"

What is it?

"It may be I tell you never."

That's alright too.

She takes her hand out from mine and holds Rin again.

"Then, if I can't do that much, there's one thing I want to tell you."

Okay.

"I want to tell you." Shuddering. "It hurts."

Shhh.

"But I can't! But it… it hurts."

I stroke her hair again.

"I'm… I'm going to tell you," she cries.

Okay.

"I'm going to tell you, Red, okay?"

Okay.

"Ready?"

Yeah.

"Now?"

Yeah.

"Okay. I'll do it, okay?"

Okay.

"I'm going to tell you now."

I'm ready.

"Are you listening?"

Yeah. I am.

"Okay, listen to me, Red."

And she hugs Rin close to her constricted heart and kisses her forehead. She strokes her ears and kisses her cheek. She embraces Rin's body and kisses where her lips would be if she had any.

Deeply.

Longingly.

Tears streaming.

Eyes closed, they put their foreheads together.

Sik breathes in shakily. She breathes out my name. And then she asks me, eyes tight, their foreheads together, shakily, and she asks me:

"Did you hear me?"

I heard you.

"Do... do you want to tell me... too?"

I do.

"Then... here. I'll... I'll let you. Because... because you're you."

Rin is softer than I expect. Squeezes with the lightest pressure. Her scent is Sik's, of sweat hugged into her over the long years. I know, without being told, this is the first time anyone else has touched her.

Just to see her in my rough hands, I feel myself about to cry.

Rin has no mouth. And so anything I do is pointless, worthless, useless, all of it. And so am I: pointless, worthless, useless. What can I possibly do for this poor wretched girl who is missing a mouth and a wing? No matter what I do, I cannot make her smile. She cannot soar.

Hold her in the crook of the neck. Pet her head. The dark hair. The wing.

Kiss her eternally shut eyes. Pick her up. Make her fly. Let her know.

What it's like.

What she's missing.

What I want her to understand.

Will you ever open your eyes, Rin? What would you see first I wonder? The blue, blue sky? The white, wide clouds? Is that what you dream of, Rin, deep in your unending dreams? There's so much more than what you see beyond the veil of your eyelids, in the mute red glow of sunlight desperate to pour in.

It's not your fault.
You were sewn this way.
It's alright.
Everything will be okay.
You aren't alone.
Rin.
Sik.
You aren't alone anymore.

I kiss where her mouth would be, where she would be smiling if only she could, and taste the hint of Sik's saliva. She sleeps on. I rock her in my arms and she sleeps on, and dreams her unnamed dreams.

Sik says I'm so gentle.
I wish that was enough.
For fuck's sake.
For fuck's sake...
Why can't that just be enough...?

#

"Tomorrow," she says a week later.

A patch of clouds hangs beyond the horizon, but the sky is already gray.

I go to inform Jackal and Quinn.

When I come home, Sik is still standing at the window.

#

"Oi, wake up, dreamers." As usual, Jackal lets herself in.

"It's the middle of the night," the chair moans with my voice.

"It's midday, ya lazy clod!"

"Same difference," the shade of Sik mutters over a cup of coffee.

"Heh, I know... thought ya two might not be able to sleep either."

Quinn taps me on the head. Waves.

"More practice?" I ask wearily.

Shakes her head no. Holds up a basket.

"Secret weapon?" Sik asks.

Shakes her head again. "Picnic," she replies.

#

It might as well be night for the lack of illumination.

The sky is dull, darkening by the hour and every empty patch is consumed by the time we reach our destination. Jackal flings the blanket over the tiles on the roof.

"Isn't this conspicuous?" I ask her.

"Naw. Told ya, we rented the place out until nightfall. Most no one shows up before then in any event," she replies. "Sit down, sit down!"

"If thieves hang out here, is there even a thing resembling privacy?" Sik scans the adjacent rooftops and the many covered windows.

"Once they see us havin' fun and eatin', they'll get bored right quick."

High up as we are, the view of both the shrine and Dun are blocked. Trust the girls to factor that into finding a place to relax.

Quinn passes us a flask of one of her special thinned alcohols. Sik takes in Jackal's reveal of savory-syrup boar dumplings with animated joy, an early treat considering the summer -- and about the only thing she can cook without charring or setting fire to the kitchen.

Quinn probably helped anyways.

Sunset arrives in browns and ambers like a theatre's colored filter that has been burned from overuse.

Sik is bold. Retells that one incident we've refused to acknowledge all this time.

In the unseen shadow of Crypt Dun, all other fears merge into the same innocuous dye, banished of the cruelty of trauma.

"It's blurry, deepness is miserable to your sense of time like that," Sik is saying, "but it was right after we found those tasty devilspots."

"I'm for ignoring this one," I tell Quinn.

She laughs silently. Relinquishes the alcohol from my grip and takes me over to the corner where we lean against pillows and contemplate the lack of sky.

"For once in forever, I was sleeping good. Then *kkksshhh!* I bolt upright and nothing. Red though, he's gone, not having any of it. So I think 'okay, I'm just scaring myself.' I fall asleep fast and then *kkksshhh!* I'm up and what what what is going on!?"

Jackal is rapt.

Surely she anticipates another tall tale of some strange and frightening creature that only Sik has ever seen or heard of, but no, no, not this story...

I look for the flask.

Quinn holds it out of reach, shakes her head no.

"Suppose you're right," I relent.

"'Red, Red, wake up, stop snoring! Something's in here with us!' I hiss in his ear. He hits me. Unconsciously. At least I hope. I fucking hope that was unconscious, Red!" she snaps at me.

"I don't remember it, so probably was," I call back.

"Well, okay, so, and then he gets up after taking his sweet ass time, and..."

It was shattertrees, to spoil your question.

Right there in the forest between us and home, a bloody *grove* of shattertrees, and we were sleeping in the midst of it. This is a lesson on not traveling when your light is gone. I don't care how comfy the ground is in comparison to what you've slept on weeks before.

"And that's when the hailstorm started!" Sik announces, as if it was fun at the time.

"Waaaahhhhh..." Jackal breathes.

Sik goes on to explain the horrors of our blind flight in intimate detail... which uproots my earlier repression.

Thanks, Sik.

You can stop digging any time.

"Look at her." Pointing my chin at the awed Jackal. "Clinging to every word..."

Quinn nudges me. "Don't you?"

"Hmf," I chuckle. "Suppose I do."

"Mm."

"Quinn, let me ask you something."

"Mm."

"When Sik was staying with you two and, um..." Is this something I should be asking? "Did she bring a toy with her?"

Quinn doesn't answer. She stares through Sik, who gestures widely and surprises Jackal more from the way she darts forward than the presentation itself, perhaps mulling the same concern. At length, she answers. "The doll."

"Rin."

"Yes."

The story continues.

We lean against each other, unspeaking.

"Kinda looks like you and Jackal," I say.

An amused flush comes to Quinn's cheeks.

"Illegitimate daughter," she says.

"I'd like to see that," I laugh. "But still... is it alright, do you think?"

She shrugs. "We choose different things." Raises the flask without taking a sip. "One is more worthy?"

"Putting it like that, I guess no."

"Hm."

"She... Sik, I think, understands the obsession is unhealthy, the emotional investment." I stop. I don't know where I'm taking this. "Well, no. I'm making an unfair judgment. It's..."

"Weird."

"Kinda."

"You."

"What, I'm weird?"

"Diggers," she says, digging in an elbow for emphasis, "obviously."

"You're harsh, Quinn."

She shrugs.

"What do you mean to say?" she asks.

"I worry."

"Hm?" Thinking. Tapping a tile as if counting the weight of each word. And then: "Do not try to replace her dear friend." A light touch as warning.

"Shouldn't we be enough?"

I don't mean we.

"Illusion," Quinn mutters.

"We are?"

She sighs, and this time does drink.

"We are all alone," she says.

"We're together now."

She ignores the comment.

"Wounded, confused, frightened. By the past. By each other. By ourselves."

At some point the story ended. Sik and Jackal are now holding their stomachs after exchanging dirty jokes.

"Is it really that bleak?"

"Crippled we," she says with a sad smile.

Passes the nearly-empty flask.

"I don't believe that."

"Be her crutch," Quinn says, "until she can run."

"But I don't want her to have to run from anything anymore."

"Mmnn." Quinn plucks the flask from my clenched fingers and substitutes her hand. "You misunderstand."

Her dark eyes are kind in the failing sun.

"You run *with* her."

"Here, Red!" Sik shouts.

"Ehh?" I startle at her sudden appearance.

"They brought dessert too. You can have this one! Here you go, Quinn."

"Mm."

Quinn's popsicle is crimson.

Mine is clear, Sik having sucked the juice out.

She and Jackal point at me from across the rooftop and laugh maniacally. So the picnic ends with a cold popsicle that tastes like nothing. It's somehow fitting and I laugh too.

And thunder chuckles at us under a breath of wind as the rain begins to fall.

#

We split up to gather supplies at home.

"Can't take much, can we?" Sik looks at the assortment of equipment spread on the table and the floor.

"The undercarriage pretty much fills our packs and that's *disassembled*. Otherwise, I think this is it." I point out the glowing blue orb that will light our way, the metallic torch in reserve, the hammer and chisel, and the two saps Quinn made for us. "That leaves..."

The Executioner blade.

"Which of us gets *that*?" she asks.

"Who's faster?"

"Me I think," she says.

"Stand there."

"Yeah."

"Go on the next flash of lightning," I tell her.

We stare out the window, rain pounding at the glass.

Tense. Arms slack.

Glancing at the sheathed weapon between us on the table.

We wait.

Tatata, tatata, tratra, tata, tratata...

Breath held.

Ta ta ta, tatratra, ta, trata ta ta...

There!

I grab.

It's already in Sik's hand. And unsheathed.

Another flash of lightning reflects off the surface.

"Two out of three?" she offers.

"Take it." I gather everything else. "And remember: absolute last resort."

#

Picker and Stealer are digging at the designated area. We nod at each other. It's begun.

Sik and I start digging too. All four of us aiming at the lifeless heart of Crypt Dun.

We tunnel deep.

Almost feels like we can make it all the way without the need for insanity... but that's about when we strike Executioner grade stonework. I call a halt with my hand.

"Distraction ready?"

They dash off and return with the waterproofed crate.

"Need help setting up?"

"Naw," Jackal says, "Quinn built it into the box." Kicks it. "I pop off both ends, light the black wicks and run my damn by damn cute little butts off."

I show her the metallic torch.

"Ohh, that's nifty!"

"Should you have it? It's reliable," I say.

Scowled crossing of arms.

"I didn't mean it like that," I clarify.

She laughs lightly. "Kiddin' ya, Red! No problems here. Ya keep it."

"Take my lantern, Quinn," Sik says. "It's brimming with high quality oil. Light it once and you're set, okay?"

"Mm."

I look at everyone. "Are we ready, ladies?"

Jackal nods for the group. "Yeah, I'm helpin' with the log, but otherwise, yeah." And to Quinn: "I know the signals by heart. Make sure ya use the tree we found."

"Yes."

"But don't take the highest branches! They seemed flimsy."

"Mm."

"And with the storm…"

Quinn smiles reassuringly.

"… okay?"

"I know."

"Yeah…" Jackal wavers a second, then grins all Picker and Stealer. "Let's do it, Quinnzy."

"Mmhmm." Grinning back just as twisted.

#

We need to move the limb farther down the road than our initial test run -- that stretch being far too waterlogged -- to where the canopy is thicker. As before, we wait until no one is coming from the Dun and…

Lanterns from the inbound cart wink out of the gloom the eyes of a fell, unblinking beast slouching its way down the corpse road towards home.

We drop the branch and sprint to the thicket.

Jackal lights off to finish preparations.

Quinn scrambles up the side of the hill.

And it's us, as it always is, just us, the two gravediggers, watching for that opening in the rain where no one looks, not guard, not Executioner, and only the blind dead await.

Sik squeezes my hand.

I squeeze back.

The cart is coming.

The cart is coming.

#

Someone touches my shoulder.

A shadow steps to my side.

Quinn.

"What's wrong?" I ask.

Shakes her head to allay my concerns. "Saw inside."

"How?"

Briefly flashes the looking-device from the other night. "Water reflection. Upside-down." Nods. "Metal gates."

"How many?"

"Three."

"Beyond that?"

"Black."

"Well, I didn't think it would be a burning festival inside."

"I'm disappointed," Sik says.

"Thanks, Quinn."

But she's already gone.

#

The city slumbered on our way to the shrine, glinting then hiding between contorting trees. Every stone lantern was unlit. There was a break in the rain and a hole in the sky where a moon should be. It silhouetted a darker shadow hunched on the final step.

"Asked ya before," it said, "so I'll do it once more." It shifted. "Are ya doin' this, Red?"

"We are."

"… what if I rescind my finder's fee?"

"You dug your own grave there," I said.

"Digger humor," Sik chimed. "Get it?"

It stood aside.

"Won't wish ya luck," it said when we passed. "If ya two had any more, I wouldn't be able to sleep with that on my conscience."

"You don't have one either!" Sik called back.

We laughed.

But I don't think we meant it.

#

The three Executioners lift up the limb.

"I wish we didn't have to go out when it's this miserable," one sighed.

Sik and I bolt for the cart and crawl under.

"Sure makes supper taste better," said another.

We take out the four parts of the undercarriage and start turning the cranks.

"Unless I'm the one cooking," joked the last.

The wood extends and the greased screws are noiseless.

"Yep, then you guys gotta toss me on the stack too."

Lower portion done. I double-check and triple-check that it holds my weight.

"Okay, okay, it's *bad*, but it's not going-to-kill-you bad."

Sik finishes and runs a check too.

"No. I just want to get away from the *stench* is what."

Upper portion latched on. Checks out.

"Oh that is painful."

Sik's almost finished.

"Yeah, that was pretty bad."

She tightens it once more and climbs up.

"Don't insult them…"

I climb too.

"… it might piss them off."

We look at each other.

"What! They smell like fresh-cut flowers they do. Each and e-ver-y one!"

We nod.

"Aaaaaand… depart!"

And lurch in the direction of a grave, as we always have.

#

The Sik-lying-in-the-cart peers down at me with a dead gaze.

"Foolish," she says.

I watch as her eye pops out, plops in the mud and is left behind.

"What are you doing?" she asks.

"Go away," one of the dead in the cart moans. "Leave us."

"Warmth," cries another. "Warmth. I can almost remember."

"Can I take," another pleads, "a part of you?"

"Foolish," she says.

The battlements flank us now. Impinging tweezers. They pluck out her remaining eye.

"This isn't what I meant."

Before me, a deep thud reverberates. Something has happened. Something is changed. The pendulum swings as far as it can -- to the point of snapping -- and slows, slows, slows, and stops with the cart. Our choice is suspended in the air. Nothing in the world stirs.

Only the Sik-above-me moves.

"This isn't what I meant at all."

She plummets to the ground with limbs in disarray, a dead doll without even a single wing, mouth and eye sockets forever paralyzed.

And the pendulum careens in the opposite, inexorable direction.

"Fools!" The dead in the cart are shrieking. "Fools!" Their dissonant chanting twists around the rumble of door and earth and cart and strangles it to a pathetic whimper.

Fool.

Why didn't I go alone?

Fool.

Why did I risk her?

"Red."

Sik.

"Red."

"Sik?"

She points at the stone floor. "We did it."

"We did?"

I look back outside.

But she's not lying there.

Not crumpled, not dead.

"Yeah," she maintains, "we're both officially fucking stupid, and…"

"And welcome to the tomb of the dead," whispers a final corpse. "You poor, lost children."

#

That's when it starts.

A whistling in the wind. Shrill, sky-piercing, followed by a subterranean explosion that rocks Crypt Dun.

The cart shakes and the oaken gate halts.

"What in high hell was that?" an Executioner shouts.

"Not so loud!" the other hisses.

They hurry outside.

Sik looks at me questioningly.

I shake my head no.

Not with the gate wide open…

We're in a narrow atrium. It's nothing like the Dun construction at Pauper's Pit. I see the three metal gates Quinn mentioned -- and also that I imagined them wrong. They aren't next to each other; they're one after the other.

Off to the side is another wooden door, ladder visible behind the slit at the top.

And outside:

"What's going on?"

"We sent someone over. Sounded like an explosion backside of—"

"I fucking got that! Find out what it is! Now!"

"We are, we are."

And inside:

"Shit, what is this,"

"Should we check?"

"They say they went, they went."

"Yeah, never leave the cart unattended. Important lesson."

"Sorry, it scared me."

"Good. Means you aren't sloppy."

"What now?"

"Hey! Can we wheel these ones in or what?"

The voice from outside: "Have to confirm this first."

"At least let me take them through a gate."

"I can't authorize that."

"Listen, I have a cartful, got it? If something's going down, I want them *inside* and we can't close the entrance now can we?"

"That's actually procedure you know."

"Fuck, man! And you're leaving me a pissing ladder as escape? Love to read that report! Hey, use my blood for ink too, got it?"

The voice outside goes dead silent, then:

"Shit. Fine, first gate. Take them through."

One of the Executioners stands in front of the metal gate and taps it three times.

After a moment it starts to rise.

The two other Executioners push the cart onwards.

"Easy forward, lads, easy forward…"

Squinting into the darkness that waits on us. How is this place laid out if not like the other? Do they patrol inside? What can we expect? Anything? I didn't want to do this blind, but I am, we're doing this blind like the Sik-at-the-final-gate, gripping the iron bars and shaking them, shaking the cart as it moves, and staring into me, head sagging about to snap at the neck and the spine will point at me an accusatory finger.

She screams.

At the world.

At them.

At me.

She screams.

"GO BACK YOU FUCKING WORTHLESS FOOLS THIS IS NOT BUILT FOR YOU THIS IS NOT FOR YOU THERE IS NOTHING HERE GO BACK THERE IS NOTHING HERE GO BACK!"

Metal clangs against metal.

"Shit."

The sound of something locked.

"The gate jammed. Stop the cart! Stop the cart!"

But the cart slams into it anyways.

The Sik-beyond-the-gate is impaled on spikes. Black ichor gushes from the wounds and countless severed hands drift on that horrible river through the second gate and the first gate and under me and away.

One hand lingers, dividing me from Sik still clinging to the undercarriage.

"Shit shit shit."

The Executioners hurry to the rear of the cart.

Another one calls from the door with the ladder. "You aren't in yet!?"

"Why did you stop the gate!"

"Fuck, this is crazy. Listen, we're closing the entrance."

"Not with us in here!"

"You, you…" The woman behind the door is hysterical. "You don't understand, there's been a detonation, something, someone, there's so much smoke, we don't know if Dun's secure. *You cannot go in*!"

One Executioner runs to the door and pounds on it.

"Let us up!"

"Nonono, I'm not opening for nothing, fuckfuckfuck."

"Open right now or I'm reporting you *immediately*!"

"Both of you stop yelling," one at the cart says.

"Yes," says the other, "we have to… this…"

"Oh fuck." The woman at the door. "Oh fuckfuckfuck, you dropped one."

"Shit, boss, get over here and help us lift. Deal with her after."

"What the fuck is going on." The woman is leaving up the ladder.

"Get down here this instant, you damn lunatic! You got a job to do!"

"I secure Dun! And Dun isn't secure, so… FUCK OFF."
They keep arguing.
"We can do this. Hundred times. Lift carefully, slowly."
"Got it got it."
"On three."
"Right right."
They kneel.
"One."
From that angle…
"Two."
From that angle…
"Thr—"
They see us.
"Sik."
"Fuck me up the ass," she cusses.

We spring out. I sap the nearest Executioner in the jaw, surprise and force knocking him on top of the green corpse. Sik jams the blade into the other's ankle and he goes down with a sickening yelp.

That woman must have left or is calling or—
The entrance is closing.
"Fuck it, run, Sik. Run!"
We run at the shutting light.
Again. Again. It's happening again.
It's Ensbryng.
It's Ensbryng, but worse.
They know we're here.
One is armed, dashing for Sik.
One is screaming up the ladder.
Shut it faster shut it faster!
A devil snickers between my hands.
It's quiet.
It's loud enough.

It halts the man gawps at me throwing it at the pile of corpses over the head of the man I knocked down blade arching high flying at me pounding boots. We can't fight. Run! Run! Run for the entrance!

The gate.

Our salvation.

Our damnation.

It shuts.

Shuddering to jarred stillness…

… behind us.

Smothered words. Shouts. Cries. Inside.

Footsteps. Orders. Fire crackling. Overhead.

Which was it? Which is it?

Twang tw-twang twang twang.

A flurry of bolts rains down.

One slams into my arm. I slip on the mud.

Tw-twang twang.

Another grazes my neck, but I chase after Sik.

Fuck!

Run faster!

Twang.

It rips through her running leg. She cries out, tumbles, scrambles to stand.

Twang.

Another crucifies her hand to the earth.

Twang.

The bolt aimed for her head penetrates my shoulder. At the same time, she pulls the foot-long metal rod -- still lodged in the bone -- out of the ground.

Twang.

The next tears through my other arm. Fuck the agony. Run! Just run!

And then a flash like miniature lightning.

Some Executioners cry out in pain.

And then every torch along the wall sputters uselessly, shrouding me and the stumbling Sik.

Twang.

It whizzes by my ear.

Somewhere before me

Sik collapses

screaming wet screams.

I rush at the sound, eyes in pain eyes blind always the same nothing changed nothing! But something grabs me and forces me a different way.

"Come!" the shadow orders.

"Quinn?" I gasp.

"Mm!" the shadow agrees.

It takes me into the tree line.

I see a sister shadow pulling Sik along.

Twang. Twang. Twang.

Her muffled screams tear through my body.

Twang. Twang. Twang.

My vision boils.

"Damn you, Quinn," I weep. "Damn you."

But I think she understands it's not her name I mean.

#

Sik stares uncomprehendingly at me as the bolt is pulled free from her stomach. Body arching. Crying deafening, even with a wad of cloth and my hand clamped down. Quinn already wrenched the bolt out of my shoulder. I think there's one left in my arm.

The shrine's floor is weeping red, streaming tears.

"Sweetie." Jackal runs crimson fingers through Sik's muddy hair. "Your organs are all torn up. Okay? Gonna run outta blood before I can get ya back, so I have to give ya an internal styptic. Okay? It's…" Jerks away. Her tears whip across my face. "It's gonna hurt even worse, okay? But it's… it's good for ya, okay?"

Sik sobs, manages to nod twice.

Quinn fills Jackal's palms with a pink, chalky powder.

"Please forgive Big Sis…" Shoving the powder, fingers digging deep, into Sik's gaping wound.

396

And she goes silent. So horribly silent. Cannot make a sound. Ripped from her. Has forgotten how. Blurry eyes stare at me, screaming wordlessly.

I let go of her mouth.

I remove the cloth.

Underneath, those trembling lips I briefly kissed once.

I hold her limp hand.

"If... you're... going... to... screw... up..." she whispers and blacks out.

#

The crying of the lot has begun.

Killjoy is in his element. The auction hall is abuzz.

We watch from the balcony.

"And who will make it an even ten-thousand? Yes, there it is. Now eleven-thousand. Eleven-thousand? Ladies and gentlemen, you know I'm looking for eleven-thousand. There, sir, thank you, you're an angel. And now twelve-thousand. Twelve-thousand. Fifteen-thousand! Ladies and gentlemen, the bidding stands at fifteen-thousand. You know I'm looking for sixteen-thousand."

"Is anyone even bidding?" Sik wobbles on her crutch, peeping over the railing.

Jackal steadies her. "Professionals," she explains. "They don't care for history's onus."

"Histrionics," I tell her.

"Yeah, that."

Beams of light illuminate dust illuminating Killjoy gesturing upon the stage, standing next to a table with five matching goblets.

Sik sneezes, then winces. "Ehh, I don't think anyone's even bidding..."

"Hardly close to the reserve," Jackal laments.

"I thought you didn't want your five percent anymore," I say.

"Oh, it's more than that." Smirking.

Sik fidgets. "I kinda… agreed to…"

"Twenty-*five* percent." Jackal sneers.

"Twenty-five!?"

"Twenty-five in the balcony!" Killjoy announces and immediately double-takes. "A bold and… surprising move, sir. But now thirty. Who will give me thirty?"

Jackal slaps my bandaged shoulder. "Ya *are* a good sport, Red. I tell ya that yet?"

Fortunately, the bidding continues to climb, but as Jackal says the reserve has not been met.

It plateaus a cool ten-thousand short.

"Bidding stands at forty-thousand," Killjoy intones. "Where are my scattergoods? Where are my friends who only enjoy the very best? This is a unique lot, ladies and gentlemen, it has a history steeped in blood it does. Who will make it forty-five? Forty-five? Forty-four? Can we start at forty-four? Forty-three?"

"Shit, it's tankin'," Jackal says.

"I can't fucking—"

"It's all right," Sik stops me.

Her hazy, candle-lighted eyes. Her face, as pale as that terrible night. I don't know what my expression is.

"It's all right," she repeats, forcing her fingers into my fist. "We'll figure it out."

"Forty-two?"

I nod and squeeze her hand.

"Forty-one?"

Jackal groans. Gives me a look over Sik's serene smile.

For the first time in hours, a hush descends on the auction house. This is it. He won't call forty-thousand again. He'll close it up. His hands begin to rise…

"One-hundred thousand!"

A woman with a long, shadow-black ponytail stands amidst the crowd.

Killjoy pounces. "Bidding is at one-hundred thousand!"

Jackal covers her eyes.

"Ai! Ai! Ai! That's done it now…"

"Huh?" Sik pipes, bouncing back and forth to Jackal and me. "Huh? Huh?"

"I knew she was gonna pull this," Jackal moans.

In the rush of the moment, the auction-goers swell and crash about. Such is the rampant curiosity of what extraordinary numbers could come next that not one notices the woman stealthily push past the flowing bodies and exit the room -- and for that matter, I am sure, the building.

"So," I start, "you two don't have…?"

"Not even close." Jackal snorts. "Well, my lovelies, let's get on. I'll buy ya dinner and… drinks are on *her*."

I take Sik in tow and we hobble after that patchwork Jackal who is tugging on a twintail and grousing at the walls and inanimate objects in her way. Killjoy's booming voice permeates the sunny, dusty hall. Before we attempt the first step, Sik lays her head on my shoulder, humming her favorite shantey.

"Screw up big," I say when she finishes.

She laughs. "It's true."

#

"Hurry up, Red, we're there nearly."

I strain to raise the dirt out.

"Okay. My turn."

Sik digs deep.

Too deep.

She can't manage to move the shovel.

"Go shallow."

"Hell… no… raaaaaaaah!" Pushes all her weight down, displacing the dirt all over the pit, and falls to the ground. Her hat pops off. She laughs.

"That really didn't accomplish anything helpful."

"Raaaaaaaaah!!!" And she shovels out an anticlimactically shallow pile. "Okay. Your turn."

It'll take a while to recover. For us. For the city. Like this pit, nothing is settled yet. But the more she tries, the redder her cheeks become. And the more I smile, the redder my cheeks become.

It's all rot. But it's all right.

Why do we dig?

Who knows.

Maybe we dig for the dead, searching for ourselves in the past. Or maybe we dig for the live, pulling each other out of the grave one dreamer at a time.

Now is a time for maybes.

But as I watch a silver smirk of moon peeking through the darkness and feel the winds rise up and fall, I know it's where the muck drags me down that I find home and the flickering image of Sik and I holding each other in the grave.

www.ingramcontent.com/pod-product-compliance
Lightning Source LLC
Chambersburg PA
CBHW071151250626
47159CB00001B/62